It's Never Gonna Stop
by Jessica Wren

# TABLE OF CONTENTS

## FROM THE DESK OF JESSICA WREN

Thank you to my support system. You all are amazing. Dad, thank you for always pushing me. You always tell me to complete what I've started. The way you show off my books and keep them on display at your home, warms my heart. You mean the world to me, and I love you, daddy. Mom, you are so encouraging and inspiring. If there were anyone I would aspire to be like, it would be you. You're so selfless, faithful to God, and loving. Thank you for all you do. I love you! Ashley, I couldn't have asked for a better younger sister. I have never been able to argue with someone and five minutes later bust out laughing. I love our rawness and our relationship. You're the hardest reader to please, lol. Thank you for your honesty and always having my back. I love you! Jaylen, you are the light of my world. My heart, pain, headache, and joy all wrapped in one. I love you! To my family and friends who always support, thank you. I love you all dearly ♥

Last, but not least. Thank you to my readers. You guys keep me grounded, humble, and I'm so thankful to you. Thank you for the reviews, purchase of paperbacks, messages, acknowledgments, downloads, book clubs, nominations, mentions and all you do. I'm forever grateful. Thank you for continuing to take this journey with me. May God continue to lead, guide, and bless you all. Hugs ♥♥♥

### Jessica Wren
♥

**You CANNOT compete with a woman
a MAN won't leave alone...**

# INTRODUCTION
# WHOSE MAN IS THIS SIS?

The bamboo sound alert notified Kensington that she had a new email message. She sat up in her king size bed and grabbed her laptop from the nightstand.

"About time!" she yelled. "Wait, I know damn well that ain't Tim's begging, dip head ass. Ewwww!" she blurted out.

She studied the photo of the familiar face that came through her messages, shook her head, and smiled.

"Baby, when I tell you that this shit is about to be good. His ugly ass even has the nerve to have on a brim." She laughed and squealed with excitement while uploading Tim's photo into her private group.

**Kissy**
19 October 2018 • Whose Man Is This Sis? • Friends

Wake up bitches! Listen sis wants to know the tea on Tim. Is he single, taken or Is he for everybody? All I know is he smokes dip and still tryna drop a mix tape since Cash Money took over for the 99 and 2000 😩 Other than that Tim is a pretty cool guy. Last I heard, he was messing with this chick name Tiffany on the north side. He has five kids and his kids mothers are Vicky, Nora, NaTasha and Mindy. He doesn't have a car and he stay on the strip all day long. He's pretty much a bum 🤷 Anyways, sis wants to know if he's available. Kissy 💋

563 Likes                                    6 Comments

👍 Like          💬 Comment          ↪ Share

"Boy, y'all wild as hell." She laughed.

Kensington Blu was the CEO of the comment reading association club. The Colony Park Hill Croft beauty lived and breathed in dysfunction. She was dubbed the queen of confusion, controversy, and drama. With all the fights, mess, broken homes, live viral videos, exposed down low relationships, health scares, and assault and battery charges that she caused, she knew she had to conceal her identity and create an alias name. She went by the name Kissy.

Everyone had their vices. Some used drugs, became sex addicts, alcoholics, and gym rats, but for Kissy, hers was good ole lay gossip. An occasional, "Bitch, did you hear about so and so?" Fueled her into birthing her own paid, messy, private group called: *Whose Man Is This Sis*

One thing Kissy understood was the power of information, and she knew how to utilize it to capitalize off a woman's emotions. When a woman's emotions were involved, they simply missed the five points of knowledge— look, learn, listen, observe and respect.

Kissy knew for a fact when it came to gossip or someone's rumored man, women would pull up, investigate, and pay for information, especially when it came to matters of their hearts. It was about control for many, the need to know, and having proof that they were right all along.

Behind the keyboard, Kissy was the 'Wendy Williams' of the social media's "Slam Book". She had the information, dates, times and evidence. All you had to do was pay her a fee to upload a photo of any man, and within minutes, the cards would fall wherever they laid with multiple women commenting on their dealings with him. The group was messy, and Kissy loved that shit.

"Boo hoo, hoo, bitch."

Kissy would laugh any time a woman from her group wrote a post about finding out her husband or man was trash. She didn't understand the meaning behind sympathy post, especially since most women stayed in the relationship anyway, even after being dogged, publicly humiliated, and disrespected.

Kissy actually found it to be hilarious. She didn't care about another woman's tears or broken hearts, and to keep shit going, she would find new ways to engage her followers. To see other women in pain made Kissy exultant. They were too disrespectful to her relationship in the past. This group was payback. She'd be damned if she would be the only one sleeping with a broken heart having trust issues, and insecurities that were always mocked anytime she showed vulnerability. She hated how other women quickly tossed around the word "insecure" as if emotionally they were so much stronger and better than the next woman.

Any woman who spoke highly of her husband or appeared happy, Kissy would download their husband's photo and make up a lie. She created fake profiles pages. Her pages names were Sade, Sophia, Kim, Monique, and Tamara. She would use three of five pages and post photos in the group with made lies about a relationship they were having. She knew sooner or later the wife would get word of the group and want access to learn more about the allege women and affairs. That wasn't even half of the things Kissy had done. In fact, that was too easy. She took it up a notch and searched random profiles of men in her city on tagged, downloaded their photos, and spread false, malicious rumors of HIV and homosexuality to triple her following. The caption would read *"Sis word is on this one. Y'all better go get tested."*

The rules were no screenshots, and no men allowed unless they were gay. Leave it to women though. They always allowed their men to gaslight them and throw the group under the bus.

Just like now trolling their women accounts, it was never a surprise to Kissy when some disgruntle ass man mad at the fact he was caught would post the most disrespectful post.

**Dedra Johnson**
19 October 2018 · Whose Man Is This Sis · Friends

Dig these blues. Y'all hoes in here is messy as fuck. Kissy whoever you are, just know that if my wife Dedra leave me behind this group, imma find out who you are. Kiara McVadd you foul lil mama. Wait til I tell Larry about this shit you posting in this group. Y'all hoes sad bruh. Lame ass AUSTIN bitches.

2 Likes                                          4 Comments

Wow          Comment          Share

"See what I'm saying? These hoes get on my nerves."

Kissy sighed loudly reading the wall post that was just posted. She worked with this Dedra chick, and people tried to tell Dedra that Tyrone wasn't about shit.

**Dedra Johnson**
19 October 2018 · Whose Man Is This Sis · Friends

Like          Comment          Share

**Kiara Mcvadd**
What? Don't @ ME. Fuck Larry! He got a WHOLE woman on the east side. Why I gotta be loyal to someone who isn't loyal to me or his kids? Y'all bum ass niggas got the game twisted. Now run and tell Larry that and tell the bitch he with, I said what's up 👋 Kissy started this group just to expose hoe niggas like you. Y'all some disease infested ass community dicks. Nothing more. That's all y'all do is work temp jobs, sell five dollar bags of weed, bum off the next nigga blunt, talk about the new Jordans, drink lean, wanna rap and talk shit. Y'all wanna be Z-RO so bad 😂 Fuck you Tyrone and ya bald headed, blue magic grease wearing, ain't got no hair in the back, fat ass mama. Nigga @ ME again.
18 October 2018 · Like · Reply

**Dedra Johnson**
Wait until I tell Larry. You know you was suppose to stay solid. You know these hoes don't mean nothing to fam. You running around with Ty Jackson of all niggas. Lil mama you already know what's up.
18 October 2018 · Like · Reply

**Bitch I Got Yo Man**
Tyrone you know what it is. Tell your girl Dedra the truth. Got that girl going crazy like that.
19 October 2018 · Like · Reply

**Bitch I Got Yo Man**
Dedra girl you married a hoe. He for everybody 😂
18 October 2018 · Like · Reply

"Now I gotta delete her ass. She got her man all up in the group," Kissy she said aloud while blocking Dedra. "Bye now. Have fun with Tyrone. Tuh! You Austin hoes are too silly for me."

So much drama would take place outside her group, and she got a kick out of it, especially whenever she visited nail shops and hair salons.

*"Y'all should have been at Gators last night. Hunny they were throwing down. You know Shonta's been messing with Bo behind Byrd's back. She caught they ass in the club grinding on each other. Baby, when I tell you that Byrd beat that ass so good. Titties were swinging everywhere."* Gossip would ring throughout the streets."

All gossip was good gossip. The more drama, the better it was for Kissy. It had everyone fighting to find ways to gain access to the group. So far, Kissy was 5,000 followers strong and growing. For her group to only be a couple of months old, Kissy was proud. Her coins were looking lovely.

Kissy's bamboo alert went off again, notifying her that she had received another email. *It's nothing like being able to call in on your state job, still get paid, and have a hustle on the side that allows you to do what you love.* She silently thought and smiled.

She clicked on the new message, and suddenly her world came crashing down. It was always fun and games until you were the butt of the jokes. Her smile instantly vanished.

| Primary | | |
| --- | --- | --- |

Would like to be added to the group.

**Nova Daniels**
to whosamanizthisus@gmail.com, me
0 minutes ago  Details

Hi Kissy! My name is Nova. I was forwarded the link and I paid the $50.00 admission fee for access to the group. I'm submitting this photo of my husband Hassan and a screenshot of my payment receipt. Hassan and I have been married for five years and I have a feeling he's cheating again. Thank you and have a wonderful day.

Reply        Reply all        Forward

"What? Noooooo!" Kissy screamed. She studied the woman's last name Daniels, and as soon as she saw Hassan and married in the same sentence, she checked out. She didn't need to check the photo attachment of Hassan because she knew.

"Arghhhhh I knew he was too good to be true. I'm so sick of these niggas. They are all the same. Ughhhhh!" she cried out.

Her heart dropped into her stomach causing her to feel emotionally sick. Hot tears of betrayal, hurt, and deceit ran down her dark brown oval-shaped face, causing black mascara to smudge and leave marks.

"Baby, I'm here. I brought you some breakfast. Sorry, it took me so long to get here. The line in Bill Miller's was crazy, plus I stopped by the 7-Eleven to get you those donuts you like!" Hassan yelled from the front of the apartment.

Kissy slammed her laptop shut, placed it in her secret spot between the mattress and box spring, and ran into the living room. She didn't care how crazy she looked at the moment.

*Whap!* Kissy slapped Hassan.

"You fucking liar! I hate you, Hassan. I hate you! You're married. You lied to me!" Kissy screamed, catching Hassan off guard.

"Kensington, baby, please! I can explain," Hassan pleaded, wrapping her in a tight bear hug. She was too devastated and drained to fight him.

Her body weakened in his embrace. Painful cries escaped her soul, and she shivered from the shock. *Hassan was supposed to be one of the good guys.*

Kissy always felt that all men were the same. She had her share of heartbreaks and disappointments, but with Hassan, she was honestly starting to believe that just maybe good men were still out there and then *BOOM!*

"You should have just left me alone, Hassan. You should have just left me alone. I trusted you! How could you do this to me? You know my story and all I've been through," Kissy whispered.

She licked her lips tasting the mild salty taste from her tears and buried her head into Hassan's chest.

This was an eerily resonant heartbreak. It was different. Hassan completed her. He made her better and gave her the space to be vulnerable. He was different but who was she fooling. A man could make you feel so high and low. *I'm never enough. Why can't a man ever love me without hurting me?* Kissy screamed internally.

"Look at me, baby." Hassan cupped her face in his hands. "I love you Kensington, and I would never do anything to hurt you."

Kissy stared into his beautiful lying eyes and bit down on her bottom lip. A lie didn't care who it told. She was pitiful in her love for him and as crazy as this sounds, she didn't have the strength to resign her love for him. *Tell this nigga to leave. Fuck him! He has a whole wife. Don't be stupid. You've already been down this path before. Tell him to leave.* Her inner voice silently encouraged her. But as if Hassan could read her thoughts, he pulled her back into him, making her lose all sense of reasoning when he slipped his hand between her legs.

"Hassan, please, stop," Kissy moaned.

"Tell me you love me, Kensington. Tell me." Hassan dropped to his knees and buried his head into her love box.

The thin-laced purple boy shorts she wore were no match to wing off Hassan's hot breath and juicy tongue. Her head threw back, and before she knew it, her hips slowly matched his tongue's rhythm, leaving her to scream out with pleasure.

Nova always believed that men were creatures of habit. There was another woman in the picture anytime his routine switched up. She had been with her husband Hassan long enough to know when his routine changed.

Her husband had taken her back to a familiar place. No matter how much she wanted to deny it, all the signs were there. He was cheating. She didn't know with whom, but she knew her husband. Something was up.

The sex was different to nonsexist most days. Hassan was either too tired, couldn't finish, or wanted to try new things in the bedroom, not to mention the long nights at the office and away from home. Then there were passcode changes to his phone and him insisting on taking his own vehicle to work.

Nova was The Human Resource/Complaint Manager, and Hassan was a Texas Works Advisor Supervisor. Nova's department had moved into the same building as Hassan's two weeks ago. Their work schedules were the same, so Nova couldn't understand why Hassan was so pressed on driving separate vehicles. Something wasn't adding up.

This morning Hassan pissed Nova off. He had left an hour before her, leaving her to be the one rushing to drop their daughter off at school. She hated the way he lacked communication and knew her day was going to be bad. She had a major attitude.

When she arrived at work, she didn't see Hassan's vehicle parked anywhere on the premises. *OH, she searched!* She smacked her lips, took a deep breath, and stepped on the elevator going to the fourth floor.

From the moment Nova sat down at her desk, she couldn't catch a break. Her morning was busy. From spilling coffee on the front of her shirt, firing four employees for approving fraudulent food stamp cases, and a headache, she was ready to scream.

Her personal cell phone rang startling her.

"Hello," she said in a panic, noticing it was her daughter's school.

"Yes. Hi, Mrs. Daniels, this is Qadira, little Trinity's elementary school principal. I'm calling you because Trinity here ripped the back of her shorts playing at recess. Is there any way you can bring her extra clothing or pick her up? Some of the children were laughing at her, and she's in my office crying," she said.

"Sure, I'll be right there."

*Damn, it's always something. I'm just going to go ahead and take the rest of the day off.* Nova silently thought and rolled her eyes. She leaned back in her La-Z-Boy Delano mahogany, leather office chair and sighed deeply.

"Ugh," Nova vociferate. She upraised her office phone to dial Hassan. When he didn't answer, she smacked her lips and tapped her long fuchsia square nails against the mahogany colored desk.

She was about to dial Hassan for a second time when she overheard two of her messy coworkers Tasha and Ashley talking. She knew their voices anywhere.

"Girl, Tyrone ass is out of pocket. I don't see why Dedra's ass doesn't leave him. He is always cheating on her. Ole girl didn't have to oust him like that though." Tasha laughed and shook her head.

"Wait and did you see the post where the dude stole that girl's money to give to another chick? I swear I can never get any work done. That group gives me life. *Love & Hip Hop* addition," Tasha laughed again.

9

"What group are y'all talking about?" another coworker by the name of Nicole chimed in.

"It's a secret group called, *Whose Man Is This Sis* Girl, that group be jumping all day." Tasha laughed.

"Damn! I heard about that group. How do you get added? Hell, I want the tea too," Nicole said. She wanted to add Hassan to see if she was his only mistress.

"I can't add you. The only one who can is the admin Kissy. Her email address is whosemanisthissis@gmail.com, and her Cash App tag is $Kissy. Here's how it works. To be a member, you must pay the $50.00 admissions fee. Email Kissy with the photo of whatever guy you're dealing with and a screenshot of your payment. She'll personally add you to the group on Facebook and upload his photo with the caption, "*Whose Man Is This Sis*"

The group has a lot of women and gay men in there. Don't be surprised if you see your male cousins' photos or your exes either. If you think that your man is cheating or doing some foul shit, the group is worth it. You'll find out everything. That group is so messy but informative at the same time. That's how I found out about my ex Quincy. If it weren't for that group, I would have never known that he was cheating on me with four different females. He now has HIV too, so when I say that group is worth it, it is," Ashley said, shaking her head.

She thought about how that could have easily been her. *These niggas ain't shit around here.* She silently fumed after seeing Ty Jackson's name mentioned.

"You okay, Ashley?" Tasha asked concerned, noticing the faraway look Ashley had.

"Yeah girl, I'm good," Ashley lied.

She tuned out Tasha and Nicole and tried to keep her emotions in check. The only thing bad about the group that she failed to mention to Nicole is every day you were subjected to become a target of painful information and heartbreak. You never knew when it was your turn, and right now Ashley was hurting. Her right leg shook, and she needed to know who this Kiara chick was.

Nova stood and shut her office door. She couldn't stand Ashley and Tasha. They were always gossiping and in some mess. She rolled her eyes and sat back in her office chair.

"I can't believe that I'm really about to pay to find out information on Hassan," she whispered and shook her head. Hearing Ashley's story definitely made her decision valid.

She pulled out her credit card, paid the fifty-dollar fee, and searched through her phone gallery for a photo of Hassan. "This will do," she blurted out while she sent Kissy the screenshot of her payment and photo.

Nova dialed Hassan's office phone again and then his cell. She glanced up at the clock on the wall and frowned. Hassan should have been in his office or at least return her call by now. She could have walked over to his department, but she didn't feel like being stopped, asked questions, or being bothered. She wasn't exactly in the right headspace.

"It could be a family emergency, and this fool wouldn't even know it," she angrily fussed.

She logged out of her computer, grabbed her personal items, and turn off the lights.

"Ladies, I'm taking the rest of the day off. I don't feel too well. You all have a wonderful day," she said to Nicole, Tasha, and Ashley.

"You too," they said while Nicole rolled her eyes behind her back. Nicole didn't care for Nova. She had this air about her and came off as if she was better than them.

There was a couple of times the ladies attempted to invite Nova out to eat or a party, but she would always decline and separate herself. It wasn't as if the office department was big enough for division.

"I don't know why Ms. Thang thinks she's above somebody. Hell, we all make the same amount of pay around this bitch. If anything, she should be trying to make some girlfriends. It ain't like her husband is a good man anyway with his trifling ass," Nicole fussed.

She was angry with the way Hassan had been acting towards her lately but realized she might have exposed her hand.

"I mean, I just heard he isn't faithful. That's all," she said clearing up her earlier remark.

"Who Hassan? I thought he was one of the good ones. He's always speaking, and from what I can tell, he seems professional with his employees," Ashley defended.

"Well y'all didn't hear this from me, but that baby Trinity is not Nova's daughter. He cheated on her, and word is the child's mother just left the baby on Nova and Hassan's doorstep. I respect Nova for raising that child as hers. Anyway, between us, my cousin Ro is one of Hassan's employees on his team. She told me that Hassan has been sending Tiff Treats and flowers to Kensington Blu. Ro said one day she checked the card on Kensington's desk and it was from him. I also checked the attendance records, and I noticed that every time Kensington called out, Hassan was either on vacation, sick, or took personal time. Y'all noticed though since we've been here at this office, no delivery to Kensington has been signed off for and both of their asses ain't here today." Tasha observed.

"Kensington Blu? I wouldn't even think she would be his type. I mean Nova is high yellow and beautiful. Kensington is average looking, and she doesn't look better than Nova at all or me, for that matter," Nicole scuffed.

"You sound ignorant, Nicole. Kensington is very pretty, and looks don't have anything to do with chemistry. Truth be told a man will sleep with anything. You would be hurt Nicole if someone said you don't seem to be your husband Sean's type because he's tall, skinny, and nice looking while you're heavyset, dark, and short. You see how messed up that sounds?" Tasha questioned. Nicole frowned and rolled her eyes.

"Yeah, that's true. Some of the chicks that Quincy cheated on me with looked like they smelled like ass, Newport's, and sardines," Ashley joked, and they all burst out laughing.

12

"I'm just saying. I don't know why Hassan would risk his position messing with his staff like that. It's so disrespectful knowing that your wife works here too," Nicole said.

"Man, I hope he isn't messing with Kensington. I just feel bad for Nova y'all. I know she's an introvert, but she's really nice and pleasant." Tasha sighed.

"Nice? She's so stuck up to me. She walks around here like she's better than us, and I just don't like her," Nicole nastily complained.

"Well just say you don't like her, because honestly, she doesn't think she's all that, you do. I see the way you roll your eyes, frown, and side-eye Nova every time she speaks or walks by. That lady has done nothing to you. That's what's wrong with black women. You don't have one reason to hate on that woman. It's like if we're not gossiping or bonding in pain, we can't stand to see someone who is vibrating on a higher frequency. Nova is always pleasant, and maybe she's uncomfortable because maybe she has had to deal with black women coming for her. I definitely know what that feels like," Tasha defended.

"I guess!" Nicole rolled her eyes. "I still don't like that bitch."

"So now she's a bitch? Oh, wow! Sis, you gotta let that hate go in your heart."

Tasha turned around getting back to work. Nicole rubbed her the wrong way. True enough she gossip and talked her shit too, but Tasha was never the one to just hate on another sister for no reason. She sensed jealousy and envy coming from Nicole. Most times, she knew women were that way for two reasons. They either wanted to be the woman or wanted what the woman had. Nicole's disdain for Hassan and Nova told Tasha all she needed to know.

"I still don't see his car anywhere. Where the fuck is he at?" Nova angrily whispered under her breath while observing the parking lot.

She opened her car door, slammed it, and started her engine. Queen Naija's "Medicine" came thundering through her speakers.

♫*My intuition never lies/*
*There's nothing you can ever hide/*
*Already got the screenshots, so there is no need to deny.*♫

The lyrics unlocked the waterfall of tears she held in from her office. *No, no, no! Stop that Nova. He wouldn't hurt you again like that.* She silently encouraged herself.

The nagging feeling intensified. Something was off, and she was nobody's fool. "I know he's cheating on me," she spoke aloud.

She pulled out her phone from her purse and felt despondent. Kissy still hadn't added her to the group, and Hassan hadn't returned her calls.

"Damn, why didn't I think of that?" Nova yelled and pressed her right hand against her forehead.

After Hassan's last encounter a year ago, she made sure to place a tracking device under his vehicle and link his email account. He hadn't given her reasons to feel suspicious until recently. Although his work hours were later, Nova excused them due to Hurricane Harvey. She knew the advisor had to do emergency cases to help assist the victims with food. However, that had died down,

14

so there wasn't an excuse for her husband's behavior. Instantly her fingers slid over to her tracking app, and her eyes widened with dismay.

"Travis Station? Why the fuck is he at Travis Station and not at work? I knew it. I knew it. I knew it. I knew it!" Nova burst out into tears.

It took a minute to catch her breath and compose herself. She was so tired of Hassan's lies, cheating, and manipulative love. He kept chipping away at her self-esteem, her dignity, and her heart. She didn't know how much longer she could allow him to dissect pieces of her heart. Every time she attempted to put it back together, it was never the same.

She dried her eyes with the backs of her hand and logged out her Gmail account, into his. She noticed a folder marked private and was pissed that she hadn't noticed it before.

Chase Bank, Nissan, T-Mobile, Victoria Secrets, transactions of different restaurant, airfare ticket information and hotel reservation notifications all rested within the folder.

Nova clicked on notification after notification and sat in her Jeep befuddled. "Where did he get the extra funds from to do all of this?" she screamed as fresh tears reemerged.

She saw three more notifications as recent as forty-five minutes ago. Nine hundred and seventy-five dollars had been paid to Travis Station Apartments. Another payment of five hundred and twenty-five dollars paid to Nissan, and lastly a payment of one hundred and twenty-five dollars to T-Mobile. "The fuck? He got me so fucked up today!" Nova yelled.

She was so engrossed in her phone that she hadn't notice Tasha, Nicole, and Ashley ogling at her. She looked up and locked eyes with them. They were smoking a cigarette. Nova frowned thinking how she had been sitting in the parking lot over thirty minutes.

It was ten o'clock morning break. She needed to get out of there before more employees saw the condition she was in. She was sure by Tuesday morning she would have many *"Are you okay?"* questions due to those three running their messy ass mouths.

Nova placed on her shades and put her car in reverse. Travis Station was ten minutes from her job, but with the way Nova drove, she got there in six minutes.

She screamed with vexation seeing that in order to enter in the apartments she needed a gate code. Her daughter's school called again. "Not now! Damn! Trinity is going to have to fucking wait!" she yelled, hitting the ignore button.

She spotted a vehicle coming out of the exit side of the gate. A pole separated the entrance and exit gate. She backed up and allowed the car to barely make it out of the exit gate before she hurried like a mad woman and zoomed through the gate before it closed.

*Beep, Beep, Beep!*

"You better be lucky you didn't hit my car hoe!" a heavyset, dark complexion woman with a bonnet on her head yelled.

"Lean forward and touch ya toes hoe. Ah ha, you can't. This ain't what you want!" Nova bellowed, honking her horn back and flicking the stranger off. She hated when someone tried her. She had the time TODAY.

On a mission, the five miles per hour speed limit was ignored as Nova turned corner after corner looking for her husband's vehicle.

"Bingo, there his car go right there!" she yelled. "Ugh, which apartment is it?"

Nova parked next to Hassan's vehicle and jumped out her vehicle deranged. If anyone saw her from their apartment windows or balcony, she must have looked absolutely psychotic standing in the parking lot, talking to herself, and looking both ways as if her head was a bobblehead.

"I'm just going to go home and get the clothes for my daughter!" she bellowed throwing her arms up in the air. She was so furious that her tears began to make its reappearance for the fourth time.

She began walking to her vehicle but halted when a vehicle parked on the other side of Hassan's caught her eye. A silver Nissan Rogue with the license plate KenBlu4 paralyzed her. "Wait a

16

minute," Nova vociferate, jumping back into her car. She had seen that name and vehicle before at her job.

She logged into her HR account and went to her employee's records. She searched and searched until she landed on her target, Kensington Blu.

Sure enough, Kensington had a silver Nissan Rouge with the license number KenBlu4. *Calm down! Breathe! It might not be her. Breathe!* Nova's inner voice encouraged. Nova remembered back two weeks ago.

*Nova's Program Manager had her, Tasha, Nicole, and Ashley (HR staff) introduce themselves to the staff. Nova walked around shaking everyone's hand. When she arrived at Kensington's desk, Nova admired how neat and pretty it was. The fresh vase of purple Cattleya flowers caught her attention. They were Nova's favorite.*

*She noticed Kensington's expensive décor. Everyone else's cubical was plain or the typical with photos of their families. Not Kensington's cubical. She had a white fur mat, customized desk accessories, motivational quotes, a mini refrigerator, mini coffee maker, and a stand with coffee cups with lids, creamer, and sugar. A see-through cabinet with all sorts of food was in a corner. A photo of Marilyn Monroe was placed against the cubical wall, and a decorative diamond bowl sat on the corner of her desk filled with different chocolates. Nova remembered thinking how Kensington's small cubical put her office to shame.*

*Nova didn't get a good vibe from Kensington. The girl was extremely pretty and confident. She reminded Nova of Ledisi. She wore weave goddess dreads, had a beautiful dark brown complexion, and her eyebrows were done to perfection. She had a gap between her white halo teeth. Her nails were long, red and matched her lipstick. From what Nova could tell from Kensington sitting down, she wasn't a big or tall woman. She gave the Kensington woman a seven.*

*Nova encouraged all the staff to update their addresses, phone numbers, and vehicle information in the system. She also went over the W-2 tax electronic forms, before she returned to her office.*

"I got you! 6600 Ed Bluestein Boulevard. Apartment number 910006," Nova whispered and rubbed her palms together. That was something she always did to calm herself.

"Hassan, right there baby. Right there!" Kissy screamed.

Love filled tears rolled down the sides of her face. She circled her hips as Hassan's tongue made laps around her creamy throbbing clitoris. He loved the way her juices soaked his beard.

He passionately slurped and vibrated his tongue. Kissy's moans grew louder and louder arousing him. He stroked his massive nine-inch, two-toned piston passionately joining in on the moans.

"Mmmm, you taste so good. Squirt for daddy, baby," he whispered seductively.

The weight of his manhood throbbed and jumped with anticipation. He slurped down Kissy's juices and sat up on his knees. She placed her legs above her head, crossing her ankles effortlessly.

"Hassan," Kissy moaned rubbing her bare love box masturbating. She took two fingers and placed them in her soaking wet pink fortress. It made a gushing sound, making Hassan's manhood starve of thirst.

"Kensington, I love this shit baby. You hear me?" Hassan whispered rubbing the tip of his piston against the folds of her wet Cyprian fountain lips.

"Ohhhh," Kissy moaned, biting down on her bottom lip and squeezing her pink-reddish nipples.

Hassan placed the tip of his dick in her opening, taking his thumb massaging her clit. He slow stroked her opening traveling deeper inside her love tunnel.

"Hassannnnn!" Kissy's eyes rolled.

She hated the way her body always betrayed her heart and mind. Hassan's lovemaking always took her to heights and depths no man had ever touched.

He laid on top of her and cuffed her hips rocking her middle while they passionately kissed. "Kensington! Kensington, a nigga about to cum baby," Hassan moaned in her ear while setting Kissy on fire when he took his tongue and fucked her ear.

Kissy screamed locking her legs high above Hassan's back. She grabbed ahold of his ass plunging him to go as deep as his manhood could reach.

*Boom, boom, boom!* The headboard knocked while the bed rocked. "When We Remix" by Tank played in the background steaming their energy to explode.

"Mmmmmmm," Hassan released.

He couldn't move. His lovemaking with Kissy always drained his energy. He stayed inside of her and allowed his manhood to pulsate. He felt her warm juices melt down and mix with his semen, making a large puddle under her. His eyes rolled and toes curled. She always knew how to please him.

Their foreheads touched, and they mouthed the words "I love you" in between their breaks of kissing. He slowly slid out of Kissy and laid right next to her. He loved her and never meant for things to go this far, but he couldn't help himself.

"I really love you, baby. I'm sorry I didn't tell you about my wife. We're separated and going through a divorce. I should have told you before, but I was afraid you wouldn't give me a chance," Hassan lied.

Kissy laid motionless while staring up at the ceiling. Her life as she knew it was about to take a serious turn. "Hassan, do you really love me?" she asked, choking back tears.

"I do Kensington. You're a great girl, and I'm happy you finally gave me a chance."

"Hassan, I hope that's true. I hope there are no more secrets or lies between us, and I hope you're really getting a divorce because you're going to be a daddy," Kissy blurted out. She had known for some time that she was pregnant, but she didn't know how to tell Hassan or feel about it.

"I got you," Hassan said before quickly rising. Kissy looked at him confused. His sudden movements felt as though they were miles apart.

"Well, Hassan, don't just leave and blow me off. We need to talk about this." Kissy sat up on her knees in the bed.

"Talk about what, Kensington? A nigga said he got you, so why are you tripping?" Hassan replied in a nasty tone.

"Say something at least. I mean, are you happy? This is your first child. I guess I thought you would hold me, not just run off!" Kissy screamed, throwing a pillow at Hassan with tears running down her face.

Hassan angrily turned his back to her. He dressed without cleaning himself or wiping her down. That was new, and Kissy took in everything.

"I'll be right back, baby. I need to pay the rent and get some weed from Ty over in building four. Come lock the door baby and stop tripping. I got you," Hassan's voiced softened before leaving out the bedroom.

Kissy didn't move. She just stared. This relationship they had was a slowly fading and Kissy would be a fool to think that it was anything more. She was his mistress and employee.

♥♥♥♥♥

"Fuck man!" Hassan yelled while punching dead air. He walked to the apartment office, paid the rent, and walked over to Ty's apartment lost in his thoughts. He couldn't believe this shit.

"What's up, my nigga?" Ty, his best friend, greeted opening up his front door for Hassan. He stuck his head out the front door to observe his surroundings before joining Hassan in the living room.

"What's up? You good fam?" The fuck is the deal? You're looking real spook or some shit. What's up?" Ty asked hyped.

21

"I fucked up bro." Hassan sighed and laid back on the sofa.

"Fucked up how? What you do?" Ty asked lighting a blunt.

"Kensington found out about Nova. I don't know how. She's pregnant too." Hassan ran his hand over his beard.

"What you wanna do? I can handle that and make the problem go away?" Ty passed Hassan the blunt.

"Nah! I cut for Kensington. I told her Nova and I are separated and going through a divorce. Damn, I knew this was going to happen. Kensington has been stressing a nigga about coming over to my crib, and Nova been questioning me about me coming home late. I just don't know how I'm going to keep up this affair. Nova's department moved to my building two weeks ago. Nova and Kensington are bound to run into each other. I just don't know what I'mma do. I've been fucking with this chick name Nicole too. I cut her off recently, and now she's tripping."

"You're cheating on Nova again?" Ty threw his arms up. "Nova is a solid woman. She's a real one. If I had a woman like Nova, ain't no way I would cheat on her. Think about it though, yo side bitch left a whole baby on the doorstep and left. Nova held you down and raised that baby like it was hers. After all your fuck ups, she stayed down and loyal. She's solid my nigga. She's bad too. Let Kensington, Nicole, and the rest of these hoes go before you lose Nova for good." Ty took a pull of the blunt. "Have you even heard from your baby mama, Yazzi?" Ty asked.

"Last I heard she was in Houston," Hassan said while staring off into space. Speaking about his daughter's mother was always a touchy subject. After all these years, he still didn't know how to feel about her or what she did.

"That's what up. Goo is having a poker game tonight. Niggas are starting at ten grand. You in?" Ty asked hyped.

"Nah, I'mma chill fam, not tonight."

*Boom, boom, boom!*

"Man, Ty, open this got damn door up. I'm so sick of you nigga. I'm about to go awffffff!" Ashley yelled, twisting the doorknob.

22

"Man, hold up! This hoe is tripping. Here." Ty handed Hassan the blunt. He stood to answer the front door, and Hassan laughed.

Ty Jackson was tall, light-skinned, had a low, tapered fade and was very skinny. He had multiple children by different women, and Hassan couldn't understand what Ashley saw in his boy. He was a typical hood dope boy. Although Ty was smart as hell and very talented, he didn't see himself going any further than the hood. Ashley was out of his league.

"The fuck is you tripping for coming over here with all that bullshit, Ashley? Aren't you supposed to be at work?" Ty yelled, stepping to the side to allow her to enter.

"Who the fuck is Kiara, Ty? Don't worry about where I'm supposed to be. That's none of your business. I told you not to play with me. If you were controlling that little dick of yours, I wouldn't have had to take an early lunch. Now, who the fuck is Kiara?" Ashley asked with her hands on her hips.

Ashley was short and cubby. She was what you would consider a redbone. She wore Jamaican Bounce 1B/33 wand curls and black framed glasses. Hassan knew her from working with his wife.

When he heard the name Kiara, he didn't think much of it. He had a cousin name Kiara, but he knew she wouldn't be stupid enough to boldly front around another man. Her children's father was crazy, but Hassan was definitely going to ask Kiara about Ty.

"Man crazy ass girl, gone on. I don't know nobody name Kiara," Ty lied.

"Wrong, your picture is all up in the group and the bitch Kiara keep commenting saying you're her man!" Ashley yelled.

"Man you tripping. What group? I don't even be on Facebook like that. You always fucking with them messy ass hoes. Get yo ass off Facebook. Talking about I'm in a group. What you talking about?"

"See," Ashley pulled her phone out, "look at the screenshots from Kiara. She confirmed it was you. So you been with her two months Ty? Really? After everything?" Ashley cried while shoving

23

her phone in his face. Ty's eyebrows danced as he read the post and comments.

"*Whose Man Is This Sis*. Man, I heard about this messy ass group. It got everybody in the city beefing and tripping. My boy Paul just told me his girl got into with this 2-3 hoe over this group. Why the fuck are you putting me in some shit Ashley, saying a nigga last name and shit? See this is why I don't be dealing with you like that. You're too insecure. You're messy right along with these hoes. I told you a nigga was solid with you. I cut for you, but I guess that ain't enough." Ty handed back Ashley her phone.

"So what are you saying?" Ashley asked with her hands on her hip.

"Say, man! I'mma leave you to your girl." Hassan said standing. This was getting way too intense and fast. He knew how his boy could go from one to a hundred real quick, and he wasn't trying to be in any of Ty's mess.

"Hassan, I didn't even know you were over there. What are you doing here? I didn't know you know Ty. How is Nova? Is she okay?" Ashley asked. She was so embarrassed that Hassan saw her out of character and worse dealing with Ty.

"Did something happen?" Hassan asked alarmed.

"I don't know. She left early today, and I saw her crying in her car during morning break. I hope she's okay," Ashley informed.

Hassan checked his phone and saw that Nova had called him and left a message. *Fuck*! He said goodbye to Ty and Ashley and made his way back to Kensington. He knew he needed to get home to Nova shortly.

Kissy laid in bed an additional twenty minutes. She heard the bamboo alert go off three more times. As much as she would have loved to entertain new members and get the latest gossip, she just didn't care about any of that right now.

Everything was going downhill for her and fast. She couldn't believe that she was in love with a married man, again and pregnant. *How did I miss the signs?*

Silent tears ran down her cheeks. She was so ashamed of herself. For years, she had worked on being a better person and overcoming everything that she had gone through in her childhood. She could never shake it though. One bad relationship after the next and just like Raheem her ex, Hassan had managed to come in and break her all the way down.

Kensington was doing just fine minding her business and here came Hassan. For months, he pursued her. She curved him every day, but after a while, his daily instant messages, ordering her food, leaving greeting cards with money on her desk, Tiff Treats orders, and weekly flowers began to win her over.

Letting her guard down, she began getting to know Hassan on a personal level. He stimulated her mind and helped her to become a more opened person with a positive mindset.

She loved his fun, laid back, goofy and charming personality. He wasn't bad on the eyes either. Hassan was tall with a caramel complexion, and he walked with an athletics stride that fit his tone muscle body. He wore his hair in two braids at times or twists. He had a stellar smile with the most beautiful set of white teeth. His beard was full, neat, and well kept, and his lips were soft and full.

Hassan was trouble for her, and she didn't trust herself with him. That's the main reason she avoided him, but his persistence and the way he showed interest in her other than a physical attraction wowed her.

Hassan had done more for her than any other man in the four months' timeframe that she had been dating him. Kissy never had to pay her bills or touched her money, and Hassan was very good to her.

Kissy admit that she did question how Hassan could afford the things he did for her. They worked for the state, and they were the lowest on the pay scale for state employees. Her little salary of $2754 didn't do shit and was barely enough to survive on. After they took out taxes, 401k, ERS retirement of 8.5%, Medicaid and other shit, Kissy was lucky if she had $1800 left over. With the way the rent was, it was hard to survive without a roommate. That was another reason she started her group.

Kissy massaged her temples. She didn't want to think of any of this right now. It was easier for her to act as if nothing happened, if even just for a moment. *These niggas ain't shit, and Hassan proved my point. It was silly of me to ever think he was different. It's time to turn it up a notch in my group.*

She rose from the bed and went to take a shower. She felt disgusted with herself. She hated the way she allowed Hassan to rock her center as if he hadn't done anything wrong and as far as the baby was concerned, she didn't know what to feel.

Having a baby by a married man was never in the deck of cards Kissy held. *How do I reshuffle the deck?*

The hot water massaged her scalp and body. She cried and allowed her thoughts to roam freely. "How could he do this me?" she screamed and slid down to the bottom of the bathtub. She brought her knees against her chest and buried her head. She was crashing.

Nova could hear her heart beating to an African beat. It was loud, powerful, and pushed her with force with each step. She breathed heavy, placed her right hand over her heart, and prepared herself for what was on the other side of door 910006.

Her hand shook. *Just go home, Nova. Kensington might now even be the one you're husband is messing with.* She silently tried to encourage herself, but her hand touched Kensington's doorknob. She gently twisted it and was surprised that it was unlocked. She walked in and lightly closed the door behind her.

She observed the fairly nice size one-bedroom apartment and admired how cute, sassy, and sleek it was.

"This is definitely the bitch's style," Nova whispered.

She loved the white plush couches with the ocean blue and gold throw pillows. A mirrored crushed, diamond-shaped ottoman sat in the middle of the living room floor on top of a gold, fluffy, oversized floor rug. An 80-inch LED white wall mount TV stand with a 70-inch flat screen adorned one wall, while the other wall caused a sharp pain in Nova's chest.

"I fucking knew it. I knew it," Nova whispered, biting down as hard as she could on her bottom lip.

The oversized photo of her husband and Kensington Blu disgusted her. Her husband had once again made a complete fool out of her. This was the last time. *She snapped!*

Nova kicked the 70-inch flat screen with all her might, knocking it to the floor. She began throwing the throw pillows, pulling the blinds down and destroying anything in her path.

"Hassan, is that you baby? What's going on?" Kissy yelled, running into the living with a towel wrapped around her body and goddess dreads.

*Whap! Whap! Whap!*

"Bitch, you thought were slick messing with my husband?" *Whap!* Nova delivered another blow.

"Get the fuck off of me," Kissy swung, popping Nova in her left eye.

Kissy studied the familiar woman's face for a second, and then it dawned on her that it was Nova Daniels, her HR manager and Hassan's wife.

"Nova, you got some nerve breaking into my home. What the fuck do you want? What husband?" Kissy yelled ready to pop her again.

"Don't act like you don't know Hassan is my husband, Kensington." Nova charged at Kissy again. The two women tussled falling to the floor.

"Bitch, I just learned Hassan had a wife. I didn't know anything about you. He just told me he was married and said y'all were going through a divorce!" Kissy screamed, rolling on top of Nova.

Hassan heard the commotion coming from downstairs and rushed to his and Kissy's apartment. He knew the sound of his wife's voice anywhere.

"Oh shit," he yelled, running to break Kissy and his wife up.

The two women breathed heavily and stared at each other with venom. They were ready for round two. Kissy touched her bloody lip and spat at Nova. "Bitch!" Kissy roared.

"You got me fucked up." Nova swung and missed, losing her balance and falling. Hassan went to pick her up.

"Weak ass bitch!" Kissy spat again on Nova.

"Ayo, chill Nova. What the fuck are you doing here? Why aren't you at work?" Hassan yelled.

"Move!" Nova jerked away from him and stood. "What the fuck am I doing here? No Hassan, what the fuck are you doing here? I've been calling your phone, and if you would have answered, you would have known I was leaving because your daughter ripped her shorts at school today. Never mind all of that. My employee, Hassan? Really? Our job? Why would you make a fool out of me like this?" Nova asked as tears ran down her face.

"Daughter? Hassan, you have kids?" Kissy asked in disbelief. Hassan held his head down and placed both of his hands in his jean pockets.

"He ain't gotta explain a got damn thing to you. How long has this been going on? Answer me!" Nova screamed. Heat flushed through her body and her nose ran. She wiped her nose with the backs of her hands. Her white blouse was ruin with makeup stains from her tears.

Kissy stood there waiting for Hassan to exclaim his love for her like he did minutes ago when he was stroking her love box. This would have been the time to tell Nova the truth and come clean about the woman she was to him since Hassan told her they were separated and getting a divorce.

She stared at Hassan with sad eyes. He diverted his eyes from Kensington and began pleading for his wife to hear him out. He had feelings for Kensington, but he loved his wife and knew that he had too much invested with Nova to lose.

A part of him felt bad. The pain he saw in his wife's eyes killed him, but he couldn't help his attraction to Kensington. She was everything opposite of his wife, and the truth was he was drawn to her aggressive, hood, stylist, sass, and messiness.

Kensington wasn't as beautiful as his wife by a long shot, but she had a good heart, and she was fun to be around. She made him feel alive, and he could be himself with her.

Nova was beautiful, but more on the reserve side. Everything with her was conditioned and routine. She didn't drink or smoke, and Hassan was tired of living life in confinement with her. He wasn't happy being a husband and father, but he had been with Nova over five years, and he respected her for raising a child he created outside of their union. The way Nova treated his daughter made Hassan's love for Nova that much greater. Although he cheated, he would never leave her.

"You're cheating on me with this trash? Hassan really?" Nova screamed.

"Trashhhh? I'm nobody's trash boo. You know what? Fuck you, Hassan! You just gone let your wife sit up here and attacked

30

me like that, then plead your love to her. What about me, Hassan? What about what you promised me?" Kissy yelled.

"Kensington, it's been real baby, but this is my wife. I want to work things out with my wife. I'm sorry for leading you on and lying to you. I was wrong for that, and I apologize." Hassan looked Nova in her eyes.

"Now, you heard my husband. I want you out of here and now." Nova ordered.

"Shut the fuck up my love, with your weak ass. Do you really think Hassan will stop messing with me? We just made love." Kissy smirked.

She refused for Nova to think she got the upper hand. Her ego and pride would not back down.

A loud bang from the front door gathered their attention. Hassan stormed over to answer it and wished he hadn't.

"We had complaints of screams and noises. Step to the side, sir," the short, black officer said while he and his partner entered the residence.

"What's going on here?" the tall Hispanic officer asked upon inspecting Kissy's bloody lip and Nova's swollen black eye.

"I want to press charges!" Nova shouted.

Hassan stood there with his mouth agape. Having his pregnant mistress and employee go to jail wasn't something he wanted to happen.

"Ma'am, let's go!" The Hispanic officer grabbed ahold of Kissy.

Hassan wanted to step in. He didn't like the way the officer was handling Kensington, and he felt he was enjoying the view of Kensington's barely covered body.

"Get your hands off of me. Hassan, do something! This is my apartment. She came in here and attacked me. I want to press charges on her!" Kissy screamed, fighting with the officer.

"Kensington, don't fight. You'll just make it worse," Hassan encouraged.

"Sir, does she live here?" the black officer whose name was Wallace asked Hassan. Nova crossed her arms and stared at Hassan while tapping her left foot.

"No sir, she doesn't. This is my wife and my apartment," Hassan lied.

Officer Wallace shook his head. He knew exactly what was going on and he was disgusted. He couldn't stand men who couldn't man up and be honest. *He got the two queens fighting and acting other than themselves.*

"Really Hassan? That's how you're going to do me?" Kissy screamed.

"Boo hoe boo. Get her out of here. You heard my husband. I want her gone!" Nova screamed.

"Let's go, ma'am!" the Hispanic officer whose name was Jose yelled.

"I will not be going anywhere. I know my rights. I receive mail here, and Hassan must legally evict me. We are common law married. Lastly, I'm pressing charges on her for trespassing on my residence and attacking me!" Kissy yelled at Officer Jose. "Get your nasty ass hands off of me. You have no right. It's going to be a problem the next time you put your hands on me without reading me my Miranda Rights. Now, I want all of you gone and now!" Kissy yelled, stepping out of Officer Jose's reach.

"She's right," Officer Wallace replied to his partner, showing him a piece of mail that was lying on the counter and pointing to this oversized picture of Kensington and Hassan.

Officer Wallace hadn't had intentions on taking either of the ladies to jail. If Kensington or Nova wanted to file a report and press assault charges, he was willing to do the paperwork, but he couldn't bring himself to send these beautiful women to jail. Jail was no place for either one. He could tell he wasn't dealing with hood rat women. By the looks, upkeep of both women, and the way they both carried themselves, he could tell this was about a man playing both women, and they just found out about each other.

"I told you!" Kensington yelled.

"Are you pressing charges?" Officer Wallace asked Kensington.

"Yes, I sure am." Kensington stared at Hassan.

"Kensington, look, don't press charges. This is my wife and mother of my child. Nova and I will just leave," Hassan pleaded.

"So what the fuck am I, Hassan? A fucking toy to be played with? You were just telling me how much you loved me and you were separated and going through a divorce. You just told me how you "got me" and were going to be here for the baby, yet you were just going to stand by and allow her to press charges on me knowing I'm pregnant!" Kissy screamed with a face full of tears.

The room got eerily quiet. Hassan looked at Nova and put his head down. Her worst fears came tumbling down on her, not again. She couldn't deal with another child Hassan created outside of the marriage. She had already lied to her family and friends about who Trinity really was. They all believed she was adopted and that Nova had infertility issues.

Rage filled Nova's body, and before she knew it, she quickly grabbed ahold of Kensington's hair. She attacked her with fury. *Whap! Whap!* Nova swung hitting Kensington on the left side of her jaw.

The two officers grabbed Nova and struggled to contain her.

"Fuck you! That baby ain't his. I hate hoes like you!" Nova shouted as the officers placed her in handcuffs and escorted her off the premises. Officer Wallace had no choice now but to take Nova in.

"All you had to do was comply, Kensington. A nigga had you, and I would have bailed you out. Now you done fucked up my marriage. I should have never started fucking with your bird ass. I want you out of my shit at the end of this month. Consider this your 30-day eviction notice!" Hassan yelled before slamming the front door.

"Fuck you, Hassan!" Kissy screamed.

The NIGGEROCITY of Hassan and his wife. She couldn't stand women who always went after the other woman. Hell, Kissy didn't know anything about this woman or the fact Hassan had a daughter.

She sat on the sofa and began shaking. She was so angry. She took deep breaths, counting backwards from ten. She couldn't believe how her Friday was turning out. This was supposed to be a great three-day weekend of love and fun, but Hassan and his crazy ass wife messed everything up.

Kissy didn't know what to do with Hassan. On the one hand she knew she needed to end things, but on the other hand, she was carrying his child, not to mention she was still deeply in love with him. She wasn't the type of woman to easily go away. Hassan was going to play by her rules or else.

She stood and went into her restroom to tend to her lip and jaw. The mirror showed a broken, scorned, and lost little girl. Kissy hate the way she looked and always felt she was ugly. The swollen jaw and busted lip added to her already deep insecurities.

She washed her face, covered her bruises with makeup, and dressed in a red onesie. She needed to move around in order to keep her mind busy and off of Hassan. If she didn't, she knew how her mental illness would take her under, and she would lead to self-harm by either cutting herself or committing suicide.

She lit all her vanilla ice scented candles and put on her Ella Mai CD. When she heard the song "Trip", her mode began to change a little.

Kissy shook her head at the mess Nova made. "This ignorant ass bitch!" she yelled while placing her TV back on its stand. She turned it on and was relieved to see that it still worked.

She placed all the throw pillows back on the couches, and she removed the long, sliding blinds that Nova had broken. She then opened three packs of gold and ocean blue curtains and hung them up where the patio blinds once were.

Once she was done, she took the large photo of her and Hassan off the wall and placed it in her hall closet. She found Marilyn Monroe quote wall stickers and placed them on the wall where the photo once was.

She smiled, liking the new touches of her living room and resided to the kitchen to begin cooking, something she was going to do earlier.

She prepared her a meal of enchiladas, ranch style beans, Spanish rice, cornbread, and a red velvet cake. She couldn't wait until her meal was done. All the stress and heartbreak Hassan was putting her through made her work up an appetite. She had to watch herself though. Stress made her eat, and Kissy had already lost a total of 80 pounds. She was proud of her shape but knew how easy it was for her body to pick the weight back up. Food was always a comfort to her other than cutting herself.

"Mmmmm," Kissy moaned, enjoying her hot meal.

Just like she knew she would, she overindulged. She was stuffed, and she finished her meal off with two glasses of Hennessy. She was feeling good and mellowed out until Hassan started blowing up her phone.

"Tend to your bitch!" Kissy yelled furious that he had the nerve to even be calling her after what he just pulled.

The fact that Hassan had chosen his wife in front of her spoke volumes Kissy. She knew how far into depression she could fall, and she wasn't trying to allow herself to go off the deep end, but this was too deep for her to shake.

"I'm never enough," she whispered and wiped the long tear that trickled down her left cheek.

The longer she sat there in deep thought her spirit went down and quickly. Her lip trembled, and the coping mechanisms of music, cleaning, and cooking did nothing to soothe the depression that crept in her soul. She needed her fix, and as if her body was drawn to it, she made her way back to her room. On her dresser, she found the double blade razor that she had used earlier to arch her eyebrows. She grabbed it.

"All the times I had been around Hassan he never spoke of a wife. How could I be so stupid?" Kissy took the razor and cut into her right arm. "There was no fucking wedding band, photos on his desk, or nothing." Kissy cut again. "I hate him!" she screamed, cutting too deeply hitting a vein. Kissy eyes bulge. "No, no, no, no, nooooo!" she cried. "Help me!" Kissy screamed realizing that she had hit a vein and was losing a lot of blood.

She hurried to wrap a towel around it. The last place she wanted to be was in a psych ward on 1:1 for trying to harm herself. She became sweaty and moist. She felt weak, drowsy, and confused.

Her breathing was rapid, and her heart pumped fast. Her bloody fingers dropped her phone twice as she struggled to dial 9-1-1. She felt herself slipping and losing consciousness.

"Today wasn't supposed to be like this," she repeated over and over trying to keep her eyes open.

Her mind and thoughts were floating. Hassan played her good. She would never have imagined that Hassan was a fuck boy. How could she? The man took her out of town, paid her rent, car note, wined and dined her, took her on long walks in the park, not to mention Hassan didn't have a wedding band, and there were never any mentions of a wife or daughter from coworkers.

He had definitely taken her for a ride, but Kissy valued that Hassan and his wife would be in for a rude awakening if she didn't die today. She was nobody to play with, and she was serious about pressing charges.

"Stay with us Ms…" was the last thing Kissy remembered before everything in her world turned black.

"Hey Denise, do we still have those extra clothing left from the clothing drive we did last month?" Qadira asked.

"Yes as a matter fact we do. It's in the janitor's closet. Why?" Denise asked.

"Well, little Trinity ripped her shorts, and I've been calling her mother, and she isn't answering. I have a meeting to attend, and Trinity has been sitting in my office the last two in a half hours."

"What size is she?" Denise asked.

"She's about a 5T."

"Okay, no worries. I'll go look and find her something."

"Thanks girl," Qadira said and headed back to her office.

Trinity was playing on her office rug playing with blocks, and Qadira smiled. Her long sandy brown ponytails swung, and Trinity's hazel eyes lit up every time she thought of something new to build. Her honey olive complexion glowed and everything. Whenever she smiled, a cute pair of deep dimples greeted you. She was definitely a cutie, and Qadira smirked thinking how Trinity would one day have men falling at her feet.

Qadira was about to take a seat in her office chair when something caught her eye. Behind Trinity's left ear was a heart-shaped birthmark. "Nah, that can't be!" she whispered.

"Ms. Q-a-weara," Trinity called out.

38

"Yes, Trinity," Qadira replied, trying to hide her laughter. The smaller children always mispronounced her name.

"Do you know where my mommy is? I'm ready to go home," she asked sadly.

"I don't know baby, but I'll try to call her again." Qadira smiled.

Trinity was so well mannered. Qadira wished she could be a mother. She couldn't have children of her own, so that's why she loved working with children.

Qadira's personal cell rung and she rolled her eyes seeing that it was her Aunt Clara. She ignored the call and sat down at her office desk.

Her cell rang again. It was her Aunt Clara calling again. "Why do you keep calling me?" she yelled, answering the phone.

"Your mama died, and these folks need to know what you want to do with the body," she coldly announced.

"What?" Qadira screamed, scaring little Trinity.

Tears ran down Qadira's face. Although her mother was a terrible mother, she was still her mother, and she felt the pain of a loss.

"Hey, girl! I found these and she should be able to fit these." Denise paused. "Oh my god Qadira, what's wrong? Are you okay?" Denise asked concerned seeing her friend in pain.

"I need to leave. My mother just passed away," Qadira cried.

"I'm so sorry." Denise hugged Qadira. "Look, get out of here. I'll hold everything down," she advised.

"Thank you, Denise!" Qadira sadly smiled and grabbed her belongings. She rubbed Trinity's shoulders and wished her a good day.

Qadira started her engine and made her way home. She kicked off her heels and heard them echo against the hardwood floor.

She grabbed a bottle of Merlot that sat on her bar and sat on her loveseat. Tears rolled down her face, and she didn't attempt to wipe them.

She sipped from her bottle and screamed. Loneliness and depression seem to always be her best friend. They were linked and her soulmate. She couldn't escape those feelings. No matter how successful she was, they seem to follow her like a dark cloud.

Her phone rang, and she saw it was her older sister, Yashira. She didn't feel like talking, so she let the phone go to voicemail. She called again.

"Ughhhhhh!" she yelled. "Hello!"

"Hey, Q! I hope this isn't a bad time. I just made it in town. Can you please open the door? I know you're home. I just called your job, and they said you took a personal day," Yashira said.

"Here I come," Qadira replied hanging up the phone. She was surprised to hear from her sister. Their relationship had been estranged for the last couple of years.

She wiped her face and did a quick look around her home to make sure everything was in place. She opened the door and gave her sister a long overdue hug.

"What's wrong with you, Q?" Yashira asked, taking a step back observing her sister.

"Aunt Clara didn't call you?" Qadira asked, motioning for Yashira to come in.

The two took a seat on Qadira's royal blue sofa, and an awkward silence fell between them. The silence lingered throughout the air as the two silently filled each other out.

Qadira took in Yashira's beauty. She had long, black Senegalese twist that tumbled down to her waistline. Black lipstick adorned her full lips making her honey olive skin and hazel eyes glow. She was 5'4 and had lost some weight placing her size around 125 pounds.

"I should have called you first Q, but I need a place to crash for a couple of weeks. I start my new job as the regional training manager. If not, I can get a hotel," Yashira said.

"Yazzi that's fine, but did you hear what I asked?" Qadira said, calling Yashira by her nickname.

"Yeah, I heard you. She called me too, but I didn't answer or check the millions of messages she sent. Anyway, what did she want?"

"Mama died."

"Are you going to finish this?" Yashira asked, drowning down the last of the Merlot.

"Yazzi, mama died!" Qadira screamed.

"So, that woman doesn't mean shit to me. She threw me out on the streets at 14 years old. She picked a nigga over her own daughter. Do you think that bitch cared about me? She didn't check to see if I had eaten or how I was doing. Aunt Clara ain't shit either. I guess I wasn't their favorite like you, little sister, precious little Qadira. So excuse me, sis, I hope that hoe rots in hell. Ain't no love lost here!" Yashira screamed and stood. She was so angry.

"That's still our mother though."

"Anddd, fuck her!"

"I know she wasn't a good mother, but will you help with the arrangements?" Qadira asked.

"Hell no, like I said, you were the favorite. That's your mother, so you bury her." Yashira pointed at Qadira.

"You're always speaking on shit you don't know. Poor little, Yashira. I was hurting too, Yaz!" Qadira screamed and stood. "This is long overdue. So let's get this shit out."

"Long overdue? Oh, you have no clue, little sister. Talking about you was hurting too. Oh really? How Qadira? You were mama's pride and joy. What did you possibly go through so bad? Huh? You always won and got the best, even now. I mean look at this home." Yashira did a spin. "Look at the car you drive, Ms. Big time school principal. You were always the better one, Q. Always! I was the trash. This was a mistake coming here. I don't even know why I took this position here in Austin, out of all places. I'm leaving," Yashira cried, heading towards the door.

"Do go, Yashira. You're always running away. You are never trash in my eyes and never were. I need you. I'm not as strong as you."

41

"Well baby sis, I pray you never have to see the ugliness of this world. You live in this bubble." Yashira pointed again before turning to leave.

"Why are you so angry with me, Yashira? Don't you know how much I love you? Why do you hate me so much? You were the lucky one. You got out."

"Because you look just like her, and every time I see you, you are a constant reminder of everything I've tried to forget. I hate her. I hate her, and I hate you for never having my back. You always made excuses for her."

"That's all I knew, Yaz. I had to. She was sick, and that's what I had to believe," Qadira cried. "I had to believe she was sick because no mother in their right mind would allow her boyfriend to strip her daughter of her innocence."

Yashira covered her mouth and turned around to face Qadira.

"Noooo!" Yashira cried. "I'm so sorry."

"I was nine years old when he crept into my bed. It was so much blood," Qadira whispered. "I wouldn't stop bleeding. He damaged me to the point that I can never have children. It happened for years. She didn't stop him. She just turned the other way. I would tune it out, and the first time I had enough money and the opportunity to leave, I did. I searched for you, and that's how I found you that night at the strip club. I love you, Yazzi. I always have. This house, my position, and vehicle mean nothing. I still have nightmares."

"I had no idea, and I'm sorry," Yashira said.

"Of course you didn't because you're selfish."

"Selfish how?"

"It's all about you. After mama kicked you out, did you ever once think, let me go check on my little sis?"

"I couldn't go back there, Q. It was nothing against you personally, but I had to mentally block him and mama out. You're taking shit personally, and I feel that's being selfish. I'm sorry I couldn't be there to protect you. I had to save myself," Yashira shot back defensively.

"I guess saving yourself is all you think about, huh? Just like how you saved yourself, abandoned your daughter, and took off. You are selfish. Not once did you ask me to care for her," Qadira cried.

"No, no, no, no. Don't go there. Just leave her out of this. Leave her out of this!" Yashira screamed. "Fuck you, Q! I can't believe you would say that. Why would I leave her with you or this sick ass family? Why, Q? Why? So you could take her around mama and that sick ass nigga? She looks exactly like me. That nigga would have harmed her. I couldn't trust you. I had to leave Trinity with her father. I knew he wouldn't leave her behind. I knew he could care for her. I knew," she sobbed uncontrollably sliding down to the floor.

Qadira felt horrible for what she just said, but it was true. She was angry with God that people like Yashira could birth children and then toss them away.

Qadira felt Yashira was wrong, and she judged her. Not for giving away the baby, but Qadira was hurt that Yashira didn't think enough of her to give her the baby.

They both had deep-rooted issues. Opening up about her past made Qadira feel closer to her sister, and she hoped that they could build a bond like the one they had when they were smaller children. She loved her sister.

Qadira sat on the floor next to Yashira and grabbed her into her arms. They both cried together. She didn't mean to bring up the baby her sister abandoned, but she needed Yashira to know that the love she always sought was what she ran from.

"I miss my baby every single day. I made a mistake. I made a mistake!" Yashira screamed. "I've turned my life around Qadira, and I want my baby back."

Yashira fought every day to forgive herself. At the time, she felt that she was only doing what she had to do. Since 14, she had to find ways to survive, and when she met Hassan, she felt he was her way out. Then he too crushed her. She found out from another dancer by the name of Ryan that Hassan was married.

Hassan wouldn't leave his wife for her, and Yashira had come too far to go back to the bottom with a baby. She didn't know how to be a mother and raising one on her own wasn't what she had asked for.

Yashira left her baby girl on his doorstep and started a new life in Houston. The money in the stripping world was good, but she wanted more.

She completed her GED and went to school for her Business and Human Resources degree. She landed a job with the Department of Human Services and worked her way up to Regional Training Manager.

She did well and built a life for herself. Throughout the years, she would keep in contact with Qadira, but building a bond was too painful for her.

After Hurricane Harvey, Yashira's two-bedroom apartment with most of her belongings was ruined. This was the third time that flooding had occurred since she had lived in Houston and she was exhausted. She asked for a transfer and Austin had an immediate opening. BPR was taking place, and they needed a trainer in the office to be hands-on with the staff. Yashira took the position but wished she hadn't. Austin had too many painful memories for her.

"Well let's make that happen, sis. Just know you can stay here for as long as you need to, and I'll do whatever I can to help you get your little girl back," Qadira promised. *I know Trinity is my niece.* Qadira silently thought.

Hassan realized Trinity hadn't been picked up from school, so he rushed to his daughter's school to pick her up and dropped her off with his relative Kiara.

"Thank you for watching her, Keke. I'll be back in a little bit," he said, calling Kiara by her nickname.

"No problem. Besides what's one more child?" She laughed and crossed her arms over her chest.

"Ayo, before I leave, let me ask you something."

"Shoot."

"You're not messing with my boi Ty are you?"

"Yeah, why and where you hear that at?"

"Keke, you know how that nigga Larry is behind you. He's going to bring smoke to anyone who messes with you, and stay out that messy ass group, man."

"I'm not worried about Larry. It's over cousin. Where was this energy when he was putting his hands on me? He does not own me. Just because we have kids together doesn't mean he owns me. That nigga runs through every bitch in the city. Why is it so wrong of me to live my life? Ty treats the children and me good."

"I hear you. Just be careful out here. I'll be back in a little bit to get Trinity." Hassan kissed her cheek and left.

He hopped in his vehicle and shook his head. Larry was crazy as hell. He sighed worried about his friend Ty.

Larry had done a lot to his cousin. She had even put him in jail three times before and had gotten a restraining order against him. The family never got into their affairs because Kiara would go right back to him.

Hassan admitted his cousin looked good. Her weight had picked up, her skin was glowing, her home was nice, and he could tell that she was really into Ty. He still worried though. Ty wasn't good for Kiara. He sold drugs and slept around with many women. To be honest, he wasn't surprised when Ashley popped up at Ty's apartment acting a fool. Hassan has seen worse than that dealing with Ty. Ty was also ruthless. He didn't mind using his gun. He was always setting someone up and robbing people. It was a part of the game, and Hassan slowed up on hanging around Ty as much, especially when he married Nova. She didn't care for Ty at all and didn't want Hassan around him.

Hassan parked the police station and had to wait a total of two hours. His lawyer advised him that Nova had been fingerprinted and processed. As soon as the judge signed off on the bond, she would be released.

He paced back and forth upset with himself that things had even come to this. *How did Nova know where I was or where Kensington lived?* He stepped outside the police station to smoke a black and mild and checked his phone. He rubbed his right hand over his face. He didn't have time for Nicole's shit. She kept calling him, and he couldn't understand what she wanted. She spoke a good game in the beginning, but she was unraveling and acting very desperate. His phone rang again, and he went on and answered it. She was beginning to become a problem, a problem that he didn't need.

"Nicole, why do you keep calling me? I told you we were done," Hassan said harshly.

"No Hassan, we're not done. So what, you thought you were just going to dump me for Kensington Blu? Did you think I wouldn't find out? You told me you loved me. Was that all a lie? I left my fucking husband for you," Nicole cried.

"You did that shit on your own. I never told you to leave that nigga, nor did I ever tell you we would be together. Don't play victim here. You knew what you were doing, and you also know I'm a married man."

"You used me!" Nicole yelled.

Hassan knew he should have never started sleeping with Nicole. He overheard her on the phone one afternoon when he had visited Nova's job at the prior location. Nicole's father had passed away, and she was the beneficiary. Hassan heard her arguing with a relative about a $75,000 life insurance policy.

The policy wasn't much, but Hassan was in desperate need of money at the time. He had a gambling addiction and had lost thousands of dollars. He had a deadline. It was either tell Nova about his gambling problem, take out money against their home, or risk being murdered.

With all the shit that he had put Nova through, he couldn't risk letting her know that he had failed her again. She was too good for him, but he also knew Nova had her limits.

Nicole wasn't his type. She was dark-skinned, overweight, and wasn't shapely with her weight. She was wide and unattractive with a nasty attitude. Hassan thought she could be beautiful with some adjustments, but at the time, he was only focused on what she had. He could tell Nicole had low self-esteem by the way she carried herself. Her light was dim, and her aura was off-putting. He knew with some sweet talks, a little attention, and cheating on Nova with someone like her would boost Nicole's ego, and he would be in.

It took all of two days for Hassan to swindle her out of her money and get between her prize box. He would be lying if he said Nicole's sex wasn't good. She knew how to please him, and she gave the best head, but he was done with her. He had paid his debts off.

Luck became on his side, and he began to have a winning streak. He paid Nicole her money back, and the money he won allowed him to afford to wine and dine Kensington.

"I used you? Come on, Nicole. Don't start that shit. I gave you back every single dime. Look, I just want to make things right with my wife. I know we work together, and I don't want any hostility or my wife knowing about us. It was fun while it lasted, but we're done." Hassan hung up the phone.

Nicole called his phone over and over six more times. He placed her number on block, and he called his boy Ty next.

"Man, I think that Nicole is going to be a problem," Hassan said worriedly.

"Why? You need me to handle that fam? You know I got you," Ty replied. Hassan laughed.

"'Preciate you boi. You stay having a nigga's back. Nicole talking about I used her and made her leave her husband. Ain't that some shit?"

"Boi, you must got some dope dick cause you got these females going wild. Anyway, what's all that noise in the background? Where you at?"

"I'm outside the jail right now waiting on Nova to be released. That's why I was calling you."

"Oh shit! They got yo ole lady?" Ty asked shocked. "What she do to end up in there?"

"Kensington." Hassan sighed.

"Damn, family."

"Yeah man! Remember when Ashley said Nova was crying earlier and had left the job?"

"Yeah, man that girl crazy as fuck. We argued for hours when you left." Ty sighed. "Man, that group she was talking about got me in some shit. Word got back to Larry about Kiara and me, and he called me threatening a nigga."

"Damn! I just left fam's house too and told her to be careful. She's cut for you. When Ashley mentioned Kiara name earlier, I didn't think she was talking about my peoples Kiara. She went through a lot with Larry. I'mma keep one hundred, do my fam right.

If you're going to keep fucking with Ashley, let Kiara go. She has kids, and I don't need Larry tryna whoop up on her and shit," Hassan warned.

"I feel that. I'm digging Kiara. It ain't nothing too deep, but I'm feeling lil mama. I'm still weighing my options with Ashley, but I ain't tryna be caught up in no bullshit with Larry over Kiara either, so I respect what you're saying. Anyway, what's going on with Nova?"

"Apparently, Nova found out about Kensington. All I know is she showed up at the apartment, and they fought. Kensington is pressing charges, and Nova found out about the baby. This is all my fault, and I feel bad man. I just don't know what to do. I love Nova, but I love Kensington too. I tried to call Kensington, but she's not answering my calls. I said some foul shit to her, but a nigga was just mad he got caught. But aye though, do me a favor and take Nova's car to the crib for me. Her door code is 4-3-5-7. She has a spare key in the armrest. I don't need her ass going back to the apartments and Kensington sees her or some shit."

"Anything you need."

"Thanks, fam and good looking out."

"I got you," Ty said before ending the call.

Hassan flicked his black and mild on the ground and stepped on it. When he looked up, he noticed Nova's sister, Ryan, walking up the sidewalk. *Damn, what is she doing here?* He silently thought, mad that Nova had involved her family in their business.

"Well if it isn't the world's sorriest nigga, Hassan," Ryan clapped walking towards him yelling.

"Yeah hoe, okay," Hassan replied.

"Hoe? Don't get disrespectful. You know what, Hassan? You don't deserve Nova. I don't know why she won't just cut ties and divorce you. My sister has never been to jail or in a fight. You got her out here looking and acting stupid!" Ryan snapped.

"Yeah, you say all that shit now, but there was a time you were screaming a nigga's name. You were so jealous of Nova that once you found out about Yashira, you pulled a hoe move. You thought exposing me would make Nova divorce me. You hate the

49

fact Nova is still with me. Shit, if you had of acted right, you still could have gotten this daddy's dope dick. I used to pay your stripping ass good back in the day." Hassan smirked. "What cat got your tongue?"

"I'm no longer the same person I was. You also know that isn't fair for you to say. I didn't even know you were her husband. Nova married you so quickly and kept us in the dark about you for months. It wasn't until she introduced us that day. Once I found out you were her husband, I stopped messing with you. It didn't make sense to confess to her that I had slept with you, because y'all were already married, and I didn't know. I wasn't about to ruin my relationship with my sister because her nigga is a whole hoe out here. Don't try to make it seem like I'm some kind of jealous, deranged woman who backstabbed my sister and slept with her man. The only thing I'm guilty of is playing like I don't know she lied to the family about the truth behind Trinity and that I know who her mother is and where she is!" Ryan yelled.

"I bet you won't tell Nova who you were though. It easy for you to judge me, Ms. Saved church lady. We both know you weren't always a saint. You used to beg me to coke up my piece so that you can suck it. I'd advise you to mind your business and stay out of ours," Hassan said through grunted teeth.

"You don't scare me, Hassan. The thing is you have more to lose than I do. You ain't shit, and that's something we both know," Ryan said before walking into the Travis County Jail.

"Watch yourself, Ryan. I would hate for tapes and photos to be released," Hassan threatened.

"Play ball, bitch. I got tapes too. Play with it!" Ryan yelled from over her shoulder.

Hassan thought about going back into the building but decided against it. "Man, fuck this shit!" Hassan yelled before turning to walk to his vehicle.

He swung by Kiara's home and picked Trinity up. He decided to take her out to eat and have some daddy/daughter time. As she ate and swung her little legs, Hassan smiled at her and thought about her mother, Yashira. Trinity was a splitting image of her.

Yashira was special to him, and he wished he would have made the decision to divorce Nova and be with her, but at the time he couldn't. Nova was and still is his stability.

When Nova met Hassan, he was down on his luck bad and had no direction. She was there for him and helped build him up as a man. His job of ten years had let him go, and once the stipend package dwindled down, Hassan went through depression. He went on job search after the job search with no luck, and his mother's sofa was beginning to become his permanent home.

*He met Nova at Auto Zone after his truck battery decided to die. She was there buying accessories for her vehicle.*

*Hassan remembered thinking she was the most pleasant woman he had ever met. The way she smiled around the store, said thank you to the sales reps and hummed made Hassan smile. Her energy was contiguous, and Hassan had never met a woman with such a great attitude.*

*He had to shoot his shot, and he was surprised that Nova gave him a chance. She didn't judge him or turn her nose up. She was kind and patient. Hassan told her about his employment background, and Nova gave him a job with the Texas Department of Human Services. Over time he worked his way up to supervisor, and together he and Nova built their own foundation.*

*He and Nova didn't date long before they married at the Justice of Peace. Actually, they pulled a Biggie and Faith Evans move. It had only been three weeks.*

*Nova's family wasn't pleased that they married at the courthouse and that they had yet to meet Hassan. They thought she had rushed things, and she barely knew him, but they were very much in love and inseparable.*

*A couple of months after their union, Hassan wondered if maybe Nova's family was right. He wasn't feeling Nova the same* way and started to believe that maybe he made a mistake. He wondered did he really need Nova now that he was back on his feet. He admitted thinking that way was part of the way she made him feel, and he wondered why Nova still had yet to introduce him to her family. He felt he wasn't good enough for Nova or her family and pieces of resentment began to build in him.

Battling his inner demons and depression, his boy Ty took him out to the strip club. That's where he met Ryan. They slept together in the back room of the club multiple times. To Hassan, she wasn't anything special, but Ryan began to catch feelings.

It wasn't until weeks later he saw the newcomer Yashira, that went by the name Yazzi, and she set his body on fire. Her olive skin glowed, while her eyes glistened in the darkness. Hassan was stuck.

Yashira gave him a lap dance, and while she danced, he studied her and asked her questions. Hearing the way she spoke and gathered her words turned Hassan on. He knew she had a story and didn't belong in the club. She gave him her phone number, and they built a friendship. Hassan fell in love with her. He had never met a woman who he could be open and transparent with without sleeping with them.

When he and Yashira finally made love, Hassan knew that their friendship and relationship would change. Out of respect for Yashira, he ended things with Ryan, and that left her sour towards him.

Shortly after sleeping with Yashira, she had gotten pregnant. Hassan tried to keep his marriage a secret while still being with Yashira. However, Ryan ruined that the day he and Nova ran into her at Walmart. Nova finally introduced them, and Ryan couldn't believe that the man she was sleeping with and had caught feelings for was her sister's new husband.

Ryan told Yashira about Nova in hopes that Yashira would tell Nova and Nova would leave him, but it didn't happen that way. Yashira told Hassan that she knew he was married because he was too predictable and had married men habits. She wasn't going anywhere, especially after giving birth to their baby girl.

*Hassan tried his best to keep up with his double lifestyle, but Yashira was wearing him thin. She fell into postpartum depression, and while she was adjusting to a brand new baby, Hassan and Nova's marriage began to blossom.*

*He was honestly in love with two women but knew he had made a mistake. He attempted to end things with Yashira and sat up an arrangement for the baby. He even wanted to come clean to Nova and confess his betrayal to her. Yashira didn't take the news well and felt that Hassan was abandoning her.*

*"You think I wanted to be a mistress and a baby mama? You got me fucked up, Hassan. I'm not raising this baby on my own," we're the last words Hassan remembered Yashira yelling at him while he walked down the stairs to her apartment.*

*Yashira must've followed him or knew where he and Nova rested their heads because the next morning when Nova opened the door, his baby girl was left in her carrier with a note attached.*

"Daddy, I said can I have some more fries please?" Trinity asked, breaking Hassan's thoughts.

B*eep, beep-beep, beep!*
"Mmmm," Kissy moaned, stirring in her sleep. She attempted to open her eyes, but couldn't.

The beeping sound was extremely loud to her sensitive ears. She heard the loud voice of her Aunt Torrie, and a nurse talking in the background.

*Ugh!* She inwardly screamed. The last time she was in the hospital, she remembered putting her Aunt Torrie down as her emergency contact.

"She's up y'all. Kensington baby, can you hear me?" her Aunt Torrie asked loudly.

Kissy frowned and nodded her head. She took her right hand and rubbed her eyes. "Can you turn the lights off? I can't open my eyes," Kissy asked.

Torrie turned the lights off, and Kissy took a while to open and readjust her eyes. They were extremely dry and itchy.

She looked around the hospital room and then down at her arm. She had stitches and a white bandage wrapped from her risk to her upper arm. She looked away. She was ashamed that Hassan had pushed her to this.

"I see you been cutting yourself again. We could have lost you, Kensington. Are you not taking your meds?" Torrie asked.

Kissy was embarrassed. Her aunt talked too much, and she was the last person she wanted to know about this. She regretted placing Torrie on her emergency contact list.

"Ms. Blu, this is Dr. Sarah," a pretty, petite, blond-haired nurse said before leaving.

"I'm happy to see you here with us. You lost a lot of blood, and we had to give you an emergency blood transfusion and stitch your arm. You'll be getting admitted tonight at ASH (Austin State Hospital) for further elevation," Dr. Sarah said.

"That won't be necessary. Kensington hadn't had an episode like this in years. It's the anniversary of her sister's death, and I'm sure she just needed to relieve some sort of pain. I assure you she's not suicidal," Torrie assured.

"I understand that, but it is hospital policy that anytime a patient attempts to commit suicide, that they be taking for further treatment and evaluation. Given Kensington's history, it's best for us all that she receives the help she needs. She could have died or lost the fetus. Kensington has already been admitted," Dr. Sarah replied snappily.

"Can I at least get a moment to clean myself up and get something to eat?" Kissy asked.

"Sure, I'll figure out something. The cafeteria is closed. I'm going to prepare your discharge paperwork from here, and your transportation will be here shortly. Kensington, please take care of yourself and the baby." Dr. Sarah said before leaving.

"Kensington, you didn't give these people my address, did you?" Torrie asked.

"No, just your phone number," Kissy replied as tears slowly ran down her face.

"You ain't going to no fucking hospital Kensington. Get out that hospital gown, and let's go. Oh, and here's your purse. The EMT's brought this from your apartment. I had to go in it to give them your insurance card," Torrie said, jumping out of the reclining hospital chair.

"Auntie, what if someone catches us?" Kissy asked, putting on her onesie.

"Your room is by the exit and away from the nurse's station. They won't even see us. Now hurry up, child. You'll just have to stay at my home for a minute because if they notice you're gone, they're going to send the police to your place." Torrie looked out the door. "Come on now," Torrie whispered.

The two ran out the side exit, and Kissy had to pause for a minute to catch her breath. She felt lightheaded and began to get dizzy.

"Come on before they drag your ass to the hospital," Torrie harshly whispered while turning back to assist Kissy.

They made it to Torrie's old school caddy and left the hospital grounds. Kissy laid her seat back. Her arm was in a lot of pain, and she was feeling nauseated.

"Don't worry about your arm. I got all kinds of shit for pain. You hungry?" Torrie asked.

"Yes, very, but please run me by my apartment real quick. I need to pack a bag and at least get my car."

"Okay, but make that shit fast."

When they arrived at Kissy's apartment, Kissy instantly knew something was off. Her apartment door was halfway opened, and she screamed realizing that the EMT's must have left her door opened.

"God, please," Kissy cried.

She had been robbed. Her living room was damn near emptied. The only thing left was her dining room table and the bedroom furniture. Kissy ran into the kitchen and looked behind the refrigerator. She began sobbing uncontrollably thanking God that her envelopes of large sums of cash were still taped in the back.

Torrie eyed Kensington with envy. No matter what she went through it seemed as though Kensington always rose to the top. Torrie wondered what Kensington did to get all that money she had. She wanted a piece, and she was going to find a way to get her hands on her niece's cash, one way or another, but for now, she was going to play the concern aunt.

Torrie angrily grabbed a suitcase and began putting clothing, shoes, and undergarments in it. She went into Kensington bathroom and saw the words *"Bitch"* and *"Slut"* written in red lipstick. *What is this bitch into?*

"Kensington, do you have any enemies?"

"No," Kissy lied.

"Come look at this bathroom!" Torrie yelled.

Kissy grabbed the three envelopes, tucked them under her arm, and made her way to the bathroom. She froze. *Who other than this Nova bitch and Hassan would have it out for me?*

Kissy refused to let her aunt see her sweat. It was something she saw in her eyes moments earlier that put Kissy on guard. She grabbed another suitcase to pack the rest of her belonging. This apartment was in Hassan's name, so if he wanted to deal with it cool, but she was out.

"Can you please help me move this mattress?" Kissy asked. She was feeling a lot of pain and was becoming extremely weak.

"Kensington, why don't you go sit down in the car? You look bad."

"I'm okay, auntie. I just need assistant moving the mattress, and then you can go. I'm going to stay at a hotel."

"No, you're not. Kensington you can barely stand. You're still on those hospital meds, and I need to be sure you're okay. At least stay one night."

Kissy didn't have the energy to argue. She grabbed her laptop, thankful it was still there, and Torrie grabbed her two suitcases.

They made their way out the front door, and Kissy saw Ty Jackson. She couldn't stand him and didn't understand why Hassan was friends with him. When they made eye contact, she rolled her eyes. She was sure Hassan had told him about her and Nova. He shot her the bird and got into a vehicle that was next to Hassan's car. *Bum ass bitch. I got something for his ass.*

She started to lock the front door but thought the hell with it. All of her electronics were stolen anyway, so whoever robbed her could come back and take the other shit. She got what she needed, and she had the cash to get what she wanted.

Her aunt put her bags in the trunk, and Kissy struggled to keep her eyes open. "Kensington are you good to follow me, or do you want me just to leave my car and we'll come back for it tomorrow?"

"I'm good, auntie. I'm going to follow you. It's just right across the light. I can make it," she slurred.

"Okay, Bo made some nachos, and it's some barbecue from Sam's on the counter. You can sleep in the back room. Don't go to sleep until you eat and get you some more meds," Torrie warned before hopping in her car.

Kissy rolled her eyes. The last place she wanted to be at was her aunt's home. She loved her aunt and all, but she hated the way she lived her life. Kissy wasn't trying to be reminded of where she came from.

When they arrived in Colony Park, she smacked her lips. She couldn't stand these niggas. All they did was stand on the strip day in and out, begging, bumming, smoking, lying about shit, drinking lean, rapping, and talking shit. These niggas disgusted her.

"Gawddddd!" Kissy yelled. "Look at this sorry ass nigga Tim, ole begging ass. Ain't even washed his ass and these niggas out here bumming off the same blunt. Ewwwww!" she said, getting out the car.

"Ayo, Kensington. What it do fam?" Tim yelled out to her. She nodded her head acknowledging him and walked in her aunt's home.

"Bo, Kensington's here. Make her a plate of food. She ain't feeling too good!" Torrie yelled when they entered the house.

Kissy went to the back room and flopped down on the old worn out sofa.

*Tap, tap, tap, tap!*

Kissy smacked her lips at the knock that came from the side window. "Yeah, what you want?" she asked annoyed while opening the window.

"Tell Torrie I want $20 of loud, a bottle of wet, and three swishers," the overweight, caramel complexion man said.

"Ugh!" Kissy yelled, slamming the window and storming off.

*Torrie got me fucked up. I got to get out of here.* She silently thought while looking around at the tiny space that was considered her living quarters.

Her nostrils flared at the strong stitch of embalming fluid. She gaged holding her stomach. The home was old and unkempt. The gray carpet had stains. It was worn with two black leather love seats. An outdated 32-inch modeled television sat on a black stand. The walls were an off white stained with black markings. It was crowded with clothing, magazines, newspapers, ashtrays, an air mattress, and a dresser. *This is some bullshit, yo!*

Aunt Torrie stayed off the strip in 2-4 Colony Park. She was the hood's candy store lady. She had your sweet needs and your fiend needs. The front window of the home was for snacks, and the back window was for wet, weed, meth, swishers, lighters, crack, pills, and any other vices to accommodate your needs.

"Torrie, it's some old fat ass nigga, talking about he needs 20 dollars' worth of loud. Look, I ain't gonna be able to do this. I'm tired, and I need some rest," Kensington groaned.

"Where the fuck are you going to go? Yo crack head mama's house? Girl, you are staying here until Monday so get rid of your little attitude and here." Torrie threw her a bag of loud. "Give this to him, and this is for you. It's a muscle relaxer and Vicodin. You should be good throughout the night," Torrie said with her hand on her hip.

"I can't take this. I'm pregnant. Won't it hurt the baby?" she asked, shocking herself. Just hours ago she had drowned down glasses of Hennessy not caring about her unborn, and now she was concerned.

"Girl, take that shit. You alright. Hell, I did worse shit than that when I was pregnant with Tony. You see his ass is alright. Either take it or deal with the pain."

Torrie was a very tall, slim woman. She was very pale and wore two black cornrows. Years of the street life and drugs had taken its toll on her, but everyone in the hood had love and respect for Torrie.

Kissy respected her aunt and didn't give her any problems. After her sister drowned, their father had left their mother for a white woman. Her mother couldn't take it and through her finding ways to cope, she'd turned to crack. If it weren't for her aunt and cousin Tony, Kissy would have starved. They looked out for her.

"Can you please have Bo bring in my suitcases, please?" Kissy didn't know if Hassan would be spiteful, track her vehicle, and have it towed.

"Yeah! He'll bring them in a minute, but Ms. Thang you're staying here until I know for sure that you're well."

"Can I at least sleep in Tony's old room? He has a bathroom in his room, and I'll be able to sleep better without the knocks."

"Yeah, that'll be fine. That baby of his comes back on Sunday, but you can sleep in there until then."

Kissy thank her aunt. She stormed back to the back room, rolled her eyes, and gave the man his drug of choice.

"Your fat ass really needs to lay off this shit. Got you out here looking a mess, gawddddd!" she said to the man before slamming and locking the window.

She entered into her cousin's Tony's room, turned on the television, and sat on the full-size bed. Kissy looked around the fair size room and shook her head at all the posters of DJ Screw, Big Moe, Big Hawk, UGK and other Texas rappers. The walls were covered. She was surprised at how neat, and clean Tony's room and bathroom was.

The door opened and in walked Bo, her aunt's friend. *Damn, I see folks don't knock around here. Rude ass!* She looked at his appearance and wondered what the hell her aunt was doing with him.

Bo appeared to be in his late 20s to early 30s. He was slim, dark-skinned, tall, and had a beard. Kissy thought he was cute but too hood and young for her aunt. It was something about him that she didn't like. She felt uneasy. He handed her a plate of food and a large cup of grape Kool-Aid. He then dragged her luggage in.

"Thank you!" Kissy whispered.

"You're welcome, beautiful. If you need anything, let me know," Bo said, taking his left hand rubbing her cheek.

Kissy's entire body stiffened. She had met "Bo's" before and was very familiar with them. Bo's were who her mother would sell her to many nights for her crack high, calling those men her uncles. He gave her a rapist vibe.

Bo lingered in the room a little too long, and Kissy swallowed hard. She wasn't in any position to fight. She already felt lightheaded, and she kept getting a dizzy spell.

He finally left, and Kissy hurried to lock the door. She sat back on the bed and enjoyed her piled plate of chips, cheese with brisket, Rotel, jalapeños, sour cream, and guacamole. "Shit, this is so good!" she yelledm going hard on her food. Nachos were one of her favorite things to eat.

She flipped through the channels and landed on *Tyler Perry's Acrimony*. She was team Melody all the way, of course. She popped her two pills, grabbed her purse, and struggled to place it under the mattress. She had over a hundred bands on her, and she be damned if someone in this home got her. She laid down and sleep soon took her over.

"My baby's here! My baby's here! I wanna see my baby. Tim 'em told me my baby's here!"

Kissy stirred in her sleep.

"Move, Torrie. I heard my baby was over here. You can't stop me from seeing my baby. You're always tryna steal my baby, hoe. She's my daughter, not yours. Kensington it's yo mama!" Kissy heard loudly. She thought she was dreaming, but the noises were definitely coming from outside her door.

"Bo, why the fuck did you let her in here?" Torrie yelled.

"Well hell, Torrie, I thought it would be okay. I mean she is your sister," Bo shot back.

"She's tweaking, Bo. I don't want Kensington to see her mother like this. She's pregnant, and the girl already tried to commit suicide," Torrie whispered.

Kissy rose from the bed. She was dazed, drained, and her arm was killing her. She looked at the alarm clock and saw that it was after midnight.

She relieved her bladder, washed her hands and did a once over. She could still hear the arguing outside her door, so she opened it.

"Ahhhhh, there go mama's baby!" Lisa, Kensington's mother screamed. She broke through Bo and Torrie and gave Kensington a tight hug.

Kissy frowned at the odor that came from her mother. She motioned to her aunt to give them a minute alone, and her mother needed a shower.

Torrie rolled her eyes and threw her arms up. Her sister Lisa was a thief and a con artist. She didn't trust her in her home, and she didn't want Kensington to get her hopes up high about her mother. Lisa was sick and would do anything to get her high.

Kensington looked at her mother and wanted to cry. She was thin, smelly, and had lost all her teeth. All of her long pretty hair was gone. Her dark skin was ashy with holes in it. She looked bad.

"Your mama loves you, baby. You're so pretty and smart. I know I haven't always been the best mother, but your mama is going to beat this addiction, you watch and see," Lisa slurred while holding Kensington's hands. Her nose ran, and her body rocked back and forth while her jaw moved quickly in circular motions. Numerous times Lisa grabbed ahold of her stomach.

"I know, mama," Kissy said, holding back tears.

As she held her mother's hands, all she felt was love. She reverted to when she was a little girl. Before the crack, before the death of her little sister, and before her father walked out of their lives. Lisa was the best mother Kissy could ask for. She wondered how her life would have been if the tragic incidents hadn't taken place.

Kissy wanted her mother more than anything and just standing there with her, soften Kissy's heart. At that moment, she wasn't mad at her mother for selling her young body. She wasn't mad at her mother for choosing drugs over her. She wasn't mad at her mother for abandoning her. At that moment, she just wanted a hug and to never let her mother go.

Kensington wiped the tears that made its appearance and turned to open her luggage. She grabbed her mother a bra, panties, socks, sweats, and a t-shirt.

"Here mama, gone in there and take you a hot bath. I'll fix you something to eat. Hygiene products are in the bathroom."

Her mother thanked her and Kissy went up front where Bo and Torrie were. Her aunt was still mad at Bo for allowing Lisa in the home. "Kensington, your mama is sick. She's no good. Just be careful, baby. I know you saw the way she kept grabbing her stomach," Torrie said.

"Yeah, I know and I will, auntie," Kissy replied sadly.

Although she knew that her aunt was right, Kissy always got on the defensive side anytime her aunt spoke ill of her mother. It made her upset because Kissy believed in her mother and believed that one day she would be free from the disease that trapped her.

"I know she looks bad. I've tried to help my sister many times. Addiction runs deep in our family. I don't know baby, just say a prayer for your mama. Pray that she comes out of this."

Kissy hated for anyone to see her cry. She walked into the kitchen and wiped her face. Her hands shook as she searched for a plate for her mother.

"You might not wanna leave her alone too long with your shit!" Torrie yelled to Kissy in the kitchen.

*BOOM!*

Kissy ran out of the kitchen. She, Bo, and her aunt looked at one another with wide eyes. "Oh shit!" Kissy yelled. She ran to

Tony's bedroom with Torrie and Bo right behind her. "Nooooo!" she screamed.

"Go chase after that bitch, Bo. I told you. I told you not to let her in her. I knew this would happen." Torrie angrily yelled.

All of Kissy's clothing was spewed throughout the bedroom. The mattress was flipped, and Kissy saw the contents from her purse lying on the floor. Her envelopes of cash were gone, along with her laptop.

She broke down crying in her aunt's arms. She was almost at her goal. She didn't plan to do her group forever. She just wanted to stack a lot of money and live a comfortable life.

Kissy knew her mother was going to sell her laptop for crack. If it landed in the wrong hands, she would be ruined. *I can't believe this is happening.* Kissy silently cried. She took a seat at the foot of the bed and placed her head in her hands.

"Here," Bo handed Kissy her laptop. "She threw this down, but I couldn't catch her. I'm sorry," Bo said out of breath. He was sweating profusely and rubbing his left leg.

"Oh my god! Thank you!" Kissy replied with a face full of tears, jerking the laptop from Bo's hands. She prayed to God that Bo hadn't opened her computer.

"Good morning, big sis." Ryan smiled, handing Nova a cup of coffee.

Nova was in the living room laying on Ryan's oversized gray sessional. She was wrapped in a peppermint-colored blanket and had on one of Ryan's t-shirts and boy shorts.

"Thank you!" Nova replied, sitting up. Ryan sat next to her.

"How are you feeling? I can't believe I'm going to be an auntie," Ryan said, smiling.

"Numb. I just need some time to sort things out in my head. I can't believe any of this right now."

"Are you ready to talk about it?"

"Not really sis. Just give me some time, but thank you, Ryan, for coming to get me from jail and taking me to the hospital. Please keep the news about the baby and drama with Hassan between us. You already know how the family feels about him. The last thing I want to do is prove them right," Nova pleaded.

"I will sis, no worries. At some point, though Nova you're going to have to realize that maybe mom is right about him."

"She is," Nova admitted. "So were you."

"When you're tired sis, you'll finally leave. Anyway, whatever happened to your ex-Brixton?" Ryan asked, folding her legs under her.

"I don't know. I heard he finally made partner at his firm." Nova shrugged.

"Have you ever thought about getting back with him?"

"I can't compete with a dead wife. Emotionally he wasn't available for me. He left me. He didn't even have the respect to face me. He sent me an email breaking up with me. Then he blocked me. I never got closure from that. Honestly, I just moved on. I met Hassan a year later. I thought he would be different, but he isn't," Nova cried. "Sis, I just don't even know what it is like to be loved by a black man, other than dad. I want my marriage to work so badly, but I'm tired. I can't take too much more."

"I know sis. I've been there. That's why I keep telling your ass to do you. Fuck Hassan! He's doing him. How many times are you going to let this nigga cheat on you and stick around? He isn't worth it!"

"This is too much. I just need some time to think. I don't want to talk about this right now," Nova reiterated, wiping her face.

"Okay! Well, are you still coming to my party next weekend?"

"Of course, I wouldn't miss it for the world." Nova smiled. "Sis, I'mma call an Uber and get on to the house. I need to see Trin and make sure she's good."

"I can drop you off. I need to get going anyway. I have to get to work."

"Okay, that'll be great."

Nova rolled her window down and enjoyed the fresh breeze that hit her face. She was doing everything in her power to stay strong and not break completely down in front of Ryan. She was already embarrassed that her sister had to come bail her out and worse hear the news of the pregnancy. She didn't even want to call her, but when Hassan didn't walk out the apartment with her when those cops were practically dragging her to the police car, she figured he stayed behind to tend to Kensington.

She had about enough of Hassan. The only thing that always kept her around was Trinity. She loved that little girl as if she was her own, and she knew if she left that she would have to leave Trinity behind. After this though, she didn't even know if her love for Trinity could make her stay. Hassan had broken her, and when she heard Kensington say she was pregnant, something in her snapped.

Their wedding anniversary was coming up, but honestly, it didn't mean much to Nova. The fact he got his mistress pregnant took away her joy of thinking about what it would be like to have a gender reveal party, the excitement of the sex of the baby, planning the baby shower, getting decorations for the third bedroom and finally becoming a mother to her own child. It was all ruined, and all she could think of is how much of a mistake this pregnancy was.

There was no way she would have a baby the same time as Hassan's mistress. *Damn, here I was paying to find out if Hassan was cheating, and he got a whole baby on the way by his employee. Now, I got to see this bitch every day. I'mma fire that hoe. Watch!*

Nova's mind drifted to her ex Brixton. She wished her sister hadn't brought him up. She had tried so hard over the years to forget about him, but she couldn't. Every time Hassan would hurt her, her memories would travel back down memory lane to the abandonment she felt from Brixton.

Brixton January was one of the best men Nova had ever been with. Financially she didn't have to worry about anything. He was kind, sweet, and always showered her with gifts, but emotionally he was cold and distant at times.

Nova learned of Brixton's ex-wife Michelle. They were married for six years. She was his first love, and Brixton loved her with every fiber in his body. Michelle had his heart, even in death.

She was murdered by the hands of her lover in a murder/ suicide. Her lover happened to be Brixton's cousin. Michelle tried to leave him and break off their relationship, but he killed her and then himself. Brixton was heartbroken. Not only had he lost the love of his life tragically, but he also had to find out the details of her betrayal. Since then, Brixton hadn't been the same.

In the beginning, Nova tried to be understanding, but it was always Michelle this and that. Brixton couldn't let her go. One minute he was angry, and the next loving towards Nova. He had a wall up, and at times, she couldn't figure him out.

Being with Brixton was emotional suicide. She felt she was walking on eggshells, but she didn't have the strength or courage to walk away from Brixton. She loved him. She was a fighter. She fought for what she believed in, and she would have fought for Brixton and never given up.

When Nova received Brixton email, her spirit was crushed. His words were short, cold, and unapologetic.

*Nova,*

*You're a great girl, just not for me. It's over. Take care!*

Nova remembered letting out a loud scream. Everything around her turned black. She was confused. She remembered trying to call every number associated with him. He blocked her, abandoned her, and up and disappeared all at once. She never got over that. She just learned to keep moving.

"Nova!" Ryan yelled.

"Huh?" Nova jumped.

"Are you okay? We've been sitting here for two minutes. I've been calling your name, and you're just staring off into space."

"My bad sis, thank you for everything. I'll see you Saturday," Nova said when her phone rang. She looked down, noticed it was Hassan, and rolled her eyes. "Bye girl! Love you!" Nova shut Ryan's car door.

"Mommy!" Trinity yelled running to hug Nova as soon as she walked through the door.

"Hi, baby! Did you eat breakfast yet?" Nova asked picking Trinity up.

"No, I just woke up not too long ago. Mommy, can I go to granny's house later?"

"Sure baby! Where's your dad?" Nova asked putting Trinity down.

"He's in the room on the phone. Mommy, can you make some eggnog pancakes, potatoes, eggs, and bacon? Please, please, pleaseeee!" Trinity placed her hands in a praying position smiling.

"Come on."

"Yayyyyyy!" Trinity jumped up and down and took off running to the kitchen.

Nova and Trinity laughed. She was always intrigued by her daughter's conversations. Her little mind would drift from one subject to the next, causing Nova to always get a good laugh in.

She and Trinity enjoyed their breakfast. Nova was happy that Trinity hadn't noticed her eye. She swooped her hair over it to try to conceal it. It looked bad, and Nova had a hard time seeing out of it.

"Good morning, baby!" Hassan said walking in the kitchen giving Nova a peck on her cheek. Nova frowned. *The fucking nerve of this nigga.*

"Ewwwww!" Trinity laughed.

Nova rushed over to the sink to vomit. *Blrgggggghhhhh, Blrgggggghhhhh!* The smell of Hassan's cologne made her extremely nauseous.

"Baby, are you okay?" Hassan asked with love.

"I guess you impregnated your mistress and your wife." Nova shot daggers into Hassan. Her voice was filled with rage and hurt.

Hassan stared at Nova. He took a piece of her hair and removed it out of her face. Nova tapped her right foot, perked her full reddish lips, and crossed her arms. She was ready to lay into Hassan.

Trinity interrupted the volcano that was about to erupt throughout the Daniels household. "Mommy, are you having another baby?" her little innocent voice asked.

Nova shook her head up and down afraid to speak. Her pain was etched across her face, and she knew if she opened her mouth nothing but sobs would escape.

"Yayyyy! I'm going to be a big sister!" Trinity yelled excitedly. Nova half-smiled.

"Trin, why don't you go wash your hands and change for your grandmother's house," Nova managed to get out.

"Yes ma'am," Trinity replied doing as she was told.

"So are we going to talk about this?" Hassan asked.

"Nope! You have some nerve, Hassan. Why weren't you there to bail me out? You know what fuck it. It doesn't even matter. Ryan was the one who bailed me out and took me to the hospital to get checked out. It should have been you there with me, but all you do is shit on me. I don't even know why I thought this time would be any different. You've actually been cheating on me with your employee, a bitch we work with. How much lower can you go? You know I thought after Trinity, nothing else could hurt me. But, year after year Hassan, it's just a new bitch and a new low. I'm so tired of your shit. Take Trinity to mother's, and I suggest you stay the fuck out my face," Nova warned before storming out the kitchen.

Hassan stood there dumbfounded. He bit his bottom lip and shook his head. Nova had never spoken to him like that before, and he knew she was fed up. He didn't know what was wrong was him. On the one hand, he wanted his wife, but a piece of him was yearning to be under Kensington. He missed her. He hated the way he had spoken to her. He knew Nova was in the wrong for popping up over at Kensington's apartment.

"Trinity baby, let's go!" Hassan called out.

The hot water ran over Nova's body releasing the pint up anger, hurt and soreness she felt. She allowed her tears to mix with the water. She could feel herself slipping, fading away, and withdrawing.

She knew she was a snapshot of who she once was. Before Hassan, she was strong, confident, and learning herself again. Now she felt like a capsule, frozen in time, distraught, lost, and used. Her heart was painted like a blooded tattoo with a brick structure. She felt dead, yet at the same time, she didn't know who she was apart from Hassan.

The hot water felt like tears of blood that fell from her broken heart. She remembered all the times Hassan told her he loved her, but now she knew it was all just a cold-hearted lie. Her love for him was blind.

Having a baby is something she always dreamed of, but not like this. She didn't want a baby to cloud her judgment. In her heart, she just couldn't do this with Hassan any longer.

*He really had this bitch in an apartment, paying her bills. Where the fuck did he get all that extra money from? I bet everyone at the office knows. I'm so stupid. I know them hoes are laughing at me. Fake asses! I bet that's why they always wanted me to go out to eat with them just so that they could pick my brain. How could he do this to me? I've worked so hard to build my professional portfolio and resume. I've never missed a day of work. I'm always on time. Never in any mess, and I'm a damn good manager. I can't believe he brought this shit to our job. A baby? I can't stay, not again! Trinity almost broke me. It took a long time to let the hurt go. Then he cheated on me again and again. I'm so tired. I can't have this baby. I'm done with Hassan!* Nova internally screamed.

"Where would I go?" she spoke aloud.

"Nowhere!" Hassan answered.

He had dropped Trinity off at Nova's mother home ten minutes away. He hurried back home and heard Nova crying. He had been quietly sitting on the toilet waiting for her to finish her shower.

Nova jumped. She was so lost in her thoughts that she didn't even realize she was sobbing loudly. She didn't even hear Hassan come in and she wondered how long he had been there.

She shivered realizing that the hot water was now cold. She turned off the shower and pulled the shower curtain back. Hassan stood and held out a towel for her. She reached for it, and he backed up.

She looked towards the towel rod and realized he had the only towel. "Will you give me the towel? I'm not in the mood for your shit." Nova attempted to jerk the towel, but Hassan backed up further. This enraged Nova.

*Whap*!

She slapped Hassan and began pounding on his chest. "I hate you, Hassan. I hate you. How could you do this to me? Why do you keep hurting me? I'm good to you. I do everything a wife is supposed to do. Whyyyyy?" Nova sobbed.

Hassan wrapped the towel around her and quickly picked her up. "I'm sorry, baby."

"Ahhhh, put me down, Hassan!" Nova screamed fighting with him. Her tiny, 5'6 frame was no match for Hassan's tall, strong body.

He laid Nova down on their king size bed and began planting kisses all over Nova's body. She tried to fight him. She was so emotionally drained, but she'd be damn if Hassan thought he was going to fuck his way out of this.

She hated the way her pussy purred. Hassan always had that effect on her body. Slowly she gave in, and she was so disappointed in herself for doing so. "Hassan stoppp!" she screamed as soon as he entered her love tunnel.

He made love to her passionately and aggressive.

"I'm sorry, Nova. I fucked up. Baby, I love you. This shit is so good. I ended things with Kensington. I told her to get an abortion, and I'm putting her on Hector's team. I'll never hurt you again. We can go to counseling. I'll do whatever you want me to do. Just don't leave me. I love you, baby."

"I love you too!" Nova moaned.

"Please forgive me, baby. Let's start over. We're about to have our baby. Tell me you're not leaving," Hassan stroked her deeply.

"I'm about to cum!" Nova screamed.

Hassan removed his manhood making Nova go crazy. He aggressively entered her again. "Tell me," Hassan ordered.

"Hassannnnnn, I'mma about to. Ohhhhhh! Ahhhh! Ahhhhh! Pleaseeee!" Nova began squirting.

"Tell me."

"I'm not leaving. I love youuuuuu! I'm cumming. I'm cumming. Ahhhhhh!"

"Fuckkkkkk!" Hassan moaned and released.

He laid next to Nova, and she placed her head on his chest. Just as always, Nova forgave Hassan, and her tears were replaced with a satisfied lustful smile. *I'm going to give him one last chance,* she silently thought before dosing off to sleep.

*That's one down. Now if only I can get Kensington to come around, we could be one happy family.* Hassan slightly smiled.

Kissy wiped the sides of her mouth and sat up in bed. The smell of bacon tickled her nostrils, and her stomach growled. She ran her hand over her tiny bulge and bit down on her bottom lip. The events from yesterday began to weigh on her. She felt so isolated in her mind.

Her phone rang, and Kissy was thankful. She hated when her mind traveled down dark, depressing paths. She realized the call was coming from The Wren's Supportive Living Center. She swallowed the lump in her throat and answered the phone.

"Hello!"

"Hi, Kensington! This is Ryan. I was calling to let you know today we're having arts and crafts day. You're more than welcome to join us if you'd like."

"Okay! Thank you! Sure, I'll love that. I'll be there soon," she replied and hung up the phone.

She heard a knock on her door, which instantly caused her to become annoyed. She wasn't a morning person, and she honestly didn't feel like being bothered. She stood, opened the door, and retreated to the bed. Her aunt walked in and sat at the edge of the bed.

"I was just coming in here to check on you. Are you hungry? I made some bacon, French toast, eggs, and oatmeal." She paused. "Listen, I'm sorry you had to see your mother like that. Just know

I'm here for you as long as you need me. I'm never too far, and you can stay here for as long as you like."

"Thank you, auntie. I'mma head out in a little bit, I need to go visit Kinley," Kissy said, turning her head.

"How is she doing?"

"As good as to be expected." Kissy shrugged.

"Okay, well don't forget to eat something, and I'll bring you some more pain meds. Be careful, and I love ya." Torrie left.

Hearing the word "love" was new for Kissy. Her aunt had never told her that before. She smiled slightly and got up to handle her hygiene.

She placed her goddess dreads in a high bun and settled on black leggings and a sleeveless baby blue tank top. She slid her feet in her baby blue and black fur slippers, rewrapped her bandage, grabbed her laptop, keys, and purse, and made her way up to the front.

She fixed herself a plate and leaned down to grab herself a cold soda that was in the back of the refrigerator at the bottom.

"Damn! Kensington is fine as fuck," Bo whispered and licked his lips while grabbing his hard erection. He looked around to make sure Torrie wasn't in sight before he boldly made a disrespectful move.

Kissy's entire body stiffened when she felt the hard bulge of Bo's penis rubbed against her backside. *Thump!* She quickly jumped hitting her head at the top shelf of the refrigerator. "Ouch shit. The fuck is you on?" Kissy snapped while rubbing her head.

"My bad baby, I was trying to move around you," Bo smirked while reaching to grab a box of cereal that was placed on top of the refrigerator.

Kissy looked down and noticed the large erection in the front of Bo's boxers. He was bare-chested, and she studied a tattoo on his shoulder blade that read "Jaybryd". She only knew of one Jaybryd in the city, a messy hairstylist, who was also a member of *Whose Man Is This Sis*.

Kissy balled up her fist. If Bo thought he was going to violate her in any way, she would kill him. Her intuition about him

75

was right. She had to hurry up and get out of her aunt's home. She knew Bo was on some rapist type of shit, and it was only a matter of time before he forced himself on her.

She grabbed her purse, left the food on the counter, and hurried back to the bedroom and locked the door. "Ouchhhh!" she moaned loudly in pain. Her arm was killing her.

She hurried and packed up her suitcases. She wasn't staying there, regardless of what her aunt said. She would move to a hotel before she slept in the same house with Bo.

Opening Tony's large bedroom window, Kissy pushed her luggage through the window and quietly climbed out. She wasn't coming back there.

"Ayeeeeee, Kensington! You looking good as fuck, Ms. Lady. Come holla at a real nigga," one of the wannabe hustlers that stood around on the strip by her aunt's said.

Kissy rolled her eyes. *That's all these bum ass niggas do all day long. Holla at a real nigga where? My gawd these niggas ain't finna worry my soul.* She silently thought while hurrying herself along. She couldn't stand to be in Colony Park.

Bo lusted after Kensington while she walked away. He grabbed ahold of his manhood a second time and needed a release. Torrie just wasn't who he desired, and ever since he's known Kensington, he had a thing for her. Having her this close in close proximity was doing something to him, and he couldn't control his urges.

He excused himself from the kitchen and went into the hall bathroom. He hurried to drop his boxers.

"Ahh, Kensington!" he moaned while stroking himself.

He looked over by the sink and saw a bottle of lotion. He stopped stroking briefly, moistened both hands with the lotion and twist, turned, and jacked off to a Jamaican rhythm in his head. *I'mma fuck that young bitch pussy up good. I bet that bitch is warm and juicy.* He deviled in his lustful thoughts. "Yeahhhhhh!" he moaned loudly watching his semen powerfully shoot ahead.

His leg shook.

"Got damn!" he moaned, taking a seat on the toilet. His piston was still semi-hard, and he stroked it again thinking of Kensington. Sweat ran down the sides of his face as his body jerked. His toes curled, and he imagined her big juicy lips wrapped around his piece. "Mmmm shit."

"Nooooo!" Torrie whispered with a stream of tears that flowed down her doleful face. The exchange she saw between Bo and Kensington brought her great sadness and anger. She felt dejected and disrespected in her own home.

She leaned against the off-white stained wall of her bedroom and slid to the floor. She could hear the pleasurable moans, and groans that Bo was giving to himself. When he called Kensington's name, a bullet of hot rage shot through her. Not many things hurt her, but this stung.

She loved Bo, and although he cheated, that never bothered her as long as he came home. She gave him a pass since he was a lot younger than she was. A piece of Bo was better than a cold bed, but this thing with Kensington burned. *Bitch knew what she was doing wearing them tight ass leggings around my man,* she angrily thought. *I should have known she was a hoe when I saw the red lipstick on the walls at her apartment. The little bitch has probably been peeping my man from day one. S*he continued with her thoughts.

She heard Bo wash his hands and then yell out to her that he was going out. She wanted to yell out to him, *"Fuck you, Bo!"* but she never wanted to lose him either. She wiped her face with the end of her worn housedress and struggled to get off the floor. She was on her way to confront Kensington if she was still there.

"Where the fuck did this little bald headed hoe go?" Torrie yelled using a spare key to open Tony's bedroom door. She looked around the room and noticed all of Kensington's belongings were gone, and even the bathroom was empty.

She went back up front and took a seat in a recliner chair. She lit a cigarette and rocked back and forth. "Where did she get all that money from and what's on that damn laptop?" Torrie questioned aloud.

A knock on her door broke her out of her thoughts. She placed her cigarette in the ashtray and stood to open the door. On the other side of the door was Nicole.

Nicole and Bo were half sister and brother with the same fathers. Torrie had met Nicole a few times and liked her vibe. "What's up, Nicole?" Torrie smiled.

"Nothing much, is Bo here?" Nicole asked.

"You just missed him. You can come in though and wait for him if you want."

"Yeah, as a matter of fact, I think I will," Nicole entered.

Nicole's nose turned up a little at the old modeled home. She was accustomed to nice things and cleaner places. She took a seat on the worn black leather sofa.

She had been to Torrie's home twice, but it was nighttime and dimly lit. This was the first time she saw the wall with all the family photos. She glanced ahead at each one, and when her eyes landed on Kensington's photo, she smacked her lips and rolled her eyes.

Torrie watched Nicole and saw her disgust for Kensington. "You know her or something?" Torrie asked, relighting her cigarette.

"Huh?" Nicole asked.

"Kensington. Do you know her or something?" Torrie asked again.

"Nah! Not really! I work with her though," Nicole replied. Her phone rang, and she was thankful for the distraction until she saw who it was.

"Where the fuck you at?" Sean Nicole's husband roared through the phone. Torrie's ears perked up.

"Why does it matter, we're no longer together?" Nicole snapped turning down the volume on her phone.

"Nicole if you think you're going to up and leave me…" click Nicole hung up her phone.

"You good?" Torrie asked Nicole.

"Yeah! Why?"

"What happened to make you leave your husband?" Torrie asked, and Nicole frowned at how forward she was.

"Well, I thought I was in love with another man until I found out that he's been messing with that bitch Kensington behind my back!" Nicole angrily spat and then covered her mouth.

"Nah, you're good. That's my niece and all, but she stays in some shit. Anyway, what's his name?" Torrie asked.

"Hassan."

"Tall Hassan that drives the green Impala?"

"Yeah, that's him," Nicole confirmed.

"Oh, so that's who she's pregnant by." Torrie frowned. She saw the loving photo of Hassan and Kensington in a closet and saw a piece of mail of his on her dresser.

"Who Kensington? She's pregnant?"

"Yup!" Torrie blew out smoke. "I've been knowing Hassan's sorry ass for years. His ass be around there at Goo's house gambling and shit. He's married too. He got a pretty wife and baby girl. The baby is by that stripper girl they called "Yazzi" or something like that. She just left that baby on the doorstep, but I don't blame her," Torrie said, realizing she was talking too damn much, but she didn't care. She was in her feelings about Bo masturbating to her niece.

Hate was building in her heart towards Kensington. Kensington reminded Torrie of her sister Lisa. She was the pretty one who always got chosen and had the best of everything.

Kensington's father James was with Torrie's first. She met him at a poker game. They dated for months and out of nowhere, he ghosted her. She didn't see James again until her sister's Christmas party.

At the Christmas party, she learned James was with Lisa and from that moment forward, she couldn't stand her sister. It wasn't as if Lisa knew about James and Torrie, because she and Torrie weren't that close. They had lived two different lives. Torrie was in the streets while Lisa was the good girl, who worked good jobs.

Torrie envied their relationship. They seem to have it all. Nice home, two beautiful girls and even after James' infidelity with a white lady named Sandy, which resulted in an outside love child, her sister still seemed to have it all. Lisa and James' marriage appeared to be stronger than ever until their youngest daughter Lexi drowned. It was too much for Lisa, and James decided to leave Lisa to be with Sandy and his daughter Bella.

A crying shoulder with Torrie turned into Torrie introducing Lisa to crack. Torrie was already on crack, and Lisa begged her to try it. She insisted because she needed something to ease her pain. One hit was all it took for Lisa. The drug took Lisa down fast, and while Torrie was able to go to rehab and shake her habit, Lisa couldn't quit.

When Torrie found out that Lisa was selling Kensington for ten-dollar crack hits, she stepped up and took her in. She made sure Kensington went to school, brought her clothes, and kept her fed. Her son Tony did the same thing. He sold drugs, and with the money, he made sure that Kensington had what she needed.

Torrie loved her niece. She was the daughter that she never had, but seeing the lust in Bo's eyes and hearing him jack off in pleasure, took Torrie back. In her mind, her niece was Lisa and now her enemy.

"These niggas ain't shit," Nicole blurred out, bringing Torrie back to the conversation. She had zoned out.

"You need to work that shit out with your husband. Hassan ain't worth two dollars. I'm surprised he's messing with you though. You ain't even his type. I ain't ever seen Hassan with someone your size or complexion. Don't play yourself. Your husband is a good man. Get your ass out the clouds and go back home," Torrie rudely said. She wasn't one to bite her tongue. "Anyway, I'm not surprised Kensington than went and got herself knocked up again by a married man."

"Again?" Nicole asked.

She was about ready to read Torrie's ass. How dare she say that she wasn't Hassan's type? However, her anger subsided when Torrie mentioned Kensington being knocked up again by a married man. She was all ears and needed as much information as she could find on her.

"Yes, again. She used to mess with this married man name Raheem Gold."

"I know Raheem. His wife Iesha is Ashley's first cousin."

"Well, Kensington had a baby by him name Kinley. She's in a state supported living center. She has CP. The doctors gave that baby about five years to live if that."

"Damn, that's sad."

"Yeah, it is. Raheem dog the mess out of her. Had her fighting, losing jobs, and doing pop up on folks. I'm surprised her ass even got a state job with the record she has. You would have thought she would have learned her lesson. That man had her in and out of the state hospital. When she left him alone, she started doing okay for herself. Well, that's what I thought until last night."

"What happened last night?" Nicole asked on the edge of her seat. This tea was too good.

"I don't know what led up to her breakdown, but the hospital called me and told me the girl tried to off herself again." Torrie shook her head. "Like I said, the little hoe is my niece, but her ass is always in some shit."

Bo walked in the door, and Torrie's entire demeanor changed. She excused herself to the back and gave Nicole and Bo their time to bond. She couldn't even look at Bo at the moment. He'd hurt her, but Torrie wasn't the one to bring her insecurities to her man. She didn't want to lose Bo, and since it appeared that Kensington wasn't coming back, she decided to let this one incident slide.

Kissy pulled up to the supportive living center and parked. She took a deep breath before she entered the building. "Hey, Kensington! How are you doing?" Ryan cheerfully asked while giving her a friendly hug.

Ryan had grown very fond of Kensington. She liked her and respected how she always made an attempt to visit her child.

Most of Ryan's client's parents had given them over to the state and acted as though they never existed, but Kensington always came to bond with her daughter Kinley.

Kinley was born with Cerebral Palsy. She had an abnormal development of her brain, and it affected her ability to control her muscles. She also had a rare bone disease, and the doctors informed Kissy that Kinley wouldn't live past five.

Kinley was mostly bedridden. She didn't talk and could barely interact with Kissy. She was two years old and very tiny. She was blind in her left eye, and at times, Kissy felt like her eggs were rotten and cursed. She didn't understand why she and Kinley were punished. "Why me?" She would always ask God.

Kissy loved Kinley but couldn't bear the sight of her at times. She felt guilty, resentment, sadness, love, shame, remorseful and like a failure all at once, but what angered Kissy the most was that Kinley resembled Raheem.

Nobody knew about Kinley except her ex Raheem who was Kinley's father and her Aunt Torrie. She carried very small, and due to the way her weight went up and down, nobody ever questioned was she pregnant, not even her employer at that time.

When Kinley was born, Kissy stayed off the scene. She spent countless hours and resources to find ways to make her child better. She even attempted to care for Kinley for a month before she gave her over to the state.

Soon after giving Kinley to the state, Kissy was laid off from her job. In survival mode, she didn't have time to grieve or feel her emotions. It finally took a toll on her mentally. She found herself in and out of psych wards for suicide attempts. She thought Raheem would be there for her, but he wasn't.

Raheem and Kissy were together for a year. He proposed to her, and they had even planned to marry. She honestly thought this man was her forever.

"I'm doing good, girl. Well, as to be expected. Kinley is going to have a new little sister or brother soon." Kissy beamed.

She couldn't believe she shared that with Ryan. She barely knew her, and the only people who knew of her pregnancy was Hassan, his wife, and her Aunt Torrie. Ryan was friendly though, and Kissy felt a level of comfort with her.

"Oh my God! This is so exciting. Congratulations!" Ryan jumped up and down.

"Thank you!" Kissy smiled and removed her shoes.

She walked over to the sink and began to wash and sanitized her hands. This place brought her comfort and pain. She loved visiting her daughter, but the memories of Raheem were sometimes too great for her healing.

*My intuition saw through his intent, and my ass still gave him the benefit of the doubt. I'm so foolish when it comes to men.* Kissy shook her head. Her mind drifted, and she thought back to the day of December 1st. That day was etched in her memory. Raheem had broken her spirit on that day, and she shifted!

*"Baby, nothing is going to fit me. Why can't we just wait until Kinley is born? I want my wedding dress and photos to be beautiful," Kissy complained while dressing.*

*She was five months pregnant with Kinley and had gained a lot of weight. She had her ideal dress in mind but had a feeling they wouldn't be able to alter it to her size.*

*"Because baby, I refuse to have my daughter born without me not being married to her mother. Besides, you look good, and I'm sure whatever dress you pick, you're going to be beautiful. I gotta run to the office, but I'll see you later." Raheem kissed her on the forehead.*

*Kissy made her way over to David Bridal and was happy to hear that they had the dress she wanted in her size at another location. She squealed with joy and thanked the sales attendance.*

*As she drove to the other location, Kissy smiled and glanced down at the stirring wheel at her ring. She couldn't wait to be Mrs. Rangers.*

*"Hi! I'm Kensington. The sales associate from the South location sent me here," she smiled.*

*"Yes! Right this way and ohhhh congratulations." The sales associate smiled. "This dress and the color is going to be absolutely stunning on you." She beamed.*

*The sales associate was right. The long, flowing, strapless canary yellow dress made Kissy feel beautiful. She couldn't wait to marry Raheem.*

*Although they both opted to skip a traditional wedding and marry in Vegas, Kissy still wanted a beautiful gown and nice wedding photos.*

*She purchased the dress, grabbed accessories and shoes, and made her way over to her favorite seafood restaurant.*

*She knew per her doctor orders, she wasn't supposed to eat seafood, but she couldn't help the cravings she was having, besides Raheem wouldn't know. She wasn't expecting to see him until later on that night.*

*She toyed with the idea of carrying out or dining in and decided to kill time. A whiff of Raheem's cologne hit her strongly. She knew his scent anywhere. He always wore African scented oils that lingered throughout the air.*

84

Like a Bloodhound scent dog, Kissy's nose led the way. "Miss, are you okay? Right this way," the waitress asked alarmed attempting to get Kissy's attention.

Kissy's heart exploded, and tears rushed her face. "This doesn't look like the office to me!" Kissy screamed yanking the white tablecloth to the floor. Glass broke, while food and drinks spilled on Raheem and his guest.

"What the fuck?" the dark-skinned beauty yelled while trying to get the red liquid substance off of her white dress.

"Ken-Ken-Kensington, what are you doing here?" Raheem stuttered.

"Who is this bitch?" Kissy screamed. She was making a huge scene and didn't care. She wanted answers, and she wanted them now. She couldn't believe Raheem would do this to her.

Kissy wouldn't have thought much about the woman or her man being out to eat if she hadn't witnessed the kiss Raheem leaned over to give her. She knew what she saw, and it clearly wasn't a friendly coworker "hey let's go grab lunch" situation. He was cheating on her in broad daylight out in the opening.

"Oh no see what we not about to do is call me out my name. I'm his wife, Iesha. Who are you?" the tall, smooth, chocolate sista asked.

"I'm his fiancée and mother to be of his child," Kissy shot back.

"Is this true?" his wife asked while staring at Raheem. Tears ran down her face, and Kissy felt bad. She didn't know Raheem was married.

"Yes! Baby, I can explain. I was going to tell you," Raheem pleaded. His wife jumped up from the table and ran out of the restaurant crying.

Raheem ghosted Kissy after that. She spent the last four months of her pregnancy alone, begging, pleading, and even bargaining.

She would call Raheem, and he would ignore her calls. Just that quickly she went from happily in love, to a lost, confused, and abandoned woman.

*It was nothing worse than telling a man your past hurt, only for him to turn around and hurt you worse. Kissy hated Raheem for what he had done to her.*

*With all the pain and hurt Kissy had been through, she thought Raheem was different. He wasn't though. He was just another man out here telling lies and breaking hearts.*

*She went down and all the self-care, appointments with her doctor and classes she took while pregnant in the beginning with Raheem, she stopped doing. She just didn't care anymore, and if she weren't so far along in the pregnancy, she would have aborted Kinley, that she knew for sure.*

*Truthfully, her aunt was the only person Kissy felt comfortable enough to know she was pregnant. She needed her, and the day that she delivered Kinley, her aunt was right there by her side.*

*Holding her baby brought her joy and sadness. She immediately knew that something was wrong with her daughter. She was so prideful and in denial. Kissy wasn't trying to hear the conditions that the doctors diagnosed Kinley with. She even screamed, "My baby is fine. Fuck you!"*

*Raheem reached out when Kinley was two weeks old demanding a DNA test. It came back positive, and Raheem told Kissy that Kinley couldn't be his because he didn't make deformed babies. She couldn't believe he would say something so heartless and cruel, and she couldn't believe all that time Raheem had lied about even having children. Kinley made his sixth child.*

*After she gave her baby away to the state, she tried to rid herself of Raheem, but he came back during her healing, apologizing and told her he had left his wife.*

*Kissy knew after how Raheem had done her, she should have told him to go on about his life, but she loved him. Things were different she thought, but Raheem sucked her back into him and spit her out damaging her heart further.*

*She began learning about all the women Raheem had cheated on her with. He had her head gone. Her days consisted of daily bullshit from women. Facebook messages from strange women, screenshots, posts laughing at her, and women harassing her and making her lose her dignity. She was fighting, following him, losing jobs, getting arrested, gaining assault charges and had protection orders against her for stalking, but the ultimate betrayal came when Raheem went back to his wife.*

*Kissy went through months of evaluations. She attempted numerous times to kill herself. If she couldn't have Raheem, life to her wasn't worth living. She never thought she could breathe without him.*

*Once she was stable enough, her mind was set on revenge and hurting women the way she had been hurt. She hadn't figured out how she was going to do it, but it was only a matter of time before her obsession with Raheem and his wife bubbled over into something else. That's how her mental condition worked. She went from one extreme to the next.*

*Kissy knew she needed to get her life in order though. Without Raheem's help, she had to move into a Motel 6. She drove a used car, and it was only a matter of time before her money dwindled, and she would have to tuck her tail between her legs and live with her aunt.*

*Her state job came in time. She was able to move into a hotel inn and do repairs on her car. She enjoyed her job and told herself to stay there as long as she could and mind her business. She had to, seeing that she lied about her criminal record.*

*Other than call centers and hospital work, Kissy had never worked for the state. She lied on her state application, and she was thankful they hadn't run a background check. Her interview process was very quick. She filled out the application on a Monday, was called on a Wednesday for an interview, and was hired that Friday. They needed workers badly, and she was happy she applied when she did, or she would have been like most people, waiting months for an interview.*

*She never intended on meeting or falling in love with Hassan. In fact, she never planned to get into another relationship period, especially with her boss out of all people, but she'll be lying if saying the attention and persistence that Hassan had in the beginning wasn't refreshing and halted her revenge plans for a long time.*

*Hassan made her believe in love. He showed her love. He took care of her. He was her friend, but now Hassan was her enemy. She was out for war.*

"Kensington, did you hear me?" Ryan snapped her fingers.

"Huh? I'm sorry, girl. What did you say?" Kissy asked. She was so embarrassed that she had tuned out. She had a habit of doing that and wondered how long she had been standing out the sink washing her hands.

"I was asking who does your hair. It's so pretty."

"Oh, thank you! I do!" Kissy smiled.

"Really? How much do you charge? I'm having my birthday party next Saturday, and I need something done to this head of mine. Can you please hook a sistah up?" Ryan pleaded.

"Sure and I'll just charge you $75."

"Whoop, Whoop! A bitch going to be too cute. Oh my god, you should totally come to my party. I mean if you're not busy."

"That sounds like a plan. I can come over Friday night if that's okay with you to do your hair. I can get the hair. Just tell me the color you want and reimburse me."

"I want 1B/33/4/27, a pretty blend of different browns!" Ryan said excitedly.

"That's going to be so cute on you. Here, put in your phone number and address," Kissy said, passing Ryan her phone.

"Here you go." Ryan gave Kissy her phone back. "Thank you! You're a lifesaver. Well, let me get little Ms. Kinley. She looks so cute in the outfit you sent. I'll be right back, let me go grab her." Ryan said.

Kissy looked around the center and smiled. It was so nice, comfortable, and cozy. She knew Kinley was in good hands, but a quick feeling of sadness swept over her. Sometimes she wished Kinley was with her, but she knew she couldn't properly provide the round the clock care.

"Annndddd here she is." Ryan smiled pushing Kinley's small bed towards Kissy.

"Aww, mama's fat baby. Hi, beautiful!" Kissy cooed while kissing Kinley. She was dressed so cute in a pink and gold short set.

"Ahhh is that a smile? Are you trying to smile for me? I love you too." Kissy beamed.

Ryan smiled and shed a few tears. The love Kensington had for her child was infectious and loving. Ryan thought how blessed Kinley was and how wonderful of a mother Kensington would make to her second child. She said a small prayer and gave them privacy while chit chatting with the other mothers.

Kissy stayed at the center awhile and bonded with other mothers and children. The center always gave her peace and a sense of belonging.

"Smile," Ryan said while snapping a photo. Kissy frowned.

She knew Ryan probably meant well, but she never wanted anyone to know her secret. Kinley was off limits, and although she loved Ryan's energy, she didn't fully trust anyone.

"Nah! I don't like that. Where is that photo going? Please delete it," Kissy said coldly. She was pissed. People seem to always violate her in her most vulnerable moments. Her mood drastically changed. She wanted to scream.

"Mama loves you, Kinley," Kissy whispered in Kinley's ear. She kissed Kinley, wiped her tears, and stood to leave.

"Wait! Kensington I'm sorry. I didn't mean any harm. I took a photo of all the mothers and children. I was going to put them up on the wall for our Christmas display wall I'm doing. I didn't mean to offend you. Please forgive me," Ryan pleaded.

"You're good. Don't worry about it. I'm just having a bad day. I'll see you on Friday to do your hair." Kissy placed on her shoes and left.

Ryan watched as Kensington got into her car and pulled off. She wondered what triggered her mood so quickly. She didn't mean any harm by the photo.

Kissy came to a stop sign and screamed to the top of her lungs. "Get him out of your mind! What you and Raheem had is over. Don't do anything crazy. You've come so far," she spoke aloud to herself. She always went through this same emotional outbreak every time she visited Kinley.

She stopped by a burger joint and grabbed herself a bacon cheeseburger, fried pickles, onion rings, peanut butter cookies, and a super large peach sweet tea. She was extremely hungry after missing breakfast and had begun to feel lightheaded and weak.

She pulled by a park and got out of her vehicle to sit at a bench. The cool breeze felt so good against her skin, and she smiled at the laughter from innocence children running around enjoying themselves.

A lone tear ran down the side of her left cheek, and she wondered why God cursed her baby Kinley the way he had. She didn't deserve that and Kissy felt it was unfair.

She wiped the tear and continued to eat. She wondered what kind of mother she would be, and if she was ready to go down this path again with a married man. Abortion often crossed her mind, and she couldn't bear the thought of having another child with a disability.

As she ate her food, she thought of her next move. Truthfully, she wasn't hurting for money, but the money her mother stole definitely sat her back. Kissy had only $150,000 in her bank account, plus five months of her 1,856.00 deposits from her job that she never had to touch thanks to Hassan. She knew his help had come to an end since Nova knew about her now, but she wasn't tripping.

She decided today would be the day that she got herself together. She browsed her phone and landed on a new condo development in Round Rock. She saw a brand new three bedroom, two and a half bathroom that was move-in ready. She contacted the agent and was happy to hear that they had an open appointment in two hours.

After she finished eating, she pulled out her laptop.

"Yassss!" she squealed, happy to see all the email messages. She checked her cash app and smiled widely seeing all the payments that had poured into her account. "I guess I'll get me a new vehicle today too," she said aloud, happy that on Tuesday, she could just leave her current vehicle at the job to give back to Hassan. She was sure Nova would be petty and make Hassan get it towed. No way was he going to continue to support her living situation on his dime.

"Ugh! I guess her ugly, fat ass is messing with Hassan too." She frowned seeing a message from this lady named Nicole she saw around the office.

She added all the requests to the group, including Nova Daniels. She searched on Nicole's Facebook page and saw a photo of her husband named Sean and clicked on his Facebook.

"Oh! Hello Sean!" Kissy smiled while creating a duplicate Facebook page of Nova Daniels. She sent Sean a message from Nova's fake page.

Kissy burst out into laughter when she saw that Sean had read the message and responded. She knew that come Tuesday morning at work, it was going to be some shit. She couldn't wait.

"Both y'all bitches done fucked with the wrong one," Kissy whispered.

Her right leg shook as she searched public police records, gathering photos and data. Bo, Ty Jackson, Hassan, Nova, Raheem, his wife, and anybody else who got on her radar had a rude awakening. She was known for shaking things up in the city, and that's exactly what she was about to do.

"I'm sorry, excuse me. I didn't mean to hit your leg with my ball," a beautiful little girl said to Kissy.

Trinity's grandmother decided to take Trinity to the park. It was such a beautiful day, and Trinity wanted to go to the play escape.

"No problem baby. Here you go." Kissy said, giving Trinity her ball.

"You're pretty! What's your name?" Trinity asked.

"I'm Kissy, what's yours?" Kissy slapped her forehead realizing what she had just said. "I mean I'm Kensington, what's your name?"

"I'm Trinity and why you have two names?" She asked with a confused face. "I like Kissy." She smiled.

"Trinity get over here and leave that lady be, ya here!" Margaret, Trinity's grandmother, yelled.

"Yes ma'am, me-ma. Bye, Kissy, it was nice meeting you!" Trinity smiled and ran away to play.

"Shit!" Kissy mumbled and gathered her things. She couldn't believe she slipped up and called herself Kissy. She had never done that before. She just hoped she never encountered the little girl again.

After leaving the park, Kissy fell ill. She didn't know if it was seeing Kinley, eating her burger too fast, or making the stupid mistake of telling a stranger that her name was Kissy. Whatever it was, she needed to lie down and fast. She called and spoke to the agent for the property in Round Rock and canceled her appointment. She checked into the Holiday Inn for three nights and made her way to her room.

She didn't do her normal routine of checking the bed for bed bugs or Lysol the bathroom. She could barely stand and keep her eyes open. She removed her shoes and crashed on the cozy king size bed.

"No! No! Get off me! Mommy, help me!" she screamed. *Thump!*

She fought so hard in her sleep that she found herself hitting the floor. Her eyes jilted open and she looked around the unfamiliar room. The clock read *10:00 p.m.*

Tears rushed her eyes, and she wiped the beads of sweat that appeared around her forehead. "Oh no please," she whispered, praying that the trauma from her childhood didn't reappear in her dreams. She closed her eyes tightly and opened them quickly. She practiced breathing exercises until she felt her heart rate return to normal.

She slowly stood up and made her way to the bathroom. "Ahhhhhh!" she moaned, reliving her bladder. "I'm so hungry," she said aloud.

While washing her hands, she stared at herself in the mirror. She could already see the weight gain from the pregnancy and her nose widening out.

She quickly turned off the light switch and grabbed the hotel's menu. She was happy to see that the hotel didn't stop serving food until midnight. She placed an order of catfish, hush puppies, shrimp, fries, and a German chocolate cake. The restaurant informed her that her meal would be delivered up in forty minutes.

After placing her order, she went through her suitcase and settled on hot pink boy shorts and a black tank top.

"Part Time Lovers" by Tink played loudly on her phone as she showered.

♫*He got a girl, and I got a man*
*When he ain't around, I'm sneaking him in*
*I know that I'm wrong, for leading them on and bringing them home*♫

"I guess that's how Hassan sees me, a part-time lover." She sadly realized.

She turned off the shower and grabbed a towel to dry off. The lyrics of the song played in her head as she moisturized her body, dressed, and turned the television to *Iyanla Fix My Life*.

"Tuh! Does her ass ever fix anyone's life?" Kissy laughed slightly amused. She thought she had issues, but Iyanla's guests never cease to amaze her.

*Knock, knock!*

"About got damn time!" she yelled getting off the bed to answer the door. Her stomach began to do flips smelling the food. "Calm down little one." She laughed while lightly running her left hand over her stomach. "Mmmmm!" she moaned, tasting the hot, crispy catfish. The flavors danced in her mouth leaving her anxious for more. She ate every last bite and drowned it down with sweet tea.

"Now how Iyanla gonna cut this girl off and tell her how she's supposed to feel? Her ass be cracking me the fuck up. She's always doing that shit!" Kissy yelled at the television. Her phone beeped, and she smacked her lips.

Kissy rolled her eyes. She wasn't thinking about stepping foot in her Aunts home again, especially with Bo there. He gave her the creeps, but she also didn't want any bad energy between Torrie and herself.

"Shit! Maybe if Tony is there, I won't feel as uncomfortable," she whispered.

She grabbed her laptop and began looking online for a vehicle. She always wanted a Silver Tahoe with peanut butter interior. She saw where she could custom build it, and she began playing around with colors, tires, and different little add-ons. When she finished adding all her special touches, her total came out to $63,235.

A feeling of euphoria came over her. She had never owned anything that was hers without the help of a man. All her life everything she had was used, borrowed, hand-me-down or given as a bargaining tool. This vehicle was hers— first owner, zero miles, and designed just for her. Her phone beeped again, and Kissy shook her head. She didn't need this right now.

"Just don't respond," she said aloud reading Hassan's text messages. Her heart ached for him, and she missed him. She couldn't lie.

"Ughhhhh," she yelled. "I'm so stupid. Why didn't I just tell him to go to hell?" She paced back and forth. Her stomach began to feel queasy and the contents she just ate made her hurry to the toilet.

*Blurppppppppp!*

She heaved in and out gagging a couple of more times. She hated throwing up. This pregnancy so far was smooth, but she prayed she didn't start feeling ill the way she did with Kinley. She stood weakly and flushed the toilet.

"Ouchhh!" she moaned grabbing her arm. She was still in a lot of pain.

After rinsing her mouth and brushing her teeth, Kissy searched in her belongings for cleaning supplies to sanitize her arm and rewrap it. Twenty minutes later, there was a knock at the door, and she knew it was Hassan. She opened the door and quickly turned to sit in a nearby chair.

Hassan walked in dressed in gray sweatpants and a white tee. *His ass knows exactly what his long, dick ass is doing.*

97

She wanted to smile and replace the frown that was etched across her forehead. Hassan brought her red roses. He also had a Walmart bag and placed the contents from inside of it on the dresser.

He brought her gummy worms, salted caramel peanuts, and Cheetos puffs, all types of chocolate candy, water, orange juice, cheese crackers, bread, and Elgin sausages. He knew her like the back of his hand.

He removed his shoes and shirt and sat on the edge on the bed in front of her. An uncomfortable level of silence stood between them, neither of them knowing what to say. Kissy stood and grabbed a water bottle, chocolate candy bar, and Cheetos.

Hassan stared at her. Her ass was sitting right in the boy shorts she wore, and the pregnancy was placing her weight in all the right places. He felt the weight of his manhood and adjusted. He noticed the bandage around Kensington's arm and wondered if Nova had hurt her. He felt extremely remorseful for how he had spoken to her and how things transpired the other day.

Kissy enjoyed her bag of Cheetos and zoned out. She always had that ability to see you but not see you. Hassan came to talk to her, and she was willing to listen, but she honestly didn't have much to say to him.

"So you just gone ignore a nigga?" Hassan said hurt.

"I mean what do you want me to say? You treated me as if I was some random. Well, maybe I am. I mean, since you're married and all. All this time Hassan, after everything that I've been through in my childhood. You were someone I thought I could trust. You made me believe in love again. My stupid ass fell right for your trap," Kissy said, shaking her head.

"Trap? Is that what you think about a nigga? I trapped you? Nah, what I feel for you Kensington is real. Yeah, I know I'm foul for not telling you about Nova or my daughter, but I just needed a little more time. That's why I got you the car and the apartment. I was planning my exit. I don't know how Nova found out about us, but I had to play things out like that because Nova and I have many assets together. My daughter is my life, and she doesn't know what's going on. Kenn, I swear I don't even sleep with Nova. I sleep in the guest bedroom. I just need you to believe in a nigga baby and give me some time to sort all this out," Hassan said passionately.

"Hassan, I can't. Stop playing with me," Kissy cried.

She buried her head in her hands and sobbed. All this was just too much. Kinley, her suicide attempt, her mother, Bo, Nova, the fight, the robbery, and Hassan breaking her heart were all too much.

Hassan stood and pulled Kensington into his embrace. He whispered in her ear and rubbed her back. Her vulnerability radiated off her body, and Hassan knew he had her back where he wanted her. He kissed her tears and then her lips. Their tongues danced slowly, and their body temperatures rose making them attack each other. Soft moans filled the space of the hotel room.

Hassan removed Kensington's tank top and boy shorts. He dropped to his knees and lifted Kensington to sit her on his face. Her legs did a split, and her hands went up giving imaginary praises above. Tears flowed steadily as Hassan feast on her love box.

"Hasannnnn!" Kissy cried out.

He stood balancing himself while holding Kensington in place. She reached and used the ceiling to place her hands.

Hassan loved Kensington's ability to be flexible and in tune with him. Sex with her was always adventurous, passionate, and it drove him to new depths and heights that he could never reach with Nova. He used one of his hands to slide down his sweats and boxers. He then grabbed ahold of Kensington's ass cheeks, removed his tongue out of her pink fortress, and slid her warm, wet, tight pussy down on his wood.

"Fuckkkk!" Hassan moaned, placing his head in the crease of her neck. She wrapped her arms around his neck and bounced up and down as her life depended on it. Their bodies were in sync, and both were in total bliss.

"Right there! I'm cumming!" Kensington screamed.

"Fuck my knees. I'm finna drop you. Ahhh shit."

"Don't stop! Don't stop! Please! Ahhhh I'm, I'm, Ahhhhhhhhhh!" Kensington loudly screamed.

Hassan's knees gave out on him, and they both fell on the floor. They laughed, and Hassan brushed a piece of Kensington's hair out her face.

"Damn baby! I missed that shit." He slapped her ass. "I'm sorry if I made you feel unimportant. I'm happy about the baby," Hassan lied.

"I love you!" Kensington said, looking away.

"What?"

"Nothing." She sat up while looking at Hassan. "I just feel if we're going to start over, I need to be honest with you about something."

"Okay." He placed his arm behind his head, giving her his undivided attention.

"Long before I met you, I had a fiancé named Raheem. We had a baby girl name Kinley. She's disabled, and I gave her over to the state. That's where I spend a lot of my Saturdays, not out feeding the homeless like I told you."

"So, you still fucking this nigga?" Hassan asked pissed.

"No! I found out he was married. He didn't want anything to do with Kinley. He said he didn't make deformed babies. He just left me to fend for myself. How could he say that about my baby?" she cried.

"That's what hoe niggas do. I want to meet her."

"Really?" Kissy smiled.

"Yeah baby, I do!" Hassan said, wiping her tears.

Kensington and Hassan talked to the wee hours of the morning. She never told him about her arm or hospital visit, and he never mentioned the red lipstick message he saw on the wall about her at the apartment. He didn't ask about the furniture or why the apartment was unlocked either. He knew the apartment had to go. Nova knew where it was, and there was no way Kensington could stay there anymore. He also had to get the car back. Once Nova had woken up from their lovemaking, they had a long talk, and Nova listed all these crazy demands.

Hassan knew if he wanted to be with Kensington, he would have to change a lot of things. Work wasn't going to be an issue, because Kensington knew it was against company policy for supervisor and employee to date. She did a good job of keeping things professional.

He made the decision that on Tuesday he would place Kensington on Hector's team and switch her out for Dedra Johnson. He really didn't want Dedra because she was filled with drama and she and her man Tyrone were always fighting, but he would do whatever he had to, to keep the peace between him and Nova.

Since BPR was coming, all staff except for the HR and Program Managers would be working from home, so he knew he could get Kensington to take the ten-hour Monday-Thursday shift and still be able to keep up his affair with her, but still, that wouldn't be for another couple of weeks or so.

When he heard Kensington snoring, he lifted her off the floor and placed in her bed. He took a quick shower, left her a note, and quietly left out of the hotel. Kensington was a hard sleeper and didn't hear a thing.

His phone beeped, and he saw it was his cousin Kiara.

"What the fuck?" Hassan yelled, reading the text message.

He rushed over to his cousin's home and banged on the door. "Kiara, it's me cousin. Let me in." The door opened, and a little figure poked its head out. It was Larry Jr.

"Mommy is hurt badly. She's in the living room," his little voice cracked.

"Go wake your siblings. Be a big boy for me and help everyone pack a backpack with clothes, underwear, and shoes. Make sure you grab your things for school too. I'm here, and I'm not going to let nothing happen to you," Hassan said, rubbing Jr.'s back and wiping the tears that begin to fall.

"Okay," he whispered walking off to do as he was told.

Hassan looked around the living room and shook his head. Everything was in disarray. "Damn, Key," he said kneeling in front of her. She moaned and sat up holding her stomach.

She burst out crying, and Hassan's heart broke for her. Larry had badly abused her. She had dried up blood above her swollen lip.

Her right eye was closed shut, and her jaw was swollen. Her light skin couldn't hide the blue and purple marks all over her body even in the lightly lit room.

"Kiara I told you this shit would happen. Larry isn't having it. I told you to leave that fuck nigga alone years ago, but you kept having babies by the nigga. Leave Ty alone. This shit is going to get you both killed. Come on. Grab a bag. You and the kids are coming with me. We'll figure everything out later."

"Thank you!" Kiara whispered. Hassan helped her to her room and went to check on the kids. *Fuck! Nova is going to kill me for bringing this drama to our home.*

Nova shivered in her sleep and wiggled her body towards Hassan. Her eyes popped open when she realized she was met with a cold side of the bed.

The home was eerily quiet. "Hassan!" she called out. She looked over at the clock on the nightstand and saw where it read *3:15 a.m.*

"Hassan!" she yelled louder while getting out of bed. She placed her feet in her slippers and grabbed her robe.

"Where the fuck he go?" she yelled out, searching the entire house. Anger crept in her spirit, and she felt herself getting lightheaded. She flopped down in the oversized comfortable gray recliner chair in the living room and rocked back and forth.

She sucked her teeth when she saw a pre-rolled blunt, a bag of weed, and a lighter sitting on the coffee table. It pissed her off how careless Hassan could be, especially when it came to Trinity. She didn't mind Hassan drinking or smoking. She just asked that he didn't smoke in the house or leave items around where Trinity could reach them. It was common sense to her, and she was tired of being the only one who seemed to care when it came to the safety and welfare of Trinity. Nova was simply tired.

As she rocked back and forth, her feelings began to take her down. She was definitely living in regret. Most days she was just existing. She didn't know who she was anymore and she felt as though Hassan really didn't love her. She yearned to know what that felt like.

"Every time I think we're on the right path, he does something to hurt me," she voiced as she wiped away a single tear that trickled its way down her face.

She heard her phone go off and jumped up. She hurried to the nightstand in the bedroom room. She thought that maybe it was Hassan messaging her. To her surprise, it was someone she never thought she would hear from again. Her fingers slipped, and she dropped the phone.

She quickly picked it back up with a shaky hand. Her heart rate increased, and she didn't know why all of a sudden she had butterflies. He always gave her butterflies, but by being married, she didn't think he would still have that effect on her.

She held her chest trying to catch her breath. "After all this time he's reaching out to me. Why?" Nova said aloud while sitting back in the recliner chair.

She didn't know how to feel. Brixton was someone she still loved and cared for, but she didn't know if she was willing to travel back down memory lane with him.

Apart of her felt as if she deserved it to herself to get closure. She started to reply when her phone rang in her hands. It was Brixton calling her from messenger. *Don't answer it, Nova. You're married with a baby on the way. Block him.* She silently thought but couldn't resist the urge. *Why not Hassan has his cake and eats it too. Why am I feeling guilty for even entertaining the thought to answer the phone?* She continued with her thoughts.

"Hello," Nova answered nervously. So many emotions ran through her at once.

"Nova!" Brixton said in a relieved tone. "I-I-I don't even know what to say. I'm surprised you answered for me." There was a long pause. "I mean after how I did you and all," Brixton remorsefully whispered.

"I'm a married woman now. All is forgiven, Brixton. Please don't call me or message me again," Nova said sternly and smiled.

She was proud of herself. Brixton always brought about a softness in her that made her lose her voice at times.

"Nova, wait! Before you go, just let me get this out," Brixton pleaded.

"Five minutes Brixton."

"I know I don't have the right to impose on you or even ask for your time after all this time. I just want to mend your heart for the hurt and confusion that I caused. I never meant for my brokenness to break you. I was a coward. I ran. I fell in love with you, and I just didn't know how to process my emotions. I'm sorry for making you feel as though you weren't good enough. I'm sorry for making you pay for the things my ex did. I'm sorry for making you live in her shadow. Most of all, I'm sorry for hurting you. I didn't realize how broken I was until you tried to love me. I tried to push you away, but you never gave up on me. I tried to make it appear that something was wrong with you to avoid the pain I felt. What I did to you was wrong. I just want to see you Nova in person to be man enough to look you in your eyes and tell you I'm sorry. You deserve that. Please Nova," Brixton expressed sincerely.

Nova sat on the other end of the phone bawling her eyes out. She felt the ice around her heart melt. He opened something in her and spoke to her heart. For so long she carried the feelings of not being good enough, and it didn't help with the pain from the infidelities Hassan put her though.

She was about to reply to Brixton when she saw the headlights from Hassan's vehicle shine through the window.

"Oh my god, I gotta go. I gotta go." Nova quickly hung up and turned her notifications on her messenger to unavailable and do not disturb. She placed her phone on vibrate and stood up to turn the lights on in the living room. A mirror hung over the fireplace, and she looked at her appearance and quickly wiped her eyes.

The key locked turned, and Nova frowned when she saw his cousin Kiara and her three children. *What the fuck is this? Hell no!* She angrily thought while giving Hassan the nastiest look.

Nova liked Kiara, but she didn't like all the drama that came with her. Anytime Kiara was around, or they were out and about, it was always fighting or some type of dysfunctional behavior. She wasn't raised like that or around people who were loud, cussed a lot, or just plain tacky in terms of how they lived their lives.

She was very protective of Trinity, and although Kiara's children were innocent in all of this, Nova didn't really care for Trinity being around Kiara's children or being at Kiara's home.

Every time Nova seemed to allow Trinity over Kiara's home, she had to break habits and behaviors patterns. It was a lot of correcting for Nova too because Trinity and Kiara's children also went to the same charter school.

Nova could admit that Kiara's children were very smart and adorable, but they came from a lot and saw too much. She sighed thinking how happy she was that Trinity had stayed over her mother's home. With all the noise they were making Nova was sure it would have disturbed Trinity out of her sleep.

Nova took in Kiara's appearance.

*I guess she and Larry are back on and he beat the fuck out of her again. Hassan has me fucked up if he thinks our home is some sort of shelter. We are not about to house a grown fucking woman and her children because her toxic ass won't do better.* Nova angrily thought. She knew steam was radiating off her body.

Nova did love Hassan greatly but didn't like a lot of what came with him. She felt she was always being punished for loving him. She never went through this much shit with Brixton. Other than him being emotionally unavailable and cold most times, Brixton did shower her with love, and he was one of the best relationships she had. She would have kept fighting for that relationship if Brixton didn't leave her.

With Hassan though, Nova couldn't really remember too many happy moments. It was always a roller coaster ride with him. First, it was Trinity, then a chick name Mya, and then there was Sherry, Tamika, Tanna, Omia, Keisha and now Kensington.

On top of Hassan's cheating, Nova didn't care for his friend Ty or his family. All of his family in her eyes were trash from his mother on down. Maybe that's a little harsh, but that's how she felt. She thought Hassan was the only decent one, but lately, she found herself questioning if loving him was even worth all the bullshit that came with him.

He was definitely pushing her further and further into her "no fucks given zone". She felt it slowly approaching as the days went on.

She rolled her eyes at Hassan and went into the guest room to place fresh bedding on the bed for Kiara. She also pulled out a queen size air mattress for the children.

She got them all settled and went back into the master suite to bed. Hassan could kiss her ass right about now. She was livid with him. He always made decisions and did things without speaking to her first.

Hassan came into the room, and she smacked her lips. She sat up and looked at him waiting on an explanation.

"Look, baby, I apologize for not communicating with you, but she's family. She and the children need to stay here a couple of days until she figures out what she's going to do."

"Hassan, I understand that's your family, and I have nothing against her, but I have Trinity to think about. You know how Larry is. He'll stop at nothing, and I don't want that type of drama around her or me for that matter. She can stay here for one week and then they have to leave." Nova laid back down.

"Trinity is MY DAUGHTER. I also know what's best for MY DAUGHTER!" Hassan snapped back.

"You're right, Hassan. She's your daughter, and from now on, I will remember that I'm not shit to Trinity but the bitch that was dumb enough to pause my fucking life and take in a child you created with some strip hoe. You're absolutely right, Hassan. She's your daughter, not mine!" Nova screamed. She ran to the restroom and slammed the door. She couldn't believe he would say something so hurtful.

"Nova," Hassan knocked on the door. "Damn!" he yelled.

"Fuck you, Hassan. Leave me ALONE!"

Hassan started to say something else but thought against it. He removed his clothing, turned off the lights and got in bed. He was too drained and exhausted. If Nova wanted to cry in the bathroom, oh well. He needed rest.

He didn't like when Nova tried to run down all these demands. Kiara was his family, and he wasn't going to just leave her to dry. He also didn't like how she insulted his ability to keep Trinity safe. She was always throwing jabs at him when it came to Trinity, and he was sick of her overprotective bullshit.

Hassan thought long and hard about his marriage with Nova. There were days where he was just tired of her and wanted to be done with her, but she was his stability. He loved Kensington, but to him, she didn't hold her own like Nova did. Her salary wasn't anything compared to Nova's, and Nova had the credit that Kensington didn't have.

Leaving Nova for Kensington would be going backwards. He had a good life with Nova. They had nice things and money in the bank for a rainy day. Even still, Hassan felt Nova controlled everything. Anytime he wanted to have fun or do something that requires withdrawing funds. She would interrogate him as if he was five years old.

That's why he gambled often. He was disappointed in himself that when he won that large sum of money, he didn't invest it wisely. He blew it all and was happy that the six months least he signed at Travis Station was ending. He couldn't keep up with all the expenses, and although he loved Kensington, she was an expense and a responsibility that he didn't really want. Now she was pregnant. He was going to have to find a way to make her abort it.

His eyes fell heavy, and he made a mental note to call his boy Ty. He knew this shit would happen. Now was the time for Ty to either keep it real or stop messing with his cousin all together.

He heard the bathroom door crack and knew Nova finally decided to get her mind right. She gently laid in the bed and sleep took over both of them.

109

*Ding-dong, ding-dong, knock, knock, knock!*

"Mama, it's me." Trinity knocked cheerfully as she and her grandmother waited patiently on the other side of the door.

"Oh shit!" Nova said, jumping out of bed. She looked at the clock and realized she overslept.

She rushed to the front door and Trinity fell into arms. "Hey, mama!" Nova said, hugging her mother and kiss on the cheek.

Margaret could always tell when something was wrong with her baby. "Nova, baby! Why don't Trinity stay here with her dad and let me take you out for the day," she offered with a motherly smile.

"Yeah ma, that sounds nice. I'll get dressed. Make yourself comfortable, mama. I'll be back in a few." Nova headed back to her bedroom.

Nova's mother could always sense when something was wrong. However, today, Nova decided that she wouldn't hold anything back. She was tired of lying and covering up the ugly truth about her marriage to Hassan. She had enough, and it was time she started being honest.

"Yayyyyyy!" Trinity screamed when she saw her little cousins Larry Jr., Alexis, and Savannah.

All the children jumped up and down, excited to see one another. Hassan smiled at their bond and love how innocent they were. They reminded him of he and Kiara when they were younger.

He noticed Nova showering to leave, and he didn't care or even ask where she was going. He didn't need her negative energy, and he wasn't going to allow her to have an attitude towards his family.

As soon as Nova dressed, she started with the bullshit that Hassan knew she would.

"Nissan is tracking the vehicle from Kensington and will be towing it today. I'm stepping out, and I don't know what time I'll be in." Nova slipped her feet into her sandals.

"I told you I was going to handle it. Why do you always overstep your boundaries? I told you I would get the car back from Kensington. Why would you contact Nissan?" he yelled.

"Are you serious right now? The fact that you put my name and credit information down to get your little bitch a vehicle is low. She's not about to drive around in my shit. You're absolutely right I told them to come and get it," Nova shot back pissed.

"If you're going to forgive me, Nova, then you have to forgive all my transgressions including Kensington. She needs that

111

vehicle. I will be honest from here on out, but she needs to make her doctor's appointments. It's getting cold, and I can't have her riding the bus."

"You act like I'm supposed to give a flying fuck about your mistress. Be happy I'm letting her keep her job. I don't want you back in Travis Station either, or it's over for good. Try me!" Nova stormed out the bedroom.

Hassan sat down on the bed and bit his bottom lip. He was about done with Nova and decided he would find a way to try to move funds out of her secret account that Nova didn't think he knew about.

He took a quick shower, dressed, and went to check on his cousin Kiara. She had showered, dressed and was moving slowly about the room. "Hey, Key! How are you feeling?" he asked taking a seat on the already made bed.

"I don't know cousin." She shrugged. "Is it so bad that I want love and want to live my life like everyone else? Larry does what he wants. I'm tired of him, and we've been over for a year. He expects me to do allow him to live his life while my children and I suffer. Cousin, I just need a new start."

"I feel you. So what are you going to do? Are you going to file charges? Since you have an emergency order, they'll pick Larry up and put him in jail. I think that will give you some time to figure out your next move."

"You're right. I'll call an officer later. I'm thinking about just starting over in another city, maybe Killeen or Waco. I want to stay here, but Larry is never going to allow me to have a life. I'm tired of him violating my space. My kids saw him rape and beat me," Kiara cried. Hassan pulled her into his arms. "How could you do that to the mother of your kids, yo? Why? What have I ever done but love that nigga? I gave him everything and all he ever did was hurt me."

Kiara was sobbing uncontrollably, and it made Hassan shed his own tears. He didn't know why men did the things they did, including him. He knew Nova was a good woman, but she wasn't enough. He was selfish and incapable to love her the way she

112

deserved. He'd be lying if he said he didn't understand Larry. If Nova ever left him or slept with another man, he hated to think about what he would do. That was just something women never understood. Once a man has marked you his, you will forever be his. Sleeping with another man is not an option.

Hassan thought about his apartment with Kensington. It was paid up for a month, and until Kiara decided what she wanted to do, he would allow her and the children to stay there.

Even though Ty stayed in the same apartments, it wasn't safe for Kiara to go back to her place, and if Larry went to jail, it would give Kiara time to sort out her next plan.

He didn't want to have bad blood with Nova until he figured out his next move. He still had Trinity to think about.

"It's going to be okay, cousin. Look file the complaint, they'll arrest him, and that'll give you time to figure out your next move. I got you, cousin. I think I got a plan, if not you and the children can stay here for a week, and next week we'll figure things out." Hassan kissed her forehead.

"Ewww." Kiara laughed, wiping her forehead and her tears away. "Thank you, cousin."

"Daddy, Daddy can we go to IHOP? Please. We're so hungry," Trinity begged, busting in the room with the other three children on her tail.

"You wanna go cousin?" he asked Kiara.

"Yeah! Let me just put some makeup on to cover my bruises," she said, looking away ashamed.

"We'll be in the living room waiting on you." Hassan stood and turned back around. "You still are beautiful and don't you forget it." Kiara smiled. She nodded her head and mouthed the words, "thank you".

Hassan helped the children get dressed and straighten up a bit. He didn't wanna hear Nova's complaints about the house being in disarray. He already knew she was going to have a fit for using money to take Kiara and her children out to eat and buying large amounts of food later on.

On the way to IHOP Hassan's phone kept blowing up. He knew it was Kensington, but he couldn't answer for her. He knew if the vehicle had already been towed, she was calling about that or going to ask him a million questions about his whereabouts.

"She's going to be hell," Kiara said shaking her head. "You know I heard y'all this morning, and cousin you're wrong. Leave these hoes out her alone. Now I know your wife really don't care for our family, and I get it. Our family is very toxic, and she's just trying to keep her home at peace, but you running around with different women ain't right. You'll have a fit if she found her someone else. She's a beautiful woman, and I know for a fact men be trying to holla at her. Tighten up, cousin."

Hassan thought about what Kiara said and knew she was right. Things with Kensington were fun, but now she was acting more and more needy. He wasn't ready to lose Nova or lose his stability. With the salary he made in Austin, it still wasn't enough to live the way he was living now. Without Nova, he'll be struggling.

He pulled up to the IHOP and was surprised that they were seated pretty quickly. The restaurant was packed as always. "Daddy, Savannah and I are going to the bathroom." Trinity ran with Savannah on her heels.

"Wait for me, I'm coming too," Alexis and Larry Jr. said running.

"Trinity is so adorable, cousin." Kiara smiled.

"Thank you! I have to give it to Nova. She does a wonderful job with her."

"She's a good woman, cousin. Why do you do her the way you do?"

"Honestly, sometimes I resent her and feel trapped. Sometimes I feel I'm with her because of Trinity. I regret picking her over Yashira, but I was looking at my stability. I love Nova, but I'm not in love with her. Now she's pregnant, and I just feel stuck," Hassan confessed.

"I hear you. So have you heard from Trinity's mother at all?"

"No."

"Daddy look, Ms. Qawera is here," Trinity said, jumping up and down.

"Hassan, oh my god, turn around slowly and brace yourself," Kiara warned.

66 **I**'m so full, girl. Thank you for treating me. I haven't been to IHOP in years. Those eggnog pancakes with my Colorado omelet was the truth. Oh my god, and the eggnog coffee took my ass out." Yashira laughed sitting back rubbing her flat stomach. She and Qadira had been sitting in IHOP eating and talking for the last hour.

"Girl, I told you. Here you were wanting to go to nasty ass Denny's. They do not go harder than IHOP ever." Qadira laughed.

"Yes they do, but IHOP kinda won me over with the eggnog coffee and pancakes. You know that's my favorite." Yashira beamed.

"Yeah, I remember just like when we were kids. You remember that time you put it all in your hair? Man mama went awfff." Qadira laughed, thinking of a funny moment.

Yashira laughed and then got quiet. The topic of their mother had always been a sour subject. Her mother was so cold to her most of her life.

Sensing her sadness, Qadira reached across the table and lightly squeezed her hand.

"I know this isn't easy for you. It isn't for me either. Thank you for agreeing to help me with mama's funeral arrangements. I need you more than you know," Qadira said sincerely.

"You're welcome, sis. Maybe this will give me closure in some kind of way. I've been running long enough. I'm even thinking about going to get help. Maybe talking to someone will help me in some way. I'm ready to break these chains inside of me," Yashira sadly admitted.

"Daddy, Savannah and me are going to the bathroom," Trinity said, running past the area that Qadira and Yashira were sitting in. Qadira grasped for air.

"Qadira are you okay? You look like you just saw a ghost." Yashira asked.

"Oh my god, this can't be happening right now," Qadira whispered.

"Q, what's going on? You're scaring me."

"Nothing I-I just think we should leave now." Qadira nervously took cash out her purse and placed it on the table.

"Okay! So are you're going to tell me why. What's going on?" Yashira asked alarmed placing on her jacket.

"Yaz, I promise I'll tell you in the car. Now isn't the time to bring it up." Qadria stood.

"Look, everyone. There goes Ms. Qawera!" Trinity and her three cousins yelled running from the bathroom area. They ran to hug her.

Yashira smiled joyfully as the children hugged her sister one by one until the last little girl hugged her. Yashira blinked twice. *It's her. That's my baby.* She silently thought as tears ran down her face. She knew she had come face to face with her daughter. She remembered every little feature about her. The heart birthmark behind her ear confirmed it.

"Come on, Ms. Qawera. My daddy's here." Trinity pulled Qadira.

Qadira looked over her shoulder at Yashira with a worried look. She had a feeling Trinity was her niece, but she wanted to be sure before she told Yashira. Now her hand was being forced.

Yashira wiped her eyes and stood. She began walking in the direction of where Hassan sat, and she felt the fine hairs on her arm stand up. *He still looks the same from behind.*

"Daddy look, Ms. Qawera is here," Trinity said, jumping up and down.

"Hassan, brace yourself," Kiara warned.

The children gathered around Qadira, and Hassan stood and turned around from the booth he was sitting in slowly.

The air around his throat seemed to instantly close when he saw the love of his life appear before him. A range of emotions shot through him. He felt love, confusion, anger, lust, and then back to love. He couldn't believe it.

"Yashira," Hassan's eyes widened with shock. "Is that really you?" he asked in an unsettling tone.

"Who's that pretty lady, daddy? She has eyes like mine," Trinity innocently asked.

"Wait, Yaz. This is Hassan? The Hassan?" Qadira asked shocked.

Yashira nodded her head up and down. She placed her lips together to keep from losing her composure. She wanted to run and grab her daughter for a hug but knew she would have to establish a relationship first. She wondered if Hassan hated her, or if he understood why she did what she did. Standing there looking at him had brought back old feelings. She loved him.

Yashira had finally given Qadira all the details behind Trinity and her father. For years, she kept him a secret from everyone, including Qadira. She didn't want anyone to know where Trinity was or try to harm her. Her years of sexual abuse, abandonment, and trust issues ran deep. So deep that she didn't even trust her own sister to raise Trinity or know her whereabouts.

Qadira knew of Hassan from picking Trinity up time from time, and she knew of his wife Nova. All this time and Qadira would have never guessed that Hassan and Nova would be connected to her niece. Matter of fact she would have never thought anything of Trinity if she hadn't of seen her up close and personal to see all the same features she had as Yashira.

From that moment in her office, she had a strong feeling Trinity was her long lost niece. The connection was so strong. However, she wanted to get more information to make sure her assumptions were correct. Now she knew that she was right.

"Yashira, Trinity is one of my students at my school. I had a strong feeling she was your daughter, but I wanted to make sure before you saw her. That's why I wanted us to hurry out of here. I didn't want to upset you."

"I understand sis. I'm not mad at you." Yashira nodded her head.

Trinity walked towards Yashira and grabbed her hand. "Why are you crying? What's wrong? You want some of the eggnog pancakes I'm about to order? You can have some, and you can sit with us, right daddy?" Trinity turned to ask her father.

"She eats eggnog pancakes too," Yashira whispered and began sobbing. She let go on Trinity's hand and ran out of the restaurant. This was just too much for her.

"Yashira wait! Trinity, stay with Qadira and Kiara. I'll be right back!" Hassan yelled running after Yashira.

"Yashira wait! Just please let me talk to you. Please!" Hassan pleaded, ignoring Kensington's call.

He chased after Yashira and refused let her go without her knowing how he felt. He caught up with her and convinced her to follow him to his vehicle so they could talk.

"Yashira, look at me." Hassan grabbed her hand. "I love you. I've always loved you," he said passionately.

"Hassan, I never stopped loving you," Yashira confessed, trying to hold back fresh tears.

"I want you to see Trinity and build a bond with her. I forgive you. I love you so much. I'm sorry I choose my marriage over you. I've regretted that decision for years."

"I would like that. How would this work though? Will your wife be okay with me seeing my daughter? Hassan, I..." Yashira began crying. "I've been so fucked up all my life. I don't want you to think I'm this monster who just left her child. I'm not. I just couldn't escape my childhood trauma. When you left to be with your wife, I was in a state of abandonment. I couldn't continue stripping with a newborn. I was afraid. I was afraid someone would harm her. I was afraid she'd end up broken like me. I knew leaving her with you that you would take care of her. That day I left her on the porch, I waited, and when I saw your wife, I broke down. I couldn't be half the woman she was. I was jealous of her and vowed to myself that one day I would come back for Trinity. Hassan, I've worked my ass off, and I know I don't have the right to come in and make demands, but all I want to do is be a mother to my child." Yashira cried harder.

"Baby, don't cry. Come here. I got you." Hassan pulled Yashira in for a hug.

Having Yashira back in his arms made everything so right. Their chemistry was stronger than ever, and before Hassan knew it, he and Yashira kissed long and passionately. Neither one of them were aware of the hell that was about to break loose.

Margaret wasn't the one to press anyone for information. She allowed her daughters Nova and Ryan to be open and transparent when they were comfortable, but for some reason, lately, she couldn't rest. She knew something was going on with her beloved Nova.

She and Nova were always close, but for some reason when Nova married Hassan, Margaret felt like Nova wasn't the same. Her light in her eyes was gone. She seemed absent-minded and often got lost in her thoughts. Her spirit was dim and although Henry, Nova's father, felt like Margaret should stay out of Nova's marriage, she couldn't.

"Baby what's going on with you?" Margaret asked Nova concerned. They had just brought dresses for Ryan's big birthday party that was taking place next weekend.

Margaret took notice of Nova's lack of interest and sunken demeanor. Her mind was miles away, and while they shopped, Nova gave one-word answers and seemed distracted.

Nova diverted her eyes from her mother, placed her dress in the backseat, opened the passenger car door, sat in the car, buckle her seatbelt, slouched down in her seat, and blew out a heavy sigh. When Margaret sat in the driver's seat and reached over to grab Nova's hand, her bottom lip began to tremble. She squeezed it tight, needing to feel her mother's touch.

Margaret knew her daughter like no other. Something was bothering her spirit, and just like Margaret knew her child, Nova began sobbing really loudly.

"Come here, baby."

Nova removed her seatbelt and drove straight into her mother's bosom. Margaret rubbed her back and allowed her to get it all out. Once Nova was done crying, she sat up in her seat and began telling her mother everything.

"Mama, I've been lying to you and daddy. Trinity is Hassan's daughter. Shortly after we married, he cheated on me with a stripper. She had the baby and left her on our doorstep. I didn't want to make Hassan look bad, so I lied about me being infertile and her being adopted. Ever since marrying Hassan, my life has gone downhill mama. It's been lie after lie and woman after woman. This time he's gone too far. I had a feeling he was cheating again. I took off work Friday and through a tracking app, tracked him down. I went to the location. Mama, I don't know what came over me, but I walked in that woman's home. I found out that he's been paying her rent, got her a vehicle with my credit information, taking her on trips and everything. The worst thing about it is, he got her pregnant. Yet another baby and she's his employee, MY EMPLOYEE. He brought this humiliation to my job. Ryan had to bail me out of jail for assaulting the woman." Nova hung her head.

"Oh, baby."

"I know, ma. He has me out of character. I'm losing it, and I found out I'm pregnant too. Now he has his family staying with us without even asking me. I'm just realizing that Hassan doesn't love or respect me. I think I'm going to file for divorce. I just don't want to lose Trinity. I love her." Nova's eyes watered.

"Baby, why did you suffer in silence so long? Did you think we were going to judge you or love you any less? Let mama tell you something. I knew you were lying about Trinity and so did your father. You're a lot like me. Always trying to see the good in people and loyal to people you shouldn't be loyal to. Did I ever tell you why Leroy stopped coming around?"

"No, ma'am." Nova wiped her eyes.

"Well, your father was a lot like Hassan. That's why I never cared for him. Your father used to put me through the same shit."

"Really? Daddy? I thought he was a stand-up man," Nova asked shocked.

"That's because I made your father look good. I smiled to cover the pain for years. Anyway, your father's job was requesting more hours from him, and he couldn't keep up with the yard work, so he hired Leroy. Leroy had a grass cutting business, and he used to cut the grass every other Friday. You remember?" Nova nodded her head. "Well, he noticed me and was one of the kindest men I've ever met. Every time your father broke me down, Leroy would lift me back up. I started having an affair with Leroy. I would send you girls off to school, and your father would go off to work, and I would be with Leroy. I fell in love with him. Your father found out our affair, and all hell broke loose. Leroy asked me to choose, and I chose your father."

"Why?"

"Because I had you girls to think about. Your father eventually changed, but I should have left. I never stopped loving Leroy. He eventually got married. Every now and again I'll see him and his wife. The way he treats her hurts my heart because that could've been me. Anyway, baby, I shared that to say, sometimes in life, you got to choose yourself. Now we all love Trinity, but baby don't let her be the reason you suffer at the hands of Hassan. I know you love her, but sometimes we have to let go and let God. I never want you girls to look back and live your life regretfully." She squeezed Nova's hand.

"Brixton called me," Nova blurred out.

"I knew he would contact you again. He's a good man, he was just unbalanced, but that man loves you. He reminds me a lot of Leroy."

"Do you think I should meet up with him and see what he has to say?"

"Most definitely. If for anything closure. Baby, you deserve better, and if you need to come back home, you're more than welcome. You're going to get through this." Margaret gave Nova a hug.

"Mama, I love you. Thank you for being there for me."

"Anytime baby! Now let's get something to eat. What do you have a taste for? Never mind I know you're going to say IHOP." They laughed.

Margaret pulled into the IHOP parking lot and struggled to find a parking spot. As always IHOP was packed. She pulled around towards the back of the restaurant and found a parking spot. She backed in, and when she turned her vehicle off, she noticed Nova grasp for air. Pain was etched all over her face.

She followed Nova's eyes and landed on Hassan's green Impala. His lips were intertwined with another woman's lips. Margaret could see the color drain from her daughter's face, and she felt helpless. "Nova baby, breathe."

"Ahhhh, I'm sick of this shit!" Nova screamed, hitting the glove department with her fist over and over. She jumped out her mother's vehicle, slamming the passenger's door and ran full speed over to Hassan's car.

She opened his car door forcefully and started ranging punches down on Hassan.

"I hate you bitch! You fucking liar! Who the fuck are you bitch?" Nova yelled and ran around to the passenger side. Yashira quickly locked her door. "Get out the fucking car, now!" Nova kicked the side of the car door and fell to the ground.

"Nova," Margaret screamed. She kneeled beside Nova and began panicking. Nova's body began jerking. "She's having a seizure, call 9-1-1!" Margaret yelled to Hassan.

Yashira looked at Hassan blankly and stepped out of his vehicle. She quickly ran inside IHOP to get her sister Qadira so that they could leave. Now that she knew Trinity went to Qadira's school, she would meet her another time, but right now, she had to get out of there.

"This is all your fault. If something happens to my baby, I'll never forgive you. You coward piece of shit!" Margaret screamed at Hassan.

The ambulance arrived, and Margaret hopped in the back with Nova. She called her daughter Ryan and her husband, Henry. She couldn't believe this was happening.

"What the fuck just happened, yo?" Hassan yelled. He didn't know what to do. Everything was coming at him so fast. He ran back into the restaurant out of breath.

"Hassan, is everything okay?" Kiara asked concerned. Hassan had a wild look in his eyes.

"Kiara, come on fam. We gotta go."

"But daddy, I'm hungry, and our food hasn't come out yet," Trinity whined.

"Trinity, not now. Do as I say and let's go. I'll stop by Wendy's or something!" he yelled.

Trinity started to cry, and Hassan felt bad. She was too spoiled at times and right now, he just didn't have the time for her whiny attitude.

Hassan stopped by Wendy's and got the children all something to eat. He noticed Kiara's phone going off multiple times and her ignoring it. He sighed thinking about what he may have gotten himself into trying to help Kiara.

When they made it back to his house, Hassan made Kiara call an officer over to file a report. The sooner Larry was picked up the better. He felt nervous with Kiara and exposed. He knew how possessive and crazy Larry was, and he was beginning to feel that maybe he should have listened to Nova.

He excused himself to his bedroom and called Ty. He needed his boy's help. He sucked his teeth and shook his head thinking about how all this shit started over a damn messy ass Facebook group. He couldn't believe Kiara would even put herself out there like that with her relationship with Ty knowing how small and messy Austin was. Hassan felt Ty needed to step in and help Kiara since he kept saying he cut for her.

"Ayo, what's up fam?" Ty answered.

"Man say, dig these blues. It's some shit going down family, and I need you," Hassan said in a rushed tone. He was trying his hardest not to break down.

"What's good?" Ty asked hyped.

"Bro, so much shit is happening." Hassan paused. "Man fam, shit is all bad. I got Kiara and her children with me. Larry broke into her house, raped, and beat Kiara in front of the kids last night."

"Bro, is you serious?" Ty yelled.

"Yes, man. He fucked her up pretty badly. I brought her and the children to my house, took them out to eat at IHOP, and my nigga you ain't going to believe who I ran into."

"Who?"

"My baby mama."

"Yazzi?"

"Yup! We sit in my car, chopping it up and started kissing and shit. Nova saw us. Man, she went ape shit crazy. She opened a nigga's door and started fighting me and shit. Then she tried to attack Yashira and fell out on the ground having a seizure. She's pregnant with my seed. The ambulance took her to the hospital. Man, she had her mother with her too, and you already know she feels I'm some hoe ass nigga, now this. I got Kiara and the kids, and we just came back to the house. I got her in there filing a report on this nigga Larry."

"I'm tied up with Ashley right now, but what you need me to do? I cut for Kiara. That's my lil mama." Ty said, getting out the bed, leaving a sleeping Ashley.

"I need you to holla at Mishonda in the office. She knows you my people. Get the key to me and Kensington's apartment. Go get some food and go by rent-to-center to have them deliver furniture. Make sure the apartment has everything. I'm tryna get Kiara em' in there by tonight. Just make sure my people straight, fam." Hassan pleaded.

"I got you fam," Ty said.

"Got who?" Hassan heard Ashley yelled and he rolled his eyes. He didn't need her ass getting in shit that had nothing to do with her.

"Damn Ashley, I told you about sneaking up on a nigga. Look it's a lot of shit going on right now, and I don't need your shit right now!" Ty yelled.

"I thought you told me that you aren't messing with Kiara anymore. All of a sudden though, that's your lil mama, and you cut for her. Really Ty? You know what Ty, fuck this relationship. All you do is lie. I'm tired of you making a fool out of me." Ashley stormed back to the bedroom.

She gathered all her things and had made up her mind that she was done. She didn't need this, and she damn sure wasn't about to lose her sanity behind Ty.

"Well, if that's how you feel, fuck it then. A nigga told you he had you and cut for you, but I'm young, Ashley. I told you in the beginning when you started fucking with me, that I wasn't ready to settle down. I ain't doing shit I wasn't doing in the beginning. If you can't stay down with a nigga, then little mama I don't need you. Now you can rock with a nigga, and we continue to chill and do us, or you can go.

Tears ran down Ashley's face. She loved Ty, but why couldn't he just choose her? She was a good woman and always did things to show him how good of a woman she was. They had good times, and she always treated him good. He confused her. He was the one always calling her to chill, come over, or go out somewhere.

"Is you rocking with a nigga or nah?" Ty asked.

"Yea," Ashley said, hanging her head. She put her things down and sat down on the bed.

"Like I told you, I cut for you. Them other bitches don't mean shit. You see who here with me now. So stop tripping. Look I gotta go handle some business. Cook a nigga some dinner or something and chill. I'll be back later, and if you're good, daddy might have a little surprise for you."

He kissed Ashley, and she smiled.

"Hello!" Ty yelled while leaving his apartment. "Man, this hoe tripping. Don't worry. I got you though. One!" Ty said, hanging up the phone.

Hassan heard a knock at the door and went to open it. *This fuck boy.* Hassan silently thought and rolled his eyes. He stepped to the side and allowed Officer Wallace in.

He left Kiara and the kids at the house and ran into Walmart to get the blankets, pillows, towels and other household hygiene products. Hassan knew that he should have gone to see about Nova, but he didn't have the energy to deal with Nova's family. He knew that she wasn't alone and would be fine. His cousin was family, and he wanted to make sure she was good first, and then he'd worry about Nova and Kensington.

As he shopped, he kept getting a funny feeling that someone was watching him. That feeling continued even as he drove home. He kept checking his mirrors but didn't see anyone. When he returned home, he was happy that Officer Wallace was gone.

A couple of hours later his phone rang, and it was Ty telling him that everything was set up. He dropped Kiara and her children off at Travis Station. He felt safer knowing that his boy Ty was there. He didn't know where Ashley was and didn't ask. He was just appreciative for Ty looking out.

He and Trinity headed back to his house.

"Daddy where is mama at?" Trinity innocently asked.

He pulled up to the red light and was about to answer her when, *boom, boom, boom!* Hassan ducked just in time as glass shuttered through his window. He heard a car burn off.

"What the fuck, yo? Trinity, talk to daddy. Trinity!" he yelled, shaking her.

"Daddyyyyyyyyy!" Trinity screamed, jumping out of her seat into his arms. He held onto her for dear life and cried.

He made her put her seatbelt back on and busted a wild U-turn in the middle of the street. He headed back to Travis Station and ran up to the apartment where Ty, Kiara, and the children were.

"Man bitches is wildin', son. Somebody just shot at a nigga. I had my fucking daughter, son!" Hassan yelled walking through the front door with a crying Trinity.

"Oh My God! What? Kids y'all go to the room and take Trinity with you," Kiara ordered.

"Word? Did you see who the nigga was?" Ty asked.

"Nah, man." Hassan shook his head and sat down. "Bruhhhh, a nigga is stressed the fuck out!" he yelled. "I had my baby with me. What if those niggas kill my baby?" Hassan said, crying.

Kiara wrapped her arms around Hassan and buried her head in his neck. She felt so bad for putting Hassan in the middle of her drama. Her cousin could have died because of her, and if that had happened Kiara would never forgive herself.

Kiara knew this had Larry written all over it. He had gone too far this time. He had been texting her threatening messages all morning. He told her he was watching her and was going to kill her and Hassan for playing with him. She was too afraid to say anything. The truth was, she wasn't safe anywhere, and she couldn't wait for Officer Wallace to lock him up. She needed peace. She just hated her cousin was in the middle.

Her phone rang, and Kiara jumped up. When she saw it was an unknown caller she hurried and hit the ignore button. "You still in communication with that nigga, Key?" Hassan asked pissed with bloodshot red eyes.

"Huh?" Kiara asked as tears began to flow down her face.

"This is my fucking life we are talking about. A nigga almost killed me and me my daughter."

"He's been texting me all day." Her phone rang again.

"Answer it!" Hassan's voice roared throughout the apartment.

"It's Officer Wallace. He said they got him. The picked him up on the south side. I don't think that was Larry who was shooting at you." Kiara said in a rush.

Hassan was in deep thought. Who other than Larry would have it out for him? He didn't have any gambling debts, and other than the occasional slip up with females from time to time, he couldn't think of anyone who may want to harm him.

His phone rang interrupting his thoughts. He looked at Ty and then Kiara. He didn't recognize the number. He started not to answer and allow the voicemail to catch the caller but decided to go ahead and answer.

"Hassannnnnnn!" he heard the bloody screams of a woman followed by a shot.

"Oh, so you're not just not going to answer my calls?" Kissy screamed, throwing her phone against the wall.

She had woke up hours ago naked lying in her bed. She saw the note Hassan left, but why hadn't he called her this morning to check on her. This is the kinda of shit Kissy was talking about, the games he played. It seemed like he was back to his games again the minute she let her guard down.

She called room service and ordered a plate of French toast, eggs, bacon, fruit, and orange juice. She was starving.

After she ate, she cleaned up the room, showered, and dressed for the day. She contacted the agent from Round Rock and made the 30-minute drive out that way.

Midway there, she had thought about canceling again. Out of nowhere, the weather had changed. It went from sunny to gloomy and began to rain. She kept going though because she needed a place to move.

When she pulled up to the condo complex, she smiled. It wasn't all the way complete, and they weren't done with construction, but the condos that were complete were absolutely beautiful. They looked like individual homes with their own fences and small back yards.

She took out her phone to dial Hassan one last time. He didn't answer, but moments later, his phone dialed her back.

"Baby, where are you? I wanted you to come with me today. I wanted to show you something," Kissy said in a whiny tone.

"I love you. I've always loved you," Hassan said so passionately.

"I love you too, baby," Kissy replied lovingly and smiled.

"Hassan, I never stopped loving you," Kissy heard a female voice say.

"I want you to see Trinity and build a bond with her. I forgive you. I love you so much. I'm sorry I choose my marriage over you. I've regretted that decision for years."

"What? Whyyyy?" Kissy screamed as tears rushed her eyes. She realized Hassan had butt dial her by accident and was professing his love to another woman.

Kissy was enraged. She was so tired of men playing with her emotions. She listened to the entire 30-minute conversation he had with another woman. She was sick. She opened her car door and vomited all the food contents that she ate earlier.

She wiped her mouth with a napkin from her glove box and took the bottled water that sat in her cup holder and rinsed her mouth. She poured the rest of the water over the vomit on the concrete to wash it away. She was devastated.

Evil scenarios played in her mind, and she let out a sinter laugh. "I got every last one of you," she said aloud and jumped from the knock on her window that startled her.

"Hi! Are you Kensington Blu?" the ginger hair, freckled, green-eyed, tall, light-skinned black woman asked.

Kissy nodded her head and smiled. She turned her vehicle off and grabbed her purse from the passenger side.

"I'm Bella. Nice to meet you. Come on in Kensington and welcome. I'm so excited to show you what we have. First, tell me what you're looking for," Bella voiced in a friendly tone.

They entered a modeled home, and Bella took out a portfolio of the property, an application for Kensington to fill out, and photos of the different units. They chatted for a moment, and Bella showed Kissy a move-in ready condo.

Kissy walked around the condo amazed. She loved the light painted gray walls, nine-foot ceiling, crown molding, faux wood flooring, granite countertops, premium shaker-style cabinetry, chef-inspired kitchens, gooseneck kitchen faucets, stainless steel kitchen appliance sets, built-in microwave, large elegant master suite, soothing garden tubs, washer and dryer connection, generous closet space, three-inch blinds, ceiling fans, wrap around patio, programmable digital thermostats, and electric heating & cooling. She also loved the canary yellow, light gray, and baby blue colors scheme that flowed throughout the condo. The furniture and decorations were definitely her style.

"I'll take it." She smiled at Bella.

"Awesome! Are you buying or leasing?" Bella asked excitedly.

"I'm buying. I want to put 5,000 down now. How soon can I move in?" Kissy asked.

"Well, I just need to do a background check, and that can take up to three to four business days." Bella smiled.

"Oh okay! Well, thank you for your time," Kissy said disappointedly.

She rushed out of the office embarrassed with tears. She hated how she could never escape Raheem. All she wanted to do was move on with her life. She knew once Bella ran her background she would be disqualified. This was always her dilemma when it came to her moving into her own place. She didn't have anyone to ask to co-sign.

"Wait, Kensington come back!" Bella yelled after her.

Kissy wiped her face and turned back around.

"Just forget it. With my record, I will never be accepted. I'm so tired. I just need a breakthrough. I hate these niggas. They'll have you out here getting records behind fighting hoes. Just forget it, Bella. My record won't pass, and I'll be disqualified," Kissy cried.

She placed her head in her hands, embarrassed that she was breaking down in front of a stranger, but she couldn't help it.

"Look I'mma be honest with you. I need you. I was told today that my sells aren't good and I was going to be let go. Let's make a deal. I'll clear your background and application and you move in and put the $5,000 down. We all go through shit in life. I need the commission for selling that unit. A bitch ain't trying to go back to stripping and shit, you feel me? I got kids, man."

Bella knew what she was doing went against everything she wasn't supposed to do, but fuck it. She needed her job, and she was willing to do anything to keep it. She knew Kensington had demons and probably a shit load of things on her record. She didn't care. If she had to forged documents, she would. She was not losing this sell, by any means necessary.

"You'll do that for me?" Kissy asked.

"You help me, and I'll help you. Shit, we sistahs got to stick together sometimes. Truth be told, we all gotta a past. Shit, I can tell you're tryna shake whatever shit you going through. These condos are nice. I lease one here too. That's another reason I need this job. I refuse to go back to the bottom. If this shit doesn't work, a bitch is robbing banks." They laughed.

"Man, thank you. I really need this fresh start. Is it possible to get the unit I saw with all the furniture?"

"That's our model unit, so I doubt that, but I can get you moved into one just like the model one you saw without the furniture."

"I need a place ASAP."

"Well, the utilities are already on through the city. On Tuesday, you would have to transfer everything to your name, but shit, lets signed these papers, and I can get you the keys today. Fuck you mean." They laughed again.

"Bitch, I like you."

Kensington talked with Bella a couple of more hours getting to know her. She learned that Bella's mother had a crack addiction just like her mother. She was half-white mixed with black. Her father left her mother and fathered two other children. She had a hard life and was trying her hardest to make it for her and her girls. She and Kissy had a lot in common, and Kissy could tell they would be great friends.

She filled out paperwork and paid her money upfront. The total of her condo was $235,000. She knew she could get the rest with her group in no time. If not, that was fine too. Her payments were low enough for her to manage.

Once she received her keys, Kissy went to Ashley's furniture and Bed Bath & Beyond to furnish her entire three-bedroom condo. She then went back to her hotel room and got on IG to find her favorite female black painter. She purchased 12 paintings and brought everything else she would need online.

♥♥♥♥♥

She ended up dozing off and was awakened by her phone ringing. She ignored it only for it to ring again.

"Yeah!" She answered with an attitude with her eyes still closed.

"Yeah? What you mean, yeah? Where are you and why aren't you here for Sunday dinner?" Torrie yelled.

"I'm good. I'm asleep. Y'all have fun. I'll get up with Torrie later." Kissy hung up.

Her aunt called again cussing her out. Kissy sucked her teeth and went on ahead and showered. She had a huge attitude because she honestly didn't want to be around Bo, and she didn't understand why her aunt was so pressed about here being there. She started just to call Tony and tell him to come through the hotel where she was at, but went on and headed to Torrie's house.

When Kissy turned on her aunt's street, everything in her was telling her to go back to the hotel. She ignored that voice and attempted to find a place to park.

"That's all these bum ass niggas do!" she yelled.

So many people were out hanging out. Women and men were playing loud music, holding pit bulls by their leashes, smoking loud, and talking shit. Kissy couldn't stand it.

She finally parked on the side on her aunt's home and said hey to all the catcalls and homies that called out to her. She knocked on Torrie's door, and her aunt answered being extra as always.

"Um, it sho'll took yo little fast ass long enough to get here. Talking about you was sleep after my ass done cooked all this food. Little ungrateful ass!" Torrie yelled loud enough for the people closest to her house to hear.

"Man, ma, back off of cuz. Damn! Being all extra and shit. You got all these hoe ass niggas all in the family business and shit. I told you about that shit!" Tony yelled, pulling Kissy in for a hug.

"What's up, cousin? Pretty ass. Come chop it up with a nigga," Tony said, pulling Kissy by the hand.

Bo frowned pissed that Tony was stealing Kensington away. He was so mad that excused himself and went to his and Torrie's room.

Torrie sucked her teeth loudly. Bo had an attitude, and she saw the way he was lusting after her niece. She wanted to cry, but her mood instantly changed when she saw Nicole pulling on her street. She smirked and squealed inside. She knew some shit was about to go down. It wasn't nothing like a jealous, scorned woman.

Tony fixed Kensington a plate of food and took it to his room where they caught up on old times.

Kissy and Tony were thick as thieves. They always had a special bond. Tony never judged her, and he was always looking out for her when he could. He even looked out for Kinley although Kissy didn't think he knew about her.

Tony was always away. He worked in the oil field and only came to Torrie's home every so often, mostly to visit his daughter. Kissy was so proud that her cousin got away from the hood to make something out of himself. He still dabbled in the drug business every now and then, but he mostly walked the straight line.

"Well, cousin it was good seeing you. I'm going to get out of here. You know I gotta make my rounds and shit. Oh here, I hope you ain't think a nigga forgot about your birthday," Tony said, placing a diamond tennis bracelet around Kissy's wrist and handing her two grand. She placed the money in her fanny pack that she had around her waistline.

"Thank, you Tony." Kissy jumped in his arms.

"You're welcome baby girl. Take care of yourself, and if you need anything, you know how to reach me. Stay up kid," Tony said leaving.

Kissy headed up front to throw away her plate and grab her something to drink. She noticed Bo wasn't in sight and her aunt was speaking to Nicole in the living area.

"Alright auntie, thank you for the dinner. I'mma about to head out of here."

"Wait a minute, shit. How you just gone stop by and only speak to Tony and not the rest of us. This here is Nicole." Torrie pointed to Nicole who was sitting in the living room.

"Oh hey," Kissy waved dismissively, "I didn't know you knew her."

"This is Bo's sister. Small world ain't it." Torrie smirked.

"Sure is," Kissy replied, taking a sip of her drink.

Nicole eyed Kissy like she had shit on her. She didn't know what Nicole's problem was. Hell, she didn't even know her at all for that matter. She only met Nicole once when she, Nova, Tasha, and Ashley's messy ass introduced themselves as the HR staff. Honestly, if anyone had the right to be funny acting it was Kissy since she knew Nicole was fucking with Hassan.

"This here is my niece, Nicole. This is Kensington the one I told you was messing with that married man Hassan and who's pregnant by him." Torrie rocked back and forth in her recliner.

"Really?" Kissy screamed. "What is your problem today? Why are you being messy spreading my business? Why would you do me like that Aunt Torrie? Ever since I stepped foot on your doorstep, you've been treating me like shit."

"Oh, so you're the little bitch sleeping with my man?" Nicole asked with her arms folded. She was hoping that the group would reveal more women, but she already knew about Kensington, thanks to Torrie and Tasha from her job.

"Bitch? Why are you disrespecting me? I don't even know you!" Kissy yelled.

"Well, I know you Kensington Blu. Word is that's all you do is fuck married men and get pregnant by them." Nicole stood. "Just like Raheem and Kinley. Bitch, play with me if you want. I got your record right here, and I'll fire you." Nicole smirked picking up the vanilla folder she had brought with her.

"Wow! To think I trusted you. You hate me that much Aunt Torrie? Why would you tell Nicole things that you know would hurt me?" Kissy fought back tears.

"It's really not a secret, just like Hassan isn't either. Y'all thought y'all were being so sneaky at the job, but everyone knows," Nicole lied. "I suggest you let this be a warning. Leave my man alone, hoe!" Nicole yelled, walking towards Kissy.

"Bitch, run up and get the fuck done up. Ain't no punk in my blood. Is this what this is an ambush? Is this the reason you wanted me to come over here today?" Kissy asked her aunt with a face full of tears.

"You dirty bitch. You're just like yo mama. I had your father first. He left me for that bitch. I was fine until I saw what happened between you and Bo. You wore them little tights disrespecting me in my own house." Torrie stood, pointing her finger.

"What? What are you talking about? Auntie, I've never disrespected you. Why are you doing this to me? You were the only one I could trust. I thought you had my back. I love you. I would never do that to you."

"What's going on here?" Bo asked, coming out of the bedroom with just his boxers on. Kissy turned her head and attempted to walk out the front door.

"Where the fuck do you think you're going, bitch?" Torrie angrily yelled.

"Torrie, you love me?" Bo asked walking towards them.

"You know I do, Bo."

"If you love me, let me have Kensington," Bo voiced, and Torrie bit her bottom lip but nodded her head.

"You got me fucked up!" Kissy yelled. She tried to open the front door but was yanked by her hair locs by Nicole.

Nicole punched Kissy in her nose, and she lost her footing. "Bitch!" Nicole got on top of her throwing punch after punch.

"That's enough," Bo said picking up Kissy.

She weakly fought him. "Put me down. Auntie, help me!" Kissy screamed while her aunt and Nicole laugh.

Bo took her to the bedroom and slammed the door. "Shut up little bitch. You thought by leaving I wasn't going to get this good pussy," Bo entered her forcefully.

"Ahhhh stop! Get off of me! Why are you doing this?" Kissy screamed. "I'm pregnant. Please stop. Please, somebody help me. Somebody help." Kissy pleaded but was drowned out by the loud music that played outside.

"Shit, this pussy is good." Bo pumped harder until he released.

He collapsed on top of Kissy, sweaty and breathing hard. She laid still. She had no more fight in her. Bo removed himself from inside of her and stood up. "Now if you tell anybody about this, I will let everyone know who the real Kissy is behind that group. Next time make sure you lock your computer." Bo smirked.

Kissy's eyes grew big. Then it dawned on her. The night her mother came over. Lisa had stolen her laptop and cash. Bo was the one who brought her laptop back to her. Kissy wanted to scream.

"You one messy ass bitch. What would make someone lie on people and break up people's homes? You know if your secret ever gets out you're dead, right? You better watch yourself Kissy, and next time I want some pussy, you better give it to me," Bo threatened before he walked out the room.

"Now little hoe that'll teach you about messing with people's man." Torrie and Nicole laughed entering the bedroom.

Kissy weakly stood and pulled her dress down. She wiped her face with the backs of her hand and attempted to walk pass Torrie and Nicole. Nicole spit on her and Torrie laughed.

"Bitch, give me that shit!" Torrie yelled yanking the diamond tennis bracelet off Kensington wrist. "What else you got? What's in that fanny pack?" Torrie asked, opening it. "Aww shit, Bo, look. Two thousand dollars, we hit the jackpot." Kissy held her head down while they insulted her. She was numb.

The front door opened and everyone's eyes widened. "What the fuck is going on? Why is the house tore up like this? Is that blood?" Tony pointed on the floor.

Tony had come back to his mother's home to get a gift for his daughter that he left in the closet. Nobody expected him to return, and Torrie knew it was about to be some shit. Tony didn't play when it came to Kensington.

"Kensington what the fuck happen to your face?" Tony yelled. He looked at Kensington's clothing and knew some funny shit was going on. "That's how y'all do my family? Y'all call her over here for some fuck shit? Give me her fucking bracelet and those bands!" Tony angrily yelled. Torrie's hand shook as she placed it in Tony's hand. "Here," he gave it back to Kensington. "Are you alright? Did they hurt you?" Tony asked Kensington.

She looked over at Bo and started to rat him out, but decided against it. She had something coming for Torrie and Bo. "No, I'm good, cousin. I'm going to get out of here. Thank you, Tony. I love you," Kensington lied, hugging him a little longer than normal.

She quickly ushered herself to the front door and swiped the .22 caliber handgun that she saw sitting by the television stand. Swallowing hard, she hurried to her vehicle, instantly breaking down. She was thankful for the tinted windows because she was a mess right now.

*hap! Whap! Whap! Whap!*
"Bitch ass nigga, what do you do to my cousin?"
*Whap! Whap!*

"Tony, stop! You're going to kill him!" Torrie yelled, trying to pull Tony off Bo.

Tony laid into Bo and threw punch after punch. "Come on, man. I didn't do anything." Bo whined trying to put his arms up as a defense.

Bo was no match for Tony. Tony was well over 6 feet tall and 300 pounds. The punches he delivered felt like a horse was stomping Bo.

"Hoe ass nigga, I will kill you behind Kensington. If I find out you did anything to her, I will fucking kill you." Tony pointed before he stormed out of the home.

"Oh my god Bo, are you okay?" Nicole asked leaning down to help Bo off the floor.

"Ahhhh fuck!" Bo moaned. "I'm good. Torrie, you just going to let that hoe ass nigga whoop up on me like that?" Bo asked.

"Bo, what was I supposed to do?" Torrie asked as tears rushed her face.

"Just the fact that you asked that let me know you ain't down for a nigga. Nicole, help me pack me shit. I'm done with this old ran over bitch." Bo struggled to stand.

"Bo, I'm sorry baby. Please don't leave me!" Torrie begged.

Bo gave Torrie a once over and shook his head. He left her home with Nicole and wondered what new chick he could live off of. His baby mama Jaybryd wasn't messing with him anymore, and after that shit with Tony, Bo knew he couldn't go back to Torrie's house.

Torrie made him feel less of a man allowing her son to whoop him like that. She wasn't a ride or die like he thought, and he knew he was done with her.

"Bo, do you have a plan?" Nicole asked, breaking Bo out his thoughts.

"Nah, can I crash with you a couple of days?"

"I'm not at the house anymore with Sean. I moved into a hotel. It's small, but I mean I guess you can crash there a couple of days until you figure shit out. I got stop by the house real quick to pick up some more clothes." Nicole turned on her music.

Bo wanted to say something further and had even thought about robbing his own sister. He hated how tight she was. He knew of the life insurance policy she had from their father dying. He needed that money. He would chill a couple of days with her and then press her for money. He hoped she gave him some because he really didn't want to kill his sister.

*Skkkkkkkkkkkkkttttttttt*!

"Fuck!" Sean screamed turning the corner wildly. He had been following Hassan all morning trying to get a clear shot. He didn't want to shoot with the baby in the car, but it was now or never.

Ever since Nova sent him that message, he had been trying to come up with a plan to kill Hassan for sleeping with his wife. He had met Hassan numerous times during Nicole's company events. He didn't understand why Hassan would disrespect him that way and sleep with his wife.

He pulled in his driveway and was shocked to see Nicole's vehicle there. He jumped out of his vehicle and placed his gun behind his back. He sighed of a sigh of relief, thinking that Nicole had come back to work on their marriage. When he entered the home, he smacked his lips.

"What the fuck are you doing here?" he yelled at Bo.

He couldn't stand Nicole's brother. He felt Bo was lazy and always used women as his come up. If it wasn't Torrie, it was his baby mother Jaybryd, or his sister Nicole. He didn't work or do anything besides lay around and use people.

"Man chill out, nigga. I'm only here to help Nicole," Bo said dismissing him.

Nicole was packing up more of her things and ignoring Sean. He sat on the bed in deep thought as he watched her move about the room as if he wasn't there. He was beyond broken that his wife didn't love him anymore.

"Nicole, man I'll be right back. I'm finna go do something real quick!" Bo yelled, leaving the house and jumping into Nicole's car.

"Can we talk about this?" Sean asked with his hands extended in a pleading manner.

"Honestly Sean, it's like I told you. You know what?" Nicole threw her hand up. "I'm not repeating myself. For years, I kept telling you I was bored. I kept trying to suggest us to go to the sex store, travel, and do new things. You always dismissed any of my ideas. All you wanna do is work, go to church, and sleep. You never want to go out, and it's like you just want me to grow old. I just want to live. That's why I've been working out, going back to school, and enhancing my life experiences. I tried to do that with you, but you wanted to stay where you were. There's no growth in that for me. I'm just done," Nicole said exhausted.

She was so tired of having the same conversation with Sean over and over again. They had been married for ten years, and Nicole was just ready for something new and exciting. Sure enough, Sean was a good man, but was there all there was to being in a relationship? She wanted more. She craved for more.

144

Although Hassan was ignoring her, Nicole loved the way he spoke to her about life. Hassan was a very positive person, and Nicole loved the way he engaged in conversation. He was so intellectual and drew you in with the words he spoke.

Nicole would try to have these same conversations with her husband, and he wasn't interested. He would often fall asleep on her, say negative things about her dreams, and some of the things she wanted to do. He would even laugh and tell her to get real. He never supported her the way that Hassan did.

She continued packing her things tuning out her begging, crying ass husband. Her mind drifted to earlier, and she would be lying if she said she felt bad for Kensington. Bo was her brother, so she was going to always ride for him, and she didn't blame Torrie either. If she had opened her doors to a relative and her relative was flirting with her man and wearing tight clothing, she would have done the same thing Torrie did. Besides, in Nicole's mind, Kensington got what she had deserved.

Nicole thought about the scuffle that Tony and Bo had. Everyone was shocked that Tony had come back to the house. Nicole knew if he hadn't, more than likely they would still be over at Torrie's home violating Kensington in some way.

She hated that Bo made the decision to leave Torrie though. That wasn't in the plans, and she honestly didn't want to deal with her brother Bo. He was a bum in her eyes. He always had his hand out and always needed something. Ever since her father died, Nicole felt that her relatives counted her coins, including Bo. She just wanted a new start. She wanted to be away from Bo and Sean, but it seemed as though she couldn't escape either one of them.

She was honestly hoping she didn't run into Sean. She wanted to be in and out to avoid confrontation with him. She did love him. She just didn't love him the same anymore and felt the marriage had run its course.

*Whap!*

"Don't fucking ignore me, when I am talking to you!" Sean snapped slapping Nicole. Her nose began to bleed. "Bitch, I gave you ten years of my life. Ten years and you think, you can just walk out on me? You couldn't even have kids. The doctors said you were ruin, and I still loved your fat ass the same. I took care of you when you were sick. I stayed true to my vows. I never cheated on you, and I came home to you every single night. After all these years, you think you're going to leave me for Hassan?" Sean yelled, and Nicole's eyes widened. "What Nicole, you think I wouldn't find out? Yeah baby girl, I have proof. I received a message myself about you and Hassan. You're sadly mistaken if you think for one minute that I'm allowing you to leave me for that nigga."

Sean pulled out his gun.

*POW!*

He shot Nicole in the knee.

"Owwwww! Sean, please!" Nicole pleaded crying.

"What's that nigga's number?"

"Sean, pleaseeeee!" *POW!* He shot Nicole in her other knee.

"Dial the fucking number, bitch!" he bellowed, throwing her his phone. Nicole sobbed as she dialed Hassan's number.

"Hasssaaannnnnnnn!" Nicole cried out before Sean jerked the phone out her hands.

"I see you dodged the bullets. Next time I won't miss." Sean laughed.

"What?" Hassan yelled. "Who the fuck is this? Bitch, I had my daughter with me. You could've killed her." Hassan fumed.

"This will be the last time you fuck my wife." *POW!* He shot Nicole in the head. "I'mma find you and I'mma kill you, nigga. Watch your back!" Sean warned and hung up.

Nicole's body laid still on the floor. Blood leaked quickly and her dead eyes stared at Sean.

"Arghhhhhh, look what you made me do bitch!" he screamed, holding the gun to his head as tears and snot ran. He began pacing back and forth, not knowing what to do.

He quickly grabbed a bag and began tossing clothes into them. He ran into the restroom for hygiene products and opened his safe to grab the three grand in cash, more bullets for his gun, and his passport.

"I love you, Nikki," he whispered, looking at Nicole's body one last time before he hurried out the house.

Torrie kept calling Bo to come back home. She bribed him with money, and Bo left Nicole's to swing by there and get the cash. If Torrie wanted to give Bo money, he damn sure wasn't going to turn it down, but he'd be damned if he went back to Torrie.

As he got closer to the hood, police cars kept passing him by. It was daylight savings and dark as hell, but Bo could see the flashing lights and its location. He parked the car on the street before Torrie's home and walked.

"Ayo Tim, my nigga, what's going on fam?" Bo hollered out to Tim who was always on the strip.

"They're saying they got your ole lady Torrie. The DEA is in there right now ripping her shit up. Somebody dropped a dime on her." Tim said, trying to catch his drool. "A nigga just came from Torrie's. You know I had to get my shit." He laughed holding up his bottle of embalming fluid and a pack of cigarettes. "Anyway, I started lighting up, and the next thing I know one-timers just started hitting this bitch."

"Damn! That's fucked up." Bo rubbed his beard.

"Just be happy your ass wasn't there. She's definitely going to do some time. Look there they go bringing her out now." Tim pointed.

Bo shook his head and hurried back to the vehicle. He couldn't believe this shit. "Oh well, shit. Torrie brought this shit on herself. I hope she doesn't call me because she on her own."

He headed back to Nicole's home and hoped that she was ready to go. He couldn't stand her husband and was happy to see his vehicle gone when he pulled up.

"Ayo! Nicole, let's go fam." He grabbed a beer. He drowned the beer and threw the bottle in the trash. "Nicole," he yelled, wiping his mouth, walking to her bedroom.

A frown was etched across his forehead. An odor of feces hit his nostrils. "Spray in this bitch or something. Damn, sis!" He stopped in his tracks. "Oh shit! Nicole! What the fuck yo? Not my baby sis man, come on!" Bo broke down crying.

He dried his face with the end of his t-shirt and searched in Nicole's purse for her phone and wallet. He fled the scene leaving the door wide open.

K issy arrived back at the hotel and parked on the side closest to her room. She used the three flights of stairs to avoid hotel guests. When she made it to her room, she took all her clothes off and ran herself a hot bath. She angrily wiped away the tears that kept falling.

"Ssssss," she moaned when her raw skin came in contact with the hot water. Her tears continually ran while she soaped her body down. The soap did nothing to take away Bo's scent off her body.

Her stomach cramped, and she stopped bathing herself when she saw the water turn from clear to red. She brought her legs up to her stomach and began screaming. "God please don't make me lose my baby. Why do you hate me so much? You're never there for me. Why do you let everyone hurt me like this? Whyyyyy?" she cried but knew her prayer fell on deaf ears when she felt a large tissue ball pass through. She knew it was her baby.

She stood and drained the bloody water. Her hands trembled while picking up the blood clots and tissue that were too big to go down the drain.

"Two pink lines. You were more than just two pink lines. I'm mystified and numb. I love you so much, even though I hadn't even had the chance to name you or hold you. It hurts. Ahhhh! This hurts!" she broke down placing pieces of heart in the toilet that sat closely to the tub.

149

She ran the shower water to make sure all the blood had been washed away. In a trance, she stood under the showerhead. Snapshots flashed quickly through her head. Visions of Bo raping her and the men from her childhood all seemed to attack her memory at once. In her mind, she was in a dark room, and they all were there laughing, taking their turns and calling her dirty names.

"Ms., are you okay in there?" a stranger knocked on her hotel door, jilting Kissy out of her traumatic state of mind.

She shook her head side to side and quickly opened her eyes. Her psychosis was setting in altering her personality. This always happened when she had a traumatic experience. It was a part of her defense mechanism.

"Yes, I'm okay." Kissy gathered the strength to say and turned off the shower water. She didn't realize she was sobbing loudly.

She wrapped her body in a towel and decided to call the Austin Police Department on her aunt and Bo. She grabbed her burner phone and voice distorter device out of the side pocket of her purse. "Yes, I would like to report guns and drugs in a home. The woman name is Torrie Wells, and the address is 8109000 Hilcroft Drive," Kissy's distorted voice said.

She turned off the burner phone and had to hurry and lean against the dresser for support. A dizzy spell lasted for thirty seconds and her heart rate increase. Blood leaked quickly, and Kissy knew she needed to go to the emergency room.

Bella was the only person Kissy could think to call. She knew Hassan wouldn't answer and it pained her to know that once again, she had been made a fool of.

She struggled to get dressed. She kept falling back down.

"You made a fool of me, tell me why?" she cried singing Me'Shell Ndegeocello "Fool of Me" song while attempting to pull a shirt over her head. She fell on the bed and began sobbing. She reached for her phone and dialed Bella.

"Bellaaaa, please come and get me. I lost the baby. I need you!" Kissy screamed into the phone.

"Hello, Kensington! Oh my god, where are you? Don't worry I'll come. I'll come get you. Just tell me where you are."

"Pleaseeeee hurry. I'm at The Holiday Inn by the Greyhound bus station," Kissy slurred. She gave Bella the room number and laid across the bed in a fetal position.

Bella was cooking when she received the phone call from Kensington. She was going to give her a call tomorrow to check on her, but she was surprised to see her number flash across her screen.

The phone call from Kensington screaming for help in her ear hurt Bella. Kensington was so distraught, and even though Bella didn't know Kensington that well, it was something about her that felt like home. She trusted her for some reason and felt a connection to her. She had never felt that connection before with any other woman.

She quickly dressed her daughters and drove like a mad woman down IH-35 to the hotels address that Kensington had given her. Her heart pounded in her chest, and she didn't know why such an urgency to help Kensington was there, but it was.

"Kensington, Kensington! Open the door! It's me, Bella! I'm here!" Bella knocked frantically.

"Ohhhhhh, it hurts!" Kissy cried slowly walking towards the door. She had lost so much blood, and the pain she was feeling was unbearable.

"Listen, Mecca and Mina. Mommy wants you to help gather all of Kensington's things. Put her laptop in her purse over there. Mecca, get all the stuff out the bathroom and put in the suitcase. I need you to hurry. Kensington is coming with us. Don't go anywhere. Do as I asked and make sure you get everything. I'm taking Kensington to the car, and I'll be right back," Bella instructed.

"Yes ma'am," they replied and moved quickly about the room.

"Please whatever you do, don't take me to Seton.." Kissy slurred.

Her eyes rolled, and she held her hand over her stomach. Bella held her around her waist. Hotel guest looked on with concern seeing Kissy's condition.

Bella situated Kensington in her vehicle and ran up the three flights of stairs. She helped her girls with all of Kensington's belongings, did a double take around the entire room and grabbed her suitcases by the handle. She checked Kensington out of the hotel.

As Kissy waited patiently for Bella, her eyes began to roll again. She was so weak, but a white tow truck with blinking lights brought her back into focus. She noticed the tow truck had her vehicle and she let out a light cry. She knew this would happen once Nova knew who she was. She had prepared and cleaned out everything in the vehicle.

A silent rage was building in Kissy, and if one thought her group was messy and setting shit off in the city, they hadn't seen anything yet. The car door opening snapped Kissy out of her evil thoughts.

"Okay, we have everything. I'm taking you to the hospital. I checked you out of the hotel, and you'll be staying with us until you're well," Bella said.

Thirty minutes later Kissy was checked into a hospital. There she was given a DNC for the miscarriage, an emergency blood transfusion, treated for the bruises to her face and her arm was stabled again.

Bella and the children stayed with her a while and then left to let Kensington get rest. She thanked Bella. No other woman had ever been so kind to her, and she was grateful that Bella came to her aide.

Her phone began ringing, and she reached towards the recliner chair that was next to her bed for her purse. An unknown caller flashed across her screen, and Kissy answered the phone.

"Hello!" she answered with hoarseness in her voice.

*"You have a collect call from The Travis County Jail. Press 1 to accept." Beep!* Kissy pressed the 1 key.

"Kensington, don't hang up. It's me Torrie. Look I'm sorry for what happened to you. I need you to see about getting me out of here. I'm in here for drugs charges. They ripped my shit apart!" Torrie yelled.

She was in jail panicking. Torrie had been selling drugs for years, and nobody ever called the laws on her. It was funny to her though that today of all days, the DEA came. She knew she was facing some serious time and the only one who could help her out was Kensington. She had attempted to contact Bo and Tony, but neither was answering for her.

"What happened today wasn't supposed to go down. I need your help. I can't reach Tony or Bo. Look there's a safe in the cemetery behind big mama's grave. You'll have to dig a little. I need you to get it to give to my lawyer," Torrie pleaded.

"I'm sorry me don't ah speak cano English." Kissy hung up.

The nerve of her aunt to be calling her and asking for favors after she let her man rape Kissy was beyond crazy. She couldn't help but let out a sob. "Why would my aunt do me that way? I can't believe she treated me like that."

Tears continued to flow down Kissy's face, and visions of Bo raping her turned her stomach in the worst way. She knew she shouldn't have gone over there. Something in her heart kept telling her that something funny was in the air. She never thought her own aunt would be the one to hurt her though.

Her Aunt Torrie was all she had and for her to set up her to be beaten and raped was something Kissy couldn't understand. Did her aunt hate her that much? This question kept running through her mind. Kissy picked up her phone and texted Hassan. She felt he had the right to know about the baby.

She placed her head in her hands and screamed. A nurse overheard her and came to her room to check on her. "Kensington. Kensington, baby, are you okay?" an older black lady by the name of Sharon asked.

Kensington let out a loud sob and shook her head no. Sharon knew that Kensington was dealing with a miscarriage and left the room to get her some pain meds and meds to help calm her down. She also brought Kensington some vanilla pudding, gram crackers, and chocolate milk.

Kissy thanked Sharon and made a mental note to send her some flowers when she was discharged. She always made a habit to be kind to those who were kind to her.

She had placed her purse behind her pillows and had gotten more relaxed in the bed. Her eyes were becoming heavy, but she wanted to see if the city was buzzing yet about Torrie's arrest. She turned on the news and smiled. *Got em'*. She inwardly jumped for joy.

Kissy knew her group was live and popping with the latest gossip. She squealed at the thought of Torrie being locked up. Bo was next. She knew to always go after a man's pocket or the one woman he really loved. For Bo that was his baby mama Jaybryd, and although Kissy didn't have no beef with her, she was going to pay for what Bo had done to her. Today's events were something Kissy just couldn't wrap her mind around. She wondered how long Torrie, Bo, and Nicole had plotted against her.

"I can't believe Hassan was messing with this fat ass bitch Nicole," she angrily blurted out.

Thinking of Hassan made her fly into another fit of rage. She reached behind her and grabbed her cell phone. She began sending message after message. She was on a roll. Finding out about Nova was one thing, but the fact that he was sleeping with someone else and she attacked her was something totally different.

Kissy wondered if Nicole was the one who broke into her apartment and stole her shit. She wondered if Nicole put those messages up on her bathroom mirror. Something wasn't adding up, and nothing to her made sense. So many thoughts ran through her mind.

Her heart ached with pain. Hassan not being there for her or answering her calls was eating at her spirit. Here she was in this dark hospital room by herself after being assaulted, and the one person she needed to tell her things would be okay wasn't there. Just like Raheem, Hassan had left her out to dry. *That's okay!* She silently thought. Her eyes started to flutter, and before Kissy knew it, she was knocked out.

Nova had been in the hospital for six hours. The doctor told Nova that due to higher levels of stress, she had an uncontrolled electrical disturbance in her brain. When she fell, she somehow landed on her side crushing her right ovary. It was a lot of trauma on the baby, but somehow the baby survived.

Nova didn't know what to feel. She was numb and what hurts the most is after all these hours, Hassan hadn't called, visit her, or even contacted her family to see if she was okay.

All kinds of thoughts ran through her head, and her stomach turned in agony. She wondered if he was sleeping with the woman that she saw in his car. She looked a lot like Trinity, and Nova's heart broke. Her mind raced with a million thoughts, and all she could do was cry. *Was that Trinity's mother? Is she back? Is she going to try to take Trinity from me? Is Hassan sleeping with her?* Question after question silently ran through Nova's thoughts.

"Sis, it's going to okay. I'm sorry Hassan is doing this to you. You don't deserve this, Nova. I hate seeing you in pain." Ryan helped Nova freshen up in the restroom.

She continued to wipe Nova's tears and held her sister in her arms as she rocked back and forth. Nova was a wreck, and after Ryan helped her back to bed, the doctors came and gave Nova another round of pain meds.

Her parents and Ryan kissed her on the forehead and told her they loved her and would be back early in the morning. Nova nodded her head at them and within minutes, she was out.

"I'mma fuck that little nigga up!" Henry Nova's father bellowed as soon as they arrived in the parking garage.

He couldn't bear the sight of seeing his little girl hurting in pain. Guilt was plastered all over his face as he thought about the person he used to be to Margaret. To see his daughter be treated the same way angered him.

Margaret started to speak but halted when she heard her name being called. She thought it was funny how nobody saw their faults until it was staring them in the face. Hassan was exactly who Henry used to be towards Margaret. Even though he had changed his ways, Margaret still regretted choosing him over Leroy. She wasn't happy with Henry and prayed that her daughter found her own way and leave Hassan for good.

"Mrs. Margaret, Mrs. Margaret!" Brixton called out loudly through the parking garage.

He was at the hospital visiting his mother who fell ill. He had just gotten off the elevator that led to the parking garage when he thought he caught a glimpse of a familiar face. *No way! God, it can't be.* He silently thought, calling out Nova's mother's name.

"Brixton is that you? Oh my, Lord. Hi, son!" Margaret hugged Brixton. "Go see about my baby. She needs you Brixton. She's in room 415." Margaret smiled and winked.

"Thank you!" Brixton hurried back to the elevator.

This time he would fight for Nova and not let her out of his life again. He would marry her, love her, cherish her, and never leave her again. He just prayed she forgave him and allowed him to correct his wrongdoing.

"Do you think that was a good idea, Margaret? The girl is married. She doesn't need to go mixing her feelings up." Henry asked.

"Yes, it's a good idea!" both Ryan and Margaret yelled.

"I'll see you guys later. I have to get back to work." Ryan gave them both a kiss on the cheek.

"I just feel the boy is confused. He loves Nova, but he also loves women," Henry defended.

"You know what Henry, that isn't an excuse. I'm not going to sit by and watch Nova become hardened and mean spirited because some nigga who can't control his dick feel it's okay to treat my baby any kind of way. I will not let her make the same mistakes I did, staying in a marriage just for kids. She has the right to be happy, and Brixton loves her. I hope she leaves Hassan for Brixton and for once chooses herself!" Margaret stormed off, leaving Henry there to wallow in his thoughts about what she had just said.

Brixton was beside himself. He couldn't believe how his day was turning over for the better. His spirits had been down due to his mother's illness, and all he could think about was how lonely he would be without her if she passed.

He never expected to see Nova. After she abruptly ended their call, Brixton thought maybe it was best just to leave things in the past, but he couldn't shake Nova.

He stopped by the gift shop and was happy he arrived in time before they closed. He brought Nova flowers, lots of balloons, bears, a journal, a necklace that read *I love you*, candy, and a card.

"Wow! That must be some special person." The gift shop woman smiled blowing up all the balloons for Brixton.

"Very," he replied, matching her smile.

When he made it to Nova's room, she was sleeping so peacefully. *Gosh, she's so beautiful.* He silently thought while placing the bears, flowers, and balloons all around Nova's room.

He had made up his mind that he wanted to be the first face she saw when she had awakened. He saw the ring on her finger but paid it no mind. A real husband would have been by his wife's side.

He left the room briefly to go to his vehicle and grab the overnight bag that he always kept in his trunk. His mother stayed in and out of the hospital, and Brixton never knew when he would need a change of clothing, so he made it a habit to always have clothing and hygiene products.

Brixton stopped by the cafeteria to grab him something to eat and stopped by the nurse's station for a blanket and pillow for the sleeper bed in Nova's room. While she slept, he made up his bed, ate, and watched their favorite show *Greenleaf* on his tablet. A few hours later, he began to get sleepy. He took out a pair of socks, his boxers, a white tee, and black sweat pants. He then asked the nurses for a couple of towels and took him a nice hot shower.

The smell of Yves Saint Laurent La Nuit De L'homme tickled Nova's nose. She hadn't smelled that familiar scent in years. *It can't be. It's only one man I know and have ever met that wears that scent.* She struggled to open her eyes, and when she did, her voice was caught in her throat. Tears rushed her eyes. She looked around the room and saw all the balloons, flowers, and bears.

Brixton came out of the bathroom and rushed to Nova's side. "Nova, you're up. I'm so happy to see you. How are you feeling?" he shot off question after question.

Nova finally spoke, and Brixton held on to her every word. She forgot how easy it was to talk to him and before she knew it, she told Brixton everything.

He was quiet and allowed Nova to get it all out. It stung him to hear she was pregnant. He wished the child was his, but a baby wasn't going to stop him from pursuing Nova. She was meant for him, and he would love the child as if it was his if she gave him a chance.

The two stayed up for hours to talk. Brixton would leave and check on his mother and come right back to Nova. She smiled and was very appreciative of Brixton. She forgot what it felt like to laugh, crack jokes, and have a best friend. That's what Brixton was to her, a best friend.

Nova used to crave this connection with Hassan, but for five years all he had done was make her life miserable. She was beginning to understand the talk she and her mother had earlier about choosing yourself, and Nova felt that it was time she did that.

"Oh, I brought you this. Close your eyes." Brixton said, placing the necklace around Nova's neck. "Okay, open them." He smiled.

"Thank you," Nova beamed with joy. She couldn't remember the last time Hassan did anything special for her or even called her beautiful lately.

"You're welcome. Listen, Nova, I know you're married, but I can't lie or hide the fact that I need you in my life," Brixton passionately expressed.

"Brixton, when you left me, you put this hole in my heart. I loved every part of you, and although I always felt I was living in Michelle's shadow, I would have fought for you. You were the best man I've ever had. You were my best friend— someone I could trust, lean on, and someone who understood me. You broke me, Brixton. I had to mourn the loss of you. I had to pick myself up and tell myself you were only a dream. I questioned my worth, my value, and I was in a state of pain for a long time. When I married Hassan, I thought he could replace you in my heart, but he couldn't. I still love you, and I forgive you too. I can sit here and lie and be mad and miserable, but the truth is I'm happy you're here. If you weren't here, I would be in this lonely hospital room by myself. You just don't know what you do to my heart. To wake up and see all of this," Nova pointed around the room, "just makes my heart smile." Nova cried.

Brixton wiped her tears.

"Your mother is the one who helped me. I've been in contact with her for years. I went to counseling, and she even attended a

160

session with me. She told me not to step back into your life unless I was ready for you. I fought hard with my demons. I joined a church and started a youth program. I made partner and built the home you always talked about you wanted. I have an account with your name on it. I have a ring for you, and I haven't had sex with any woman since you. I love you Nova, and I need you. I don't care how long I have to wait for you. I will wait." Brixton shed tears.

"What about the baby?" Nova whispered and looked away in shame. "Would you think I was a bad person if I wanted to terminate the pregnancy?" Nova asked.

"I think a baby is a blessing no matter how it was conceived. At one point, you loved your husband, and the baby was made with love. Don't allow resentment to sat into your heart Nova, and don't let what Hassan, me, or anyone has done to you change who you are. I done that with Michelle and unfairly took that out on you. The Nova I know always wanted to be a mother. I will help you through this and love the baby all the same. It's a part of you. I will stand by your side with any decision you make, and no I don't think you're a bad person if you decide to terminate. All I ask is you bless me with more." Brixton smiled.

"I didn't know my mom was in contact with you. She's so sneaky." Nova laughed. "She speaks very highly of you. She hates Hassan."

"I know and so do I. You deserve better."

Nova and Brixton talked until they both fell asleep.

When the morning came, Nova was stable enough to go home. She was still sore from the fall, but she was up on her feet again. For the first time, she hadn't concerned herself with worrying about Trinity. She honestly hadn't thought of her or Hassan. When Hassan stressed that Trinity was HIS DAUGHTER, something inside of Nova broke. She knew it was wrong of her to take her resentment out on Trinity, but she couldn't help the disconnect and pain she now felt.

How could Hassan say something like that after Nova had sacrificed, lied, and giving her all to a child that was forced upon her? It was a slap in the face, and her mother made her realize that she was not obligated to a child that wasn't hers and a man who constantly disrespected her.

She was done with Hassan. After the incident that happened yesterday, that was the last straw. To have her daughter there eating while he sat outside cheating on her with another woman was it.

Hassan had made no attempt to contact her or check on her and his child. That was it. She didn't need Brixton to make her see that she and Hassan were done either. She was serious, so serious that she was going to the courthouse to file for divorce.

She decided from here on out she was going to be happy for her. That also meant terminating this pregnancy. She wanted no parts of Hassan. She had nothing left inside of her to give. She heard what Brixton had said, but she was putting herself first.

In her mind, she would be the only one emotionally suffering inside, and what if things didn't work with Brixton, she would still be tied to Hassan forever. That was just something she wasn't willing to go through.

Brixton was who her heart desired. She loved him, and she couldn't help that. He was different. He had a light in his eyes and a presence that had a glow. He was a man of God, a leader, a protector, a provider and he waited for her and came back for her. She respected that, and it was easy to open her heart again, not to mention his love for her mother as well.

Nova hadn't laughed like she had with Brixton in years. He was a breath of fresh air. She was a firm believer that with the right person, everything fell in place and that's how it was with Brixton. It was natural, and everything with him had come back full circle. *I'm not letting him get away, and for once, I'm choosing me.*

She called her parents to let them know that she was being discharged and that Brixton was giving her a ride home.

Her mother was happy while her father attempted to shame Nova telling her that it wasn't a good idea for a married woman to be with her ex. She blew him off. A piece of her didn't even view her father the same anymore.

She and Brixton said their goodbyes to Brixton's mother, and Brixton took Nova out to eat for breakfast. It was as if the two hadn't missed a beat and they picked up where they left off at.

"Ahem! Hello Nova, Does my son know you're out smiling and bullshitting with another man?" Erica, Hassan's mother, asked.

Erica had spotted Nova across the restaurant and didn't appreciate her grabbing another man's hand and laughing. She felt it was disrespectful to her son, and she was about to get to the bottom of it.

"Actually, I wouldn't care if he did. If you'll excuse us, I would like to get back to our conversation. Thank you and have a nice day." Nova smiled.

"Wait until I tell my son about this shit, you slut. I told him you weren't about shit. I never liked you!" Erica yelled being all ghetto.

Nova rolled her eyes. It was just like Hassan's mother to be loud and ghetto in a nice restaurant. This is why Nova couldn't stand to be around Hassan's family. They were trash in her opinion.

"Good day, Erica!" Nova smiled, and Erica stormed off.

She and Brixton continued there breakfast and conversation. When they were done, Brixton swung Nova by her home, and they both promised to stay in contact.

Brixton leaned in to give her a kiss and Nova's body was set on fire. She remembered the lovemaking that she and Brixton use to make and the way he just kissed her had her yearning for more.

"I love you Nova, and I'll see you soon," Brixton whispered as their foreheads touched.

"Mommy," Nova froze and tensed up.

"What the fuck? Who the fuck is this nigga? You got this nigga at the house?" Hassan screamed.

"Daddy, stop yelling!" Trinity cried.

"You know how to find me, Nova," Brixton said, kissing her on the cheek.

He smirked at Hassan as Hassan sized him up. *Fuck boy!* Brixton silently thought while getting in his car.

"Trinity, go to your room now!" Hassan yelled, storming in the house.

Nova calmly sat in the recliner chair rocking back and forth as Hassan shot obscenity at her and threatened Brixton. Nova just stared at him. The shit was funny to her. He had a lot of nerve.

"Hassan, you saying all that but ain't really talking about anything. Let switch tones. What bitch shot at you? Let's start with your truths first." Where was Trinity when you were shot at? Why didn't you come to the hospital? Shall I go on?" Nova asked with her hands on her hips.

Hassan put his head down. He knew he should come clean with Nova. Trinity was going to tell her everything anyway, and he was just tired of all the lies.

"Nova, sit down. I'll start from the beginning." Hassan said while taking a seat on the sofa.

"Where are Kiara and her children at?" Nova asked.

"I moved them into the apartment Kensington had. I told you I'm not messing with her anymore. I've been truthful about that. I already paid this month rent, so I told Kiara she could stay there for a month and then decide what she wants to do." Nova nodded.

"Well, I'm calling Ryan to come get Trinity. I don't want her here to hear what we're about to discuss." Nova stood. "I'm going to take a shower and call Ryan. Please get Trinity's clothing and backpack ready for tomorrow."

Sean drove around for hours with no real destination in mind. He couldn't believe he shot and killed his wife. The way her dead eyes stared at him began to haunt him, and he needed a drink before he lost his mind. He stopped by a little hole in the wall and sat at the bar.

"Yeah, give me a shot of Brandy and keep them coming!" he yelled to the bartender whose name was Mark.

As soon as the warm liquor hit his soul, Sean couldn't stop.

"Ahhh!" he yelled fanning for the bartender to keep more coming. His pain began to ease, and he was feeling too good to stop now.

"I think you've had enough, Sean. Maybe I should call your wife Nicole to come down here and get you," Mark the bartender said. He had been bartending for years, and the only time he knew of Sean to drink this heavy is when something on his home front was interrupted.

"She's gone, man. Can you believe her big ass up and left me? Talking about she's bored with me and in love with another nigga, after all the shit I went through. Do you know I settled for her? She can't even have kids, and I stayed with her. I never cheated. I treated her right, and this is how she does me?" Sean slurred. He was so drunk that he started to wail out crying.

Other people in the establishment stared at Sean. He was making an ass out of himself. "What the fuck y'all looking at?" he yelled at two women that were standing close by him.

"Come on, man. Let me call you an Uber. You're drunk, Sean. You need to sleep it off, buddy." Mark came from around from the bar trying to escort Sean out.

"Get your hands off of me." He swung at Mark and missed. The two young ladies on the dance floor looked at Sean and burst out laughing.

"You little hoes. Come here." Sean swung again missing and doing a full circle until he fell. He struggled to get off the floor, causing everyone in the club to burst out in hysterics.

"Come on. It's time for you to go," Mark said grabbed Sean by his arm.

"Man, get your gay ass hands off of me. I'm not your bitch!" Sean insulted and spat on Mark.

"I will fuck you up." Mark bellowed losing his composure. He didn't tolerate disrespect.

The low budget rent a cop came and threw Sean out the club. "Get off of me!" Sean yelled and wrestled with his jeans pocket for his car keys. "Ah, ah," he fought.

Once he sat in the car, he was so exhausted and worn down from today's event. He ended up crying himself to sleep in the parking lot of the club as Johnny Taylor's "Last Two Dollars" played.

*Tap, tap, tap!*

"Club hours are over. Get the fuck out of here!" Mark yelled, knocking on Sean's window.

Sean jerked his head back and forth and shot Mark the bird. He looked at the time and saw it was past two in the morning. He was starving, so he stopped by Jack in the Box for something to eat.

"I wanna go home!" Sean burst out crying while eating his Jumbo Jack in the restaurant's parking lot. He missed his wife so much.

After he finished eating, he pulled in the parking lot of Nicole's job and parked where nobody would see him. He toyed with the gun in his hand and thought about just ending his life.

"Hassan must pay!" he screamed.

He stepped out his vehicle to relieve his bladder and sat back in the driver's seat. He leaned his seat back and fell asleep until the sun had awakened him.

"Ahhhh!" He stretched sitting up in his seat, rubbing his eyes. He looked down at his hand and saw the gun that he was clutching so tightly. "Damn," he whispered, rubbing his head. He had a major headache and had a hard time remembering how he ended up at Nicole's place of employment.

The parking lot was bare, and Sean realized that he had about another hour to wait before his target Hassan arrived at work.

He checked his clip and smiled at the six rounds of bullets. "I'mma kill that bitch for fucking with my wife."

He would wait for however long it took, but he wasn't leaving without making sure Hassan was dead.

Nova made it to work earlier than normal. The truth was she couldn't take being around Hassan any longer. She was still in a lot of pain and should have just called in or went to stay over at her parents; hell even a hotel would have been fine after the night she had.

She didn't get any sleep at all. She and Hassan had a shouting match all night. The truths he threw at her were too much to bear, and she cried for hours. She didn't know what she was thinking of showing up at work. Work was the last place Nova should have been after learning of the affair her husband had with Nicole. She thought Kensington was a blow to her ego, but to know that he had slept with Nicole multiple times behind her back hurt her to no end.

Nova always felt Nicole had it in for her, but she couldn't put her finger on why. She would always catch Nicole's side eyes or seemingly hostile responses and questions. Nova also didn't like how Nicole seemed to buck her authority and was insubordinate to the changes in policies. She received a lot of pushback from Nicole and negative energy. Now she knew why.

She felt like a fool. All the times Nova would talk to Hassan about her days at the office with Nicole's attitude and rudeness would turn into Hassan gaslighting her, making her feel as if she was being overly sensitive. Yet, he knew the whole time why Nicole was acting the way she was.

Aside from the affair Hassan was having with Nicole, Nova found out that Nicole left her husband Sean to be with Hassan, which led to Hassan coming clean to Nova about his gambling addiction and how the affair with him and Nicole started, also answering her questions of where he had the extra funds to finance Kensington. Nova didn't know what to think or say, especially when Hassan revealed that it was Sean who shot at him.

This information was too much for Nova, and she didn't feel safe around Hassan, at home or at work. She couldn't believe he brought this drama to their doorstep and Nova was still worried about this Larry and Kiara situation, even though Hassan told her he took care of it.

His confessions weren't as painful as Hassan revealing that Trinity's mother Yashira was back in town. She was the woman Nova caught him kissing. She blacked out and began swinging wildly on Hassan when he revealed Trinity met her mother. She was thankful that Trinity was with her sister.

Her thoughts ran wildly. She wondered if Hassan had picked the school that Qadira was the principal at to reunite Trinity with her mother one day. Even though Hassan swore up and down that he didn't know Qadira and Yashira were sisters, Nova didn't believe him. Her marriage was over. There was nothing worth salvaging. It was over. She couldn't do it anymore.

*Knock, knock!*

"Good morning Nova. These came for you." Tasha handed Nova a bouquet of red roses and a box of tiff treats.

"Oh! Wow! Thank you!" Nova looked at the time. She hadn't realized that an hour had gone by with her sitting in deep thought.

"You're welcome! How was your three day weekend?" Tasha asked, inspecting Nova's appearance. Her eye was still swollen from the fight that she had with Kensington.

"It's was good," Nova lied. "Well girl, I'm going to get back to work." Nova smiled politely while pulling the card off the roses.

"Okay! Oh, have Nicole called you or called in? She still hasn't arrived."

"No, I haven't heard from her."

"Oh okay! That's weird. She normally beats Ashley and me here. Anyway, Kensington Blu, Terry Wright, and Donald June all called out today. A new BPR trainer by the name of Ms. Harris will be arriving within an hour. She's paired up with Hassan this week and Hector next week," Tasha informed Nova and gently closed her office door.

At the mention of Kensington Blu's name, Nova smirked. "I wish I could have seen that bitch face when they towed my shit," she whispered and laughed.

She started to call Tasha back in her office to get the first name of Ms. Harris, but her phone beeped, and she saw that it was her sister Ryan. "What's up, sis?" Nova asked.

"Nothing much, just checking on you. Are you okay? Trinity said before I picked her up last night that you were crying. She told me something about a window shattering and her cousin Kiara having stains all over her body. Then she said something like she met a woman who looked exactly like her. Nova, what's going on?" Ryan asked concerned. "I tried to get mama to tell me, but you know how mama is. She feels if a person is ready for you to know something they'll tell you." Ryan sighed. "I just want to know what's going on with you."

"Where are you right now?" Nova asked.

"I'm actually not far from you. I dropped Trin off not too long ago and ran a couple of errands. I'm off today."

"Let's meet at that Mexican restaurant off of 290. I'm not really feeling work today. I should have called in," Nova confessed with watery eyes.

"Okay, I'll see you there."

Nova sat back in her chair and stared at the roses. If they were from Hassan, she didn't want them, but she decided to read the card.

*Nova, I love you. I hope this brightens your day and I hope your spirits are lifted and you're in a better space today. I can't get you off my mind. Let's do lunch sometime this week. I miss you, and I'm thinking about you. -Brixton-*

Tears fell from Nova's eyes, and she couldn't help but to silently sob. "I love you too Brixton, more than you know." She exhaled.

Once Nova composed herself, she sent an IM to Ashley and Tasha letting them know that she was taking the rest of the day off. She grabbed her roses, note, and cookies and signed out her computer.

When she reached the first floor, she stepped off the elevator and thought her eyes were deceiving her. *Nah! That couldn't be him.* She thought she caught a glimpse of Sean walking through a side entrance. Everything in her wanted to stop and verify if that was him, but she kept going about her way.

*Tap! Tap! Tap!*

Hassan tapped on his large office window when he spotted Nova walking in the parking lot to her car. "Where the fuck is she going?" he shouted a little too loudly.

He spotted the roses and cookies Nova was carrying, and jealousy and rage rose in his chest. He dialed Nova's cell phone and squeezed his stress ball as hard as he could when he saw Nova check her phone and ignore his call. It angered him that she ignored him the way she had. She hadn't said two words to him all morning.

He knew he needed to get his attitude in check, but his mind was all over the place. Rotating the ball between his fingers, he stared at Kensington's empty desk. He was happy she called in but wondered how to move forward with her. She had blown his phone up with all kinds of crazy ass messages, and he knew that a lot of drama was about to unfold with Kensington. He just felt so overwhelmed and stressed. He knew he should have called out too, but he had a new BPR trainer that would be arriving at any minute.

He was upset that his Program Manager wanted him to be the one to introduce the new trainer and show her around the building. "Ugh!" he moaned and stood to leave his office for coffee that was located in the employee's break room.

Hassan was so frustrated that he wasn't aware that the plastic coffee cup had a tiny hole in it. When he went to sip, droplets of brown stains fell onto his white collared shirt. "Fuck man!" Hassan whispered, hurrying over to the sink for a paper towel and soap to remove the stains.

He walked back to his office with his head down focusing on cleaning the stains. "Oh my god, Hassan!" Yashira excitedly yelled, covering her mouth; causing other staff around to look up from their computers being nosy.

"Yashira? What are you doing here? Wait, you're *the* Ms. Harris?" Hassan asked shocked.

"I am," she smiled. "I'm the new training manager for BPR."

"Wow! I can't believe this. That's wonderful. I didn't know." Hassan smiled widely and then frowned. "Yashira, what's-what's wrong? Are you okay?" Hassan asked concerned, seeing the faraway look in Yashira's eyes.

"Hassannnnn, behind you!" Yashira cried.

"Ahhhhh!" Staff members screamed, running out the second exit door. Hassan slowly turned around and came face to face with the barrel of Sean's gun.

Sean's hand shook. His eyes were dark but steady on his target. Tears ran down his face. He reeked of alcohol and musk. His hair needed to be cut, and his facial hair was telltale signs of a man who hadn't slept or showered.

"You think you can just fuck a man's wife with no consequences?" Sean yelled.

"Man, I'm sorry. It was only once. I'm with my wife, Nova. I swear I'm not sleeping with Nicole," Hassan said with his hands up.

"Your wife Nova is the one who contacted me and told me you were sleeping with my wife. Do you know Nicole had up and left me because of you? Said she was in love with another man after all the shit I did for her." Sean cried and wiped his nose with the back of his hand. "I killed my fucking wife, and now I got to kill you."

"You don't have to do this. Please, he's my daughter's father. Please just let him go." Yashira cried. Hassan took that at his chance to try to get the gun away from Sean, but it went off.

*POW!*

"Ahhhhh!" Yashira screamed. "No, no, no, no, no! Hassan, look at me. Baby, look at me!" Yashira cried noticing the blood leaking from Hassan's chest.

Sean stared at Yashira and Hassan. He began sobbing as he cradled the gun. He could have run, but he was tired. He wanted his wife, and when the realization that she was never coming back hit him, he opened his mouth and pulled the trigger.

*POW!*

N ova pulled up to the restaurant and pulled out her phone. She was about to dial Ryan to see how close she was but rolled her eyes when she saw the message from Hassan she had ignored.

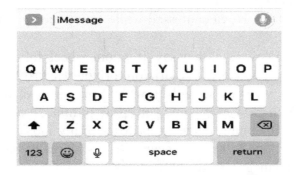

"I'm done with you!" Nova yelled aloud.

She pulled out her compact to check her face. Her eye was still swollen, and the other eye gave signs of lack of sleep. She refreshed her foundation and smiled when she saw her sister Ryan.

Her sister reminded of Jennifer from *Basketball Wives*. She was tall, lean, with a caramel complexion and she wore a long black wavy weave. The one-piece jean jumper set she wore, hugged her small frame in all the right places.

"Hey, sis!" Ryan excitedly yelled when she saw Nova walking towards her.

"Hey!" Nova gave her a long embrace.

Ryan could tell her sister had a lot on her heart. "Come on. Let's go eat." Ryan took her sister's hand.

"Is it too early for a margarita?" Nova asked playfully, and they laughed. She low key was serious as hell.

Moments later the two were seated, and Nova got lost in her head again. She thought of Brixton and about how good it felt to see him. She wondered what he was doing and how his day was going.

"Novaaaaaaa!" Ryan sang out.

"Yes."

"The lady asked do you know what you want to drink," Ryan voiced.

"Oh yes, my bad. Is it too early for a strawberry margarita?"

"Yes," the server laughed.

"Okay, let me get a strawberry lemonade." Nova smiled.

"Girl, you're a trip." Ryan laughed. "Anyway, who were you thinking about smiling like that."

"Brixton," Nova confessed while eating a chip with salsa on it.

"You know what they say. If it comes back full circle, then it is meant to be. I actually love Brixton for you. He takes care of your heart. That's who you should be with. You still love him, and he loves you. You glow every time you speak of him." Ryan smiled.

"I do love him. He just sent roses to my job. I just feel like I'm damaged goods now. I mean what do I really have to offer Brixton. Hassan has really broken me. All the lies, cheating and things he has put me through, I just can't do it anymore," Nova confessed.

"So what are you going to do?"

"I want to file for divorce from Hassan and get an abortion. I honestly just want to start over. I don't want anything to do with Hassan."

"What about Trinity?"

"She isn't my daughter. She's his daughter. Hassan has made that very clear."

Ryan looked down at the menu. She had known all along that Trinity belongs to this stripper named Yazzi she used to dance with back in the day.

*Yazzi was the new girl that Ryan had shown the ropes to. Ryan thought they could be friends, but jealousy got in the way of that. Yazzi was beautiful, and all the male customers started to come just to see her. She would get all the ballers and money, making the other strippers hated her.*

*Nobody in Ryan's family knew that she once stripped. She had a very bad coke addiction and the money she made from stripping supplied her habit. Hassan was Ryan's customer during hours and off hours. She had caught feelings for him and thought they could have something. Things seemed cool until Hassan met Yazzi. Just like with all the other men, Yazzi stole Hassan too. Yazzi started to dance less and Hassan frequented the strip club less and less. Ryan fought for her feelings to go away. She tried to act as though things didn't bother her, but when she learned that Yazzi was pregnant with Hassan's child, anger got the best of her.*

*She confronted Hassan, and he basically laughed in her face. He called her all kinds of strip hoes and told her she was crazy to think they could ever have something. She didn't understand what was so special about Yazzi. She was a strip hoe too, but Ryan knew she had to move on.*

*Ryan knew that Nova had married, but as close as they were, Nova had yet to introduce her new husband to the family. She met Hassan by accident at the infamous Walmart.*

175

*She overheard Nova's voice on the next aisle. "I thought that was your voice. Hey, sis! What are you doing here?" Ryan laughed, shocking Nova.*

*"Sis, now back me up. Tell this fool ketchup goes on eggs." Nova laughed, and Hassan had turned around. Ryan almost dropped her phone.*

*"Ryan, this is my husband Hassan, and this is my sister Ryan." The two shook hands, and their eyes trailed off.*

*"Sorry, I just up and got married. Everything happened so quickly. I want to host a dinner though once our new home is ready." Nova beamed.*

*"Okay! Well, keep me posted. Well, let me run. It was nice meeting you, Hassan."*

*Ryan hurried to her vehicle and burst out crying. She wasn't the one to betray her sister or sleep with someone's man. She thought that if she told Yazzi that Hassan was married, it would get back to Nova and Nova would leave, but she stayed. Ryan couldn't believe the amount of lies Nova would tell to her family to cover for Hassan. She knew Trinity was his and couldn't understand why Nova stuck around for the mistreatment Hassan gave. She couldn't stand him and wanted better for Nova.*

"I hear you, sis. Well, you got to take care of yourself first. You know mama stay preaching that." Ryan laughed while continuing to look at the menu.

"Yeah, but did hear you what I said? Trinity isn't mine, she's Hassan," Nova repeated.

"Yeah, I heard you. I already knew though Nova. We all did. You're not a good liar. We accepted Trinity and never mentioned it. I just felt you would say something when you were ready. I love her though, and whatever you decide to do, I will be right there." Ryan smiled.

"Thank you, sis. I'm just ready to be done with Hassan. It's too much. I found out he is sleeping with a coworker of mine name Nicole, not to mention the other coworker Kensington he slept with. He got her pregnant, and now he has his cousin Kiara in our mix with her drama with her child's father. I just can't do it anymore."

Nova shrugged. "Sis, I'm all cried out. I didn't even tell you about Trinity's mother being back and how I caught them kissing. That's how I ended up in the hospital. I tried to fight them and fell out and had a seizure. That bastard didn't even come to check on me." Nova shook her head and then smiled. "Brixton was there the entire time for me." She rubbed her necklace.

"Wow! I didn't know you were going through all of that. I heard you mention a lady named Kensington. I know a chick name Kensington. She's pregnant too. Wait I got a photo of her. Is this her?" Ryan asked showing Nova the photo of Kensington and Kinley.

"Yup! That's her." Nova frowned. "Who is the baby and how do you know her?" Nova asked still looking at the photo on the phone.

"Well Nova, don't say anything. It's really against HIPPA, but I'll share this with you. She's a parent of a disabled child. The little girl she is holding is her daughter Kinley."

"Wow! That's so sad. I don't know what I would do if my child were disabled to point I couldn't care for them."

"Yeah, it's a lot of work. It breaks me down sometimes when women have to make the hard decisions to give their child up. Aside from that though, Kensington is a great mother. She's so dedicated. She comes to visit her daughter every single Saturday. She helps with bathing and feeding, and she's so loving and patient. I've gotten the chance to know her, and she's a nice person. However, you know you're my sister, and I'm loyal to you. Whatever you need me to do, I'm down. Matter of fact she's doing my hair Friday for my party. You should pop up." Ryan suggested.

"I might just do that."

"So what about Trinity's mother? Are you going to allow her to see Trinity?"

"Honestly the way Hassan kissed her, I don't have a chance. He has never kissed me the way I saw him kissing her. He loves her. At this point, I'm just ready to end it all. I can't do it anymore." Nova said and stared ahead. "What? Nooooo!" Nova cried.

"Nova, what's wrong?" Ryan asked concerned while reaching across the table to grab her hand.

Ryan noticed Nova's phone blowing up, but Nova's eyes were fixated straight ahead. Ryan followed Nova's eyes and turned in her seat.

"Oh my god!" Ryan yelled, cupping her mouth with both hands. "Nova, breathe and answer the phone," Ryan encouraged.

"Hello!" Nova cried.

"Nova, this is Tasha. Nicole's husband Sean shot Hassan. He was transported to Seaton. Get there now. It isn't looking good. He's lost a lot of blood," Tasha cried through the phone.

Nova hung up, and she and Ryan ran out of the restaurant. "Oh god, please don't take my husband!" Nova cried.

"Come on sis. I'll drive. We'll come get my car later," Ryan suggested grabbing Nova's car keys.

"Thank you!" Nova cried. She was in no shape to drive.

Ryan rushed to the hospital as quick as she could. She could tell her sister's mind was racing by the way she rubbed her hands against her pants.

Nova began praying. Just moments ago, she was ready to leave Hassan, abort her baby, and had even fantasized about being with Brixton. Her mind was foggy as she constantly repeated the same prayer in her head.

"God, please watch over Hassan. Please let him be okay. Please don't take my husband. I love him. Please God spare him!" she cried.

Ryan hurried and parked in the parking garage, and they ran into the ER. "Please, my name is Nova Daniels. My husband Hassan was shot and brought here. Is he okay? Can I see him? Please, someone, help me!" Nova screamed.

"Nova chill, I got this. Hi, we're the family of the gunshot victim Hassan Daniels that was brought in," Ryan said calmly.

"Yes come right this way. We have a second waiting area you can wait in. Hassan is in surgery to remove the bullet from his chest. His prognosis is good. He has lost a lot of blood and is receiving a blood transfusion. We're going to keep him here a couple of days for monitoring. He should be out of surgery soon. Right this way," a short, petite, blond-haired female nurse said.

"See sis. You can breathe now. He's going to be fine," Ryan said, rubbing Nova's back.

Twenty minutes had passed, and Nova was a nervous wreck. She was happy to hear that Hassan was fine and was going to make it.

She thought about Nicole and her husband Sean. She couldn't believe Sean was behind this. She shook her head and then slouched in the seat. *Why didn't I go check earlier to see if that was Sean? I knew that was him. If I had gone to check, I could have stopped this.*

"Okay, thank you."

"You're welcome, Mrs. Daniels."

Nova's head shot up, and Ryan stood to her feet. "The fuck? She isn't Mrs. Daniels. This is Mrs. Daniels." Ryan pointed to Nova.

"Oh." A tall, Asian, male doctor looked between Nova, Yashira, and Ryan. "My apologies, I assumed this was Hassan's wife because she came in with him. I'm sorry for the mistake, Mrs. Daniels," he looked at Nova, "Hassan's surgery went well. He's been placed in room 505. I'm Dr. Lee if you need me. I'll leave you good people now."

Yashira and Nova stared at each other not knowing what to say. Nova's mind ran full speed with questions in her head. Everything was so confusing to her.

"Excuse me. We're looking for the family of Hassan Daniels." Two tall, dark, lean, well-dressed black men said.

"Yeah, well who are you and who wants to know?" Ryan asked hostile with her hands on her hip.

"Ma'am, I'm Detective Lu, and this is my partner Detective Eric. Anytime a victim has been involved with a shooting, it's routine that we investigate," Detective Lu said, handing Ryan his card. She read the information while tapping her foot and purring her duck lips together.

"Well, my sister don't know nothing about no shooting. She wasn't even there," Ryan huffed.

"Sis, it's okay. They're just doing their jobs. I'm Nova, Hassan's wife." Nova stood and shook the detective's hands.

"I'm Yashira, the mother of his child, and I was there when Hassan was shot," Yashira butt in.

"Andddd nobody asked you shit. You meant to say the mother of his child who abandoned her newborn daughter and left her on my sister's doorstep to raise!" Ryan yelled. "What are you doing here anyway? You don't just get to pop up all these years later and act like you've been here all this time."

"Look, Ryan. I don't know what your issue is with me. Let's let the past stay in the past. If Nova wants to sit down with me for clarity, I'm open to that. I don't owe you shit though." Yashira crossed her arms.

"That's enough. I can't do this right now. You know what sis, I'mma stay here and talk with the detectives. Give me your car keys, and I'll catch an Uber to the restaurant to pick it up. I'll meet you and Trinity later at your place," Nova reasoned.

The tension was too thick, and she had questions of her own for Ryan. She wondered how this Yashira chick knew who she was. They seemed very familiar with each other, and although Nova knew Yashira's name, she hadn't seen the women before other than the IHOP incident.

"Yeah okay, but you call me if anything pops off, Nova." Ryan kissed Nova on the cheek.

"Shall we?" Detective Eric asked, pulling out a notepad from his suit jacket pocket while pointing to the seats to sit down.

Nova looked at Yashira and took in her appearance. She had Hassan's blood on her clothing, and she could tell Yashira was worried about Hassan. Her heart broke knowing that almost six years of her life would be rewarded to a woman who caused her so much pain the day she left her child on her doorstep.

"Ah Nova," Detective Lu said gently touching her shoulder, breaking her out of her trance.

"Huh?" Nova jumped.

"May we?" Detective Lu asked, pointing to the chair.

"Oh! Yeah, okay," Nova whispered and bit down on her lip.

The four took a seat, and Nova's right leg danced uncontrollably. She always did that when she was uncomfortable. She took both of her hands to rub her knee, and the nervousness she felt began to calm a little.

"I'll start with you, Mrs. Daniels. Where were you at the time of the shooting?" Detective Eric asked.

"I had come in early to work and decided to take the rest of the day off. I wasn't feeling too well. I met up with my sister to eat."

"Your coworker Tasha said you seemed distracted this morning. She said you received roses and Tiff Treats. She said you left shortly after the delivery. Was there something bothering you, Nova? Who did you receive the delivery from?" Detective Lu asked.

"I was very distracted!" Nova angrily spat, taking the detectives back with her sudden demeanor.

"How so?" Detective Lu pressed.

"I found out that Hassan has been having an affair with Nicole and another worker named Kensington. He even got that bitch pregnant. I came to work early to get away from Hassan, but being at the office was just too much, so I left. The delivery was from an ex-boyfriend. Happy?" Nova yelled.

"How did you find out about Hassan being shot?" Detective Eric asked.

"From the news, that's all I know. Is anyone going to tell me the full details now?" Nova yelled, looking between Yashira, Detective Lu, and Detective Eric.

"Well, you should know that Sean said you had been messaging him and told him about the affair Hassan was having with his wife. He said you told him and that's why he killed Nicole and had to kill Hassan for messing with his wife!" Yashira yelled.

She was tired of Nova acting like she didn't know why Sean was there or what happened. In her mind, she felt Nova set Hassan up to be killed by Sean. How else did he have access to the building, unless she let him in?

"Whatttttt? I never messaged Sean. I didn't even know Hassan and Nicole were even sleeping together until last night. What were you doing at the office anyway?" Nova stood.

"I'm the new BPR trainer." Yashira stood as well crossing her arms.

"You're Ms. Harris?" Nova asked shocked.

"Yes!"

"So, let me get this right Yazzi or whatever the fuck your name is. Not only do you fuck my husband, but you also leave your bastard daughter on my doorstep to raise, and now you're back to ruin my marriage and steal my child. Then you have the fucking nerve to work at my building with my husband? Hoe, you have another thing coming. Fuck this! I'm out. Fuck Hassan too. I hate you. Just leave me alone!" Nova screamed, running down the hall to the elevator. She pulled out her cell phone and screamed into the receiver for Ryan to turn around and pick her up now.

Nova sat on the emergency curb with her head between her knees. She cried hysterically and didn't care who saw or heard her.

"This ain't right, God! This ain't right!" Nova screamed, rocking back and forth. She wondered what she had done so horrible for things in her life to be this painful.

*Honk, Honk*!

Ryan pulled up and jumped out of the car. "Sis, come on. Get in." She assisted Nova into the passenger seat.

"Sis, I'm done," Nova said, wiping her face with her hands. "I don't care if he lives or dies at this point. Can you believe he has Yashira, Trinity's mother, working there? So, not only do you sleep with Nicole, but you play as though you don't know why this woman would have an issue with me as if it was me tripping or something. You sleep with Kensington, get her pregnant, finance her an apartment and car with my credit to now having Trinity's mother, an ex-stripper who left her daughter on the doorstep and left, working with us? I can't. This dysfunctional ass shit is not for me. I'm not a ride or die, and I'm not about to lose my mind over this tired trifling ass nigga." Nova shook her head. "Look, it's after ten, and I know that restaurant is serving drinks by now. Take me there, please." Nova buckled her seat belt.

The two went back to the restaurant, and Nova noticed how Ryan hadn't said two words. Something was up, and she had a feeling she was about to get more painful news. She sat back in her chair and massaged her neck before looking at Ryan.

"Spit it out sis. I know you. How do you know Yashira? The way you acted at the hospital, gave you away. I wanna know everything and now."

Ryan ate a piece of her enchilada, wiped her mouth, moved her plate to the side, and placed both of her hands on the table. "You sure you wanna know?"

Nova nodded.

"All I ask is you give me the respect to finish saying what I have to say. Don't cut me off, run out, or make a scene. Let me tell you everything, and when I'm done, I hope you still love me the same," Ryan sadly said.

"At this point sis, I don't think anything else can hurt me." Nova sipped down her margarita and motioned for the waiter to send another one.

"Yeah, I'm not too sure about that." Ryan dropped her head.

"Come on, Ryan, get to it!" Nova snapped.

"I was a coke head and stripper. I met Hassan at the strip club. He was my customer, and we slept together many times. When he met Yashira or Yazzi as everyone knows her by, he stopped messing with me. He had fallen in love with her and had gotten her pregnant. I didn't know Hassan was your husband. I would never hurt or betray you on purpose. It wasn't until that night I ran into you guys at Walmart that I knew he was your husband. You were so happy and in love. I didn't know what to do or how to tell you. I told Yashira about you being married to Hassan. I was hoping that she would confront Hassan and you would find out. It didn't happen that way. I knew Trinity was her daughter, and I knew that Yashira moved to Houston and had been there all these years. I hate Hassan. This is why I never really came around or always wanted you to come over to my place. He's no good for you. My truth is I never touched him again the day I found out about you being his wife. I'm no longer on drugs nor do I strip. That was years ago. I'm sorry for betraying and hurting you. I take full accountability and responsibility. I hope you don't hate me or leave me. I love you, Nova. You're my best friend and sister. Please forgive me," Ryan cried.

Nova sat stiff. She rubbed her hand over her belly and began to cry. She couldn't help it. Her sister and her husband, she wasn't expecting this.

The two sat at the table with their head down. Tears ran rapidly as they both were trapped in their own pain and truths. Nova's phone rang, and she noticed it was Trinity's school. She took a napkin and wiped her face before answering. "Hello!" she sniffled.

"Mrs. Daniels, this is Qadira. I just saw on the news about Hassan. I haven't told Trinity, but I was just calling to make sure you and Hassan were okay," she expressed with concern.

"He's okay, and your sister Yashira is by his side. Trinity will be picked up on time. Thank you and goodbye. Oh and another thing, all this time I can't believe you, your sister, and Hassan would play me like this. You knew all along that Trinity was your niece and you smiled and faked in my face!" Nova angrily spat.

"I didn't know Trinity was my niece. Yashira and I hadn't spoken for years. Our mother passed away Friday and Yashira showed up asking if she could stay with me to start her new job. I swear, I didn't know. I just found out," Qadira cried.

"Just stop it. I'm so sick of everybody making a fool of me. I don't deserve this." Nova hung up and looked at her sister.

"Ryan, I'm not even mad at you. Thank you for telling me. Do you mind watching Trinity tonight? I just need some alone time to think. I gotta get out of here. I feel like I'm suffocating." Nova grabbed her purse. "Oh, here are your car keys. I'll take mine and don't worry about anything. Hassan and I are over. I just need to get myself back to me, whatever that means. Right now, I'm just lost. I don't even know who I am anymore," she cried and left out of the restaurant.

As Nova drove home, Ashanti's "Foolish" song played on the radio. Foolish for Hassan is exactly how she had been since the day she met him.

If Nova was honest with herself, Hassan only did what she allowed. What she had allowed continued and her self-esteem is what kept her bond to Hassan. She knew the day that Trinity was left on her doorstep she should have left. An outside child should have had her packing her bags, but instead, she stayed.

Being with Hassan taught Nova that a woman could never say what she would or wouldn't do when it came to love. She never would've thought that she would stay, lie to her friends and family about Trinity, and even held off on her and Hassan having a child to keep the lie a secret. She was surprised that she ended up pregnant with all the precautions she took.

When she arrived home, Nova walked straight into the kitchen. She poured herself a large glass of wine and sat in the recliner chair. Her phone rang and rang, but she ended up turning it off. She just wanted to be left alone with her thoughts.

Her eyes watered again when she saw the oversized family photo of herself, Trinity, and Hassan. She couldn't believe her family and marriage was broken the way it was. She would never have thought that marrying Hassan would cause her so much humiliation and embarrassment. It was one thing to suffer in silence and be able to smile through the pain while pretending you are okay, but it was another level of pain when publicly everyone knows your secrets and that your marriage is a joke.

Men never had to deal with the opinions and whispers from other women on how stupid they were for staying, the shade, jokes, sympathy looks, and the gossip women had to endure. They mostly got a slap on the wrist or even a "congratulations" if they publicly apologize, sent flowers, or tried to somehow make amends.

Nova knew she couldn't continue to wallow in depression. She knew what she had to do and she had made up her mind that she was leaving all of this behind her. She leaned forward, grabbed the remote control off the coffee table, and turned on the news. Her mouth fell wide open.

*"Breaking News! This is Samantha reporting live from the residence of Nicole and Sean Smith. Earlier this morning a neighbor's dog ran loose and entered the Smiths home. The neighbor reported a foul odor and called the police. When the police arrived, they found the body of Nicole Smith. The victim had been shot three times. Her wallet and phone were missing. Hours later, we're told her husband Sean Smith was found dead at a state office. He attempted to kill another employee whose name we won't release. Allegedly, the shooting was due to infidelity. The suspect turned the gun on himself. We are told the shooting victim is in surgery and expected to make a full recovery. We'll update you further as more details arrive, back to you Joshua."*

Nova sat there numb. She didn't know if she were going or coming. She felt like she was in a bad dream, except this was real and her reality now.

She turned off the television and made her way to the shower. Somehow, water always seemed to bring Nova back into focus. She made the water steaming hot and stepped in it. The hot water instantly seemed to wash away all the day's events.

She rubbed her necklace and thought of Brixton. She smiled. He was the one person who seemed to bring a little light to her crazy dark world.

She turned the shower off when she heard someone ringing her doorbell. She wasn't in the mood and took her time drying off. She brushed her teeth, washed her face, moisturized her body, and brushed her hair. She figured whoever was at the door would go away, but she was wrong.

"Damn it. Hold on shit. Who is it?" she yelled.

Nobody answered and that pissed Nova off more. She peeked through the side window and smiled when she saw Brixton standing there.

"Brixton, what are you doing here?" she asked puzzled opening the door.

"Are you okay? I've been calling you ever since I saw the news," he asked in a rushed tone.

Nova turned her back and sat on the sofa. Brixton joined her. "Nova, talk to me." He rubbed her back.

"Can you just hold me tonight?" Nova asked with tears running down her face.

"I'll do anything you want me to do, but not here. Come on. Pack you a bag and come home where you belong, Nova."

"Brixton don't waste your time with me. I'm broken. I don't know how to put things back together. I have a lot of baggage and drama. A man like you deserves better than me. I'm not the same Nova you once knew. My spirit is broken, and I'm lost. I don't even know who I am anymore. I feel so disconnected from God. If I prayed, I don't even know if he would answer or hear me. You should go on. Just leave me alone. You're better off without me," Nova sobbed.

"That's why I'm here. I'm strong enough for the both of us. I'm here to restore your heart if you let me." Brixton kissed her lips and held her. "I'm your friend, protector, and comforter. I won't leave you. I won't pressure you. I want to offer you peace, a new start, and I'll be there every step of the way for your healing. I will wait for you. Just come home," Brixton pleaded with so much love and compassion.

Nova looked up at Brixton and looked in his eyes. All she saw staring back at her was a man who was a man completely in love with her. She couldn't say no. She felt safe with Brixton, a feeling she had yearned for.

"Come on, Nova. I'll take care of you. Get dressed and grab what you need. I'll be in the car waiting on you my queen."

"Okay!" Nova whispered.

Twenty minutes later, Nova had double-checked the home making sure she had what she needed. She kissed a photo of Trinity and cried.

As much as Nova wanted to fight for Trinity, she couldn't. She belonged with her mother, and Nova wasn't going to stand in the way of that. She was honest, and with the resentment, issues, and pain she felt she knew she needed to heal and having a relationship with Trinity wasn't good for her spirit anymore.

"I love you Trinity, and I'll always carry you in my heart," Nova cried before closing and locking the door.

Brixton smiled at her and stepped out of his vehicle, to grab Nova's belongings. He placed her items in the trunk and opened the passenger side for Nova.

As soon as Brixton was about to place his car in reverse, Erica Hassan's mother pulled up behind him blocking him in.

"Aht, Aht. Get out the car, bitch!" Erica yelled. "Really? My son was shot, and all you can do is sneak off with another man. What kind of wife are you? You should be at the hospital with your man." She stood on the side of Nova's passenger window yelling.

Nova stepped out of the vehicle and snapped. She was sick of tired of Hassan's mother. "I'm not in the mood today! What are you doing here? What do you want?" Nova yelled.

"Hassan asked me to come here to check on you. He asked for you."

"He'll be alright. He has you and his mistress. Tell Hassan I'm done with his dirty ass," Nova said and hopped back in the passenger seat. Erica stormed off to her vehicle, and Brixton pulled off with Nova fuming in the passenger seat.

When they arrive at Brixton's home, Nova was impressed. A smile crept across her face and tears made their way down her face.

"You remembered?" Nova cried.

"I did. I told you to come home. The home we always said we would design and build. Everything is how you envisioned. I love you Nova, and I knew one day I would come back for you. I just had to grow into the man you needed me to be. I hate how we men often times don't appreciate you when we have you. It's selfish to hurt a person and then come back and ask for forgiveness. I should have cherished you the first time. The truth is Nova I need you. You complete me. I won't stop fighting for you. I love you. Come on. Let me show you the inside." Brixton kissed her hand and came around to open her door.

*Skkkkeeeerrrrtttt!*

"If you think for one minute, I'mma let you do my son any kind of way, you got another thing coming, Nova!" Erica yelled.

"Are you fucking serious?" Nova bellowed. "Are you following me now?"

"You are dead ass wrong. You're supposed to be there through thick and thin, sickness and health. How dare you leave my son in the condition he is in. He could've of died and you act like you don't care. Maybe Yazzi was right. You set my son up to be killed. Well, it didn't work, and you will pay!" Erica burnt off, leaving black smoke behind.

Nova sighed loudly and rubbed her forehead. She knew this drama was just getting started. She couldn't believe Erica had followed them. She knew as soon as Hassan got out of the hospital, Erica would give him this address.

Nova knew she was Hassan's meal ticket and without her, he was going to fail. She didn't care though. Hassan brought this on himself. She no longer cared of felt guilty anymore. If Erica thought she was a cold-hearted bitch now, wait until she sells her home.

"Ms. Blu, Ms. Blu," the doctor sang.

Kissy stirred in her sleep. She was so tired. Throughout the night and early morning, nurses continued to get vitals on her, draw blood, and talk loudly throughout the halls.

She couldn't get comfortable, and every time she did, she was constantly woken up. She prayed Bella's home was better than this place. Her back was screaming for a comfortable bed. She needed sleep.

"Yes!" Kissy struggled to sit up and open her eyes.

Everything looks great on your chart. We did find Chlamydia and lots of tearing in your vaginal area. I'm going to prescribe you Azithromycin for the infection. For the pain Fentanyl and Ibuprofen 800mg. Please follow up with your OBGYN and primary care physician," the short, Caucasian female doctor said and sat on the edge of Kissy's bed. "Kensington, I'm not going to ask you to confide in me, but you have a lot of tearing. I've treated many sexual assault victims. The tearing with the bruises on your body, tells me all I need to know. Your medical history is in the system. You just attempted to harm yourself days ago. Are you taking your psychosis medication?"

"Yes," Kissy whispered as tears ran down her face.

"I figured you were going to say that, but your bloodwork says otherwise."

"Kensington, I'm going to write a script for your medication. Please take them. The trauma from the rape and miscarriage will make you have an episode. You could be really dangerous to not only to yourself but other people as well."

*Oh, people have no clue what I have planned.* This doctor was getting on her nerves. She had to play this broken victim role, when all she really wanted to do was take the pen, she saw in her doctor coat pocket and stab her with it. She was sick of white doctors trying to push crazy pills down her throat. She was fine.

The doctor stayed another 10 minutes before she left. Kissy called Bella, and Bella told her she would be there in 30 minutes. She showered and gathered all her things. She opened her room door and waited for Bella's call to let her know when she was downstairs.

"Oh my god! It's was just awful. What would make someone go to a state office and open fire like that? Then they're rumors going around that the wife Nova had her husband Hassan set up to be killed. How else did the shooter get in the building?" Kissy overheard someone say.

"Look it's back on the news. Turn it up," another woman said.

Kissy jumped out of the recliner chair, grabbed the call button, and pressed the power for the television. Her mouth fell open as she heard the news about Hassan being shot. Tears rushed her eyes as she thought of the inevitable.

She exhaled when the news reporter confirmed that Hassan would make a full recovery. Her phone rang, and she saw it was Bella. She turned the television off and made her way to the vehicle.

"Hey, girl!" Bella hugged her. "How are you feeling?"

"I don't know really. I guess things haven't really hit me yet. You know?" She shrugged. "I'm starving. I know that." She laughed.

"Shit, me too. Let's go grab something to eat at Texas Land and Cattle," Bella suggested.

"Ehhh! They're alright but not really my style. What about Texas Roadhouse? I love their bread with that cinnamon butter and their fried pickles.

"Where did I get Texas Land and Cattle from? I would've been mad as hell if I looked at the menu and didn't see fried pickles too. I meant Texas Roadhouse." They laughed.

"We're too much alike. Anyway, where are the girls?"

"They go to extended care and then the boys and girls club. I won't be picking them up until seven tonight."

Kissy's phone vibrated in her hand for the millionth time. She looked down at her phone and smiled at all the notifications from Facebook, her email account, and Cash App. She knew so much drama was popping off in her group. She loved how her group was the census, news, gossip center, and daily entertainment. Her group never slept. It was addicting, and she felt she had missed out on so much.

"Girl, what do you be into? I swear your phone goes off like every two seconds." Bella laughed.

"Girl it's this crazy ass group I'm in, and that bitch stays jumping. My notifications be crazy." Kissy laughed.

"Ah, shit! You ain't even got to tell me. I already know cause it's only one group that I heard got these bitches going crazy in the city. You must be talking about *Whose Man Is This Sis*, right?"

"Yup! How you know?" Kissy asked.

She never remembered Bella's submission into the group. She always kept a close tab and record of everyone she accepted. She knew how messy her group was, and it was important for her to have information and faces to match everyone she accepted.

"Everybody knows about that group. That's all everyone talks about. I'm not in there."

"Why?" Kissy asked.

"Mentally I'm not equipped to deal with the fuckery. I have to protect my mental health. I'm an ex-user. Stuff like that will set me off. I'm trying to stay straight for my girls. My life consists of work and them."

"I understand."

"Nah, it's deeper than the surface. After I got my girls back from the system a second time, I vowed to go to school, get a good job, stop stripping, hoeing, and using. I used to be on that shit bad. My mama's still on it. She be in the hood or on 12th sometimes. Shit is hard out here, man."

Bella pulled up to the restaurant.

The two were seated quickly and ordered drinks and fried pickles. "Oh, this is so good!" Kissy yelled, taking a bit of the bread. She and Bella laughed.

"You are cool as hell, Kensington. It's something about you. I'm comfortable around you. I never really hung with females before. I don't know really what it's like to have a best friend or sister. I used to envy women who had those girl bonds and took girl trips."

"I hear what you're saying. Honestly me either. My life consists of survival," Kissy said thinking about how she never really had anyone except Torrie and Tony.

"Tell me more about you. Kids? Man? Family? I mean I know we got to know a little bit about each other, but not in depth," Bella pressed.

Kissy paused buttering her bread. She set the knife down, wiped the corners of her mouth with a napkin, and stared at Bella. Something about Bella made her feel safe.

Kissy thought about the other day. She didn't even know why she had called Bella, but she came and was there for her. She never had that, someone to show up for her. The way Bella and her daughters stayed with her for hours and made sure she was situated in the hospital, showed acts of kindness that opened Kissy's heart. She was grateful and dedicated to Bella. Bella showed her loyalty.

"Ahem," Kissy cleared her throat. "I'm from Austin, born and raised. I came from a two-parent home and life was great until my sister drowned. I was supposed to be watching her, and I was, but my sister always wanted to play. We were playing hide in go seek. I was the counter. I counted until ten. I couldn't find her. Somehow, she must've slipped outside in the back of the house and slipped in the pool. I didn't know she went outside. We weren't allowed back there without supervision. When I found her, it was too late. She was dead. Mama and daddy argue for months. My mother never wanted that home because she felt it was unsafe, but my father wanted it because of the pool and the man cave it had. He was supposed to place a cover on the pool or gate but never got around to it. My mother blamed him, and I blamed myself. He eventually left us for this white lady and never looked back. I heard they had a child too together around my age, but I don't know for sure. Anyway, when my dad left, my mama lost it and couldn't pull herself together. She turned to crack and sold everything in the house for it. When all the material things to sell ran out, she sold me for ten-dollar hits, one man after the other.

When my aunt saw what was going on, she came and got me. She took me in, but her home was dry of love. She ran a hood candy store, and she was barely around. I kicked it with my cousin Tony mostly, but he sold drugs, so he was always in and out. After I graduated, I got me a little hole in the wall apartment and work temp jobs here and there. I fucked around with different guys, but I had my first heartbreak by a nigga who I found out was married. I had his child, but she's disabled. I wasn't able to care for her, so I had to give her to the state. Then I meet Hassan only to find out he's married too. My life is fucked up. The one person that I thought had me folded on me." Kissy shook her head.

"Hi! Are you ladies ready to order now?" a short, nerdy looking woman asked.

"Let me get a ah, chicken fried chicken with extra gravy, steamed broccoli, very soft with cheese, a loaded mash potato, and a cowboy cooler," Bella said.

"And for you, ma'am?"

"I'll have the 6 ounce sirloin with ribs and shrimp. For the sides, I'll have a Caesar salad and sweet potato. For the drink, I'll take another cowboy cooler as well."

"I'll get that right out."

"Wow! Your life sounds so similar to mine."

"How so? What's your story?"

"Shit, which part?" Bella did an uncomfortable laugh. "Well, I know that I told you a little bit about my mother, Sandy. She came from a rich white family. You know the type that hates blacks. She met my father, and my grandfather begged her to end the relationship with him. She didn't, so he cut her off financially. The money ran out of my mom's saving, so it wasn't no point for my dad to be there anymore. He left my mom for another white lady. He has two kids by her, but I don't know them like that. Anyway, it was just my mom and me for a while. I was the mixed kid with the matted curly hair. She honestly didn't know how to take care of me, but she did what she could. I grew up on the east side in the projects, and mama resented me. She tried to go home, but those white folks didn't want some nigger child. She struggled. Hell, we struggled many times. She met this white man, and he basically told her they could have their own family, but I wasn't welcomed.

She gave me to the system like it was nothing. I was in and out of foster homes and was the top of the pick with my light skin and curly hair. I endure so much sexual trauma and abuse that once I turned 14, I ran away. I was homeless. A bitch was eating out of restaurant trashcans. I went to Walmart often just to steal panties, pads, and take hoe baths. A pimp found me, took me off the streets, hooked me on heroin, and had me stripping and turning tricks. I had my first baby at 16 and then the other at 18. I couldn't tell you who their fathers are. My pimp was killed, and once again, I was on my own with two babies.

We stayed in a rundown motel, and for money to get high, I would turn tricks right there in the room while they were in the bathroom or closet. I went to jail a few times, and my kids were taken twice. I got off that shit and vowed to walk a straight line for my girls. I got my GED, took night classes, and got my associates degree. I landed my current job and with the company was able to lease on the property. I fought hard for my babies. I finally got them back eight months ago. That's why I told you that you are my angel, Kensington. I haven't had a sell in three months, and the manager was literally about to fire me. If you haven't signed, I'm scared to think where I would be. I can't lose my girls again," Bella cried.

"Bitch, and you won't. I got you." Kissy reached across the table grabbing Bella's hand.

"Thank you, Kensington."

"Thank me." Kissy pointed to herself and shook her head. "No, thank you. You were there for me. I was so scared and in a lot of pain. I can't believe my aunt set me up to be raped by her boyfriend. I still can't figure that out. That's why I dropped that dime on her. I hate her and she will pay."

"That was you?"

"Yup!"

"My kind of bitch!" Bella laughed. "So, what about that nigga that raped you? I know you not about to let him walk around," she asked.

Kissy thought about Bo and what method she'd use to get her payback. She had to be careful though because he had information on her.

"I don't know yet. All I know is that this shit isn't over. I have something for everyone who has crossed me."

"Well, I'm down. Listen between you and me. I have poisoned a couple of people before. So if you tryna get back, get back let me know," Bella whispered.

"Bitch, don't tempt me." They laughed.

"Whew! Bitch, I'm full." Bella rubbed her stomach.

"Me too."

"You got your scripts?" Kissy nodded. "Well, let's go by the pharmacy. By the time your meds are ready, it'll be time to get the girls. Didn't you say your furniture should be delivered too tonight around 8:15?"

"Oh shit! I forgot all about that." Kissy laughed.

"Me and the girls will help you set up if you're up to it. You're staying with us tonight though. You need to rest. Besides, the girls have been asking about you. I know they'll love to see that you're okay." Bella smiled.

"That's so nice. I gotta stop by the restroom before we leave."

"I was just about to say that." Bella laughed.

When Kissy stood from the table, she kept getting this weird energy. She felt someone was watching her. She had the same feeling the moment that she and Bella entered the restaurant. Every time she would look around, she didn't see anyone.

"You good?" Bella asked meeting Kissy outside the restroom.

"Yeah, I just keep getting this weird vibe that someone is watching me."

"It's probably just the meds messing with you from the hospital." Bella played it off, and they walked towards Bella's vehicle.

"Bella, Kensington!" a woman's voice yelled. They turned around.

Bella and Kissy stared at the familiar face that they hadn't seen in years. She had aged quite a bit, but her features were etched in both Bella's and Kissy's memories.

"Madea?" they both said surprised and then looked at each other.

"Yes. Live in the flesh." She laughed. "I thought that was you girls. I was staring hard. Y'all look just like my son James. I'm happy to see you two together. It's good to know that even though y'all parents are junkies you ladies are doing well. Y'all look good," she admired.

"Sisters? You know my Grandma Madea?" Bella asked Kissy.

"Yeah, I know her although as a child, I was too dark and ugly for her. She treated my sister special though. It is what it is, but wait, hold up." Kissy threw her arms up. "Sandy. Sandy. Sandy. Sandy. I don't know why it didn't click. My mother said Sandy's name so much that I don't know how I didn't pick up on it. Your mother was the one my father left us for. I knew it was something in my spirit about you. I was instantly drawn to you and had a connection. I've never felt that. Now that she mentioned it, we do have some of the same features." Kissy realized and then turned her attention back to Madea. "Where have you been all this time?" Kissy asked.

"Living my best life in Dallas and have been for years. Unapologetically," she smirked and played with her gold Rolex watch.

"So you didn't think to come check on your family? Your granddaughters knowing that your son and our mothers weren't shit!" Bella yelled.

"Look, don't beat me up okay. I raised James and sacrificed my youth. I wasn't trying to raise grandchildren too. I had to choose myself. Well and look at ya, y'all turned out alright. I kept my ears on the ground and asked about y'all time to time. Kensington, I knew you were with Torrie, and although she did her thing, I knew you would be fed and have a roof over your head, and Bella I tried to keep track of you as long as I could. I heard you had gotten mixed up with Rick and well, I'll leave that alone. I apologize for not staying in contact." Madea bit her bottom lip.

"You act like I wanted to get mixed up with Rick. You know what, it's cool. Keep that same energy though. Come on, Kensington." Bella grabbed Kissy's hand.

"Wait! I'm in town for our cousin's funeral. Please take my number," Madea said, writing her number on a piece a paper that she took from her purse.

Kissy looked at the number and then back at her grandmother. There was so much she wanted to say but thought against it. *How could her grandmother and father just abandon them and leave them like that for years? What did she want now? Why now?* Kissy screamed in her thoughts.

"I-I I'm sorry. I wasn't there. Please forgive me," Madea cried.

"Forgive you? Do you have any idea the hell I've endured? While you were living your best life, I was sucking dick for survival. Fuck you! Die and keep that same energy!" Bella screamed and walked off.

Kissy stared at Madea. She always yearned for her family's love, but she didn't trust anyone. She felt she was left to the wolves.

"Please let me make it up to you. Let me back in. I'm sorry for all the hurt I've caused. I'm sorry for not being there. I'm sorry for the ugly things I said to you as a child. I hated myself for so long that you were a reflection of me. You're beautiful, Kensington. Please don't hate me." Madea pleaded.

"It's too late. Take care of yourself," Kissy said, walking away.

"Mama, I need to talk to you," Ryan cried as soon as she entered her parent's home.

"Why don't you fix Trinity something to eat, Henry? Ryan and I will be in the sunroom."

"I saw the news. Have you heard from your sister? How is that boy Hassan doing?" Henry asked.

"Grandpa, where's daddy?" Trinity asked.

"Uh, I'll let your mama answer all your questions later. Come on. Let's go get something to eat."

"But Grandpa, I want my daddy," Trinity cried while folding her arms and stomping.

"You just stop that right now girl, ya hear. Now I done told ya. Come on here!" Henry yelled.

Margaret stared at Trinity for a moment, and a long silent tear fell from her eye. It hurt to know that the fate of she and Trinity's relationship would change. She loved her.

"Ma, don't do that. Come on," Ryan said, rubbing her back.

The two headed to the sunroom and Ryan looked around at all the loving photos of her and Nova. She burst out crying thinking about how their relationship could be ruined.

Ryan had held her secret about Hassan in for years. How could she expose him without exposing herself? Every time she would look at Hassan or seen him guilt gripped her spirit.

"Come here, baby." Margaret patted the sofa for Ryan to sit next to her.

"Mommm, I'm such a horrible person. I hurt Nova mama, and I don't ever think she's going to forgive me or look at me the same. I can't lose her. I love my sister. She's my best friend. It hurts mama," Ryan cried, resting her head on her mother's lap.

"Baby, what could you have possibly done to be so horrible?" Margaret asked concerned.

Ryan sat up and wiped her face with the backs of her hands. She was tired of pretending to be this straight-laced woman. Her past haunted her, and she was ready to finally come clean about who she was.

"Mama, please don't judge me." Ryan cleared her throat.

"Never baby."

"Years ago, I was addicted to drugs. I stripped to supply my habit, and Hassan used to be one of my customers. We've slept together, and I used to dance with Trinity's mother. I knew Trinity was Hassan's daughter. I didn't know he was Nova's husband until I ran into them. I never slept with Hassan again. I don't dance anymore or do drugs. I've changed my life. Hassan has threatened to blackmail me of videos and photos too. I wanted to tell Nova for years, but mama, after she would cry about his affairs and go right back, I left it alone. Hassan isn't worth me losing Nova over. I didn't know, and I would never intentionally hurt my sister. Mama, you know that," Ryan cried again.

"I know you love your sister. She'll come around, baby. I'mma tell you like I told your sister, I knew baby about your past. Well, not Hassan, but I knew about the drugs and stripping," Margaret confessed.

"You did?" Ryan asked with wide eyes.

"Sure did." Margaret nodded.

"How mama?"

"Your daddy's friend Mr. Fred said he saw you in there one night dancing as naked as a jaybird. He said he saw you were on that stage high as a kite. He left and came right over here to tell your father. Like I told Henry, we raised you. What you and Nova do is your business, but I think your father and I sheltered you girls too much. We didn't prepare you for the world. Baby, I knew that boy Thomas you got with was nothing but trouble. I had to let you find your own way, and you did. When two people want to be together, it's nothing you can do to stop them. You were so in love, young, and wet behind the ears. Look at you though. You have changed your life around, and I'm proud of you. Nova will come around, baby. Don't you worry about that." Margaret smiled.

"I love you, mama." Ryan kissed her cheek.

"I love you too, baby. So where is Nova? Your father and I saw the news. We've tried calling but figured she was with him at the hospital."

"Nova is um." Ryan sighed. "Ma, we went to the hospital, and Trinity's mother was there."

"Why?" Margaret asked pissed.

"Apparently she's back and took a position at Nova's job. She was there when Hassan was shot. I was with Nova when Yashira and I had words. When we left, Nova asked me how I knew her and I came clean. I told Nova everything. She told me she needed time to herself and wanted to be alone. That was hours ago. She won't reply to texts or answer my calls. Oh, and get this. Trinity's school principal is her aunt. So, in Nova's mind, all this has been planned and plotted. Plus, you know she's pregnant too. She also told me Hassan slept with her coworker named Nicole. Apparently, Nicole's husband Sean found out, and he went up to Nova's job to kill Hassan. He killed his wife too and turned the gun on himself. I just hope Nova is okay."

"She will be baby. Just keep praying for her. I'm going to miss that little girl in there." Margaret's eyes traveled to the door.

"I am too. Listen, ma. I have some things to take care of at the office. I have to get going. Do you mind if Trinity spends the night here?" Ryan asked.

"Not at all baby, I got her. You go on. Lord knows this might be my last days with this child," Margaret whispered.

"Ma, things will be alright. I love you, and I'll see you soon. Thank you for watching Trinity. Love you." Ryan kissed her mother and left.

When she pulled up to her center, she smiled. She had worked so hard to get here and although she wasn't proud of her past, she was happy that she was able to pull herself out the mud and be a successful businesswoman today.

She entered and shook her head when she saw her employee, Tyrone. For a big and tall man, he was handsome. "Hey, Tyrone! How you doing?"

"As best as I can be. Ms. Lady." He placed a trash bag in the trashcan.

"What's going on? It must be something with you and Dedra again. Come on." Ryan motioned for him to follow her to her office. "Excuse the mess."

Ryan had photos everywhere for the Christmas board she was about to work on. Before Tyrone sat down, he noticed the one with Kensington and picked it up. "Kensington, you know her?" he asked.

"Yeah, I'm surprised you haven't seen her. She comes around every Saturday. Oh, that's right. You only work through the week. Little Kinley is her baby." Ryan smiled.

"Oh okay!" Tyrone placed the photo back down.

"How you know her?" Ryan asked.

"She works with Dedra. Plus everyone from the hood knows she Torrie's niece."

"Oh! Small world. I know Torrie. You're talking about 2-4 Torrie?"

"Yeah! You heard they got her? Somebody dropped a dime on her. People from the hood are saying it's that nigga Bo she was fucking with. They're gunning for him too. I don't know if he knows, but Torrie got mad respect in the hood. That lady is like everybody's T-Lady. She fed and helped a lot of niggas out. It's funny how all these years she been serving fiends, and her house never got busted. All of a sudden this nigga Bo ain't nowhere to be found."

"I bet he had something to do with it. That's why he ain't going around there. Anyway, fool." Ryan's laughed. "What done happened now between you and Dedra?"

"Shit, what ain't? Dedra left a nigga. She joined that group called *Whose Man Is This Sis,* and all those hoes in there were giving a nigga up, dragging my name. I mean yeah, I mess around, but I ain't ever leaving Dedra for none of these bird bitches. I mean even me and you fucked around, and you ain't never did no hoe shit like that."

"Boy cause I don't want you. You're just some good dick on the side. That's all. These females act like they aren't emotionally attached to you, but their feelings be hurt. They want to be Dedra and take her place. They see the things you do for Dedra, and they want that. I, on the other hand, know what it is."

"That's what I'm talking about. I'm real and upfront with all my hoes. I tell them the real. I can't believe they had a nigga name blasted all through the group. They had my picture in there and everything. I've even seen my homies in there. Whoever this bitch Kissy is, is messy as fuck, man. The shit I saw in that group is going to get that girl killed. She better hope don't nobody ever find out who she is. If I find out I'mma fuck her up, on my mama, and that's word as bond. The bitch had HIV status paperwork, mugshots, videos of niggas fucking, and photos of niggas coming outta bitches houses. Man say I was like what kind of fuck shit is this? Somebody's gonna fuck around and end up murdered. She's playing with people's lives." Tyrone shook his head.

"I'mma join that group too just so that I can see what's going on."

"Man, I'm telling you now, it's some shit. Anyway, I'mma holla at you later. I got to do this last run of cleaning and pick my little mama up from school. Dedra done kicked me out, so I'm staying at my mama's house."

"Well, homie I got three bedrooms. You're more than welcome to crash at my place. Just don't be catching feelings. I don't care how many times we fuck. You got to go home."

"You cold, Ryan. You are not like these other chicks. Yeah though, I'mma take you up on that offer. I'll call you later."

"Alright, boy." Ryan smiled.

She leaned back in her chair and wondered what the hell she was thinking. Tyrone was cool and all, but she hoped Dedra never popped up at her home. She honestly didn't want him, but there were times Tyrone hinted around to having feelings for her. She laughed because Tyrone played hard talking about his other women, but Ryan wasn't sweating him, and a piece of that bothered him.

Tyrone was so used to dealing with drama-filled women that he didn't know how to take Ryan. The truth was, after Thomas and Hassan, Ryan learned not to operate with her emotions. She only used men and women for her own sexual gratification and wants. The minute anyone expressed feelings, she ghosted them. Love was not something she was willing to take a gamble on.

Ryan shook Tyrone out of her thoughts and finished working on her board. It came out beautiful, and she was proud. She placed the board up in the main area, faxed off some paperwork, made her rounds speaking to her staff, and left.

She placed a call to Nova and left her a message.

"Hey sis, I was just calling to check on you. I love you. Please don't shut me out. You're all I have. You mean everything to me, Nova. I'm dying without you. Please just texted me or something," Ryan cried and hung up.

Her phone beeped moments later, and she smiled at the message Nova sent.

"Kensington, girl, here your phone go." Bella passed Kissy her phone. "It was just ringing and ringing. Your ass must be on it from the pills the doctor gave you." She laughed.

"Thank you! Where are the girls?" Kissy asked.

"At school, sleepy head. Oh, the news reported earlier that your job office would be closed for the rest of the week due to what happened."

"I forgot all about my job." Kissy laughed.

"Don't forget Ashley's Furniture will be at your condo at ten since they couldn't make it last night."

"Yes, mother," Kissy replied, and Bella took a pillow and hit her with it. They laughed.

"I'm heading to the office. It's some waffles, eggs, and bacon in the fridge to cook or cereal if you're hungry."

"Okay! Thank you." Kissy sat up.

"Question?" Bella pointed.

"Shoot."

"How are you feeling about the whole Madea situation and finding out we're sisters?"

"I mean, it's still weird you know. I'm surprised I didn't put two and two together sooner. My mother spoke of Sandy so much. I remember her and my dad arguing about Sandy and a baby. She knew about you. My dad told her about you. They tried to work through things, but once my sister died, he left us. With everything that happened in between, I forgot all about having another sister. I still have a lot of anger issues and emotional trauma from my childhood. I used to blame Sandy too. I often wonder if dad had stayed how my life would have turned out. When my mom got on crack, I called Madea a couple of times. I begged her to come get me. She used to promise me that she'll come. I remember waiting for her at the Greyhound station once for five hours. I had my little backpack of clothes. She never came, and that's when I realized it was all a lie. Eventually, she changed her number and lost contact all together. She looks good though, but I'm cool on family reunions and shit. It's too late. I can't pretend that things can go back to how they were. What about you? How are you feeling? I'm still tripping off the fact that we're sisters."

"To be honest, I don't know." Bella took a seat on the bed. "I didn't sleep well last night at all. I'm angry and hurt. I've tried to bury those feelings but seeing Madea broke my heart. I remembered how good she used to treat me. She was kind, fun, and loving. Then one day, she just left me, and I never heard from her again. I always felt unwanted, unloved, and like I was a burden. Seeing her again brought back those feelings. I'm just happy God saw fit for me to meet you. You and my girls are really all I have." Bella smiled while touching her necklace and playing with the cross.

"I feel that. Well, since we're being honest and getting to know each other, I think I should be open and tell you I deal with mental illness. I hear voices, I suffer from depression, and my personality can alter. Sometimes I'm afraid of myself. I cut myself as a way to release the pain and fear."

"I know. I saw the prescription medication. It's nothing to be ashamed of, Kensington. Just take your medication. I suffer from mental illness too, and I have HIV," Bella confessed.

"HIV?"

"Yes. It's undetected, but I caught it from hoeing."

"Damn, you're so young."

"HIV does not discriminate."

A long silence filled the air and Kissy couldn't pretend any longer. She was breaking inside, and her mind couldn't wrap around why all these painful things were happening to her.

"Bella, I-I wanted my baby. What would make my aunt hate me so bad to do that to me, and Hassan, he just dropped me like I wasn't shit. He hasn't even checked on me or texted me back. I'm just so tired of people hurting me and lying. Now Madea, I just can't take anymore." Kissy began crying.

"Oh sis, come here. It's going to be okay," Bella promised while hugging Kissy.

"Thank you, Bella." Kissy wiped her eyes.

"You're welcome, boo. I'mma get to the office. If you need me, you know where I'll be."

"Okay! Oh, wait, whose funeral was Madea talking about?" Kissy asked.

"Do you know who Qadira and Yashira are?" Bella asked.

"Yeah, I met them twice when I was younger."

"Well, their mother Vanetta passed away, and that's our father first cousin. Madea and Vanetta's mother were sisters. Vanetta is Madea's niece," Bella informed.

"Oh okay! Well, when is the funeral?"

"I think Thursday or Friday, one of them days."

"Oh shit!" Kissy slapped her forehead.

"What?"

"Nothing I just forgot, I'm supposed to be doing this girl hair on Friday. I need to go buy the hair store."

"Well, let me get out of here boo."

Kissy showered, dressed, fixed her a bowl of cereal, and checked her voice mail messages.

"*Good morning, Ms. Blu! This is Jeffery from Chevrolet. Your vehicle is ready. Please call us back and let us know what address to deliver your vehicle. Thank you, and I look forward from hearing from you.*"

Kissy squealed with joy and immediately called Jeff back.

She checked the second voicemail and rolled her eyes hearing Torrie's pleads to help her. Torrie could die for all she cared. She was going to go to the cemetery for sure and dig up that money for herself. She wasn't thinking about Torrie. She got what she deserved.

Kissy skipped over a few more messages and halted when she received a message from Bo. He was threatening to expose her if she didn't give him some money and sex. She made a mental note to ask Bella about the poisoning she spoke of. She was going to lure Bo and kill him.

She peeped in her group, and as usual, it was pure entertainment. She frowned up at one post mentioning her and Tony's name. She hurried and deleted the post and was upset that she hadn't been as active in her own group.

**Jersey Mai**
22 October 2018 · Whose Man Is This Sis · Friends

Ayo...did yawl here about what happened the other day in the four? They got Torrie ass. Somebody dropped a dime on her.

1.1K Like                                    6 Comments

Wow            Comment            Share

**Jersey Mai**
22 October 2018 · Whose Man Is This Sis · Friends          •••

**Lucy Baebee**
That's fucked up. They say the hood looking for that ho ass nigga Bo too. Torrie been in the hood for years and nobody ever messed with her. All of a sudden they saying Bo ain't nowhere to be found.
22 October 2018 · Like · Reply

**Sasha V.**
Ain't that Jaybryd baby daddy? I can't stand that nigga. He use to mess with my homegirl. Used her up and ran her bank account dry. He ain't shit.
22 October 2018 · Like · Reply

**Natalie**
Damn, I know Kensington and Toni ass sick right now.
22 October 2018 · Like · Reply

**Bitch I Got Yo Man**
That's what happens when you mess with these bum ass niggas 🤷 Bo known for using women. That's why Jaybryd left his ass. Torrie too old for that shit. Had his bum ass living with her and driving her shit. Now she on lock and that nigga on the prey again.
22 October 2018 · Like · Reply

**Queen Aria**
Wow! Who says something like that? 🙄 We really should mind our business.
22 October 2018 · Like · Reply

**Amber Nicole**
There you go being all extra and shit. Just stfu. Nobody likes you 🙄

For as long as Kissy had her group, her name had never been mentioned. She closed out of her laptop and walked over to her own condo with her luggage in tow. She breathed in the fresh air and took in the clean vibes the place gave her. The smell of fresh paint made her smile. "I did it!" she yelled. She was proud of herself for finally having something she could call her own. *I will never be misplaced again.* She silently thought and jumped when her doorbell rang. She peeped through the peephole and jumped up and down.

"Ms. Blu! Sign here, and this baby is all yours," Jeff said.

Kissy signed her paperwork, and Jeff walked her through the vehicle. When he left, Kissy broke down in her vehicle thanking God. She couldn't believe how her day was turning out. She was so proud of herself.

She pulled out her manual and looked over a couple of features before she saw the Ashley's Furniture truck pull up. The movers were in and out as she directed them to which room the furniture belonged to.

Her morning went fast, and before she knew it, it was already one in the afternoon. She had so many packages in her living room from all the orders she placed online. She was beat, but Kissy was the type that hates to start one thing and not finish.

Around four o'clock, Kissy showered again and stepped out to grab her something to eat. While at a red light, she briefly glanced to her left and caught a glimpse of Raheem's wife Iesha pumping gas. "Bitch!" she screamed, turning into the gas station once the light turned green.

She followed Raheem's wife in traffic for nearly an hour, until she pulled into a newly built housing development in Onion Creek. Iesha parked her silver Kia Sportage in the driveway, while Kissy parked a house down on the opposite side of the street. She saw a red Mustang parked in the driveway and assumed it was Raheem.

She sat there for hours, plotting out what she wanted to do. Evil scenarios popped in her head and she smiled thinking of seeing the horror looks on their faces as she tortured them. She imagined the begging and pleading they would scream out.

Headlights flashed her way, and Kissy ducked down in her seat just enough to still see over the dashboard. The white Nissan Rogue turned into Raheem's driveway and parked behind the Kia Sportage.

"Ugh!" she yelled reaching for her asthma pump to control her breathing. There he was. He still looked the same as she remembered. Morris Chestnut could have been his twin.

"Baby, you're home!" His wife ran outside and gave him a loving embrace.

Tears rolled down Kissy's cheek as she witnessed their love. Why couldn't that be her? "I'm going to kill you and that bitch!" Kissy screamed, hitting the horn.

Raheem and his wife both turned to look in her direction, and she ducked all the way down. "Fuck it!" she screamed, cranking her vehicle. She gripped the gun she had stolen from Torrie's home the day she was raped and removed the safety. *TAT! TAT! TAT! TAT! TAT,* she fired turning the corner wildly almost losing control.

Ashley heard the shots and instantly thought of her cousin Iesha. Iesha had just stepped outside to greet Raheem.

"Oh my god! Nooooo! Iesha!" she screamed, running outside.

She caught a glimpse of a white Tahoe wildly turning the corner and called the police. Raheem and Iesha bodies laid lifeless on the ground.

"Hey, sis! I didn't think you would be here. You've been at the hospital so much," Qadira said walking in the house.

She poured herself and Yashira a glass of wine and joined Yashira on the sofa. She took in her sister's appearance. She looked worn, stressed out, and worried. She had bags under her eyes, and she looked as though she hadn't slept in days.

"Thank you!" she sipped from the glass. "You know, I just keep seeing that man's eyes. He was so hurt by Hassan's actions of sleeping with his wife. It made me think of the pain I've caused Hassan's wife. All I keep thinking is that could've been me. He mentally snapped. Looking back, I realized how hurtful my own actions were."

"Well, how is Hassan doing?"

"He's doing well actually. I'm happy the bullet didn't hit his heart."

"Me too. So much craziness has been happening lately. Did you hear about the killing that happened over in Onion Creek?"

"Girl, yes! They were just talking about that on the radio. They're saying that Iesha was pregnant too. It's just so awful, and the only lead they have is a white Tahoe." Yashira shook her head.

"That's crazy. I hope they catch whoever did this. Oh girl, well let me tell you the drama that has come my way." Qadira rolled her eyes.

"Oh, gawd! What now?" Yashira sipped her wine.

"I called Nova and told her I was sorry for what happened to Hassan. Girl, she starts yelling at me, saying how I basically knew Trinity was my niece all along and I was in on this whole setup between you and Hassan."

"What? Wow!"

"Girl yes! A mess. I hope she doesn't bring her ass up to my school. I will call them people on her in a minute."

"Damn!" Yashira sighed. "I just keep seeing my little girl's face. She's so beautiful," Yashira said staring off.

"Ohhhhh, close your eyes. I have something for you." Qadira jumped up and pulled out a picture from her purse. "Okay! Open your eyes."

"Oh my god!" Yashira cried. "Thank you, sis."

"You're welcome. I took this photo of Trinity today and printed it. Now you have a photo of her."

"You're the best, sis." Yashira hugged Qadira. "Listen, I'm going to go see Hassan in a few. All of this is just so unreal. When I took this position, I never thought I would run into Hassan again. Is it wrong to have feelings for him again?"

"I just think you shouldn't get so wrapped up in Hassan again. I mean he's married, and the whole thing just seems very messy. I think you should just focus on Trinity. I don't want you to get your heart broken. I mean if he was willing to cheat on his beautiful wife, he'll do you the same way. I mean look at why he's in the hospital now, for messing with a married woman. He hasn't change Yaz, and I don't want you getting sucked into his bs. I mean you just said how the man who shot Hassan was broken and hurt because of his actions. You and Hassan have done enough to Nova. You're beautiful Yaz, and you can have any man you want. Let it go."

"I hear you, sis. Are you ready for the funeral tomorrow? Madea contacted me."

"Yeah, she called me too. She said she ran into James' daughters Kensington and Bella. I see Bella from time to time though. Her girls Mina and Mecca attend my school. We don't really talk though. It's awkward, and I can tell she's been through a lot too."

"Wow! I haven't heard those names in years."

"I honestly forgot all about them. I remember Kensington and Lexi coming to Madea's when we were little. I think I met Bella once when we were younger, and then we exchanged words briefly when she enrolled her girls."

"Same here. Our family has always been distant though. As long as I have you, I'm good." Qadira shrugged. "Anyway, I have mixed emotions about the funeral. I have a lot of anger in me towards mom. Then, on the other hand, I'm grieving because mom is gone. I just don't know what to feel."

"Well, you've done a beautiful job with the arrangements. The service is going to be good. Mom would be proud of you. Did her sorry ass nigga even attempt to help?"

"Nope, but he called me wanting to know what I discussed with the lawyer who contacted me."

"A lawyer?" Yashira frowned.

"Yeah! Mom left a will for you and me. She left us the house and $150,000 a piece in a life insurance policy. Who would have thought, with the way she had us living all those years that she thought anything of us to leave us money?

"Well I don't want that house, so we can sell that shit and split the money."

"I'm cool with that. The lawyer said our checks would be sent here in two weeks."

"That's good. I finally can find me a nice home somewhere and get a bigger vehicle for myself."

"Or you can just stay here." Qadira smiled. "I mean sis, what am I going to do with four bedrooms? I'm in the house by myself. It's been nice having you here."

"It has been nice being here with you too sis. Thank you for your support and being there for me. I really appreciate you. I love you!" Yashira said, tearing up.

"I love you too with yo crybaby ass." They laughed.

"Well, sis don't wait up. I'mma go see Hassan. I don't know when I'll be in later. The doctors are talking about releasing him." Yashira kissed Qadira on the cheek and headed for the hospital.

"Remember what I said," Qadira pointed.

"I hear you."

When she arrived to Hassan's room, he was sleeping peacefully. She sat in a nearby chair and pulled out a book she brought from Barnes and Noble by Jessica Wren called *I Was Made To Love You.*

She teared up and wondered if guys like Avantae really existed and if women like Mia Symone could really change. She saw so much of herself in Mia Symone. She was selfish and went after what she wanted.

Yashira sometimes felt the heart just couldn't help who it wanted, no matter how hard you tried to fight feelings. So, she understood Mia Symone well. It was also ironic how Mia Symone was also a stripper, who met Jaceyon at the club, caught feeling, and later found out he was married to her cousin Ceanna.

Mia Symone's story was so similar to hers in many ways, and a piece of Yashira didn't blame Mia at all. She wondered if she and Hassan could really be a family and if it was even worth getting back involved with him.

She wiped her tears reading the pain Ceanna was going through. She couldn't imagine being pregnant with twins by her husband and then hearing her cousin gave birth to her husband's child. She had to close the book. It was just so much truth hitting her in the face.

Hassan's door opened and in walked his mother Erica, cousin Kiara, and Ty Jackson. She smiled and gave them all a friendly hug. They were all aware of who she was, especially Ty. He frequented the strip club often back in the day.

Hassan eventually woke up and they all ordered food. They laughed, played cards and were enjoying themselves until Nova opened Hassan's room door.

Nova soaked in the nice, warm bubble bath Brixton ran her. She prayed, meditated, cried, and was thankful that he didn't bother or interrupt her. He simply gave her the space to think and breathe. That's what she wanted and needed.

After she dressed, she joined Brixton in his man cave. There they enjoyed a competitive game of *2K*. She laughed at his facial expressions every time she beat him. "I still got it!" she yelled while laughing.

Although the sexual chemistry was strong between the two of them, they decided to hold off and be intimate in other ways. Connection and communication was an important factor for both of them. This is why they were so good together.

"Nova, I think you need to go get Trinity and have a talk with her. She needs to see her father. I understand you're hurting, but you cannot be a part of her life, be the only mother she knows, and just leave her like that. She doesn't deserve that Nova. Don't let what Hassan has done change you into someone you aren't. I know you love that little girl."

"I do!" Nova screamed. "Don't you think I'm hurting too? I love her. She was my baby. How do you think it feels when you've given up your happiness and life to raise a child that isn't even yours only for her father to throw it in your face? It hurts to look at her.

Then to know Hassan was cheating on me with her mother. I just can't, Brixton," Nova cried.

"You can. You will regret your decision. Listen, Nova, it's time to go get Trinity. She needs to see her father, and if you want to hand her over and be done, I understand, but you remember how it felt when I just abandon you. You wanted answers. Don't be a coward like me. Little children don't understand. She's innocent in all of this."

Nova thought about what Brixton was saying and knew he was right.

"You're right. I guess I just know how all of this will end, and I just wanted to get everything over with now. I know I'm going to lose her or she will be some ploy in Hassan's games. I'm just done with him and that marriage. I just want to be happy again and heal," Nova confessed.

"I understand baby, but you can't rush the process. Now come on." Brixton extended his hand.

Brixton drove Nova to her mother's house. He smiled at the light in Trinity's eyes when she saw Nova. She talked Nova's ear off about her day at school and whatever else was on her little mind. Brixton couldn't wait until Nova bore his children. She was a great mother.

Brixton allowed Nova to catch up with Trinity while he and Margaret laughed and talked in the sunroom. Henry was there but basically just rolled his eyes and asked rude questions. Margaret had had enough.

"Henry, what is the problem?" Margaret asked annoyed.

"You know how I feel, and this isn't right. Nova is still married, and she's flaunting Brixton around and bringing him to my home. I don't support this," Henry huffed.

"No disrespect sir, but I love you daughter."

"Son, I understand that. My daughter is still a married, pregnant woman. So you're telling me you're willing to raise another man child?" he asked with raised brows.

"Yes, sir I am. If Nova decides to keep this baby, I will raise it as my own. I love Nova. I brought her a home, vehicle, and she has an account. I'm a lawyer, a well-paid one at that, and I plan to love, spoil, and heal Nova."

"Hmmm." Henry frowned.

"Why wouldn't you want that for Nova, Henry?" Margaret asked.

"Because the man can change, I did. We niggas cheat, Margaret. That's what we do. A wife is supposed to stick by her husband's side through thick and thin. No man is perfect!" Henry roared.

"Well, you see where that got you didn't you?" Margaret crossed her arms.

"Woman you best watch how you're talking to me in my home."

"I should've left yo ass years ago. You could never be the man Leroy was to me. All your lying and cheating, creating outside babies with your whores. Yeah, you couldn't take it when a real man came along to love me. That's why you hate Brixton so much. He's a real man, something you'll never be. You can't stand to see Nova happy. As long as she holds Hassan down is all your sorry ass care about. I'm happy she's leaving that nigga. She deserves better!" Margaret yelled.

"I should've let him take you. You're nothing but an old hag. You ain't good for nothing. You're just old, fat, and always complaining!" Henry yelled and stormed out of the house.

"Come here, mom. It's okay." Brixton pulled Margaret in for a hug. Listen, you know you can always come stay at the house. I made a guest home in the back just for you and my mother. I would love for you to come." Brixton kissed the top of her head.

"Mom is everything okay? What were you and daddy yelling about?" Nova asked.

"Brixton will tell you. Listen, don't worry about me. Get Trinity over there to the hospital. She's been asking about her daddy." Margaret dried her tears.

Nova gave her mother a hug and her, Trinity, and Brixton made their way to the hospital. The ride was quiet. Both Brixton and Nova were in their own worlds.

Brixton couldn't believe that Henry treated Margaret that way. He thought about his own father and remembered how he would get drunk and beat him and his mother. His mother stayed in the toxic marriage for ten years before she married another man who was also abusive.

Brixton swore he would never treat women that way, and with his first wife Michelle, he didn't. He was so kind, gentle, and loving towards her. He gave her the world, and he had no clue that she was sleeping with his cousin.

The day he got the call that Michelle was killed broke his heart. She was the love of his life, and she could do no wrong in his eyes.

When the details of her murder were revealed to Brixton, it killed him. He would never have thought that his wife would betray him like that. He had so many questions about the affair. When, why, and how? That it literally made him sick to his stomach.

His family was close-knit. He was an only child, and his aunt had two sons Wallace and Patrick. He and his cousins grew up together and were more like brothers than cousins. In fact, that's what they told everyone.

It was a time he and his cousins all lived together. They did everything together from sports to attending the same college. His cousin Wallace decided to go into law enforcement, while Patrick decided to study to be a computer engineer, and he went off to law school after graduation. They were three successful young, good looking men with their entire lives in front of them.

Brixton would never have imagined Michelle and Patrick having an affair. It took him a long time to heal from that. Not only had Patrick killed himself and his wife, but shortly after his Aunt Mable was killed in a drunk driving accident.

That was too much for his cousin Wallace. He decided to leave the state and be a police officer elsewhere. He cut off Brixton and his mother, and just like that, their family unit was broken into pieces.

All Brixton had was his mother and then here came this beautiful, vibrant, positive woman Nova. Her beauty instantly took him, but her smile began to turn something in Brixton. He loved her, but he admitted he wasn't healed or over his first wife.

Brixton thought about the day he regretted the most. The day he sent Nova that email broke his heart. He hated that he'd hurt her in the process of his healing. What he did was selfish and wrong. However, Henry was wrong. One thing Brixton wasn't was a cheater. He would never cheat on any woman, especially Nova.

It took so much discipline to be insulted by Nova's father like that. He had met many Henry's in his life. They always accuse Brixton of being a "simp" for the way he respected and honored black women.

Brixton looked over at Nova and knew he would never treat her poorly or speak to her the way Henry spoke to Margaret. He would protect and provide for the both of them if need be.

Margaret was a second mother to him. She helped him many days. She always checked on him and his ill mother. In fact, those two had become good friends, and whenever his mother fell horribly ill, Margaret would come by and style her hair, help bathe her, and often cooks meals for them. She was an angel to Brixton, and he doesn't know how he would've gotten through a lot of days if it hadn't of been for Margaret.

Brixton pulled in the parking garage and helped Trinity out of the backseat. He then went around to help Nova from the passenger seat. He kissed her on her cheek, and she smiled at him.

"Don't worry things will be fine. I'll be visiting my mom in her room. You know where to find me, baby. If anything pops off, you know where I'll be." Brixton walked Nova and Trinity to Hassan's door.

"Bye, Mr. Brixton!" Trinity said while opening Hassan's hospital door.

"Bye love!" Brixton waved.

"The fuck. I know Nova didn't bring that fuck boy here and have him around my daughter!" Hassan yelled.

"I told you," Erica sassed.

Nova entered Hassan's room and instantly regretted it. Erica, Kiara, Ty, and his baby mother Yashira were all in Hasson's room, watching football. The smell of Taco Bell, weed, and stale body sprays lingered in the air. Nova felt hot and lightheaded.

"I told you she wasn't no good. Here you are in the hospital, and she's floating around the city with another man. What kind of wife is that?" Erica yelled.

"Daddy!" Trinity yelled running behind Nova to hug Hassan. "I love you, daddy. When you coming home?" she asked, kissing him on the cheek.

"Ah, be careful, baby," Hassan groaned. "I'll be home soon."

"That's if he has a home to go to." Erica scuffed while glaring at Nova with her hands on her hip.

"Bitch, I'm about sick of you. Now I've tried to be respectful, but enough is enough!" Nova yelled.

"Bitch! Who are you calling a bitch?" Erica screamed.

"You, actually." Nova pointed.

"Ahhh damn, you know what let's go get some candy from the cafeteria. We'll be back y'all." Kiara took Trinity. She knew her Aunt Erica too well, and she was about to start swinging at any moment. Trinity did not need to see that.

"So what's up then?" Erica threw her hands up.

"Ma, chill. She's pregnant!" Hassan yelled. "What I wanna know is, did you call Sean and tell him I was messing with Nicole? Are you the reason he shot me?" Hassan sat up in his bed. "Who is this nigga that I keep hearing about, and why are you just now coming to see about your husband?"

"What no? I would never do no shit like that, and Hassan if I wanted you dead, I would have arranged that when your stripper girlfriend left her baby on my doorstep." She glared at Yashira. "Stop fucking playing with me in front of folks. I'm so sick of you. I don't even have Sean's number. Do you honestly think I would want anyone to know you were sleeping with Nicole? Think about it. For going on five years, I've lied about who Trinity was to keep your secret and appearances for this marriage. As much as I hate you right now for all the shit you put me through, I would never want Trinity to grow up without her father. I would never hurt you the way you've continually hurt me— mistress after mistress, your gambling, your lying, all of it, Hassan. I took it. I be damn if anybody in this room says shit to me because I was a damn good wife and woman to you. But now Hassan, now I'm done. It's over. I want a divorce. I'm getting rid of this baby, and Trinity should be with her real mother. I'm happy you're okay Hassan, but I can't take anymore. You have broken me, and you win. I can't do this anymore. My things are moved out of the home. I'm selling the home since it's in my name and my credit. You have 30 days to find a place to live. The joint account is closed, and all your money totaling $400 is there. I'm resigning and starting over. From here on out what you do and who you do it with isn't my concern. Being with you taught me, Hassan, that it's never gonna stop. I'm tired of your games. I'm done. Take care of yourself!" Nova cried, exiting the room.

"Damn family. She's really done." Ty sighed and slouched in his seat.

He felt bad for Hassan. Nova was a real good woman and person. Ty knew that Hassan would never find another woman like her. Women like Nova were rare, and he often envied Hassan for finding someone like her.

"Nova, wait!" Hassan yelled.

Yashira looked at Hassan and shook her head. She thought about the conversation she and her sister had earlier. She'd admit she ignored her sister's warning. She loved Hassan and was low key happy Nova was getting out the way, but seeing Nova broken and confessing all the emotional trauma she had went through with Hassan, made Yashira think. Did she really come this far in life just to be sucked into Hassan's bullshit?

"Nova!" Yashira yelled out to her while running to catch up with her. "Wait, please!"

"What do you want? You got him. Congratulations. You won!" Nova yelled, fighting back tears.

"Not like this. Please, Nova. I know I don't have the right to ask you of anything, but can we just talk, please. Just give me ten minutes," Yashira begged.

"I really don't have anything to say to you. Ugh! Why is this bitch taking so long?" Nova forcefully pushed the elevator button. The doors finally opened and Nova stepped on with Yashira behind her.

"I said leave me alone. I don't want to talk to you!" Nova yelled in Yashira's face.

"I'm sorry. Please just let me explain," Yashira cried.

"You've ruined my entire life. How can you explain that?" Nova broke down, placing her head in her hands.

"Can we please just sit in the cafeteria and talk? I swear to you I never meant to hurt you."

Nova didn't respond, but Yashira followed her anyway. Across the cafeteria, she spotted Trinity and Kiara. She sat at the table and began playing with her nails. It was awkward, but Yashira felt she had to not only tell her side of the story but also thank the woman who raised her daughter.

"I saw you the day I left Trinity on your front door. I studied you. I couldn't be half the woman you are. You did an amazing job with Trinity. While it was selfish on my part and caused you much pain, I'd be lying if I said I wouldn't do it all over again." Yashira shifted in her seat. "I was just some stripper who had lost her way. I

227

didn't have anything to give to Trinity. When I met Hassan, he confessed later that he was married, but I was already pregnant and in love. He led me on thinking we would be more, but he left me. That's not how it was supposed to be. I couldn't raise Trinity. I was suffering from Postpartum and needed help. I thought I was doing what was right, Nova. I'm sorry you were hurt in the process. I went to better myself. I always wanted to come back for her one day, but not like this. I swear I didn't know you and Hassan worked at the building I was transferred to, nor did I know about my sister being her principal. My sister and I hadn't talked for years due to all the sexual trauma and abuse I endured. I'm not asking you for any sympathy. I just want to know if I can be in my daughter's life. If you say no, I understand," Yashira cried.

"I never thought a day would come where I would be turning my little angel over." Nova cried while looking over at Trinity. "I love her so much, and now everything is just broken. I don't deserve any of this. I knew though that there would come a time that you would come back. Hassan has always loved you. You're the one he wants. He regretted marrying me. He hates that he needed me all these years. She's your child."

"She's our child," Yashira corrected.

"You deserve to know her." Nova sniffled. "Come on."

"Mommy," Trinity cheerfully said, eating her ice cream.

"I thought you were getting candy." Nova smiled.

"I did, and cousin KeKe got me some ice cream too. Y'all want some?" she asked.

"No baby, but Trin, hunny, I want you to meet someone." She and Yashira took a seat.

"I know youuuuu," Trinity sang. "You're the lady who looks just like me." Trinity smiled. Kiara, Nova, and Yashira laughed.

"Well, baby this here is your mother, Yashira." Nova pointed.

"But how when you're my mommy?" Trinity asked confused.

"Well now you have two mommies, and she's going to be helping raise you now. Your dad and I are no longer going to be together."

"But whyyyyy?" Trinity asked, getting upset.

"Well munchkin sometimes adults fight, and they have figured out together they aren't good for each other, but that doesn't change the fact that they love you. In fact, now you'll just have more people to love you. You have Yashira, your dad, your Grandma Erica, and all your little cousins too." Nova smiled. "In fact, you'll be staying with your other mommy tonight." Nova looked over at Yashira.

"Really?" Yashira excitedly asked, and Nova shook her head.

Trinity was quiet for a moment and then smiled. "You wanna see my Barbie collection at home?" she asked Yashira.

"I would love that." Yashira smiled.

"Well, mommy is going to get out of here. I love you, Trin. Be a good girl for your mother and do as she asks." Nova kissed her forehead and hugged her. She quickly turned to walk off before she completely broke down in front of Trinity.

"Nova," Yashira chased after her, "I just want to say thank you."

Nova gave Yashira a once over and nodded her head. She didn't have anything else to say. She was so ready just to get out of there. She hurried to the elevator, and when the doors opened, she ran into Ty.

He started to step off, but stayed on and rode the elevator back up with Nova.

"Look, Nova, I don't you don't really like me, and I understand. I mean a hood nigga around your husband when you're trying to keep a good home and shit. I get it. I just wanted to say though I apologize for how Hassan did you all these years. Believe it or not, we got into many times behind you. I think you're special and a real woman. For what it's worth on behalf of my boy, I'm sorry for all the hoe shit he put you through. You didn't deserve that, ya naw what I mean? I don't blame you for moving on. Take care of yourself Ms. Lady and stay up. You feel me? If you need anything, I got you. Word is bond, ma," Ty said sincerely, and Nova smiled.

He was so hood to her and as high as a kite, but she could tell he was genuine with his words. She appreciated him for saying that. "Thank you Ty!" she reached to hug him.

She waved bye when the elevator stopped on Brixton mother's floor and made her way to be with her man. The closer she stepped towards the room, she noticed nurses frantically hurrying to the room. "Oh, God no Brixton!" She took off running down the hall.

"Ma'am, please stay back. Sir, you must leave the room!" Nurses yelled at Brixton and Nova.

"Mom, mom. Do something! She was just fine. Mom! Mom!" Brixton screamed.

"Brixton," Nova cried, holding him in her arms.

"She's going to be okay. She's going to be okay. Come on, let's pray," Nova whispered. "Our father, please watch over her. We know that you are the healer of all things. Please heal her body, father. Please protect her and let her know she has loved ones all around her. Amen."

"Amen," Brixton whispered when his mother's door opened.

"Brixton, she's stable. She had a seizure. That was one of the side effects from the new medication. The doctor is going to take her off that. We'll be watching her throughout the night," A nurse informed.

"So will we. We aren't going anywhere." Nova looked at Brixton wiping his tears. "I love you," she whispered as tears left her own eyes.

Kissy watched the news and listened to the radio faithfully. She would be lying if she said she felt an ounce of remorse for killing Raheem, his wife, and their unborn child. They had killed her spirit long ago, and if she could, she would do it all over again, no regrets. *The bitch had what was coming. They've lived in marital bliss long enough, so fuck them.* Kissy evilly thought.

The only evidence they had as of right now, was a brief description of a white Tahoe and the use of a .22 caliber handgun. Other than that, they didn't have much to go on, but Kissy knew she needed to get rid of the gun. She figured she would bury it.

She made a quick stop to Walmart and purchased a shovel, duffel bag, flashlight, and toolbox. While dark, she traveled the 45-minute distance to her big mama's grave that was located in Cedar Creek deep in the country.

She adjusted her eyes to the darkness, light fog, and dim lighting of the cemetery. She parked her truck in front of an old low white wooden fence and unlocked the hatchet.

She fussed at herself for not wearing the proper foot attire. She could feel the mist from the grass and dirt covering the bottom of her shoes.

The dirt trail led to the big oak tree, and she could tell it was the correct tree because years ago her aunt carved a T on the side of it.

Sweat beads formed around her forehead as she quickly dug. She was hot, paranoid and she looked around in the dark frantic. She kept telling herself to breathe. A piece of her wanted to leave and wait until the morning, but she kept going.

She tried to tune out the sounds of what she thought were rattlesnakes ready to attack. A couple of times she stopped moving to calm herself before she lost her nerve.

Her eyes widen with fear at the thought of horsewhip snake beating her to death. She remembered the old white outhouse that her big mama had and how one hot summer she went to use the restroom. Something kept beating on the window. She looked out and saw the tail of the snake hitting the glass. She took running with toilet paper in her ass.

She shook her when another thought froze her with fear. She turned around quickly squinting her eyes. Wild hogs ran freely and were vicious if they attacked you. "You're safe. Just keep digging," she coached herself, attempting to slow down her racing heart.

Her mind wandered again, and laughter escaped her lips when she thought of her cousin Tony running from being chased by a wild hog.

At the time, Kissy didn't know how dangerous they were. As Tony ran she chanted, "Run Tony. Run," with laughter.

Their big mama Bernice heard little Tony running and quickly grabbed her shotgun. *POW!* The wild hog dropped. She frowned thinking how her big mama made her and Tony help her clean the hog. It was one of the most disgusting things she ever had to do. "Ewwww," she blurted out, remembering how the adults ate hog maw for dinner.

She returned to digging.

*Thump!*

"Yes!" she whispered when her shovel hit something hard. She immediately fell to her knees and began digging as fast as she could.

She pulled the old rusted lock box out of its hidden spot and entered the code her Aunt had given her. "What the fuck was Torrie into?" she whispered picking up false ID, passports, a handgun and lots of cash.

She frowned when she saw her name, her mother's name, and Kinley's name on life insurance documents for 250,000 each. "Grimy ass." Kissy shook her head.

She placed the contents of the lockbox in her duffle bag and placed the lockbox along with the gun she used to kill Raheem and his wife back into its hidden spot; covering it back with the dirt and placing the heavy rock back by the tree.

She jumped back into her vehicle, upset that she was tracking dirt into it. "Ugh!" she yelled in frustration, making a mental note to go by a car cleaning spot in the morning.

As she made a right turn from the dirt country road, to get back on Hwy 71, she could have sworn she caught a glimpse of Bo in Nicole's vehicle headed in the direction of where she had just come from.

"Oh my god!" she yelled, speeding up.

She jumped on the toll road, looking through the rearview mirror every other second. Her heart pounded. *I know that was him.* She silently thought.

When she arrived home, she set her alarm and checked all the doors and windows. "Yes, bitch!" she squealed placing the duffel bag on the table and counting the money. She hit the jackpot. In the duffle bag was five hundred thousand dollars.

*Ding, dong!*

Her doorbell rang. She grabbed the pistol from the bag and hurried to look through the peephole. "Just a second!" she yelled once she saw it was Bella.

She hid the duffle bag along with the gun and looked around to make sure everything was okay before she opened the door.

"Girl, what's up?" Bella asked walking in. "Oh, shit! Bitch, this is nice." Bella admired the furniture and decorations.

She flopped down on the couch with an opened bottle of Hennessy in her hand. Kissy took in her demeanor and frowned. "Uh, you okay? Where are the girls?"

"They are at a sleepover with their friends." Bella propped her feet. "You got some food. Bitch, I'm hungry."

"I ain't about to cook this late, but I'll order a pizza or something." Kissy jumped online to order Dominos. "Anyway, are you going to tell me what's up?" Kissy took a seat next to Bella.

"They fired a bitch today."

"What? Why?"

"Those bastards said I was stealing company funds." Bella drank out the bottle.

"Girl, give me that. Your ass is already lit." Kissy took the bottle. "Well, did you?" she asked.

"I didn't have no choice. I got kids, and that little check wasn't paying shit. Rent takes damn near everything. Now they want me out of here. Talking about I got a week to move out of my unit. Shit and go where? I knew I should've left my babies in the system. I can't do shit right. I'm a fucking failure. They're talking about pressing charges," Bella cried.

"You're not a failure."

"Yes, I am. They are keeping my last two checks to pay back the company. I don't have no money. How are my kids going to eat? Where are we going to go?" Bella placed her head in her hands and sobbed.

"How much do you owe them back?"

"Eight grand," Bella admitted.

"Eight grand, Bella?" Kissy yelled.

"I know, don't judge me."

"I'm not, and you know that. Listen, I'll help you pay that off, and you and the kids can stay here. I'm not about to let y'all starve and be homeless. We'll figure it out together." Kissy smiled.

"Really?" Bella asked.

"Yes. Shit, I ain't about to let you or my nieces suffer. I got you." Kissy got up to answer the doorbell.

She signed the receipt for the pizza and gave the young guy a tip. "What's up, Kensington? It's me, Mike, Ms. Dee's grandson," the young pizza deliver said.

"Oh hey! How are you? Tell your grandmother hi." Kissy ended the conversation while rolling her eyes. *Great, now somebody knows where I live.* She silently fussed while closing the door.

"You good? Why are you so quiet all of a sudden?" Kissy asked Bella while taking a bite of her pizza.

"I was just thinking. What if I worked for you?" Bella asked.

"Work for me? What do you mean?"

"Come on, Kensington. I know your secret. You're Kissy the chick over the group. Sorry I couldn't help but snoop through your phone when you fell asleep. You really should put a lock or something on your phone. You're wide open and should be more careful," Bella slurred.

Kissy stared at Bella for a moment. She couldn't believe how sloppy she had become. Now two people knew her secret, and while Bella was her long lost sister and had helped her through a traumatic experience, Kissy didn't really know Bella from a can of paint.

"I know what you're thinking. You don't know my ass for shit. I won't tell your secret though. You can trust me," Bella assured.

Since Bella knew her secret, Kissy decided that she needed to keep Bella close. She didn't feel an ill spirit coming from Bella, and something told her she could trust her. However, given Kissy's past with others and the way her aunt betrayed her, she didn't fully trust anyone.

She and Bella ate, laughed and cracked jokes until one in the morning. Kissy thought about allowing Bella to stay over and sleep off her alcohol, but she thought about the duffle bag of money and remembered how her mother stole from her. She wouldn't make that mistake again.

"Well sis, I'mma about to go to bed. Be careful babe walking to your condo. I'll stop by tomorrow and help you bring things here." Kissy hugged Bella.

"Thank you for everything, Kensington." Bella waved goodbye.

Kissy watched Bella walked until she could no longer see her. She closed her door, set the alarm, and made sure all the windows were locked.

She had a nagging feeling that someone was watching her. It was the same feeling she had the day she and Bella were out to eat and ran into Madea. She still questioned if that incident was coincidental, or if Madea had been purposely following them. She shook off her thoughts, turned her lights off, and retreated to bed.

An hour later Kissy had woken from a bad dream. In this dream, Bo and Hassan were trying to kill her. She had a feeling that she was going to die. The feeling was so strong that she jumped on her ERS account at work and made Bella her beneficiary. She didn't stop there. She made Bella the power of attorney for her and Kinley. If something did happen to her, Bella and her girls would be fully provided for and taken care of.

She warmed up a couple of slices of pizza, grabbed her a soda and retreated to her bedroom. She settled on the ID channel and secretly lusted after the actor who played the lead detective on *Murder Choose Me*. He was so fine to her.

*A*ccount *closed. Please go to your bank for further assistance.*

"What the fuck?" Bo punched the ATM.

He had been using Nicole's debit card for the last couple of days, and the last available amount was fifteen thousand.

"Closed? Nah!" He entered the bankcard back into the Wells Fargo ATM. The machine kept the card and Bo was furious. "Bitch!" He kicked the machine.

He paced back and forth in front of the machine and wondered how he could get the card back. His phone rang. "What the fuck does this bitch want from me?" he yelled, seeing the Travis County Jail number flash across his screen.

"Man, what the fuck you keep calling a nigga for?" he yelled at Torrie.

"Bo, where have you been? I need your help, baby. Please come get me out of here. Nobody is answering for me. I need to get out of here!" Torrie cried.

"With what? A nigga is broke. I can't even go anywhere right now. Niggas is gunning for my head because they think I set you up. A nigga is stressed the fuck out!" Bo yelled.

"I know you wouldn't, baby. Listen, I have to get off the phone now, but I have some money hidden in a cemetery. I told Kensington days ago, and she still hasn't bailed me out. I need you to go get my money and get me out of here. It's half a million."

Bo looked up towards the sky and mouthed "thank you". His funds were dwindling and he knew sooner or later he would be homeless with nowhere to go if he didn't think of something soon.

Bo jumped into Nicole's vehicle and headed in the direction of the cemetery. Driving down highway 71, Bo thought about his sister Nicole. The news had been constantly airing the love triangle story between her, Sean, and the "mystery" coworker.

That's all the radio, Facebook, talk shows, and the news focused on lately, that and the murders of Iesha and Raheem. It was such outrage and outpour of concern, but Bo knew it was only one person responsible and connected to everyone and that was Kensington.

He returned his thoughts to Sean. He didn't care for Sean, but a piece of him understood why Sean did what he had. He was a good man to his sister, and Bo didn't agree with how Nicole gave Sean her ass to kiss.

Nicole was big as hell, and Bo felt she was lucky to have any man that wanted or loved her the way Sean did. He was good to her. He never cheated, and although he wanted children and Nicole couldn't have them, he never shamed her or went out and had his own child. He was dedicated and loving to Nicole, and Bo felt Nicole was in the wrong.

Bo was her half-brother. His mother was Nicole's father mistress, so Bo was never accepted into their family. When they got older, he attempted to build a relationship with Nicole, especially when his mother passed away. They were cool, and their relationship began to grow, but Bo felt Nicole blamed him for her mother and father's divorce.

She never came out and said it, but during conversation, she would always bring it up, hint around it, and then act passive aggressive about it.

He admitted there were times he and Sean also didn't see eye to eye. Sean was always in his business, and Bo felt he had a simp mentality when it came to black women, always saying what a "real man" was and how "real men" did this or that. Bo wasn't trying to hear any of what Sean was talking about. Women to him were dumb. They made it too easy for him to use them and live off them. Why change now when he had been doing the same thing for years?

Sean knew his game and made sure Nicole wasn't one of his victims. She would help when she could, but what angered Bo is when their father passed. He left all the money to Nicole, and Bo didn't get a dime. He felt Nicole was selfish for not considering him or at least giving him some money. After all, they had the same father. Ever since their father passed, Nicole had been acting funny and thinking she was better than the rest of her family, even Sean. She had dropped a little weight, started cheating, and had gotten a new vehicle. Bo envied her. Now that she was gone, the only thing Bo had of use was the vehicle that she had paid off, and the five hundred dollars he had withdrawn earlier.

He followed the directions that Torrie gave to the cemetery, and as he turned on the dimly lit country road, he could have sworn he caught a glimpse of Kensington in an all-white Tahoe. *Nah, that can't be her.* He silently thought and kept driving.

The cemetery was dark and creepy. Bo adjusted his eyes and used the flashlight on his phone as a guide. He found the tree Torrie told him about and quickly began digging.

"That's what the fuck I'm talking about!" Bo yelled excited when he came across a big lock box. He didn't bother trying to hide any evidence of where he had dug. He hurried to Nicole's vehicle and made it back to the Crown Plaza hotel he had been staying at.

His room was messy and overcrowded with all the shoeboxes and shopping bags he had. He moved his clothing off the bed and sat the lock box next to him. He entered the combination and rubbed his hands together. "A nigga about to be on!" he excitedly said.

"Bitch!" he bellowed, removing the gun from the box and throwing the empty box across the room. He didn't know what to do now.

He sat the gun on the nightstand and laid back on the bed. He was extremely exasperated that Kensington had beaten him to the cemetery. "I knew that was that bitch. I should have followed her.

What the fuck am I supposed to do now?" His only solution was to blackmail Kensington for money. He dialed her.

"Stop calling me!" she screamed and hung up.

"Bitch!" Bo yelled while rubbing his growling stomach. He was tired of playing games with her.

He hopped back into Nicole vehicle's and stopped by Domino's Pizza. As he exited the restaurant with his pizza in hand, he ran into his little cousin Mike, who was entering the restaurant from a delivery.

"Oh shit! What's up, little cousin?" Bo asked Mike and hugged him.

"Shit nothing, trying to make this bread. You know prom and graduation are coming up, and I'm trying to get my money together," Mike proudly announced.

"That's what's up. Come outside boi and chop it up with me. I ain't seen you in a while. How is your grandmother doing?" Bo asked while leaning up against Nicole's car.

"She's doing as good as to be expected, still bat shit crazy." He laughed. "What's up with you? I heard about what happened in the 4 with Torrie. I know you wouldn't do that though. Niggas are asking about you though, so be careful, cousin," Mike warned.

"Good looking fam." Bo slapped hands with Mike, ending it with a snap.

"Oh, guess who I ran into?"

"Who?" Bo asked, taking a bite of his pizza.

"Ms. Lisa's daughter, Kensington. Man, she looks so good. She's living well too. I'm trying to get on her level." Mike smiled. "You think she would give me a chance?" Mike laughed.

"Boy, you wild. Little young ass," Bo teased. "Last time I saw Lisa she was on that shit bad."

"Yeah, I be seeing her and old crazy ass Sandy over there on 12th and Chicon sometimes, her dad James too. It's messed up how Kensington don't have anyone." Mike shook his head.

"Yeah, it is. Her aunt has been calling me from jail asking if I've seen her. She's been trying to get in touch with her. Where's she staying at?" Bo asked.

"She stays in these brand new condos in Round Rock."

"Round Rock?"

"Yeah, her place is bad too. She done came up."

"You said it's some new condos?" Bo asked with a raised brow.

"Yeah! They aren't complete yet, but some of the units are ready. Man, she's so pretty. I always had a crush on her." Mike smiled.

"Alright, young buck." Bo laughed.

"Mike, you have another delivery!" Mike's manager yelled outside the door.

"I gotta get going, but it was good seeing you. Oh and here is Kensington address." He wrote it down on a piece of paper. "Tell her I said, 'what's good' when you see her." Mike hugged Bo.

Bo hopped in the vehicle fuming. He felt a little disrespected by Mike's manager. He wanted to say something to the man but thought against it. He didn't want his cousin to lose his job. He stared at the address Mike had given him and smiled.

"Got you hoe," he whispered cranking Nicole's vehicle to head back to the room.

He watched a little bit of the game and snacked on his pizza. Nicole's phone lit up while it was on the charger and he grabbed it. A couple of notifications from Facebook and *Whose Man Is This Sis* rested on the home screen.

Seeing that Nicole's phone was free of password restrictions, Bo decided he was going to play mind games with Kensington. He started by changing Nicole's name on Facebook, deleting all her social media photos and then he trolled Kissy's group. He knew Kissy had too much to lose, and if he played his cards right, she would come to him.

The bamboo sound alert sounded off loudly multiple times on Kissy's phone. She frowned rolling her body over in the bed and sitting up. The sun shined brightly peeking through the sheer curtains lighting up the room. Kissy yawned and stretched her body.

She warmed up a Jimmy Dean breakfast sandwich in the microwave and grabbed her laptop. While her sandwich was warming, she decided to post in her group.

*Hey, what's up guys!* the caption read.

She strolled through the latest gossip and read most of the comments. The hot topics were the murders of Raheem and his wife, Hassan getting shot, Nicole being murdered by Sean, Sean killing himself, Torrie's arrest, Larry being released from jail, and who was cheating on who.

*Ding!* The microwave chimed.

Everyone had an opinion on things they really knew nothing about, but Kissy was amused, to say the least. As she ate, she saw a couple of bait post threatening to reveal her identity, and she instantly knew it had to be Bo. It didn't take her long to track down who was behind the fake photo and name, especially when Bo hadn't deleted the RIP post off Nicole's wall. "Dumb ass nigga." She laughed.

She saw some of the comments pressing Bo to reveal her identity, but Kissy knew Bo needed her and she wasn't about to play these games with him any longer. She thought about just shutting the entire group down since she had more than enough money now and she could relocate and start over, but the drama fed her soul.

"These niggas ain't shit!" Kissy yelled.

Everyone was familiar with Quedarius "Quincy" for short. He had infected multiple women in the city, but since Paris wasn't from Austin, she didn't know who to look out for. Kissy shook her head.

"Whew, let me get off of here." She closed her laptop.

Opening the bottom cabinet in the kitchen, she grabbed the duffel bag and smiled. She couldn't believe she had so much money in her hands but knew she had to think of a location to stash it. If she opened another account, it would alert the IRS, and she couldn't add the money to the account she already had because she would run into the same problem. The most she could deposit was $9,999 without incident.

"Shit think, think, think." She paced back and forth. "Nah," she blurted, looking up at the attic. "Wait!" she yelled, remembering that her box spring was made of wood.

She removed the mattress and retrieved her toolbox to disassemble her king size bed. She placed the half a million neatly inside the box spring and screwed the cover to the box spring back on. She then placed her mattress back on top and felt secure knowing that her money was hidden.

Her doorbell rang, and she looked over at her alarm clock and frowned. "It's too early for this shit," she whispered, looking through the peephole.

"Good morning, sis," Bella said, walking in.

"Aht, Aht Bella, it's early as fuck. I'm not a morning person." Kissy rolled her eyes with her hand on her hips.

"Girl, you will be. Wait until your nieces start bugging you on the weekends and shit." Bella laughed.

"What's up? What's brings you by so early?" Kissy asked, taking a seat on the sofa.

"I was up packing, and then I got in my feelings."

"Feelings about what? I told you that I'd help you, and you and the girls can stay here."

"Yeah, I know. I just…" Bella paused. "I've been talking to this guy name Tyrone, and his wife and me got into this morning. I didn't even know he was married. He has met my children and everything. I'm just taking an L in every direction." Bella shrugged.

"Tuh! Bitch, first of all, if you were in my group, you would know Tyrone is a whole hoe out here in these streets. You didn't take an L. Shit if anything, you won. He ain't shit. I work with Dedra, and he stays putting her through all kinds of shit. Just take the L and move on."

"I wish I could." Bella reached in her pocket and pulled out a pregnancy test. "I'm pregnant. I just took the test. That's why I came here so early." She sighed. "I needed someone to talk to."

"Does he know you're HIV positive?"

"No. I tried to make him wear a condom, and we did the first time, but he removed it saying that he needed to feel me. His chances of contracting it are low though. Even if I took an HIV test, it would come back negative."

"Well, shit that's his bad then." Kissy shrugged. "Are you keeping the baby?" Kissy asked with raised brows.

"I don't know yet."

"Well, whatever you do, I'm down." Kissy grabbed ahold of Bella's hand. "I'm going to go see Kinley, do you want to come?"

"Yes! I would love to see my niece." Bella smiled.

The two hopped in Kissy's vehicle and drove to the center. Normally Kissy would see Kinley on Saturdays, but Kinley had been on her mind heavy.

Maybe it was because the news kept airing the story of Raheem and his wife being murdered, she didn't know, but she couldn't get Kinley off her mind.

"You okay?" Bella asked, noticing the sad look on Kissy's face.

"Bella, sometimes I envy the fact your daughters are normal. I envy the bond you have with them. I hate seeing my baby like this. She can't even move or breathe on her own. I wonder if she even knows who I am. I feel like I'm making her suffer. I want her so bad, but my baby can't even do anything on her own. She'll never get to run and play or swim or call me 'mom'. Every time I see her like that, it breaks me. Her own father didn't even want her," Kissy cried.

Bella handed her a napkin from the glove compartment. She felt bad for her sister. She couldn't imagine what Kissy was going through.

"I'm sorry, sis. I wish there was something I could say or do."

They entered inside the facility and the first thing that Kissy noticed was the Christmas board that Ryan said she was putting together. Although it was nice, she didn't like it, and she felt exposed. She wanted to rip the picture of her and Kinley down.

"Oh my god! Is this her?" Bella asked Kissy while pointing to the photo. Kissy nodded her head. "She's so beautiful. She must look just like her father though."

They heard someone rolling a trashcan behind them and quickly turned around. Bella's eyes danced with fire, while Kissy avoided eye contact.

"Oh shit!" Tyrone yelled removing his Beats earphones. "What it do, Kensington?" Tyrone said, smiling.

"Hey, Tyrone! What are you doing here?" she asked.

"I work here," he proudly replied.

"Oh okay!"

"I'm sorry about your Auntie Torrie, that's fucked up. Torrie's a real one, you feel me? How you holding up?" he asked.

"I'm holding. You know I don't fold. I'm solid."

"That's what's up? Is that your little girl in the photo?" he pointed already knowing the answer.

"Nah, that's my little sister. I'm just coming up here to make sure she's good," she lied. She didn't need Tyrone spreading her business.

"What Lisa has another baby?" Tyrone played along.

"Yeah, she did and you know she's on that shit, so my little sister came out disabled," Kissy continued with her lie.

"Soooo, you're just going to act like you don't see me standing here?" Bella bellowed pointing her finger at Tyrone.

"Come on, Bella, this is my job. Don't do that shit here. You got people all in a nigga business and shit." Tyrone frowned.

"Yeah, whatever. You need to tell your bitch to learn her place. I don't appreciate her calling me this morning. You told me you weren't married. Why would you lie to me like that?" Bella teared up. "I'm pregnant."

"Mannnn, yeah okay." Tyrone walked away.

"Come on, Bella. Fuck him," Kissy encouraged.

When they arrived at Kinley's room, Kissy closed the door, and Bella broke down in her arms. "It's going to be okay, sis," Kissy promised. "I have someone I want you to meet," Kissy whispered to Bella.

Bella dried her eyes and looked over towards Kinley. "Oh my god, look at my beautiful niece," Bella cooed gently picking Kinley up. She planted kisses all over her tiny body. "Auntie loves you," she sang. "I'm in love" She smiled over her shoulder at Kissy.

They visited the center for an hour and then left to grab lunch at Dairy Queen. "How many times are you going to call him?" Bella asked.

"Huh?"

"Hassan. How many times are you going to keep calling him? Why don't you just go to him?" Bella asked, eating her fry.

"I don't know." Kissy shrugged.

"Here, what's his number?" Bella asked, pulling out her phone.

Kissy gave Bella Hassan's phone number, and she called his cell from her number. "Bitch here, he's on the phone," Bella whispered, passing Kissy her phone.

"Hassan, how are you? I've been trying to get ahold of you." Kissy asked.

"Yeah, I can't talk right now. One." Hassan hung up the phone.

"Bitch!" Kissy screamed a little too loudly.

"Fuck that! You should just go pop up on him. You already know the hospital he's at. Act like you're a concerned employee and show your badge if they need identification. Shit, I'll ride out with you." Bella said hyped.

"Fuck it! Let's go." Kissy slurped down the last of her sweet tea.

Bella stayed in the car while Kissy went inside the hospital. She smiled thinking Bella must have done this before. The front desk asked for her badge information.

"Breathe," she whispered and exhaled when she arrived at Hassan's room.

The door was slightly ajar, and she peeped in. Her fists instantly bawled when she saw a beautiful woman kissing Hassan. A little girl who resembled the woman was also there.

Kissy looked a little more closely and knew she had seen the little girl somewhere before, but couldn't recall where. When she heard her call Hassan "daddy" tears welled up in her eyes. There Hassan was with another woman and his daughter.

♪*I just need someone to love me. When it's hard to, I can trust with all my issues. Someone who is patient and consistent. I need good sex and commitment.*♪ Monica's commitment song roared through Kissy's phone, causing the little girl to look her way.

"Hey, I know you, you're Kissy," she said excitedly while getting out of her seat.

"Oh shit!" Kissy whispered and took off running down the hall. She couldn't risk Hassan or anyone else knowing who she was.

When she made it to her vehicle, she was out of breath. She breathed heavy as sweat poured from her forehead. She blasted the AC and hurried to get out of there.

"Damn, that was close!" she yelled.

"Uh, you okay?" Bella asked alarmed.

Kissy shook her head no when her phone rang. It read private caller. She ignored it, and it rang three more times. "What?"

"Bitch, don't what me. Where you at?" Bo asked.

"None of your fucking business."

"You must think I'm playing with you Kissy. I need some money. Send me a thousand right now through Cash App: $BoBo4.

"Fuck you, Bo." Kissy hung up and turned her phone off.

"Kensington, pull over before you kill us," Bella suggested.

Kissy pulled over to the side of the road and broke down crying. "He was with another woman and his daughter. That's why he hadn't been answering for me. I lost our fucking child, and he doesn't even care."

"It's okay, sis. In due time, everyone will have what's coming to them. Just wait and see," Bella promised.

"Hey, Eric!" Detective Lu yelled while entering in Eric's office.

"Yeah, what's up?" Detective Eric looked up from his papers.

"The bank notified me that they placed a hold on Nicole Smith debit cards. Photos of a Bobbie "Bo" Jackson were taken at the ATM in the Muller shopping center. He has the victim's vehicle too. He's the half-brother of Nicole."

"Hmmm, things with this whole case aren't adding up."

"I agree! It's a whole shit show, and the captain is on our asses." Detective Lu sighed and took a seat.

Detective Eric looked at all the photos in front of him trying to piece together all the key players involved.

"We have Nova and Hassan Daniels, Sean and Nicole, Bobbie Jackson, Yashira Andrews, Kensington Blu, Brixton January, and Ryan Taylor."

"Let's start with Nicole. We know she was found murdered. Her cell phone and wallet are missing. Sean shoots Hassan and then turns the gun on himself. How does Bo Jackson end up with Nicole's possessions?" Detective Lu asked leaning back in his chair twirling a black ballpoint pen.

*Knock, Knock!*

"Hey, guys! What's up?" Amber asked, stepping in Eric's office.

"Anything yet, Amber?" Detective Lu asked.

Amber was working undercover in the *Whose Man Is This Sis?* group. So much violence, and fights had happened in the city, and every time a suspect was detained, the private group was always mentioned.

"Okay! Get your pads ready. Here's what I've seen in the group and heard on the streets. Nicole, Yashira, Kensington, Hassan, and Nova all work together. Hassan and Nova are married. Hassan had a baby by Yashira, or Yazzi as everyone knows her by. She just moved here from Houston. Anyway, Nicole is married to Sean. Bo is Nicole's half-brother. Nicole had an affair with Hassan. Are y'all following me so far? This shit is messy," Amber emphasized.

"Keep going." Detective Eric encouraged.

"I was able to get a warrant for Sean's and Nicole's Facebook messages and phone records. Nova, Hassan's wife, sent a message to Sean informing him of the affair Nicole and Hassan were having. The morning of the shooting, Nova received a delivery of flowers from Brixton January an ex-lover also an attorney at Stubblefield Law Firm. It is confirmed that Nova met with her sister Ryan at the time of the shooting. The video shows Sean entering through a side entrance that wasn't closed all the way. This eliminates Nova. She used the front entrance."

"This is good. Keep going." Detective Lu said.

"Whew! Okay! So now, Kensington is Hassan's employee. They've been having an affair." She flipped a piece of notebook paper. "An arrest was made due to Nova trespassing and assaulting Kensington. Nova, Nicole, Ashley Williams, and Kensington Blu all are members of *Whose Man Is This Sis.* Amber smiled.

"Ashley Williams, the shooting victim Iesha's cousin?" Detective Lu asked perplexed.

"Yes."

"Good work, Amber. I'm still wondering though, how Bo ended up with Nicole's possessions." Detective Eric uttered.

"Kensington, I've heard that name before." Detective Lu insisted, rubbing his bald head.

"Kensington Blu. She was stalking-" Detective Eric paused. "Oh fuck me!" he yelled. "Kensington was stalking Raheem and his wife. She had to be admitted in a state facility. Torrie Wells is her aunt. That's who she had been released to."

"Well get this," Amber inserted. "Bo and Torrie are an item."

"Get the fuck out of here!" Eric yelled.

"Hey, Eric and Lu, ballistic tests report just came back and you're never gonna believe whose prints are on the .22 caliber bullets belong to that killed Raheem and Iesha Gold!" Jim their supervisor yelled.

"Who?" they all asked shocked.

"Torrie Wells."

"Hot damn!" Detective Eric yelled.

"Well, she was locked up at the time so that would only leave..." Amber paused.

"Kensington or Bo!" they all yelled in unison.

"We've got a ping off Nicole's cell phone. It's near the Crown Plaza at University Station!" Sarah bellowed from her desk.

"Let's go get the son of a bitch." Detective Eric said, placing on his coat.

"Try to get us an IP address on the computer being used behind that group if you can, Sarah. We need to find out who is behind the screen!" Detective Lu yelled while he and Detective Eric headed out.

♥♥♥♥♥

"Thank you for lunch, Auntie," Kiara said as she and Erica entered her apartment.

"You're welcome, baby. It's the least I can do. How are you and the children holding up?" Erica asked, taking a seat on the sofa. "It's nice in here. I like the way you have everything set up," she complimented.

"Thank you, Auntie." Kiara smiled. "We're good. I mean, of course, it's an adjustment, and it takes a while to get them to school now from here since I don't have my own vehicle yet, but we're making it. Plus, Ty helps out a lot with anything me and the children need." Kiara opened the living room blinds.

"Do they ever ask about their father, Larry?"

"No, not really. They're scared of him more than anything, especially after Larry raping and beating me the way he had in front of them. I'm still embarrassed to look at my children. Sometimes I feel Larry Jr. looks at me differently. I feel weak and unsure of myself a lot of times. Ty has been good with them though." Kiara smiled and sat on the love seat.

"Well, I'm happy you finally left him alone. I hate you got mixed up with Larry. He stole your youth. Your mother and I should have pressed charges on him. There was no reason for an older man to be preying on a young girl."

"Looking back, you're right. I was so in love and dumb behind Larry. I regret how my life turned out. I love my children, but if I could do it over again, I would have aborted my first child and went off to the Navy like I wanted to. I always wanted to see the world and better my life. I never thought I would be trapped in Austin. Larry really played on the death of my dad. I was hurting and felt alone. In the beginning, he was just a listening ear. Then it turned to him buying my things for school, and then eventually taking my virginity. I didn't see how manipulative he was. He was training me and molding me into a person he could use and control. The only thing good I did was made sure I graduated high school." Kiara smiled and shrugged her shoulders.

"Yeah, but we should have done something to stop it." Erica frowned.

"Auntie, what was there really to do? Mom was grieving over dad's death and trying to care for eight kids. You had your own thing going on."

"I just feel like we failed you, especially when I think of all the abuse Larry put you through."

"Sadly, I don't ever think I'll escape him. Ty is the only man I've been with other than Larry, and I'm honestly terrified of what Larry is going to do when he's released. I know he's going to kill me one day." Kiara saddened, reaching for her vibrating phone in her pocket.

"Oh my god! It's Larry. He's going to kill me." Her leg nervously shook. "I knew he was going to find a way out. They never keep him long, even after the orders have been violated. I just want to be left alone."

"Don't answer that. That's not going to happen. We're going to protect you." Erica assured, blowing the situation off. "What's your take on everything that is going on with my son?" Erica asked.

"Honestly, Auntie," Kiara fired up a blunt, "I feel bad for Nova." Erica frowned. "Wait!" Kiara put her hands out. "Now, I know you and the rest of the family don't care for Nova, but I honestly think nobody has ever given her a fair chance."

"Tuh!" Erica scoffed.

"She's not like us and doesn't come from our background. We all judged her for that. A piece of us envies the fact she was raised on love and not survival. She's different, and her spirit is different."

"Nobody is jealous of her stuck up ass."

"Then why are you and everybody so mad at her then? She hasn't done anything to anyone, and she's always pleasant."

"Because she thinks she so much better than us."

"I don't really see that though, Auntie." Kiara blew out smoke. "However, she's still a woman first, and although I love my cousin Hassan, he's trash. I know that's your son, but look at all the shit he has done. You coddled him because he help pays your bills. You're mad at Nova because we all know Nova is Hassan's bread and butter. That house they're live in is something we aren't used to, the cars, everything. Even Trinity stays fly. Nova is the one who upgraded Hassan, and he knows, and we know that without her, Hassan ass is going to be right back on your sofa, barely making it on his salary. Other than that though, he is just foul on so many levels. Nova raised that baby as if it was hers. We all saw, and we all judged her to for staying. Even after all of that, he cheats, lies, and gets other women pregnant who work with Nova. Then he gets shot by their coworkers' husband, and now Yashira is back. You know after all of that, I don't blame Nova one bit for leaving. Besides, everyone knows who Brixton is, so why would she throw away a good man like that to stay with Hassan?" Kiara took a pull of the blunt.

"She's his wife, for better or for worse. She's pregnant too, running around like she doesn't have a care in the world. She can't just throw my son away like that. He put in work too. Talking about she's selling the home. I hope Hassan sues her for child support and spousal support," Erica huffed.

"Why? Trinity has a mother and let's be real, Hassan wants to be with Yashira. Plus they haven't been married for ten years, so he won't get spousal support in Texas."

"Well watch when I tell you, Nova got what's coming to her."

Kiara was about to say something else when there was a knock at her door. *Thank God! Saved by the door. Her ass is tripping. Get a fucking job. Hassan is not your man. You're just pissed that your money train is leaving.* She really wanted to give her aunt a piece of her mind but didn't want to be disrespectful or hurt her feelings.

"Babyyyyy!" Kiara squealed and jumped in Ty's arms.

Ashley's apartment had a major water leak. For the time being, she had been staying with Ty, and she was beginning to wear out her welcome. She was smothering him, and Ty was extremely exhausted from trying to keep up with all his lies.

He was going back and forth between Kiara and Ashley. He liked them both but was becoming more and more attached to Kiara. She was fun, funny, a great cook and mother. He also loved the fact Kiara was also resourceful and self-sufficient when it came to her babies and working the system.

Then there was Ashley. She was smart, a book nerd, funny and intelligent. He loved her spirit. She was sweet, kind to everyone, a hard worker, and she really knew how to cater to and please her man. It's just she bothered him too much, and she wasn't his peace. It was something about her that made him have a love/hate energy with her. Not only that, but the death of her cousin Iesha had taken a toll on her and emotionally Ty wasn't the type of man who knew how to console a woman through pain.

Ashley was having nightmares and had fallen into depression. Detectives had come by Ty's place a couple of times to question Ashley about the murders of Raheem and Iesha. Ty had a huge issue with that. He didn't mess with the police.

He looked at the clock and knew Kiara kids were in school, which would have given them some much-needed alone time.

He heard Ashley turn on the shower and knew it was now or never to leave. He hated how she always questioned him and wanted to know where they stood. He couldn't wait until her apartment was ready, and she went back to work. She was working his nerves.

"Baby, I'mma about to take care of some business. I'll be back in a little while!" Ty yelled.

"Okay!" Ashley replied and waited for the front door to close.

She jumped out the shower fully clothed and hurried out the front door. She had to catch up to Ty to see where he was going.

*Whew!* She inwardly screamed. She worked up a sweat damn near jogging trying to follow Ty. He was a fast walker and more fit than she was.

Ty rounded the corner to building nine and Ashley ducked behind a large bush. *Get it together, Ash. He's probably just about to sell some weed.* She encouraged herself to stay calm. All that went out the window the second Ashley heard a woman's voice yell, *"Just a second."*

Her hands began to tremble. Her pain was evident and etched across her face. Tears made their way down her cheek as she watched the love of her life publicly display a sign of affection.

"Hi, baby!" Kiara gave Ty a long kiss in the doorway.

Ashley wondered if she should confront Ty and Kiara or just leave things alone and leave Ty for good. Her ego and petty side wouldn't allow that, and before Ashley knew it, she began taking photos of Ty and Kiara.

She thought about confronting Ty with the photos later but thought what good would that do. He would just call her all kinds of "crazy bitches" for following him.

She decided she would vent her anger elsewhere and posted the photos in *Whose Man Is This Sis* with the caption reading: *Look at this shit. This is the type of trash ass bitches Austin have. I have told Kiara that Ty was my man. She continues to disrespect me, so I'mma about to beat this hoe ass.*

Members began commenting on the the post Ashley made. Some were encouraging her to go live, while others took up for Kiara calling Ashley dumb, desperate, and pathetic.

"Pathetic," Ashley whispered pissed off. Pathetic was definitely something she was not.

These women didn't know her, so how dare they judge her and call her names. She was the victim. How dare they take up for Kiara and not her?

Ashley wasn't having it. When she heard the apartment door close, she began recording live in the group. "Yeah! I'm at the bitch Kiara's house now. She's about to see what time it is!" Ashley yelled while pounding her fist on the door. Comments began hyping her up, and her live stream went from 100 views to 1,500 views in a matter of seconds.

She wasn't a fighter, and she prayed Kiara wasn't either. She would die if she got her ass whooped on a live video. Austin would never play that shit down.

She banged on Kiara's front door.

"Who is it?" Kiara angrily shouted attempting to look through the blocked peephole. *Boom, boom, boom, boom!* Ashley continued to bang.

Kiara swung the front door open, and Ashley locked onto her like a vicious pit bull. She wasn't letting up.

Ty attempted to pull Ashley off Kiara, but she was too heavy. "Man you tripping. Get off her, Ashley. The fuck is wrong with you? Is you following a nigga?" he asked out of breath.

"Ty, I trusted you," Ashley cried.

She picked her phone up and turned the camera on Ty.

"Fuck you, Ty. You told me you weren't messing with her. You lied to me. This bitch lives in the same complex apartment. Why have me at your apartment if you knew you were going to sneak over here? That's fucked up!" Ashley screamed.

"The fuck you got that camera in my face for? You tripping." Ty helped Kiara off the floor.

"That man doesn't want you. Go home with yo fat ass!" Erica yelled.

"Y'all see this shit? See how these niggas lie. They ain't shit." Ashley sniffled while looking in the camera. "Never trust these niggas out here. They're for everybody."

"Bitch!" Kiara screamed, pulling Ashley's new lace front wig. The wig came off leaving Ty stuck between anger and laughter.

"Ayooo!" he yelled distracting Ashley leaving her open and caught off guard.

Larry got word through his little cousin that Kiara and his children were staying in Travis Station Apartments, and that she was still messing around with Ty Jackson. He didn't want to believe it, but it was true.

He had been following Kiara and her Aunt Erica all morning, and now he was parked outside of her apartment, looking through her window. Her blinds were open giving Larry a full view of her living room.

He smoked on his blunt while listening to ZRO "I Hate You Bitch". That was exactly how he was feeling about Kiara. She had disrespected him by messing with another man.

Everyone in Austin knew not to mess with him or his women. Kiara was his, and she was off limits. He had been her first, last, and only. He didn't care how many women he slept with, Kiara was his and only his.

He wondered who leased the apartment she was in and how she had the resources to move. Everything in the apartment from where Larry was sitting looked brand new and Larry knew Kiara was broke. He made sure of that.

Throughout the years, he purposefully blocked any chances of Kiara working or moving ahead. It always amazed him how she somehow always got on her feet with their children. Her homes were always nice and clean. Kiara never had much furniture, but she always made what little she had work. She always had a house full of good food, and their children stayed dressed and looking nice.

Kiara was resourceful and smart. Larry didn't like that one bit. He purposely trapped her with his children to keep her indebted to him. He cut down on her having friends and really didn't want her having contact with her family. Somehow, though, she always proved to him that she didn't need him.

Larry had put her out in the cold before, beat her, and did all he could to break her; but she always came back stronger and with a fight in her. The only thing he hadn't done was put her on the hoe strip or dope her up. He had thought about doing that to her many times but didn't want another man inside of her. His anger flared thinking of her being with another man. He exhaled while watching her smoke weed talking to Erica. He was pissed at the choice in clothing she wore. Kiara knew to always cover up.

After an hour of watching her, he pulled out his phone and called her. He watched as she rolled her eyes and ignored his call. He was done playing her. He reached in the glove compartment for his gun and checked to see if it was fully loaded.

As soon as he opened his car door, he saw Ty walking towards Kiara's door with a woman following closely behind him.

He closed his car door and waited to see what was going on. He watched as Ty and Kiara kissed while a short, redbone woman hid behind a brush while snapping photos. "The fuck this bitch into?" he whispered.

He gripped the gun tightly while his right leg shook. His blood was boiling. He couldn't believe Kiara and this nigga Ty would openly disrespect him after he had warned the both of them.

Larry didn't know who the other woman was and she wasn't even his beef, but today she would be at the wrong place at the wrong time. He sat for a moment and wondered how he should approach the situation. If he opened fire on Kiara, he would have to kill three other people as well.

"Fuck it!" he yelled, exiting his vehicle.

Larry could hear the commotion the closer he got to Kiara's apartment. The door was wide open, and Larry could see the redbone chick throwing punches. He shook his head. Kiara could never fight but stayed in shit.

*Click, Click!*

"Now that I got y'all fucking attention. Nigga, didn't I tell you my bitch was off limits?" Larry pointed the gun at Ty.

"Ahhhhh!" the ladies screamed.

"Nigga I suggest you use that bitch if you're going to point it at me," Ty said unbothered.

"Just leave, please," Erica begged.

*POW!*

He shot Erica between the eyes. Blood splatter rested on Kiara's face and shirt. Erica's body dropped instantly making a loud thumping sound. Ashley and Kiara both screamed, and Kiara dropped to the floor cradling her dead aunt's body.

"What have you done? Why?" she cried.

"Kiara, this is how you repay me?" Larry yelled.

"Repay you with what? You did this to me. You stole my youth. You trapped me. My life has been hell since the day I met you. You never loved me. You used my father's death against me. You played with my mind, my heart, and my soul. This was all a game to you. You only wanted to control me. I hate you. I hate everything about you. I just wanna be free. I want you to leave me alone. I don't need you or love you!" Kiara sobbed uncontrollably while rocking back and forth with her Aunt's body.

"You heard what she said."

"What? Hoe ass nigga."

*POW!*

He shot Ty.

"Arghhhhh fuck!" Ty moaned, holding his stomach. "You bitch!" Ty lunged at Larry.

*POW!*

Larry shot him again causing Ty to fall.

"Kiara, I'm sorry ma," Ty said with a mouth full of blood. He began shaking until his body laid still.

"Noooooo!" Ashley screamed. She kneeled down and cupped Ty's face.

*POW!*

Larry shot Ashley. She fell forward, and her body rested beside Ty.

"Get the fuck up now, bitch." Larry yanked Kiara by her braids.

She fought with him while he threw her on the sofa. He viciously punched her over and her again causing her screams to get caught in her throat. "Take your fucking clothes off."

"You don't have to do this," Kiara cried weakly standing.

"Nawl bitch, you wanna be a hoe, so I'mma treat you like one!" he roared.

Kiara removed her clothing while Larry unzipped his pants. He slapped her across the face causing her to fall back on the sofa. He roughly turned her over and rammed his massive large dick into her anus. She yelped out in pain, and her body instantly jerked.

"Turn over and suck my dick," Larry ordered.

Kiara could see his manhood covered in her blood and feces. She gagged, and tears ran down her face. She was humiliated and embarrassed. She looked up at Larry, and all she saw were dark, cold eyes staring back at her.

"Open your mouth, bitch!" Larry roared.

Kiara did as she was told and bit down as hard as she could. *POW!* Larry shot her in the head, instantly killing her.

Ashley tried not to scream. She had lost a lot of blood but knew she had to play dead if she wanted to make it out alive. Ashley was so upset with herself for being in this situation. Ty wasn't worth losing her life over, and she couldn't believe that she had allowed herself to go down a slippery slope of lust, lies, denial, and betrayal.

She didn't know how much longer she was going to be able to withstand the pain or bleeding. She felt lightheaded and started to feel herself drifting. She prayed to God to send her help and just when it seemed as though he had given up on her, she could hear them.

"We have one still alive with a faint pulse," an EMT announced.

W*hat am I'm doing?* Yashira silently thought. She rolled over and laid on her back. She stared up at the ceiling, disappointed that she made love in another woman's bed.

"Good morning, beautiful." Hassan smiled while kissing her on her cheek.

"Good morning. This was a bad idea. I don't know what I was thinking." Yashira sat up in the bed.

Hassan had been released from the hospital and, he was able to get Yashira to stay over with him in his and Nova's home due to his cunning, manipulative ways.

"What's the matter, baby?" Hassan asked.

"Everything. I can smell her. Her perfume is embedded in these sheets. Hassan, I don't like this. It doesn't feel right. I'mma get ready to take Trinity to school, and I'm going to Qadira's to get ready for my mother's funeral later." Yashira got out of the bed.

Hassan jumped up, came around to where Yashira was and stood in front of her.

"Baby, we can talk about this. I can buy some new sheets. I'll even get a new bed. Listen, you, Trinity and me we're family now, just like we wanted. You can move here, and we can work something out. Just please." Hassan pleaded.

"Hassan, this is the home you shared with your wife. Why would I want to stay here? She hasn't even been gone a week, and you already have another woman in her bed."

"Since when do you care about, Nova?"

"That's not fucking fair, Hassan. I was young, damn near homeless, a stripper, and I didn't know you were married until I was already too deep in. I can't believe you. That was just hurtful."

"Baby, I'm sorry. I didn't mean it like that. I love you, Yashira. I do. Listen, go get ready for your mother's funeral and just meet me back here tonight. That way we can talk about everything."

"Okay, I can do that," Yashira agreed.

She wiggled out of Hassan's reach and rolled her eyes when she left out the bedroom. The short stroll down the hallway to Trinity's room made her uncomfortable. Photos of Nova, Trinity, and Hassan stared out her, reminding her that she was just a guest. This arrangement wasn't going to work.

"Trinity, sweetie, it's time to wake up baby," she sweetly sang.

"You want some breakfast?" Hassan asked standing in Trinity's doorway while she combed Trinity's hair.

"I do, daddy," Trinity announced.

"Is your chest and arm okay? You need to rest it."

"I'm fine, and you should know by the way I worked you last night," he teased.

"Hassan," Yashira fussed and pointed to Trinity.

"Daddy, where's mommy? She said y'all are not going to be together anymore and that mommy is going to be my mommy now."

"Well, that's true, pumpkin. You're with your mother now, and Nova won't be around anymore."

"But-but-but what about my little brother or sister?" Trinity asked sadly.

Yashira looked away. She was feeling out of place and like a third party. She knew Trinity would have to get used to her, but she wondered if she could fill Nova's shoes. A piece of her knew she would always live in her shadow.

They ate breakfast, and Yashira dropped Trinity off at school. She was happy Hassan didn't come and allowed her to have space with her daughter, for that short timeframe. All of this was so unreal to her. She dreamt of this moment for years. It was bittersweet though because the man she thought she saw in Hassan years ago wasn't who he was today.

She pulled off with Nova in her thoughts and humbled herself. She was thankful that Nova gave her an opportunity to know her daughter. She had done such a great job raising her, and although Yashira was grateful, she wouldn't do a thing differently. She knew the moment she saw Nova that Trinity would be in good hands.

She made a left turn and sighed loudly. Today was the day of her mother's funeral, and she didn't want to go. She hated her mother, and she honestly didn't care that she was dead. The only reason she was going was to support her sister, and even then, Yashira didn't know how to feel about that.

She quickly showered and dressed. She did a once over in the mirror and stared at the reflection staring back at her. She was torn and all over the place. Her phone chimed, and she saw that it was a message from Hassan. She suspired and thought about Nova. It was something about Nova's broken spirit and sad eyes that taunted her.

Nova's words from the hospital constantly played in her mind. She asked herself if she really wanted to get tangled in his web again. She resented Hassan when he chose his wife all those years ago. The way he gaslighted her and promised her security, only for him to abandon her, in the end, took her a long time to heal from. Honestly, she still didn't think she was over everything Hassan put her through.

"You ready, sis?" Qadira asked, knocking on Yashira's bedroom door. Yashira opened the door and smiled.

"Not really but it's time."

"Well, you look really pretty. Aunt Clara called and said they are at the funeral home already waiting on us."

"I hope her fake ass don't start all that hollering and shit. Ugh! I really don't want to be around these people."

"Sis, I know. Honestly, me either. I just feel if we don't go, we'll regret it years later."

"Nah! Sis, never mind. Come on. Let's go before I change my mind," Yashira huffed.

The two rode in silence. They were both lost in their own thoughts. When they arrived at the funeral home, Yashira's stomach began to turn. She began sucking on her thumb, a childhood habit that she never broke when she was nervous.

"I see you still do that." Qadira laughed. "Sis, it's going to be okay. I won't let nobody hurt you." Qadira squeezed her knee.

"What the fuck is he doing here?" Yashira whispered, seeing her mother's boyfriend. She instantly began shaking.

She thought of all the times he sexually abused her and the smirk he permanently wore every time her mother would call her "fast". She hated him, and her mood instantly changed. She didn't want to be there.

She spotted her Aunt Clara walking towards their vehicle and rolled her eyes. Her aunt was another one that she couldn't stand. All these people in her family stood back and watched her be mistreated and did nothing. She had nothing to say to them.

"Y'all come on. Damn! It's about time y'all got here, got me in there muthafucka waiting!" Aunt Clara yelled waiting by the car. Yashira rolled her eyes and smacked her lips.

"I can't stand this White Diamond perfume wearing hoe. I'm telling you to handle your auntie Q because if her old ass gets out of pocket, trust and believe I won't spare her feelings," Yashira warned.

"I hear you! Sis, come on. Let's get through this." Qadira reached to grab Yashira's hand.

"I don't think I can do this. It's too much pain. I hate her." Yashira broke down. Qadira wiped her tears and sat with Yashira in the car for an additional five minutes.

"Come on, shit." Aunt Clara grabbed the car door handle, opening Yashira's car door.

Yashira got out of the car facing her aunt. She took in all her features and thought how much her aunt had aged. *That Hennessy is fucking her up.*

"So you're just going to stand there? Hug your auntie and stop acting like a stuck up bitch." Aunt Clara grabbed Yashira tightly.

"I'm good on you." Yashira pulled back.

"Good on me?" Aunt Clara pointed at herself. "You know what?" Aunt Clara was cut off.

"Come on guys; let's walk inside." Qadira defused the storm that was silently building.

♥♥♥♥♥

Yashira stared at the casket of her mother the entire ceremony. Everyone around her, including Qadira was shedding tears. She felt apathy. Her anger wouldn't let her feel anything for her mother. She had been dead to Yashira many years ago.

"My sister! Oh lawdddd, my sister! Bring her back. God, why did you take my sister?" Aunt Clara cried, making a scene.

"Fake ass bitch," Yashira whispered, and Qadira tapped her leg.

"What?" Yashira asked.

She stiffened when family and friends came around to view the body. She hated when anyone touched her or reached to shake her hand. It was all bullshit to her.

"Oh, Vanetta! I'm so sorry. I love you!" Madea hollered out, and Yashira threw her head back. She couldn't take much more of this nonsense.

She couldn't deal with people and their fake ass drama. Madea was another one Yashira didn't care for. She remembered trying to tell Madea what her mother's boyfriend did, and Madea actually had the nerve to tell her to pray for his demons. *His demons? What about her?*

"Netta baby, I miss you, and I'm sorry," Bart their mother's boyfriend cried. He turned towards Qadira and Yashira with his arms out.

"Bitch, get the fuck away from me. You dirty bastard!" Yashira screamed, causing everyone to gasp and grab their chest in shock.

"I'm sorry," Bart expressed and went to take a seat.

Yashira's right leg shook, and the movie *Woman Thou Art Loosed* came to the front of her mind when Michelle shot and killed Reggie. If she had a pistol, she would have pulled it out and shot Bart. She saw red.

"I'm ready to go. I can't do too much more of these grimy niggas," she whispered harshly to Qadira.

The funeral wrapped up quickly, and Yashira went to stand by Qadira's car. She wasn't about to skin and grin with these people.

"We're going to the burial and afterwards to Aunt Clara house," Qadira informed, approaching Yashira.

"Nah, you go ahead. I'll just call an Uber or Hassan." Yashira looked away.

"I'm sorry, sis. I should have respected your boundaries. You said you didn't want to come, and I selfishly forced your hand, disregarding your feelings. I know seeing Bart was a trigger," she cried.

"It's cool, sis. I just got to get out of here." Yashira walked away, dialing Hassan.

He wasn't far away because he was already on his way to support her at the funeral. "Aww thank you, Hassan." Yashira smiled at the bouquet of red roses and card that Hassan had given her.

"You're welcome, baby. I'm sorry I missed it. How are you holding up?"

"You didn't miss anything. I hate I came. I'm ready to get out of here." She placed her seatbelt on.

She stared out the window as Hassan drove and felt suffocated. *Ugh! Why did I call him, instead of Uber? I need to be alone!*

Hassan wasn't on her good list either. She didn't trust him. He was over accommodating, too eager, and something was telling her to stay far away from him. She really wanted to get to know her daughter but felt Hassan kept making things about him, about them, and Yashira really wasn't on that.

The night he came home from the hospital, he kept interfering with their time. Yashira felt he was selfish. He already knew her daughter, and she wanted a chance to get to know her without feeling like it was a supervised visit or some type of family bonding.

Yashira also peeped how Nova was the breadwinner and the one who financially held things down. Yashira would never do that, especially not with a grown ass man. She had her own money, a nice vehicle, good job, and her mother left her money. She wasn't hurting for anything, and she'd be damn if she got with Hassan and be burdened carrying him and his family. She was very aware of Erica, Kiara, and others like that. She wasn't interested in filling Nova's position.

For years Yashira dreamt of this very moment with Hassan, but after seeing the devastation he caused, all she felt was apathy. She realized all this time what she once felt was limerence. However, the reality was Hassan wasn't right for her and no matter how hard he tried, she would always wonder if he would disrespect her the way he had Nova all those years. There was a saying, *"how you get them is how you lose them."* Yashira believed it.

"You okay, baby? I know laying your mother to rest must have been hard, but ever since I've been released from the hospital and we've made love, you've been withdrawn from me. Did I do or say something wrong? Hassan asked compassionately.

Yashira rolled her eyes. This is what she was talking about. Hassan thought everything was about him. He hasn't asked her one time how she felt about seeing Trinity. It was all about him attempting to make her comfortable with him, but he was forgetting the fact she hadn't seen her daughter all this time. He kept forcing himself on her and almost dominating the situation to his benefit. If he thought for one second she wanted to play Nova's role, he was wrong.

"Hassan, I really have a lot on my mind. If you don't mind, I really would like to take Trinity to Qadira and my place for some one on one time. I really would like to get to know my daughter."

"Why does it feel like you're trying to push me to the side? I thought being a family and being together was what we wanted. Why can't you just move in the house or we go get a place together to raise our child?"

Yashira wanted to answer his question, but they pulled up to Trinity's school. She smiled seeing her baby laughing and playing with her three little cousins and two other pretty little girls.

"Mommy2 and daddy!" she screamed, running to the vehicle, opening the door.

"Daddy, can my friends Mina and Mecca come over?" she asked placing her hands together pleading.

"Not today, baby. Maybe this weekend. Uh, Larry Jr., where's your mom at?" Hassan asked looking around. It wasn't like Kiara to not be on time.

"I don't know. I keep calling her on the phone you brought me. She's not answering, Grandma Erica either. They dropped us off this morning. I'm hungry. Can we come with you?" Larry Jr. asked.

"Yayyyy, please daddy?" Trinity asked.

"Yeah! Come on." Hassan sighed.

"Yayyyyy!" all the children yelled and jumped in the back seat.

Yashira shot daggers at Hassan. She crossed her arms and thought about how inconsiderate he was of her feelings. Her mother just passed, and even though she didn't like the woman, she still would have liked a hug and understanding. *Why would he invite all these kids?* She angrily fussed.

She frowned thinking how once again time alone with her daughter was stolen. Instead of being able to ask Trinity about her day, help her with homework, and cook, Yashira now had a total of four children.

She wasn't feeling this. She should have just caught an Uber home. Nova's home made her uncomfortable, and she wasn't even going to speak on the millions of family photos that Hassan hadn't even attempted to move or take down.

Her phone beeped, and she saw a message from her sister. She replied setting off a chain of back and forth messages.

"Who is that?" Hassan asked in a jealous tone.

"Huh?" Yashira frown.

"Who are you texting back and forth? Smiling and shit."

"Uh, it's not that deep," Yashira sassed and placed her phone in her purse.

When Hassan pulled up to his home, Yashira suspired, and she didn't move at all. She watched as the children ran to the front door.

Hassan grabbed his door handle, but stopped once he noticed the displeased look on Yashira's face. He was getting really aggravated with her. He couldn't read her, and he didn't understand the sudden changes. She was sending him mixed signals. One minute she's crying saying she loved and missed him all these years, to now seemly interested in Trinity only.

"What's the issue, Yazzi?"

"Please don't call me that." She looked out the window.

"Well, are you coming in?"

"Yeah, just give me a minute. I'll be in there in a few. It's been a long day. I just need some time."

"Well, why don't you come in, and we can take a bath together and talk about it."

"Hassan, that's the thing. I just need to sort out my feelings. This doesn't feel right."

"What doesn't feel right, Yashira? I thought this is what we wanted, to be a family. I'm finally getting a divorce, and you can have me to yourself. What's the problem? Damn!" Hassan yelled.

"Daddy, these papers were on the door. Can I have the keys to unlock the door?" Trinity said as she knocked on the driver's window with documents in her hand.

He passed Trinity the keys and stared at the documents in disbelief. He couldn't believe Nova was actually serious and going through with this divorce. "That bitch!" he bellowed, hitting the dashboard.

Hassan looked over at Yashira and softened his mood. He loved her, but he also needed her. She was his backup plan since Nova left him. He couldn't afford the home and taking care of Trinity too.

"What's on the documents?" Yashira asked, eyeing Hassan's left hand.

"Nova filed for divorce. She gave me a 30-day eviction notice, and she's also giving me full custody of Trinity."

"Well, since she's pregnant, the judge isn't going to grant the divorce until after the baby is born. They have to do a DNA test and also hearing for child support." Yashira informed.

"She terminated the pregnancy. She actually killed my baby to be with that fuck boy lawyer of hers and had him draw up these documents."

"Well, you're over her, right? I mean that's what you say Hassan, but emotionally you're still involved with Nova, or you wouldn't be so angry right now. So, what am I Hassan, the rebound again?" Yashira cried.

"Yazzi, I mean Yashira, don't do that baby. You know I love you."

"Listen, go on ahead, Hassan. I'll be there in a minute." Yashira waved him off.

He looked at Yashira for a moment and bit down on his bottom lip. She stared back with empty eyes. For the first time, she finally saw who Hassan really was, and she believed him. The rose-colored glasses were off.

She waited for a few minutes when he exited the vehicle before she let out a loud sob. Her phone began buzzing.

"Hey, Q!" she cried. "You must have felt my energy."

272

"I just made it home and saw you weren't here. Are you okay, sis?" Qadira asked taking her heels off and taking a seat of the sofa.

"No, not really. I just don't know sis. I love him, but I can't do this. You were right about him," Yashira cried.

"Sis, what's going on? Where are you?"

"I'm with Hassan but sis, I can't do this. We just had a fallen out, and I just want to leave, but I feel like I have to be careful because I don't want him to take Trinity from meee!" Yashira broke down.

"Sis, calm down and tell me what's going on."

"You were right, Q." Yashira sniffled. "Hassan is a user. I thought he and I could have something, but not like this. He has it in his mind that since Nova is gone, I can move into the home, and we can be this family. I thought that's what I wanted, but he's selfish, and after Nova broke down about everything he put her through, I realized I don't want to be her. She's broken. He hasn't even allowed me to bond with Trinity. He keeps interfering with our time, making it about him and inserting himself in our conversations every time. Q, he already knows her and I'm trying to build my own bond with her. I just feel overwhelmed and disgusting too. I had sex with him in their bed, and I just feel really low. Hassan thinks I don't see through his shit. He has nowhere to go. Nova gave him 30 days to be out the home and sis. You should have heard his mother Erica and Hassan plotting ways to get money out of Nova. He has put her through hell," Yashira vented. "Oh my god sis, why is he watching me through the window?" she yelled.

"You need me to come over there?" Qadira asked.

"No, sis, I just needed to get that off my chest. I'll be there later. I love you and thank you for listening."

"Anytime." They hung up.

Yashira exited the car and froze when a dark blue crown Vic pulled into the driveway behind Hassan's vehicle.

"We're looking for Hassan Daniels." Detective Eric sternly said.

Hassan saw the two men and stormed through the front door. "Is there any reason you two clowns are on my property?" Hassan yelled. He was no stranger to Detectives Eric and Lu.

"Hassan, we're sorry to inform you. There has been a shooting. Your mother, Kiara, and Ty are all dead.

B o stared at the address on the piece of paper Mike gave him and looked up to make sure he was in the right spot. He silently plotted his move while he sat outside of Kensington's condo. He groaned with anger when he realized he forgot to bring the pistol that was in the lockbox.

Kensington's front door opened, and Bo slouched down in his seat. He peeked over the dashboard and frowned.

"Girls let's go, we're going to be late!" he heard Kensington yell.

"What the fuck? Who are they?" Bo whispered as he watched Kensington, a fair-skinned chick, and two little girls climbed inside of a white Tahoe.

Bo followed closely behind Kensington. She dropped off the two little girls at school and drove to a hair store. He wanted to run up on Kensington then, but a cop car sat across the street from the supply store.

"Fuck!" Bo yelled, looking at his gas tank.

His funds were running low, and he knew he didn't have enough gas to follow her back to Round Rock. "I'mma get you soon bitch, just watch!" he bellowed backing out of the parking lot of the beauty supply store.

He stopped by Waffle House and ordered an egg omelet, two pecan waffles, hash brown, bacon, and apple juice before he got gas and retreated to his hotel room.

As he ate his breakfast, the news ran the clip about Raheem and Iesha Gold's murder. "This bitch is so sneaky and clever!" he yelled, referring to Kensington.

He knew Kensington the one was who committed the murders. She had a white Tahoe, and he knew she had motive. Torrie had told Bo all about Kensington and Raheem's relationship.

Nicole's phone rung and Bo frowned. "What the fuck?"

He stood and walked over to the phone. It displayed a weird number, and Bo knew it had to be some kind of bill collector. He sat back on the bed when his own cell phone began ringing. He hurried to answer the call.

"Bo, did you get it?" Torrie asked.

"She got to it before me, but don't worry. I know where she stays." He slurped down his apple juice.

"Let me worry about her. I got one better," Torrie whispered. "I don't have a lot of time. One of the guards is allowing me to use her phone, but check this out. I have a policy on Kensington, Kinley, and Lisa. They're $250,000 each." Torrie smiled.

"Oh yeah!" Bo asked, rubbing his hands. "Kensington got too many people around her, so she may be a challenge to get to right now. I would have to track Lisa down in a crack house, but how can I get to Kinley?"

"Kinley will be your best bet. She's at The Wren's Supportive Living Center. Security there is light from what I can remember. Say you're her father Raheem. Kensington has Raheem name listed as a visitor in case he ever wanted to see her. Nobody knows that the Raheem that was killed on the news was Kinley's father. Where a cap or hoodie. Avoid the camera in the main lobby. Kinley's room is at the end. The fifth door on the right. Don't unplug anything. It'll set off an alarm, but you know what to do. I gotta go, here comes the guard for her phone. Love you, baby." Torrie quickly hung up.

Bo threw on some gray sweats with a black hoodie. He grabbed Nicole's car keys and headed for the center. When he made a right turn, he noticed a dark blue crown Vic heading towards the hotel. He didn't think anything of it.

♥♥♥♥♥

"The bastard didn't take the bait." Detective Lu said. He had dialed Nicole's cell phone to see if Bo would be stupid enough to answer it.

He and Detective Eric parked in front of the hotel and looked around for Nicole's champagne colored four-door Altima. They didn't see it.

"He isn't here," Detective Lu said, entering the hotel behind Detective Eric.

"Hi, Detective Eric Washington and Lu Staples. We're looking for a residence you may have housed here by the name of Bobby "Bo" Jackson. We have a search warrant." Detective Eric flashed his badge to the front desk receptionist.

"Give me a second," Natalie nervously said. "Let me see if I can pull up anyone by the name." She paused. "What's this about?" Natalie asked.

"Police business ma'am. Do you have him here?" Detective Lu rudely asked.

"Yes, I see here we do. He's in Room 315. I'll walk you gentlemen up in case Mr. Jackson isn't in the room, right this way."

Detective Lu knocked twice on Bo's door with no answer. "If you're looking for the gentleman who has been staying in that room, he left about 20 minutes ago," a hotel guest said.

Natalie opened the door and returned to the front desk. She wondered what Bo had done that required a warrant to search his room.

Detectives Eric and Lu entered in Bo's room with their guns drawn. "Bobby Jackson, we have a warrant!" they shouted. When they noticed that the coast was clear, they placed on gloves and began searching Bo's room.

"Look what we have here." Detective Lu picked up the .22 caliber handgun.

"Bag it," Detective Eric said happily.

"Hey, look what I found over here." Detective Lu held up Nicole's wallet and phone.

"Well, I'll be damn."

"What do you think we're going to find on this phone?" Detective Lu asked.

"We're about to find out. Thank God it doesn't have a password on it." Detective Eric commented.

They strolled through Nicole's phone and landed in *Whose Man Is This Sis*. The live video that Ashley had recorded was playing, and Detective Lu and Eric watched the live stream with their mouths agape.

They watched and listened to the live stream until the end, frustrated that they couldn't see a clear visual on the male assailant but could on hear his voice.

"Got damn it!" Detective Eric bellowed.

As they attempted to view the live stream again, but the video was blocked, and the group was no longer available.

"Hey, Amber! What's going on with the group? We're trying to access it from Nicole's phone, and she's locked out," Detective Lu informed.

"I can't get in it. They can't trace the IP either. The group has been deleted," Amber informed.

"I need you to have Sarah, put a trace on Nicole's vehicle. When you find it, have Nissan disable the engine."

Bo nervously signed into the visitor's log and made his way back to Kinley's room. He smirked at how easy it was to get into the center. The staff was lazy, overweight, consumed with the latest gossip, and not paying attention.

He quietly shut Kinley's door and walked over to where she was. He bit down on his bottom lip attempting to calm his nerves. Everything in him was telling him to leave. He had two little girls of his own, and although he hasn't been present or seen them as of late, he couldn't imagine anyone harming them.

A single tear rolled from his left eye. Kinley looked up at him with her one good eye and Bo could feel her begging him not to harm her. He walked away and then went back over to her. He took his right hand and placed it over her face. "I can't do this," he whispered, removing his hand.

He stared at all the plugs and guilt consumed him. He didn't want to harm Kinley, but he felt she was his only option to make it out. "I'm sorry. Please forgive me," he said before suffocating little Kinley to death.

He smoothly hurried at the center without incident. Once he made it back to Nicole's vehicle, it wouldn't start. The engine had been locked. "Fuck!" Bo yelled. He saw a bus coming and ran to jump on it.

His phone rang, and he saw it was Natalie from the front desk calling. "What's up beautiful?" Bo asked in a rush tone.

"Bo, two detectives just came by here looking for you. They had a search warrant to search your room. They just left," she informed.

"Damn! All my shit is still in the room." Bo sighed.

"What's going on?"

"I don't know, man. I have no clue why they would have a search warrant for me. I haven't done anything. Look, Natalie, I need your help ma. I know you say you cut for a nigga, and I need to know if that's true." Natalie paused for a second.

"Yeah, I got you. What you need?" Natalie asked.

"Shit for starters a ride. My car broke down. A nigga ain't got no money or a place to go. All my shit at the room."

"Where are you? I'm clocking out."

"I'm heading towards Capital Plaza, just meet me at the Ross. I'll be outside beautiful, and please get my shit out of the room for me."

"I got you. Wait so does this mean we're official now? I mean I know we just met, but are we together?" she asked.

"Yeah, baby! A nigga cut for you," Bo lied.

"Okay, see you soon, baby."

Bo hung up the phone and took a seat on an outside bench on the side of Ross. "Man that was too easy. Black women are easy as fuck. All a nigga gotta do is slang some dick and tell them what they wanna hear. That's cold, boy."

He watched as bystanders walked to the stores minding their business. He frowned his nose up a couple of times at plus size women who walked by. Bo couldn't stand to see large women, mainly because his mother was large. She was one of those proud, big women, and Bo admitted she kept herself nice. It was all good until her health began to decline. Bo couldn't understand why she wouldn't lose the weight or workout. She ended up getting bigger and bigger until her weight and complications ultimately took her life.

He felt big women were a disgrace, but he loved targeting them and preying on them because he felt they were easy, just like Natalie. She was a cute girl to him, but her weight was a turn-off. However, he knew he needed a backup plan, and she took the bait. A little attention had Natalie screaming Bo's name in a matter of two hours.

His phone chimed with a text from Natalie letting him know she was coming around the corner from Walgreens. He stood and walked the sidewalk to meet her at her car.

"Hey, baby." He leaned over to kiss her. She smiled, and Bo knew he had found his next victim to leech off of.

"Sistahs, y'all got a couple of dollars to spare a brotha? I'm just trying to get something to eat," a man called out to Bella and Kissy as they were exiting the beauty supply store.

"Bella, just keep walking. I can't stand these niggas. Every time they call you sistah they want something, always begging and shit!" Kissy spat.

"Kensington, he sounds familiar." Bella stopped and turned around.

"Bella, come on. Ugh! These begging ass niggas get on my nerves. I swear." Kissy fussed pulling out her car keys from her purse.

"It's dad!" Bella exhaled. Kissy stopped walking and turned around.

"Dad!" she exclaimed while her eyebrows danced.

A lonely tear slipped from her left eye. The last time that she'd seen her father he was healthy, tall, and good looking with smooth skin. He always reminded her of the actor Rockmond Dunbar, but the man before her now was a shell of who he used to be.

"Yeah! Hey girls. You gone hug your old man?" he asked, extending his arms.

Bella and Kissy looked at one another, then back at James and gave him a quick hug. Bella gagged from his body odor. She attempted to hold the vomit that crept up in the back of her throat, but she couldn't, causing her to regurgitate on the sidewalk. "I don't feel too well," she whined, wiping her mouth with the back of her hand.

"You look just like Sandy. She would be proud. It's good seeing you," he said, scratching. "You got some change for your old man?" he asked, begging again.

"Ugh! Kensington, come on!" Bella angrily yelled, pulling Kissy by her arm.

They sat in the Tahoe staring at their father, who was now harassing two other black women that went into the hair store.

"That's fucking sad. Our mothers and father ain't shit. I just wanna get the fuck away from here. Austin is nothing but a painful vicious cycle. I just want my girls to experience a life of happiness and stability. I feel like I'm suffocating here. Now, I got this legal shit on my back and pregnant with this nigga's baby. I just feel I'm never gonna make it," Bella cried.

"That's not true, Bella. You will be fine. You have me now, and I won't let anything happen to you or my nieces. As far as me though, I don't know." Kissy sighed.

"What do you mean?" Bella asked looking over at Kissy.

"I think I may be in trouble Bella. I have to see how everything is going to turn out."

"Does this have something to do with Raheem and Iesha's murder?" Bella asked. Kissy looked out the window. "Look, I'm not judging you. I've killed before too," Bella confessed.

"What?" Kissy asked shocked.

"Yes, my pimp Rick and two other working girls. I poisoned them and burned down the house. I robbed him. That was the only way I could escape with my girls."

"So you're the one who murdered him?"

"Yes, and I'll do it again. Sometimes you feel you have to do what you have to do." Bella shrugged.

"Yeah, well it was me. I don't know what came over me. I was fine that day, and then I saw Iesha and followed her. I waited for hours outside their home. I swear I was about to leave, but then he showed up. Something in me broke all over again, and before I knew it, I was pulling the trigger."

"Honestly, I get why you did it. I can see why you killed that nigga after seeing Kinley and knowing how Raheem turned his back on you. Aht, Aht. You not about to live all nice, while I'm struggling and my child is sick. No sir." Bella crossed her arms.

"There's more Bella," Kissy confessed.

"There is?" Bella frowned.

"I stole Torrie's money, and once Hassan finds out that I'm Kissy, it's going to be over for me. His daughter knows who I am."

"Kensington, I'm going to propose something, and I want you to hear me out."

"Okay, what is it?"

"What if we changed our identities and left the state?" Bella proposed.

"And go where?"

"Anywhere. I have a friend name Juan that will get us passports, birth certificates, and an ID for five grand apiece. He can even switch out this Tahoe and the color if you want him to. He has a chop shop."

"Fuck it. Let's do it. Can we get them done now?" Kissy asked.

"Hell yeah!"

"Call him," Kissy instructed.

As Bella made the phone call to Juan, Kissy's phone beeped. She checked her notifications and entered into her private group. She flinched, watching the video that Ashley posted. "What the fuck?" she cried, covering her mouth.

She thought back to the day Kiara posted about Larry and Ty. She put two and two together and knew the guy doing the shooting had to be Larry, even though she couldn't see his face.

"Kensington, okay he said we're good and to come through," Bella announced, hanging up the phone. "Oh my god! What's wrong?" she asked, and Kissy passed her the phone.

Bella studied the video and became visibly upset. This is why she never joined her sister's group because things like the video were triggering for her. She closed out the video and clicked on a member by the name of Amber and sighed. Shaking her head and laughing, she passed Kissy back her phone.

"Sis you have to get rid of that group, your phone, and laptop. A murder has been committed. They're going to track the IP address, and you'll be charged with some type of internet felony. I'm pretty sure of it. Next time, do your research before accepting people in the group. That chick Amber is the fucking police."

"What? How you know that?" Kissy asked alarmed.

"She interviewed me once about a murder on the south side. Listen, I don't know if you're aware Kensington, but your group is everywhere. Too much shit has happened and now this. I'm sure they're on to you with Amber in the group. If they aren't, they will be soon. Delete the group, sis," Bella urged.

"You're right," Kissy admitted. "I wish I could see the man's face in the video. I'm pretty sure it's Larry though."

"That's exactly who that is," Bella informed.

"That's fucked up." Kissy sighed. "I work with that chick Ashley. If she's still alive, I already know the police will be questioning her. Ugh! I don't wanna let my group go. This bitch be jumping, but here it goes," she pouted, deleting the Facebook group and deactivating her personal page.

"Delete everything off your phone and laptop. Here give it to me. I'll do it while we drive. I'm ready to get the fuck away from here. Dad is a waste. Look at him begging and shit." Bella pointed. "Ugh! I hate him and my mother. The shit is sad to watch, man," Bella cried.

"I know. I just don't even feel anything anymore. I'm so numb."

"Me too. The only thing that keeps me going is Mina, Mecca, and now you. I just wanna be happy and free of pain." Bella dried her face. "Anyway, Juan lives in Dove Springs."

"Cool. I can swing by Ryan's afterwards to do her hair. Everything is in the same area." Kissy said, backing up. She took one last look at James and shook her head before pulling off.

"You probably should get new devices. After I delete everything, I'm going to power them off. You need to get rid of these," Bella warned.

"I will. It's nothing anyway. They aren't in my name. It's in Hassan's name." Kissy winked. "I operated everything under his name. Even the email address is under his name.

"You're smart as fuck. My kind of bitch. No traces back to you." Bella smiled.

"I hate I'm taking a 5K loss on the condo though."

"Well, it's yours and will be there. Just throw out all the food, when we leave. It'll be good."

As Bella deleted everything off the phone and laptop, Kissy thought about her daughter. Something was bothering her, and she couldn't figure it out. It was as if she could hear her daughter Kinley calling out to her. She kept getting a feeling something bad was going to happen.

She remained silent for the rest of the drive to Juan's home. Something wasn't right, and she could feel it, or maybe it was the guilt she was feeling for getting ready to leave Kinley behind.

"Ah, Kensington, you okay?" Bella asked, snapping her fingers.

"Huh?"

"Are we going in or were just going to sit here. You're in la la land again." Bella laughed.

"I just keep getting a funny feeling that's all."

"Well, everything is going to be all good. Juan is going to get us new paperwork, and we can kiss this miserable ass city goodbye. Come on." Bella encouraged.

"This bitch is nice," Kissy whispered to Bella admiring Juan's home. "Bitch, you have fucked him before, haven't you?" Kissy laughed.

"Mind your own bed and stay out grown sluts business." Bella winked and laughed.

Kissy was impressed with all of Juan's illegal businesses. She walked around Juan's huge garage of brand new vehicles and was able to switch her Tahoe for a Silver Suburban.

"Bitch, I told you." Bella laughed as they pulled away from Juan's home.

"This hoe is fire." Kissy hollered admiring the internal design.

She banged Cardi B's "Money" song as loud as the stereo would go, and she and Bella rapped the lyrics. "Cardi at the tip-top, bitch kiss the ring and kick rocks, sis uh!" they yelled.

"Bitch, Cardi ate that verse." Bella laughed.

They pulled up in front of Ryan's home and admired the beautiful landscape. The flower combination of pink, blue, and yellow flowers danced around the healthy watered grass. The external of the home was brown and beige with a hunter green door.

Kissy knocked on Ryan's door, and then looked behind her at Bella who seemed to be a bit distracted. "Ayo Bella, you good sis?" Kissy asked.

"Yeah, I'm just tripping. I could have sworn Tyrone has a vehicle like that." She pointed towards the brown four-door Buick.

"Oh really? Well, I don't see why he would be here."

"Yeah, I ain't tripping though. I'm cool. It probably ain't even him," Bella brushed it off.

"Heyyyy boo!" Ryan singed answering the front door, wearing a light green tank top and black boy shorts.

"Hey boo. This is my sister Bella. I hope you don't mind."

"No, you're good. It's nice to meet you. "Ryan extended her hand to shake Bella's. "Have y'all eaten? I'm cooking some asparagus, steaks, mash potatoes and a pineapple upside down cake."

"That sounds yummy." Kissy rubbed her stomach, and they laughed.

They settled down, and Kissy started on Ryan's hair. They engaged in small talk and caught up on reruns of *Love & Hip Hop: Atlanta.*

"So would y'all be able to forgive y'all husband for an outside child and still stay with the nigga?" Bella asked, referring to Kirk.

"Hell nawl. I don't see how these bitches do it. That's what happened to my sister though." Ryan said.

"What? You talking about the outside baby?" Bella asked.

"Yup!"

"So, did she leave?" Kissy asked.

"Yes, she sure did. Finally, I couldn't stand her husband. All he did was cheat and hurt her."

"What made her finally leave?" Bella asked, looking at Ryan.

"She joined this group and found out her husband was cheating with his employee and got her pregnant. Then she found out he was sleeping with another employee too. Niggas are trash. She did all she could for him, even raising his daughter as her own."

Bella looked at Kissy, and Kissy looked at her. They instantly knew who Ryan's sister was. The story was too familiar for it not to be Nova.

"Hurry up and finish this bitch's head," Bella mouthed to Kissy as soon as Ryan looked away.

The timer on Ryan's oven went off, and she jumped up to get the food out of the oven. Bella and Kissy use that opportunity to speak to each other while Ryan was away.

"Bitch, I know her ass is talking about Nova. Ask her who her sister is? Nah, watch I'mma ask her and play like my cousin work with Nova," Bella whispered.

"What y'all whispering about?" Ryan asked, coming back to take a seat. "The steak is almost ready," she confirmed.

"I was telling Kensington, that your sister story sounded so familiar," Bella said.

"Well, she should know. She's the one I'm talking about." Ryan stood. "Yeah, Kensington, Nova is my sister. The only reason I'm not tripping is because Nova has moved on. You're fucked up for what you did though," Ryan calmly said with her hands on her hip.

"Well, I'm not about to beef over no dick. I didn't know Hassan was even married. How could I? He paid for my apartment, furniture, car note, cell bill, and laptop, and took me places. What married man you know have that kind of time or money? I work with him and saw him every day. He approached me, buying me flowers and shit. I had no clue about Hassan, and nobody has even taken the time to see how I feel about any of this. I'm just labeled as some home wrecking hoe, and nobody has even heard my side, especially your sister. What's fucked up is her breaking into my home and attempting to beat my ass over Hassan. I lost my baby, and Hassan hasn't even attempted to check on me or anything. Yet I saw him booed up with Yashira at the hospital. So since you know I'm the Kensington that Hassan was messing with, you lured me here to do your hair. What you thought, you were about to whoop my ass or something?" Kissy asked.

"I didn't find out about you until the day Hassan got shot," Ryan said when her doorbell rang. She turned to answer it.

"Bitch, let's go. Fuck her and her hair with her bald-headed ass. The bitch tried to pull a fast one. I surprised that ass when I showed up too. Her ass was probably gonna try to fight you, jump you, or something. She's on some bullshit. Something is up."

"You hear that?" Kissy asked Bella.

"Yeah, it sounds like Ryan is at the door arguing with someone. I told you. This chick is on some bullshit. You can't trust these Austin bitches. Didn't you say she's over the center Kinley is at too?"

"Yeah!" Kissy confirmed and halted mid-sentence.

"Move! Bitch I know he's here. Move!" Dedra pushed past Ryan.

"You got ten seconds to leave before I call the police!" Ryan yelled.

"Tyrone! Tyrone, bring your bitch ass out here. I know you're here!" Dedra screamed.

"First of all Tyrone isn't here. His car is broke, and he took mine to run to Home Depot. I want you to leave. Second of all the only reason he is here is because I'm his supervisor, and he had nowhere else to go." Ryan stood in Dedra's face.

"That's a weak ass bitch move to show up at another woman's home!" Bella bellowed.

"Bitch, I will whoop your ass. I knew you looked familiar. You're the ugly bitch my husband is messing with. I found your pictures of your stinky ass pussy in my man's inbox." Dedra charged at Bella.

"What's up, hoe? Come on." Bella swung.

*Whap! Whap! Whap!*

Bella learned how to fight years ago. So many times the older girls in the home would try to fight her and steal her money, especially when they came up short for Rick or "daddy" as they would have to call him. She was giving Dedra the ass whooping of her life.

Ryan and Kissy attempted to break the two up, but Bella and Dedra were like squalls of heavy driving rain. They broke Ryan's lamps, turned over furniture and broke her coffee table. She was livid. Her front door opened and Tyrone walked in dropping the bags he had in his hands.

"Oh fuck!" he yelled and shook his head.

"Tyrone, get your bitch up out of here nigga. I told you that I didn't want any drama in my home. Listen, get her and y'all get the fuck out now!." Ryan screamed.

"Ayo, chill!" Tyrone yelled, pulling Bella and Dedra apart. "The fuck is wrong with you yo? Why you tripping, Bella?"

"What nigga? I don't even know this bitch. I was here with my sister while she was doing that messy ass hoe's head." She pointed at Ryan.

"Messy?" Ryan squealed, pointing to herself.

"Yeah! Messy hoe. You knew who my sister was. You lured her over here. Man, let's go Kensington. Fuck you, Tyrone. You're a bitch. You played with me the whole time. Don't worry about me or my baby. We're good. Come on Kensington. Bella grabbed her purse.

"Baby?" Dedra ululated, looking at Tyrone with a face full of tears.

"Yeah, a baby. Come on sis." Bella grabbed Kissy's hand scudding across Ryan's living room, towards the door.

"Tyrone, I want you and Dedra out of my home. You can forget about your job muthafucka. You're fire. Now get out!" Ryan screamed.

"Breathe, Bella," Kissy said, rubbing Bella's back once they got in the Suburban.

"Ugh! That bitch got my left cheek." Bella snarled, looking through the mirror.

She set her back against the passenger seat and released her tears. "I hate men, sis. They are all the same. I wanna kill Tyrone so bad for playing with me." Bella jerked up, reaching for the glove box.

"Bella, no!" Kissy held her hands. "Not like this. We're leaving and getting out of here. Tyrone will get his when he least expects it. Be cool."

"I'm ready to go. Let's just go, sis, tonight. Let's just go home and pack. Let's just fucking go." Bella broke down.

"Fuck it. Okay! Tonight we will leave. We'll get the girls, swing by and see Kinley, and then we're out," Kissy assured.

"We have a gunshot victim. Ashley Williams, African American female, age 25. She has a weak pulse and has lost a lot of blood!" Nurse Sarah yelled.

Detective Lu and Detective Eric burned holes in the soles of their shoes as they paced back and forth in the hospital's waiting area.

After informing Hassan of the murder of his loved ones and accessing the crime scene, Detectives Eric and Lu headed straight for the hospital. They prayed Ashley made it through so that she could assist them in their investigation.

If they didn't get a lead on the suspect, they feared he would walk free. Ashley's statement would be critical in moving forward.

The video she recorded was of no use. It never picked up the suspects face. They got a tiny glimpse of an Islamic tattoo on the suspect's right forearm. Other than that, they had nothing. The video disappeared when the group was shut down.

"This is fucking ridiculous!" Detective Lu yelled frustrated.

Their captain was on their back wanting answers that they couldn't give. Nothing was making sense, and it was one senseless act of violence after the other. Detective Lu's phone rang, and he hurried to answer it. Detective Eric stared impatiently, waving his arms waiting to know what was going on.

"You have got to be fucking kidding me. Tell the judge we need a warrant right fucking now for his arrest!" he screamed and hung up the phone. "Son of a bitch." Detective Lu punched dead air.

"What's going on?" Detective Eric asked alarmed.

"Bo Jackson signed in a visitors log as Raheem Gold at The Wren's Supportive Living Center. Cameras captured him suffocating a little baby to death. The baby name is Kinley Blu. The mother is Kensington Blu. Nicole's vehicle is parked there at the center. A witness stated they seen Bo getting on the 300 Govalle bus. Amber tracked down the bus driver, and you aren't going to believe this."

"What?"

"The bus driver said that Bo was dropped off at the Capital Plaza. The driver said he took a 30-minute break and that he saw Bo get into Natalie's vehicle. He said he's sure it was her because he and his wife frequent the hotel occasionally."

"Got damn it. She played us," Detective Eric huffed.

"This has been one hella of a day." Detective Lu sighed frustrated.

The footsteps behind them gathered their attention. "Ahem! Gentlemen, I'm sorry to inform you. We did all we could but, Ashley Williams didn't make it." Dr. Lee sadly announced.

"Thank you, doctor," they said and left.

Hassan wailed on the front steps of his home. He had been sobbing in the same spot since the detectives broke the news. He couldn't believe his mother, cousin Kiara, and his best friend Ty was gone.

Yashira sat by his side and rubbed his back. She was ready to go and felt this was all too much for her. She didn't want to sound or seem insensitive, but this isn't what she imagined coming back to Austin. In fact, she didn't know what she thought it would be like, but this was just too heavy for her. She had to release her bladder, and she was a tad bit upset that the front of her blouse and pants were soaked with Hassan's tears. She looked up towards the clouds and rolled her eyes. She knew she was being petty, but she was just over it.

She heard her daughter Trinity walk up behind her. "I want my mommy. Why is daddy crying?" She burst out into tears.

Yashira tried to move from Hassan's grip, but he held her down tighter. That infuriated her. She wanted to see about her daughter and check to see if she was okay.

Trinity ran away towards the kitchen and grabbed the phone off the hook. She dialed Nova's number by heart but received a dial tone. She then called her grandmother and next her Auntie Ryan.

"Okay baby! I'll call your mama, and I'll be there okay. Dry your tears, baby," Ryan said.

"Okay! I love you, Auntie," Trinity sweetly singed in the phone.

"I love you too. Bye, bye!"

Ryan sighed deeply and dialed Nova. The call went through. She frowned because moments ago Trinity said the number didn't work.

"Hey, sis! I was just about to call you. Are you still having your party?" Nova questioned.

"No. I'mma cancel it. How are you feeling?" Ryan asked.

"'I'm okay. Sore. Brixton has been taking good care of me though. How about you? Why are you canceling the party? What's up? You okay?" Nova questioned.

"Nope." Ryan's bottom lip shook.

"What's going on?" Nova worried.

"You won't believe the day I had."

"What happened, Ryan? You're scaring me." Nova sat up.

"Is she okay?" Ryan heard Brixton ask in the background.

"Tell my future brother in love not to worry. Anyway, so you remember I told you that Kensington Blu was doing my hair for my party, right."

"Humph." Nova hissed.

"Let me back up. You know my employee Tyrone that I was telling you about?"

"Yeah, Dedra's husband. Lawd, that couple is a mess." Nova laughed lightly.

"Well, anyway, she put him out again and he had nowhere to go, so I offered him a room temporally."

"Ryannnnnn."

"Sis, I know. It was a bad idea. Anyway, Kensington shows up with this chick name Bella. Come to find out it's her sister. So she's doing my hair, and we're watching *Love & Hip Hop: Atlanta*. It was on the scene about Jasmine telling Kirk about the baby. The chick Bella starts asking "what if" questions, and I couldn't help but confront Kensington about y'all situation with Hassan. So, we're getting into when my doorbell rings. It's Dedra, looking for Tyrone. Tyrone wasn't there though because he drove my car to Home Depot. Anyway, the chick Bella and Dedra get into it because Tyrone has been sleeping with Bella. Man sis, these bitches tore my home up. Tyrone finally came and broke them up, and the chick Bella reveals she's pregnant."

"Both Bella and Kensington are birds of a feather. Always getting pregnant by somebody else man. Typical!" Nova bitterly spat.

"I put all they asses out. I thought I would be able to relax after all that, but Trinity just called. Nova, please tell me you didn't block the house number."

"I did," Nova confessed. "Anyway, what's going on?"

"I'm getting ready to head that way now. Trinity called me crying. She said she needs you. Something about her Grandmother Erica and Kiara being killed. Wait hold on. It's on the news now. Turn it on!" Ryan yelled.

"What?" they both yelled in unison while watching the breaking news.

"Brixton and I are on our way over there now. I'll see you there." Nova hung up.

"Whyyyyyy?" Hassan screamed. "Why you take my mama?"

"Hassan, baby I have to pee?" Yashira finally said. Her bladder couldn't hold another round of this.

"You don't give a fuck about a nigga." Hassan bellowed, jumping up.

"What are you talking about? I just sat here on this dirty ass step, ass sore and all for over two fucking hours consoling you. My mother had her funeral today, and that's all you can fucking say!" Yashira snapped.

She could hear the children crying, and she felt awful. She and Hassan turned their attention to Ryan who just pulled up.

"The fuck are you doing here?" Hassan yelled at her.

"My niece called me to come get her. Listen, I didn't come here for no beef. I'm sorry to hear about what happened to your family," Ryan said.

Moments later Margaret and Henry pulled up and parked next to Ryan and then Nova and Brixton. "Mommy!" Trinity cried, running pass Ryan, Yashira, and Hassan.

"Hey, baby!" Nova cried.

Yashira stood on the porch and watched the interaction between Nova and Trinity. A twinge of jealousy was evident and etched across her face. She felt out of place. She wondered if her coming back was the right thing to do.

Ryan stood next to Yashira on the porch, and Margaret joined them. She cut her eyes at Ryan to silently tell her to make amends with Yashira and now wasn't the time to be petty. If Nova has moved on in Margaret's opinion, Ryan should too. Yashira was here and was going to be around.

"Look, Ryan." Yashira faced her. "I get it. I apologize. I was young, inexperienced, and in love. I apologize if I hurt you. I just want to move forward and be a better person for Trinity."

"You're right. Hassan isn't worth it. Are you with him?" Ryan asked.

"I thought coming back and seeing Hassan again, I would want that, but I never saw the pain and devastation that I put Nova through. She broke down at the hospital, and all I could think about is I didn't want to be her. I had no clue Hassan put her through so much. It just doesn't feel right. You'll never be happy bringing misery to others, and that's something I had to learn. All I want to do is be a good mother to Trinity, but I don't think I can." Yashira sadden.

"Just give it time. She has to get to know you. Let things happen naturally. She'll come around." Ryan smiled.

"You think so?" Yashira asked hopeful.

"I know so."

"I just fear Hassan will keep her from me. He has it out for Nova. He's very angry at her for leaving him and cutting him off financially. I'm not going to be his bread and butter, and he can't stay with me. That's all he's been talking about is moving together and being together. He's suffocating me. I can't even bond with Trinity without him making it about him or us. I can't do this."

"When you get a chance, see if you can talk to Brixton. Maybe you can get some type of custody or visitation. Things will work out."

"I will and hey thanks." Yashira smiled, rubbing Ryan's shoulder.

They looked over at Hassan who was seething in anger watching Nova and Trinity. Brixton stepped out the vehicle and Margaret went to greet him, while Henry went to hug Hassan.

Margaret shot Henry an evil glare. She couldn't understand how he could easily forgive the pain that Hassan had put their daughter through. She understood his family was murdered and she was sorry for that, but Henry preferred Hassan over Brixton, and that's what she had a problem with.

In Margaret's heart, she was completely done with Henry. After the blow up they'd shared days prior, they hadn't said two words to each other. The only reason they came today together is because Trinity called crying. After today though, Margaret would take Brixton up on his offer. She had already started packing her clothes. She was done.

"Just give Nova some time son. She'll come around. I know you love her." Margaret and Brixton heard Henry tell Hassan.

Hassan dried his face and looked over at Nova again who was engaging in a loving conversation with their daughter. He needed her. "Nova, I need to talk to you," Hassan pleaded, walking towards Nova.

"She doesn't have anything to say to you. She only came to check on Trinity. The rest is history," Brixton warned.

"Son, this has nothing to do with you. This is between Hassan and his wife!" Henry roared.

"Yeah! She's still my wife, nigga. I'll talk to her if I want to. You're on my property. Hoe ass nigga," Hassan replied.

"Not in front of Trinity. Hassan, we only came to give our condolences and check on Trinity. Other than that, I don't have anything to discuss with you. It's like I told you, you have 30 days, well less than that now, to be out of my home." She turned her attention back to Trinity. "Baby I'm leaving now, but your mother is here and will take good care of you."

"Noooo, please don't leave me. Please!" Trinity cried.

Nova looked over at her mother, and then Ryan and Yashira who was still standing on the front porch. She really didn't know what to say or do, and she felt torn. She missed Trinity too, but she had too many feelings she needed to sort out. The last thing she ever wanted to do was take her anger out on Trinity. Being around Brixton and having him pray with her though was slowly helping Nova to heal and come back to herself.

She rubbed her stomach. She was still in pain from the abortion and cramping. Her mother saw the discomfort look on her face.

"Why don't we all go inside and try to figure this out. Trinity, have you eaten yet?" Margaret asked.

"No, ma'am. My cousins and I are hungry, granny. Can we order a pizza?"

"Yes, baby! That sounds good. Come on."

Nova looked over at Brixton, and he nodded his head to go on. That's what she loved about him. His patience, understanding, and the fact he understood that everything wasn't about him or feelings. Brixton was about right or wrong, and to him, Trinity was a priority as well.

The women all went into the home, while Henry, Hassan, and Brixton stayed outside.

"Brixton you're disrespecting this man's home. You shouldn't be here!" Henry angrily spat.

"It's like I said. I love Nova, and I'm not going anywhere. I'm going to marry her. She will be the mother of my children. She doesn't have to work, and I will never misuse, mistreat, or cheat on her. You had five to six years with her. All you did was break her down. Even now, you have your baby mama here. I know you have slept with her and more than likely in the home you shared with Nova. You continually abuse, harm, and hurt her. I will no longer allow you to hurt her. She's mine now!" Brixton yelled.

*Whap! Whap! Whap!*

"Hoe ass nigga. Are you fucking my wife? She's mine. She will always be mine." Hassan fought with all his might.

Brixton grabbed Hassan and placed him in a headlock. "Yeah bitch, talk that shit now! I can snap your fucking neck," Brixton threatened.

"Come on! That's enough. Let him go. He can't breathe. You're going to kill him," Henry worried.

Brixton let him go, and Hassan stumbled backwards while rubbing his neck. He breathed heavy while balling his fist. He charged at Brixton again, and the two began to throw blow for blow.

"Oh my god! They're fighting!" Ryan yelled.

Nova and Ryan ran out the front door screaming for Hassan and Brixton to stop. Yashira stood in front of the large window and shook her head. She was happy the children were in the back playing. She couldn't believe Hassan and Brixton.

Again, another wave of jealousy hit her, this time knocking her in the face. Hassan and Brixton were fighting over their love for Nova, that much she knew, and it was something she couldn't compete with or wanted to.

She pulled out her phone and dialed Qadira to pick her up. She went into Nova's room, changed out of the soaked clothing she wore, and packed the few items she had there. Everyone was so engrossed in the arguing and fighting that nobody saw Yashira walk right past them. She stood on the side of the house, and when she saw Qadira turning the corner, she began walking towards her.

"Sis, this is some bullshit. Let's go!" she yelled, placing on her seatbelt.

Qadira drove past the home, and Yashira sucked her teeth. She would just have to find another way to bond with Trinity, but today wasn't the day.

"You sure, you're ready to leave?" Qadira questioned, pulling up to the stop sign.

"Yeah, it's just too much. Hassan's mother, cousin, and best friend were killed. He's losing it, and he snapped on me because I wasn't stroking his ego. I'm just not in the mood, sis. I had a long day, and my feelings are hurt. No matter how hard I try to get space and time with Trinity, it's ruin or overshadowed. Please just get me away from here," Yashira cried.

Ryan saw Yashira and Qadira pulling away from the stop sign and shook her head. She felt Yashira was selfish. She ruined her sister's spirit for years behind Hassan. Now that she had him, she didn't want him. *Now she wants to run after she sees what my sister has dealt with for years. How dare that bitch feels that she gets to pick and choose her happiness when it was she who fucked a married man, had his child, and abandoned the child on my sister's doorstep. Now that Nova is done and has given Yashira her blessing, she doesn't even want Hassan. Keep the same energy you had when he wasn't fair game in the beginning.*

Her phone vibrated in her pocket, and she looked at the ID and saw that it was her job calling.

"Hello," Ryan urgently answered, excusing herself back in the home.

"Ryan, it's me, Pamela," Pamela announced out of breath.

"Pam, are you okay? What's going on? What's all that noise in the background? What is happening there?" Ryan asked.

Pamela was an employee of Ryan's. She was on shift when Bo killed Kinley. She had seen him sign in and then she took a phone call outside arguing with her boyfriend.

"Ryan, something bad has happened." Pam cried. "Turn on the news. Kinley Blu was murdered. The police are here, and we've been trying to reach Kensington, but her number is no longer in service."

"What? I'm on my way!" Ryan screamed.

She covered her mouth watching the footage of Bobby Jackson entering Kinley's room and murdering her. She was furious and sick to her stomach.

"Where the fuck was my staff? How did this happen?" she screamed in agony.

She knew her job would be in jeopardy, causing a huge state investigation. She could lose her funding, be sued by Kensington, and lose everything she had worked for.

"I can't do shit right." Ryan began to sob loudly.

She rushed out of Nova's home sobbing, gaining the full attention of Margaret, Nova, Brixton, Hassan, and Henry.

"Ryan! Ryan! What's wrong?" Nova asked running over to Ryan.

"Bobby Jackson killed baby Kinley at my center. The police are there now. I'mma lose everything." Ryan sobbed uncontrollably.

"Kinley? Are you talking about Kensington Blu daughter?" Hassan asked, causing Nova to snarl in his direction.

"Yes," Ryan cried.

"I'm not going to even ask how you know this baby HASSAN!" Nova snapped.

"Ryan, come on, I'll take you. If the police are there, I'm sure they're going to question you. I'll be your legal backup if you need me. Let's go," Brixton instructed, opening his back car door for Ryan and going around to the passenger side to open the door for Nova.

"Mom, here you go. I made this for you. These are your personal keys. Whenever you're ready, you're welcome. Everything is set up for you and mother." Brixton kissed Margaret on the cheek and stared Henry down.

"She won't be needing those. Her ass ain't going nowhere!" Henry yelled at Brixton while pointing his finger.

"I wouldn't be so sure of that. By the way mom, Leroy's wife passed last night. He has contacted me to handle the will she left. I'm pretty sure they'll be plenty of time to rekindle an old romance. I'll be sure to give him your number and make sure he calls you. I'm sure Leroy would never hurt or disrespect you. Word on the streets is you were always the one who got away." Brixton winked at Henry and got in the vehicle.

He was tired of being disrespected by Nova's father and furthermore he was tired of Henry feeling comfortable enough to disrespect his wife in front of others.

Henry looked at Margaret and angrily shook his head. He wasn't going to allow her to go off and be with her lover. He hopped in his vehicle and left Margaret there.

"Margaret, go with Ryan, Nova, and Brixton. I'm going to drop the kids over at Yashira's home. This isn't your concern anymore." Hassan nastily stated.

"The children are waiting on a pizza. Why don't you go see about your family and let me stay with them?"

"I said go." Hassan evilly eyed her.

Margaret regretfully left Trinity and got into Brixton's vehicle. They watched as Hassan yelled and kicked dirt towards Brixton's car.

"Arghhhhhhh!" Hassan stormed in the home.

"Jr.!" he yelled.

"Yes, cousin?" Larry Jr. ran into the living room.

"I'mma take a shower. Look here's $40. The pizza delivery should be ringing the door. Give him the entire thing. Lock the door after he leaves and make sure everyone eats." Hassan ordered, handing Jr. the money.

"Yes, sir."

Hassan drew a hot bath and poured a bag of peppermint Epsom salt in the water. He lit a blunt and gulped down a sip of Hennessy. The burn of the warm liquid caused tears to rush his eyes, and he cried his soul out.

"Man, not my mama man. Come on," he sobbed.

He knew Larry had made good on his threat to kill Kiara. He blamed himself for not protecting his family more. He had heard Larry was released from jail, but everything dealing with Yashira and his daughter clouded his mind.

He was angry and blamed Yashira for everything. If she hadn't come back, Nova would have never had a seizure or left him to be with Brixton. His mother, cousin, and homeboy would have still been alive if he wasn't so worried about her. Hassan felt Yashira used him and she bailed on him now that it was her time to hold him down and they be a family. It was because of her that his life was a mess. She had always been the reason things with him and Nova was shaky.

The day she left Trinity in his doorstep and took off, Hassan knew Nova would never fully forgive him, and now that Nova was fully gone, Yashira didn't want him.

"Grimy ass bitch!" Hassan roared, taking another swig from the bottle. He drained the water from the tub, dressed and went to join the children to eat.

"Daddy where are mommy and mommy 2?" Trinity innocently asked.

"I don't know baby. I'll figure it out later. For now, let's just eat."

"Hey look! I know her. It's Kissy." Trinity pointed at the television.

The news reporter showed the photo that Ryan took of Kensington and Kinley at the center. They were airing the story of Bobby Jackson murdering her.

"What did you just call her?" Hassan questioned.

"Kissy. I saw her at the park when I was with grandma, and she came to the hospital daddy when you were there with mommy2," Trinity informed.

Hassan ate his pizza in silence. Screenshots in his memory began to play out like a movie. He was very aware of the name Kissy but never thought Kensington would be the "Kissy" who broke up homes and stirred up a lot of drama.

"Ayo, this bitch has been playing me the whole fucking time!" Hassan bellowed and looked over at the children who were staring at him.

"Y'all just eat and when you finish, draw y'all baths up. Girls y'all can bathe in the big tub, and Jr. you in the other one."

He rubbed his face. He decided tonight would be the night that he paid Larry, Yashira, and Kensington a visit. At this point, he had nothing to lose. He had lost everything important to him.

Bo walked around Natalie's three-bedroom home and admired the layout and color scheme of each room.

In one of the rooms, Natalie had turned it into a women's den and movie theater. The ceiling was painted black, and the walls were a dark gray and black glitter color. Photos in black and white of black Hollywood actresses such as Mother Jennifer Lewis, Dorothy Dandridge, as well as many others decorated the walls. A red and black popcorn stand was housed in a corner. A diamond-studded bar lit with a red led light occupied a corner with any of your favorite brown and clear liquors. Four large oversized leather red recliner chairs greeted you, while you had your favorite candy snacks and a huge jar of pickles on a shelf begging you to take one.

Bo was in awe of the room and knew that it would be one of his favorite spots of the home. He could see himself laid back, enjoying a hood movie, while sipping Grey Goose, a fresh batch of popcorn brewing, inhaling good dro smoke, while Natalie sucked him off until he bust.

The second bedroom had two twin size beds, a dresser, and flat screen. The colors were gray and pink with an elephant theme. The room was cozy and cute, but Bo was thinking of a way he could make that his man cave. Besides, now that he was here and Natalie's man, no company was allowed.

The master bedroom was too girlie for Bo. It had a purple and gold theme with photos of black women with natural Afro hair. He wanted to change the colors to red and black like the other room.

The living room was perfect to Bo. Gold and royal blue was the color scheme, and he admired the artwork of black kings in royal blue suits. He loved the royal blue sessional with the gold throw pillows. Everything was classy, and with the candles lit, the living room could have easily made a front and center magazine fold.

He settled in the home and hung his clothing in Natalie's closet. While she cooked, he took that as his opportunity to bathe and unwind. A heavy feeling came over him, and he tried not to think of it. Killing Kinley did something to him. He wasn't a killer, and he had children. He felt sick. He brought his right hand up to his face and began crying. "I'm so sorry," he cried.

Natalie danced around the kitchen grooving to Tony, Tony, Tone's "Anniversary" song. She was in such a good mood with high spirits. She really liked Bo and could see them together for a long time, and the sex was amazing.

She prepared a meal of meatloaf, red potatoes, string green beans, corn on the cob and garlic bread. While Bo bathed, she waited on her meal to finish cooking and made her way to the movie room. There she poured herself a glass of pineapple Paul Masson.

She turned on the television in search of something to watch until Bo got out of the tub. She settled on *Law & Order: SVU,* and in the middle of a good scene, her TV show was interrupted. Bo's photo was plastered on the screen, and Natalie's mouth was wide open in shock. She closed the door and locked it while turning the volume down and sitting in front of the television to hear.

*"Police are looking for Bobby "Bo" Jackson. The suspect is said to be armed and dangerous. He is wanted in the connection of the murder of Iesha and Raheem Gold and baby girl Kinley Blu. The suspect was last seen at the Capital Plaza getting into a black, four-door Malibu. Please call the police if you have any information."*

"Hey baby, is the food ready?" Bo asked, knocking on the door.

Natalie hurried and turned the television on Netflix to *Paid In Full*. She opened the door calmly being sure not to alert Bo of what she just learned.

"Why you got the door locked?" Bo questioned annoyed.

"I'm sorry, baby. It's a habit of mine," Natalie innocently said.

"Okay, well from now on don't lock no doors. That makes me feel you're hiding something from me."

"Oh, no baby never that." Natalie kissed him.

"Alright, that's what I like to hear, with yo fine ass." He smacked Natalie on her flat behind and wanted to laugh. "It smells good as fuck in the kitchen." Bo beamed.

"Thank you, baby." She kissed him again. "Mmmm, you smell good. Baby, make us some drinks and roll us a blunt. I'mma about to set the table and check on the food." She smiled.

As soon as she rounded the corner, Natalie quickly and quietly grabbed her car keys, purse, and cell phone. She exited through the garage door careful not to make too much noise. She quickly rushed out of the garage and dialed 911.

"911 operator, what is your emergency?"

"Yes, my name is Natalie. Listen, Bo Jackson is at my home now." Natalie hung up.

She didn't worry about giving her address. She knew it was in the system due to her ex-lover Larry whooping up on her all the time. Her phone startled her when it began ringing back. It was Bo. She took a deep breath to calm her nerves before answering it.

"Natalie, baby, where you go? You had a nigga calling your name and shit, searching for you all over the house," Bo hostilely asked.

"Baby, I'm sorry. I should have communicated. I just came right here to the Dollar General. I needed some seasoning that I forgot. Everything is almost done. You need anything, baby?" she sweetly asked.

"Yeah! Get a nigga some hygiene products," he said.

"Okay, I will." She quickly hung up.

"Breathe Natalie, breathe Natalie," she coached to herself.

She waited at the corner until she saw police vehicles. She waved them down and asked them to turn off their sirens. She didn't want to alert Bo in any way.

She pulled back into her garage, leaving the garage door open and leaving the entrance to her home unlocked. Bo was standing in the kitchen with her gun that he must've gotten out of her bedroom.

"Where are the Dollar General bags at, bitch?" he roared, pointing the gun at her. "Hoe, you thought you were going to set me up. Yeah, I saw the news. Bitch, give me your car keys and your money! You should have minded your business."

"Here, please don't hurt me," Natalie begged, handing Bo her purse.

"Too late, bitch."

*POW!*

Bo shot Natalie in the head instantly killing her. Her body dropped, and Bo rushed out the garage door.

"Get on the fucking ground now!" The police yelled with their gun drawn on Bo. He dropped to the ground without a fight. He knew it was over.

Detective Eric and Detective Lu waited for Bo in the interrogation room. They knew he would be the one to finally put the pieces of the puzzle together.

The door open and two police officer along with Bo walked in. Bo sat in the chair and placed both of his hands on the table.

"Man, look. I'll tell y'all what you wanna know. Just get a nigga a blanket, coffee, and something to eat. It's freezing in this bitch," Bo complained.

An hour later Bo was singing like a Wren hummingbird. He told them about the infamous Kissy being Kensington Blu. He told them about his and Torrie's relationship and how it was her who proposition him to murder Kinley for the insurance money. He told them about Sean killing his sister Nicole, and the way he ended up with her possessions. He told them about the relationship his sister was having with Hassan. He informed them on the drama between Ty, Larry, Ashley, and Kiara. He also promised them that he had nothing to do with Raheem and Iesha's murder.

"The problem with everything you're saying Bobby, is it all points back to you. The gun we found in your hotel room matches the bullets that were used to kill Iesha and Raheem. Your prints are on the gun. You're going down Bobby Jackson, not to mention the first-degree murder of Natalie, and Kinley Blu, a fucking baby who couldn't even walk or talk. You're a monster, and you disgust me. They're going to eat your black ass alive in prison, and I'mma see to it that your life is fucking hell. You piece of shit!" Detective Eric yelled, jumping across the table lifting Bo by his shirt. He head butt him multiple times losing his cool. "You piece of shit!" he continued to scream.

Detective Lu and other officers had to pull Eric off Bo. He knew his partner would soon crack, especially when little Kinley was murdered.

Detective Eric hated men like Bo. His wife and daughter were murdered and sexually assaulted. They were tortured for hours, and he wasn't there to save them. He blamed himself. He wanted to kill Bo for what he has done. If they hadn't pulled him off Bo, he was sure he would have killed him.

"Get the fuck off of me!" Detective Eric angrily yelled, pushing everyone off him. He picked up his chair and threw it at Bo before exiting the room.

"Take him. We're done here," Detective Lu said to the officers.

He went outside and saw his partner pacing while smoking a cigarette. He approached him, and Eric looked at him with sad eyes.

"Two years on this date, my fucking family was stolen from me man. It's not a day or second that goes by where I don't think of them," he sadly expressed while tears covered his face.

"I know man. I'm so sorry. Detective Lu hugged his partner.

"I'm okay. I'm okay. Thanks, man. Come on. Let's get to The Wren's Supportive Living Center." he dried his face.

"Hi girls!" Kissy and Bella sang as soon as Mecca and Mina entered into the vehicle.

"You got a new car?" Mina excitedly shouted.

"Yup!" Kissy laughed.

"I like this one better. It's so big back here." Mecca smiled.

Bella looked over at Kissy, and she nodded her head for her to go ahead and address the moving situation.

"Girls, how would you feel about going on a road trip?" Bella asked.

"A road trip. What's a road trip?" Mina asked.

Kissy laughed at how adorable Mina was. She wore two pigtails, had freckles, fair skinned, and she was missing her front teeth.

"I know what it is?" Mecca knowingly said.

"Uh-uh know you don't," Mina sassed.

"I'm older than you, and I know everything," Mecca boasted.

"Girls, okay." Bella rolled her eyes. "You see what you're going to have to go through?" Bella laughed pointing at Kissy. "Anyway girls, when we get home, I need you to pack all your clothing and shoes. We're going to be leaving," Bella confirmed.

"Leaving? I can't leave. What about my boyfriend and my friends?" Mecca asked.

"Boyfriend?" Kissy and Bella threw their heads back.

"First of all don't ever put no nigga—" Bella was interrupted.

"Bella. Aht, aht. They're kids." Kissy laughed, causing Bella to laugh.

"Shit, I forgot who I was talking to hell. I was about to give a hoe lesson." Bella slap hands with Kissy. "Girls, mommy got fired from her job. That's why we had to move in with Aunt Kensington. She's got a new job, and we have to move."

"But what about all my toys?" Mina whined.

"Here, open this. I have a gift for both of you." Bella smiled passing the girls two individually gift bags.

"Ahh!" the girls screamed.

Kissy had purchased Mecca and Mina their own personal tablets, Beats headsets, cases, and iPhones. She also purchased Bella a tablet and phone, and she brought herself new devices as well. Since Bella and Kissy agreed upon Colorado to move, they all received area codes from Colorado.

"Thank you, mama and Aunt Kensington." The girls beamed.

"Coolllll, I get to make my own cases!" Mecca yelled, pulling out the stickers to the clear cases.

"Yup and you girls can work on them while we're on the road. You also have headsets and iPad pen to draw on your tablets." Bella smiled.

She looked over at Kissy and smiled. She mouthed the words "thank you" and touched her heart. Tears flooded her eyes, and Kissy grabbed her hand and squeezed it.

"Things will be alright, sis. Now let's go eat Kissy said, and everyone agreed.

They stopped at Amaya's and enjoyed a great dinner of Enchiladas, tacos, and nachos. They laughed and joked. Kissy hadn't remembered ever feeling this comfortable or close with anyone in her life. For the first time, she felt free and safe.

"Girl why are all these people staring at us? Every time I look up, someone is ogling in our direction?" Bella said annoyed.

"Okay, so you caught that too?" Kissy rolled her eyes.

She glanced over to her left and made eye contact with Tasha, one of her HR representatives at her job. Tasha waved, and Kissy waved back and turned her attention back to Belly and her nieces.

Tasha was shocked to see Kensington. So much had happened with their jobs and coworkers that Tasha really didn't want to go back to work. Two of her coworkers in HR were dead. Hassan was shot. They had a suicide in the office, and she just learned moments ago that her coworker Kensington's daughter was murdered. The job seemed to be bad luck, and she was thinking of being transferred or sending in her resignation.

She couldn't believe how calm and posed Kensington was, especially after the news just showed the photo of her and her baby Kinley. Tasha would have been devastated if her daughter was murdered. A piece of her wondered if Kensington even knew what was going on. By the looks of other stares in the restaurant at Kensington, Tasha wasn't even sure she knew.

She dapped the corners of her mouth with a napkin, took a sip of her sweet tea, and made her way over to Kensington's table.

"Ahem, hi Kensington. I just wanted to offer my condolences," Tasha softly said.

"Condolences? I'm confused." Kissy frowned.

"Kinley. She's your daughter, right? You were just on the news," Tasha informed.

"What are you talking about? How do you know my daughter? What news are you talking about?" Kissy yelled, getting upset.

"You don't know?"

"Know what, bitch? What are you talking about?" Kissy stood. She was irate.

Tasha pulled out her phone and clicked on the local news channel. She pushed play on the video that had being airing.

Kissy held her chest with one hand and stomach with the other. Bella stood to view Tasha's phone as well. A loud sob erupted from the pit of her soul. "My baby, he killed my baby!" she screamed.

A photo of her and Kinley flashed across the screen, and Kissy lost it. Bystanders began shedding tears for Kensington.

"Come on, Kensington. We have to get to the center. Girls, get your things and help me with your auntie," Bella urged.

Bella assisted Kissy in the passenger side and situated her girls. She went back to pay, but the manager charged the food on the house. Random "bless you" and "I'm praying for you all" greeted her while she exited the restaurant.

Kissy sobbed the entire way to the center. She knew her baby was calling out to her earlier. She felt something was wrong. She knew it.

"I know my aunt put Bo up to this for that insurance policy, but little does Torrie know I canceled all three of the policies she had. I'm the only one who will be collecting any money, and she had my child killed for nothing!" Kissy angrily yelled.

They pulled up to the center, and Kissy jumped out of the car. A police officer attempted to stop her, but she fought with her.

"Get the fuck off of me. That's my baby!" she screamed.

"Let her through," Detective Eric and Lu ordered.

"Kinley. Where is she?" she screamed. She saw Ryan and ran up to her. "Where is my baby, bitch? You did this. I hate you. I hate you!" Kissy swung wildly while being held back by the detectives.

"Kensington, I'm sorry." Ryan cried. "I wasn't here. I just got here myself."

"I want my baby." Kissy sobbed falling on the floor. "Whyyyyy? How did this happen? Answer me. I trusted you and this place. Why did this happen? My baby. Whyyyyy?" she screamed at Ryan.

She saw someone rolling a small bag and jumped off the floor. "Kinley. Give me her." Kissy yanked the bag and opened it.

"Ahhhhhhh!" She fell to the floor. "I'm so sorry. I'm so sorry." She rocked back and forth holding Kinley.

It wasn't a dry eye in sight. Seeing Kissy break down over the murder of her child was gut-wrenching.

"Get my sister and nieces so that they can say goodbye!" Kissy yelled.

She stared evilly at Brixton and Ryan who were standing off to the side. "I want answers. Where was the staff? Why didn't her alarms go off? How was Bo able to slide past security? What about the cameras?" she bellowed.

"Ms. Blu, we have Bo in custody for the murder," Detective Eric informed.

Bella and the girls ran over to Kissy, and all took turns holding, kissing, and grieving over Kinley. When they were done, Kissy kissed Kinley one last time and placed her body back in the bag. "I want her ashes," she blurted out.

She stood, and she and Bella hugged a long time. When she released Bella, she dried her tears, and they began to make their way out.

"Ms. Blu, we need you to come down to the station for questioning."

"Fuck you and your questioning. I don't have shit to say to anyone, and Ryan you better find another job bitch. I'm suing this place. I trusted you with my baby's life, and you let this happen," Kissy pointed, and they left.

Detective Eric and Lu looked at each other and then back at Ryan. She looked at Brixton, and he nodded that he will handle things. It was going to be a long night, so Brixton sent Nova and Margaret home.

"You all ready?" Detective Eric and Lu asked Ryan's and Brixton. They nodded. All the staff members were called into the back, and Ryan sighed thinking how they failed Kinley.

She knew this was the beginning of the end for her. Her fear was coming true. Kissy was suing, and she didn't blame her. She would have too. Kinley was such a joy and a special baby. What Bo did to her broke Ryan's heart.

♥♥♥♥♥

Bella got into the driver seat and looked over at Kissy. She had a blank stare and Bella worried about her mental state.

"Kensington, we don't have to leave tonight. We can wait until everything is situated with Kinley."

"I have to get out of here. I can just have Kinley's ashes shipped to where we are. As far as her policy, they can wire the funds to my bank account, and once I get them, I'll close that account and have everything transferred to my new account. I'm definitely suing," Kissy informed, staring out the window.

"Sure, sis. Whatever you wanna do, I'm down." Bella pulled away from the center. She took a right down a dimly lit street and got a funny feeling that someone was following them.

She looked in the backseat and saw Mina and Mecca sleeping. Once she pulled up to the stop sign, they were rear-ended from behind.

"What the fuck?" Kissy and Bella yelled at the same time. They both began to remove their seatbelts when sheer terror stared Kissy in the face.

"Hassan!" Kissy yelled, attempting to roll her window up. Bella tried to reach for the gun that was in the glove department but was too late.

*POW! POW! POW! POW! POW!*

Hassan shot Kissy multiple times.

*Skeeerrtttttt!*

Bella turned the corner quickly almost losing control.

"Kensington, please don't die on me!" Bella screamed. "I need you. We need you. I love you so much."

"Bella, I-I love you." Kissy coughed. "In my room, inside my bed frame, is half a million dollars. My paperwork and Kinley's paperwork is in my drawers. You and..." she coughed. "You and the girls will be set forever. Make them pay for my, baby. I love you," Kissy whispered before closing her eyes.

"No! Wake up we're here!" Bella screamed, pulling in the driveway of the emergency room.

"Somebody, somebody, help me!" Bella sobbed. "My sister was shot. Help me!"

Bella and her girls stood off to the side crying while emergency staff pulled Kissy's body out of the Suburban.

"She's dead," a doctor confirmed Bella's fear.

Forty-three

Hassan made sure the children were situated before he left home. He checked his gun and sat in his car to recollect his thoughts. He was so angry, but most of all heartbroken. He seemed to be losing everything and everyone around him. First, it was his wife, then his mistress, his mother, cousin, and best friend. The only one he thought was solid and loyal was Yashira. He never thought that she would turn on him and leave him when he needed her the most.

Yashira had to have known the stress her absence caused him and the pain his wife felt, knowing that no matter what she said or did, she couldn't compete with someone I couldn't let go of.

Now that Hassan was free and all hers, she didn't want him, and he couldn't take the fact she left him when he needed her the most. She was selfish, different, and wasn't the same woman he had loved all those years.

He wondered how he would raise Trinity and his three little cousins on his own. He only had four hundred dollars to his name, and he wouldn't get paid until next month. He was so angry at Nova for leaving him the way she had and cleaning out the bank account. He had nowhere to go, and he didn't like the fact that she had moved on and didn't seem to care anymore about him or his daughter.

He envied the fact Nova had a man like Brixton. His mother had described the big home she now lived in, and the vehicles that were parked in the driveway. She also didn't have to work again, and she had leveled up. Hassan wanted a piece of that.

Cranking his vehicle, he made his first stop over to the hood to Goo's home. He was having a poker game, and Hassan knew that Larry would eventually show up. Hassan didn't care about being seen. He had come to murder Larry.

"What's up, boi? I'm sorry to hear about your peoples?" Random dudes said to Hassan when he entered Goo's home.

"'Preciate you," Hassan mumbled.

It didn't take long for Larry to show his face. He came in Goo's home loud, flashy, and boastful as he always was. He looked in Hassan's direction and smirked, before making his way over to Hassan.

"I just want to extend my condolences." He arrogantly stuck his hand out to shake Hassan's.

Hassan shook Larry's hand and pulled him in for a hug. He removed the gun from the back of his jeans, placed it in Larry's stomach, and pulled the trigger.

*POW!*

"That's for my mother muthafucka!" Hassan bellowed.

Larry stumbled backwards, holding his stomach. He couldn't believe that he had been shot and caught slipping. He looked at the blood on his hand and then back at Hassan. He stared at the smoking gun and knew this is where he would take his last breath.

*POW!*

Hassan shot him in the head.

Bystanders stood by and watched. They didn't blame Hassan for killing Larry, and they wouldn't snitch on him. Everyone who was familiar with Larry and some was able to watch Ashley's live video in *Whose Man Is This Sis* group. They knew that it was Larry. Even though you couldn't see his face, the Islamic tattoo on his forearm was a dead giveaway.

Hassan looked over at Goo and the other ten men that were in the home and nodded his head. "Y'all don't know shit and ain't seen shit. Where this bitch Kensington at?" Hassan asked.

"Ain't nobody seen her around fam," Tim slurred.

318

"Check it, if y'all get to her before me, dome that bitch. She's KISSY," Hassan informed.

"What the fuck? Get the fuck out of here. Kensington is Kissy? If I see the bitch, it's on sight!" Goo yelled.

Kissy had started a rumor that Goo was sleeping with men and was HIV positive. It took Goo a while to clear up the rumor, and even still, niggas looked at him funny, and some gay men had even tried to shoot their shot with him.

"Ayo, go by that center. They keep airing this shit on the news. I bet that hoe is there," Terrance one of the men in the house said.

"ONE!" Hassan yelled before exiting the home.

He ran to his vehicle and dialed Kensington's phone number while burning off. He frowned when the operator stated that it was disconnected. "Where the fuck is the bitch at?" he yelled out in frustration.

Hassan crossed over the light and saw the big apartment sign reading Travis Station. He entered the apartment complex and sat outside the apartment where everything changed his life. Yellow tape was around the complex, and Hassan sobbed loudly thinking of his mother and cousin being killed.

He didn't know what to do anymore, but he promised he would avenge their death. That's why finding Kensington was so important to him. All this time she was Kissy. She was the reason for all of this in the first place. If it weren't for her group, Ty and Kiara would still be alive, and he and Nova would still be together.

The Wren's Supportive Living Center would be his best bet to find Kensington. When he pulled up, news vans were everywhere, and so were the police. They had the parking lot blocked off, so Hassan parked directly across the street.

After waiting for an hour, he spotted Kensington, a fair chick, and two little girls entered into a silver Suburban. He cranked his vehicle and followed the truck down a dimly lit street. He looked around and saw that there were no residential homes or other vehicles in sight.

When the Suburban came to a stop sign, Hassan used that as his opportunity to kill Kensington. He bumped the back of the Suburban and quickly jumped out and rounded the passenger side.

"Kissy. Yeah! You thought I would never find out. It's because of you bitch that my entire family is gone. Meet them on the other side."

"Hassan, I'm so sorry. Please don't kill me," Kissy begged.

Hassan saw Bella reaching for the glove compartment and let off rounds in Kensington before he sped off.

"Get it together, nigga!" he yelled, hitting himself on the head.

He wasn't a killer, but he couldn't explain the rush he felt catching two bodies in one night. It felt good and powerful seeing the light drain out of someone's eyes. He couldn't stop now if he wanted to. He was on a mission and wouldn't stop until he completed it.

Pulling up in Qadira's driveway, Hassan frowned at the red Hummer that was parked next to Yashira's car. He peeked his head inside the car and saw a work badge hanging from the mirror that read *Charles*. His insecurities instantly began to get the best of him.

He walked up the four front steps and gently turned the doorknob surprised that the door was unlocked. He entered the home and crept down the hallway to Yashira's room. He could hear a male's voice, muffled with Yashira's moans.

His heart ached. He couldn't believe Yashira was cheating on him. *Charles? Who is this nigga, and when did she meet him? Is this the reason she left earlier? Had she been playing me the entire time?*

"Ahhhh. Oh my god! Hassan, what the fuck are you doing in my home?" Qadira screamed.

She ran towards him and attempted to fight Hassan, but she was no match for him.

*POW!*

He shot her between the eyes causing Yashira's room door to fly open.

"Qadira. Noooooo!" Yashira screamed. She hadn't even noticed Hassan standing off to the side.

"So this was the reason for you leaving me?" Hassan asked, pointing his gun at Charles who had his hands up.

"Hey man, I don't know what's going on here. I just met her off Tagged, a couple of days ago. Please let me live. I have a daughter man," the man begged.

Hassan motioned for him to leave and the man hurried out of the home. He looked down at Yashira who was on the floor cradling her dead sister. She looked up at him.

"You gone kill me next, Hassan?" she asked with a face full of tears.

"You played me." Hassan slid down the wall sitting on the floor.

"No, you played me. What you thought I was going to be Nova's replacement? You thought I was going to allow you to treat me the way you treated her? Never HASSAN! All I wanted was my daughter, NOT YOU!" she cried.

"I know that now, but that's not how this ends."

"So you're going to kill me and then what, Hassan? Spend the rest of your life in prison? You know that's where you're going, right?"

"I love you Yashira, and if I can't have you nobody will, not even Trinity," Hassan shot her.

He stood and looked down at Yashira and Qadira. "Fuck!" he screamed and ran out the front door. He froze seeing the flashing lights and gun drawn on him. This isn't how this was supposed to end.

"Get on the fucking ground now!" Officer Wallace yelled.

Hassan had two choices. He thought about running or shooting at the cops but what good would that do. In one swift second, Hassan placed the gun in his mouth and pulled the trigger. *POW!*

"I now pronounce you man and wife. You may kiss the bride."

Cheers of congratulations ringed throughout the flower garden of Brixton and Nova's home. Margaret kissed Leroy, and he gave her a coquettish grin. So much love and happiness radiated off their beautiful smiles. It was infectious, and they were living proof that you could find love at any age.

Ryan, Nova, and Tammy (Brixton's mother) all stood to the side in their light blue bridesmaid's dresses. They clapped while shedding tears. Seeing their mother and friend and in a jovial space made their hearts swell. Lord knows they needed good news. So much had transpired last year that almost rocked their family to the core.

Hassan's death was very hard on Nova and her healing. Although she hated him and was in a loving relationship with Brixton, she still had so many questions. She never got the closure she needed and knowing that he was gone forever hurt her.

She went through months of counseling. She attended some sessions alone, some with Brixton, and others with Ryan. They had to build their trust back up again and work through all the betrayal Nova felt. Brixton also encouraged her to go to support groups for divorce and spiritual counseling to help with her resentment issues.

As promised he was there every step of the way, and any time Nova fell, he picked her right back up.

They adopted Trinity and later found out they were expecting their own little bundle of joy. Their home was filled with love and Brixton couldn't wait another minute.

"Nova," the pastor called.

Nova passed her flowers to Ryan and went before the pastor. Margaret and Leroy joined hands and smiled.

♫*You don't know, babe when you hold me and kiss me slowly. It's the sweetest thing...*♫ "Best Part" by Daniel Caesar played.

The guests began cheering as Brixton kneeled behind Nova. She slowly turned away and began shedding tears of joy. Margaret kissed her on her cheek and Leroy hugged her, giving them their blessing.

"Nova, you are my world. I love you. Will you do me the honors of marrying me here and right now?" Brixton asked, wiping his tears.

"Yes," Nova nodded.

Trinity gave Nova a hug and as the pastor had Nova and Brixton repeat after him, Trinity stayed on the side of them.

"I can't believe we're married now, Brixton. I love you." Nova beamed. "Y'all got me." She laughed and pointed at Ryan, Tammy, Leroy, Margaret, Brixton, and Trinity.

"Look there goes Grandpa Henry," Trinity pointed and ran to hug him.

"Let me." Margaret calmed an upset Leroy down. She walked over to where Henry stood.

"You look good, Margaret," Henry complimented.

"Henry, what are you doing here?" Margaret asked with her hand on hip.

"I just came to give you these." He handed her flowers.

"Look, I'm sorry about how I treated you all these years. You are a good woman, and you deserve to be happy. I should have cherished you while I had you. I never thought I would lose you. I'm lonely without you, and I miss you. I'll always love you. Well now, I bets to get going," Henry cried and left.

Margaret turned and walked back towards Leroy. She kissed his lips and told him she loved him. What Henry said was sweet, but a little too late.

"Congratulations," filled with love and kisses surrounded the two newlyweds, as people took turns rubbing Nova's protruding belly.

Things in their lives could've been more complete than it was at this very moment. Nova's journey proved to her that with the right man by your side, healing and being loved wholeheartedly was possible. With the love and strength of Brixton, Nova was able to feel safe and secure. She was no longer lost and filled with despair and hopelessness. Brixton had come in and restored her faith and heart. She could truly say she was happy.

Ryan mixed and mingled a little more with the crowd until she felt ill and needed rest. She retreated to a large room in Nova and Brixton's home that was now her living quarters. So much devastation had happened within a year, and she honestly was just trying to find her way.

After the murder of Kinley, her Aunt Bella Blu sued Ryan. They settled out of court for 1.3 million dollars. Ryan ended up losing her state funding and had to close her center down. She lost everything, including her home.

Nothing was worse than having your health fading. A simple flu revealed that she was indeed HIV positive. She knew it had to have come from either Tyrone or a guy she had met and had a one night stand with by the name of Quincy. She didn't know which one, but all she could do is take accountability for her actions.

"You alright, sis?" Nova asked poking her head in the door.

"Yeah, sis I'm sorry. The meds make me sick sometimes. I felt lightheaded and needed to lie down."

"It's okay, and I understand. Guess what?" Nova beamed.

"What?" Ryan asked excitedly.

"Brixton's cousin Wallace wants to date you."

Ryan had met Wallace a couple of times when he came over for dinner. He and Brixton were rekindling lost time and making up for it. She liked his vibe and good looks, but she never thought he would take an interest in someone like her.

"Does he know I'm positive?" Ryan asked.

"Of course, you speak about the virus all the time. He told Brixton he saw you at a teen conference speaking about it, and he went to learn about a prep pill."

"Wow!"

"See I told you, there's still hope for love. I love you, sis." Nova hugged Ryan.

"I love you too and congratulations." Ryan smiled.

Nova went back to her guest and Ryan refreshed and met Wallace in the garden. *Maybe there's hope for new beginnings.*

Bella settled out of court and rewarded 1.3 million dollars for the wrongful death of Kinley Blu. Her life had changed for the better thanks to her sister Kensington. Not only did Bella receive the $500,000 that was stashed in Kensington's bed, but she was also the power of attorney of Kinley and Kensington's life insurance totaling $250,000 each policy, not to mention the $200,000 that was in Kensington's personal bank.

Her life was bittersweet, but she chose to look at the blessings, instead of the losses. She walked around her 4,500 square foot home in a buoyant mood. She wished Kensington was here to share this moment with her. She missed her dearly.

Although her life was bittersweet, Bella was thankful for all the blessings she had, including her baby boy Cannon. She was so in love. She and her little family settled in Colorado, and there she started her new life with her new identity. Her past was behind her, and she looked ahead of her with her head held high. She was living proof that things could turn over in a blink of an eye.

Bo was sentenced to life in prison for the murders of Kinley, Natalie and evidence found against him in the murders of Iesha and Raheem.

Torrie was sentenced to a total of ten years in prison, due to her drug related charges and her sister Lisa is still battling her crack addition.

# THE END
## I HOPE YOU ALL HAVE ENJOYED IT.

## STEP INTO THE WORLD OF THE AUTHOR

The incomparable Authoress Jessica Wren is known for her critically acclaimed series, *The Worst Thots Ever, I Was Made To Love You: The Ceanna & Avantae Story, YOU, Salvaging What's Left Of Me* and now she brings you, *It's Never Gonna Stop*. Authoress Jessica Wren is a native of Austin, Texas. She has been penning her stories since the age of fourteen. In 2005, she received her Creative Writing Degree. In 2016 and 2017 she was listed as UBAWA's Top 100 Urban Author. She has released a total of seven books. One being a collaboration with twelve other women. In the collaboration *Women Withstanding All*, Authoress Jessica Wren gets personal with her story *There is Life After Divorce*. In 2018, *I Was Made To Love You* became available in all major bookstores as well as Audible. This Authoress keeps growing and perfecting her craft. Outside of writing, she loves to paint, design, plan events, travel, and spend time with her love ones. Get to know the Author and stay connected.

Send Author friend request to Jessica A. Wren
Email: contactshopjessicawren@gmail.com
Author Page: Books By Jessica Wren
Twitter: wren_jessica
Instagram: Authoress Jessica Wren

CPSIA information can be obtained
at www.ICGtesting.com
Printed in the USA
LVHW021521230819
628745LV00009B/323/P